CUGEL'S
SAGA

CUGEL'S SAGA

JACK VANCE

TIMESCAPE BOOKS
Distributed by Simon and Schuster
New York

A Timescape Book
Published by Pocket Books, A Division of Simon & Schuster, Inc.
Simon & Schuster Building
Rockefeller Center
1230 Avenue of the Americas
New York, New York 10020

Use of the trademark TIMESCAPE is by exclusive license from
Gregory Benford, the trademark owner.
Simon and Schuster is a registered trademark of Simon & Schuster, Inc.

Designed by
Irving Perkins Associates
Manufactured in the United States of America

1 2 3 4 5 6 7 8 9 10

ISBN 0-671-49450-3

CONTENTS

CHAPTER
I

FROM SHANGLESTONE STRAND TO SASKERVOY

1
FLUTIC

IUCOUNU (known across Almery as 'the Laughing Magician') had worked one of his most mordant jokes upon Cugel. For the second time Cugel had been snatched up, carried north across the Ocean of Sighs, dropped upon that melancholy beach known as Shanglestone Strand.

Rising to his feet, Cugel brushed sand from his cloak and adjusted his hat. He stood not twenty yards from that spot upon which he had been dropped before, also at the behest of Iucounu. He carried no sword and his pouch contained no terces.

The solitude was absolute. No sound could be heard but the sigh of the wind along the dunes. Far to the east a dim headland thrust into the water, as did another, equally remote, to the west. To the south spread the sea, empty except for the reflection of the old red sun.

Cugel's frozen faculties began to thaw, and a whole set of emotions, one after the other, made themselves felt, with fury taking precedence over all.

Iucounu would now be enjoying his joke to the fullest. Cugel raised his fist high and shook it toward the south. "Iucounu, at last you have exceeded yourself! This time you will pay the price! I, Cugel, appoint myself your nemesis!"

For a period Cugel strode back and forth, shouting and cursing: a person long of arm and leg, with lank black hair, gaunt cheeks, and a crooked mouth of great flexibility. The time was middle afternoon, and the sun, already half-way into the west, tottered down the sky like a sick animal. Cugel, who was nothing if not practical, decided to postpone the remainder of his tirade; more urgent was lodging for the night. Cugel called down a final curse of pulsing carbuncles upon Iucounu, then, picking his way across the shingle, he climbed to the crest of a dune and looked in all directions.

To the north a succession of marshes and huddles of black larch straggled away into the murk.

To the east Cugel gave only a cursory glance. Here were the villages Smolod and Grodz, and memories were long in the Land of Cutz.

To the south, languid and listless, the ocean extended to the horizon and beyond.

To the west, the shore stretched far to meet a line of low hills which, thrusting into the sea, became a headland. . . . A red glitter flashed across the distance, and Cugel's attention was instantly attracted.

Such a red sparkle could only signify sunlight reflecting from glass!

Cugel marked the position of the glitter, which faded from view as the sunlight shifted. He slid down the face of the dune and set off at best speed along the beach.

The sun dropped behind the headland; gray-lavender gloom fell across the beach. An arm of that vast forest known as The Great Erm edged down from the north, suggesting a number of eery possibilities, and Cugel accelerated his pace to a striding bent-kneed lope.

The hills loomed black against the sky, but no sign of habitation appeared. Cugel's spirits sagged low. He proceeded more slowly, searching the landscape with care, and at last, to his great satisfaction, he came upon a large and elaborate manse of archaic design, shrouded behind the trees of an untidy garden. The lower windows glowed with amber light: a cheerful sight for the benighted wanderer.

Cugel turned briskly aside and approached the manse, putting by his usual precautions of surveillance and perhaps peering through the windows, especially in view of two white shapes at the edge of the forest which quietly moved back into the shadows as he turned to stare.

Cugel marched to the door and tugged smartly at the bell-chain. From within came the sound of a far gong.

A moment passed. Cugel looked nervously over his shoulder, and again pulled at the chain. Finally he heard slow steps approaching from within.

The door opened and a pinch-faced old man, thin, pale, and stoop-shouldered, looked through the crack.

Cugel used the suave tones of gentility, "Good evening! What is this handsome old place, may I ask?"

The old man responded without cordiality: "Sir, this is Flutic, where Master Twango keeps residence. What is your business?"

"Nothing out of the ordinary," said Cugel airily. "I am a traveler, and I seem to have lost my way. I will therefore trespass upon Master Twango's hospitality for the night, if I may."

"Quite impossible. From which direction do you come?"

"From the east."

"Then continue along the road, through the forest and over the hill, to Saskervoy. You will find lodging to meet your needs at the Inn of Blue Lamps."

"It is too far, and in any event robbers have stolen my money."

"You will find small comfort here; Master Twango gives short shrift to indigents." The old man started to close the door, but Cugel put his foot into the aperture.

"Wait! I noticed two white shapes at the edge of the forest, and I dare go no farther tonight!"

"In this regard, I can advise you," said the old man. "The creatures are probably rostgoblers, or 'hyperborean sloths', if you prefer the term. Return to the beach and wade ten feet into the water; you will be safe from their lust. Then tomorrow you may proceed to Saskervoy."

The door closed. Cugel looked anxiously over his shoulder. At the entrance to the garden, where heavy yews flanked the walk, he glimpsed a pair of still white forms. Cugel turned back to the door and jerked hard at the bell-chain.

Slow steps padded across the floor, and once again the door opened. The old man looked out. "Sir?"

"The ghouls are now in the garden! They block the way to the beach!"

The old man opened his mouth to speak, then blinked as a new concept entered his mind. He tilted his head and spoke craftily: "You have no funds?"

"I carry not so much as a groat."

"Well then; are you disposed toward employment?"

"Certainly, if I survive the night!"

"In that case, you are in luck! Master Twango can offer employment to a willing worker." The old man threw open the door and Cugel gratefully entered the manse.

With an almost exuberant flourish the old man closed the door. "Come, I will take you to Master Twango, and you can discuss the particulars of your employment. How do you choose to be announced?"

"I am Cugel."

"This way then! You will be pleased with the opportunities! . . . . Are you coming? At Flutic we are brisk!"

Despite all, Cugel held back. "Tell me something of the employment! I am, after all, a person of quality, and I do not turn my hand to everything."

"No fear! Master Twango will accord you every distinction. Ah, Cugel, you will be a happy man! If only I were young again! This way, if you please."

Cugel still held back. "First things first! I am tired and somewhat the worse for travel. Before I confer with Master Twango I would like to refresh myself and perhaps take a bite or two of nourishment. In fact, let us wait until tomorrow morning, when I will make a far better impression."

The old man demurred. "At Flutic all is exact, and every jot balances against a corresponding tittle. To whose account would I charge your refreshment? To Gark? To Gookin? To Master Twango himself? Absurd. Inevitably the consumption would fall against the account of Weamish, which is to say, myself. Never! My account at last is clear, and I propose to retire."

"I understand nothing of this," grumbled Cugel.

"Ah, but you will! Come now: to Twango!"

With poor grace Cugel followed Weamish into a chamber of many shelves and cases: a repository of curios, to judge by the articles on display.

"Wait here a single moment!" said Weamish and hopped on spindly legs from the room.

Cugel walked here and there, inspecting the curios and estimating their value. Strange to find such objects in a place so remote! He bent to examine a pair of small quasi-human grotesques rendered in exact detail. Craftsmanship at its most superb! thought Cugel.

Weamish returned. "Twango will see you shortly. Meanwhile he offers for your personal regalement this cup of vervain tea, together with these two nutritious wafers, at no charge."

Cugel drank the tea and devoured the wafers. "Twango's act of hospitality, though largely symbolic, does him credit." He indicated the cabinets. "All this is Twango's personal collection?"

"Just so. Before his present occupation he dealt widely in such goods."

"His tastes are bizarre, even peculiar."

Weamish raised his white eyebrows. "As to that I cannot say. It all seems ordinary enough to me."

"Not really," said Cugel. He indicated the pair of grotesques. "For instance, I have seldom seen objects so studiously repulsive as this pair of bibelots. Skillfully done, agreed! Notice the detail in these horrid little ears! The snouts, the fangs: the malignance is almost real! Still, they are undeniably the work of a diseased imagination."

The objects reared erect. One of them spoke in a rasping voice: "No doubt Cugel has good reason for his unkind words; still, neither Gark nor I can take them lightly."

The other also spoke: "Such remarks carry a sting! Cugel has a feckless tongue." Both bounded from the room.

Weamish spoke in reproach. "You have offended both Gark and Gookin, who came only to guard Twango's valuables from pilferage. But what is done is done. Come; we will go to Master Twango."

Weamish took Cugel to a large workroom, furnished with a dozen tables piled with ledgers, crates and various oddments. Gark and Gookin, wearing smart long-billed caps of red and blue respectively, glared at Cugel from a bench. At an enormous desk sat Twango, who was short and corpulent, with a small chin, a dainty mouth and a bald pate surrounded by varnished black curls. Under his chin hung a faddish little goatee.

Upon the entrance of Cugel and Weamish, Twango swung

around in his chair. "Aha, Weamish! This gentleman, so I am told, is Cugel. Welcome, Cugel, to Flutic!"

Cugel doffed his hat and bowed. "Sir, I am grateful for your hospitality on this dark night."

Twango arranged the papers on his desk and appraised Cugel from the corner of his eye. He indicated a chair. "Be seated, if you will. Weamish tells me that you might be inclined to employment, under certain circumstances."

Cugel nodded graciously. "I will be pleased to consider any post for which I am qualified, and which offers an appropriate compensation."

Weamish called from the side: "Just so! Conditions at Flutic are always optimum and at worst meticulous."

Twango coughed and chuckled. "Dear old Weamish! We have had a long association! But now our accounts are settled and he wishes to retire. Am I correct in this, Weamish?"

"You are, in every last syllable!"

Cugel made a delicate suggestion: "Perhaps you will describe the various levels of employment available and their corresponding perquisites. Then, after analysis, I will be able to indicate how best I can serve you."

Weamish cried out: "A wise request! Good thinking, Cugel! You will do well at Flutic, or I am much deceived."

Twango again straightened the papers on his desk. "My business is simple at its basis. I exhume and refurbish treasures of the past. I then survey, pack, and sell them to a shipping agent of Saskervoy, who delivers them to their ultimate consignee, who, so I understand, is a prominent magician of Almery. If I shape each phase of the operation to its best efficiency — Weamish, in a spirit of jocularity, used the word 'meticulous' — I sometimes turn a small profit."

"I am acquainted with Almery," said Cugel. "Who is the magician?"

Twango chuckled. "Soldinck the shipping agent refuses to release this information, so that I will not sell direct at double profit. But from other sources I learn that the consignee is a certain Iucounu of Pergolo. . . .Cugel, did you speak?"

Cugel smilingly touched his abdomen. "An eructation only. I usually dine at this time. What of your own meal? Should we not continue our discussion over the evening repast?"

"All in good time," said Twango. "Now then, to continue. Weamish has long supervised my archaeological operations, and his position now becomes open. Is the name 'Sadlark' known to you?"

"Candidly, no."

"Then for a moment I must digress. During the Cutz Wars of the Eighteenth Aeon, the demon Underherd interfered with the overworld, so that Sadlark descended to set matters right. For reasons obscure — I personally suspect simple vertigo — Sadlark plunged into the mire, creating a pit now found in my own back garden. Sadlark's scales persist to this day, and these are the treasures which we recover from the slime."

"You are fortunate in that the pit is so close to your residence," said Cugel. "Efficiency is thereby augmented."

Twango tried to follow Cugel's reasoning, then gave up the effort. "True." He pointed to a nearby table. "There stands a reconstruction of Sadlark in miniature!"

Cugel went to inspect the model, which had been formed by attaching a large number of silver flakes to a matrix of silver wires. The sleek torso stood on a pair of short legs terminating in circular webs. Sadlark lacked a head; the torso rose smoothly to a prow-like turret, fronted by a particularly complex scale with a red node at the center. Four arms hung from the upper torso; neither sense organs nor digestive apparatus were evident, and Cugel pointed out this fact to Twango as a matter of curiosity.

"Yes, no doubt," said Twango. "Things are done differently in the overworld. Like the model, Sadlark was constructed of scales on a matrix not of silver wires but wefts of force. When Sadlark plunged into the mire, the dampness annulled his forces; the scales dispersed and Sadlark became disorganized, which is the overworld equivalent of mortality."

"A pity," said Cugel, returning to his seat. "His conduct from the first would seem to have been quixotic."

"Possibly true," said Twango. "His motives are difficult to assess. Now, as to our own business: Weamish is leaving our little group and his post as 'supervisor of operations' becomes open. Is such a position within your capacity?"

"I should certainly think so," said Cugel. "Buried valuables have long engaged my interest!"

"Then the position should suit you famously!"

"And my stipend?"

"It shall be exactly that of Weamish, even though Weamish is a skilled and able associate of many years. In such cases, I play no favorites."

"In round numbers, then, Weamish earns how many terces?"

"I prefer to keep such matters confidential," said Twango, "but Weamish, so I believe, will allow me to reveal that last week he earned almost three hundred terces, and the week before as much again."

"True, from first to last!" said Weamish.

Cugel rubbed his chin. "Such a stipend would seem adequate to my needs."

"Just so," said Twango. "When can you assume your duties?"

Cugel considered for only a moment. "At once, for purposes of salary computation. However, I will want a few days to study your operation. I assume that you can provide me adequate board and lodging over this period?"

"Such facilities are provided at a nominal cost." Twango rose to his feet. "But I keep you talking when you are surely tired and hungry. Weamish, as his last official duty, will take you to the refectory, where you may dine to your selection. Then you may rest in whatever style of accomodation you find congenial. Cugel, I welcome you into our employ! In the morning we can settle the details of your compensation."

"Come!" cried Weamish. "To the refectory." He ran limping to the doorway, where he paused and beckoned. "Come along, Cugel! At Flutic one seldom loiters!"

Cugel looked at Twango. "Why is Weamish so animated, and why must one never loiter?"

Twango shook his head in fond bemusement. "Weamish is a nonpareil! Do not try to match his performance; I could never hope to find another like him!"

Weamish called again: "Come, Cugel! Must we stand here while the sun goes out?"

"I am coming, but I refuse to run blindly through this long dark corridor!"

"This way, then: after me!"

Cugel followed Weamish to the refectory: a hall with tables to one side and a buffet loaded with viands to the other. Two men sat dining. The first, a person large and thick-necked with a florid complexion, a tumble of blond curls and a surly expression, ate broad beans and bread. The second, who was as lean as a lizard, with a dark leathery skin, a narrow bony face and coarse black hair, consumed a meal no less austere, of steamed kale, with a wedge of raw onion for savor.

Cugel's attention, however, focused on the buffet. He turned to Weamish in wonder. "Does Twango always provide such a bounty of delicacies?"

Weamish responded in a disinterested fashion. "Yes, this is usually the case."

"The two men yonder: who are they?"

"To the left sits Yelleg; the other is Malser. They comprise the work-force which you will supervise."

"Only two? I expected a larger crew."

"You will find that these two suffice."

"For workmen, their appetites are remarkably moderate."

Weamish glanced indifferently across the room. "So it would seem. What of yourself: how will you dine?"

Cugel went to inspect the buffet at closer range. "I will start with a dish of these smoked oil-fish, and a salad of pepper-leaf. Then this roast fowl seems eminently edible, and I will try a cut off the rare end of the joint. . . . The garnishes are nicely turned out. Finally, a few of these pastries and a flask of the Violet Mendolence: this should suffice. No question but what Twango does well by his employees!"

Cugel arranged a tray with viands of quality, while Weamish took only a small dish of boiled burdock leaves. Cugel asked in wonder: "Is that paltry meal adequate to your appetite?"

Weamish frowned down at his dish. "It is admittedly a trifle spare. I find that an over-rich diet reduces my zeal."

Cugel laughed confidently. "I intend to innovate a program of rational operations, and this frantic harum-scarum zeal of yours, with all shirt-tails flying, will become unnecessary." Weamish pursed his lips.

"You will find that, at times, you are working as hard as your underlings. That is the nature of the supervisorial position."

"Never!" declared Cugel expansively. "I insist upon a rigid separation of functions. A toiler does not supervise and the supervisor does not toil. But as for your meal tonight, you are retired from work; you may eat and drink as you see fit!"

"My account is closed," said Weamish. "I do not care to reopen the books."

"A small matter, surely," said Cugel. "Still, if you are concerned, eat and drink as you will, to my account!"

"That is most generous!" Jumping to his feet, Weamish limped at speed to the buffet. He returned with a selection of choice meats, preserved fruits, pastries, a large cheese and a flask of wine, which he attacked with astonishing gusto.

A sound from above attracted Cugel's attention. He looked up to discover Gark and Gookin crouched on a shelf. Gark held a tablet upon which Gookin made entries, using an absurdly long stylus.

Gark inspected Cugel's plate. "Item: oil-fish, smoked and served with garlic and one leek, at four terces. Item: one fowl, good quality, large size, served with one cup of sauce and seven garnishes, at eleven terces. Item: three pastries of mince with herbs, at three terces each, to a total of nine terces. A salad of assorted stuffs: six terces. Item: three fardels, at two terces, to a total of six terces. Item: one large order of quince conserve, valued at three terces. Wine, nine terces. A service of napery and utensils: one terce."

Gookin spoke. "Noted and calculated. Cugel, place your mark at this point."

"Not so fast!" spoke Weamish sharply. "My supper tonight is at Cugel's expense. Include the charges to his account."

Gark demanded: "Cugel, is this correct?"

"I did in fact issue the invitation," said Cugel. "I dine here, however, in my capacity as supervisor. I hereby order that 7the charges for sustenance be waived. Weamish, as an honoured ex-employee, also eats without charge."

Gark and Gookin uttered shrill cackles of laughter, and even

Weamish showed a painful smile. "At Flutic," said Weamish, "nothing is left to chance. Twango carefully distinguishes sentiment from business. If Twango owned the air, we would pay over coins for every gasp."

Cugel spoke with dignity: "These practises must be revised and at once! Otherwise I will resign my position. I must also point out that the fowl was underdone and the garlic lacked savor."

Gark and Gookin paid him no heed. Gookin tallied the charges on Weamish's meal. "Very well, Cugel; once more, we require your mark."

Cugel inspected the tablet. "These bird scratchings mean nothing to me!"

"Is that truly the case?" asked Gookin mildly. He took the tablet. "Aha, I notice an oversight. Add three terces for Weamish's digestive pastilles."

"Hold up!" roared Cugel. "What is the account at this instant?"

"One hundred and sixteen terces. We are often rendered a gratuity for our services."

"This is not one of the occasions!" Cugel snatched the tablet and scribbled his mark. "Now be off with you! I cannot dine in dignity with a pair of weird little swamp-hoppers peering over my shoulder."

Gark and Gookin bounded away in a fury. Weamish said: "That last remark struck somewhat close to the knuckle. Remember, Gark and Gookin prepare the food and whoever irks them sometimes finds noxious substances in his victual."

Cugel spoke firmly. "They should rather beware of me! As supervisor, I am a person of importance. If Twango fails to enforce my directives, I will resign my post!"

"That option is of course open to you — as soon as you pay off your account."

"I see no great problem there. If the supervisor earns three hundred terces a week, I can quickly discharge my account."

Weamish drank deeply from his goblet. The wine seemed to loosen his tongue. He leaned toward Cugel and spoke in a hoarse whisper. "Three hundred terces a week, eh? For me that was a fluke! Yelleg and Malser are slime-divers, as we call them.

They earn three to twenty terces for each scale found, depending on quality. The 'Clover-leaf Femurials' bring ten terces, as do the 'Dorsal Double Luminants'. An 'Interlocking Sequalion' for either turret or pectorus brings twenty terces. The rare 'Lateral Flashers' are also worth twenty terces. Whoever finds the 'Pectoral Sky-break Spatterlight' will gain one hundred terces."

Cugel poured more wine into Weamish's goblet. "I am listening with two ears."

Weamish drank the wine but otherwise seemed hardly to notice Cugel's presence. "Yelleg and Malser work from before dawn until dark. They earn ten to fifteen terces a day on the average, from which the costs of board, lodging and incidentals are deducted. As supervisor you will see to their safety and comfort, at a salary of ten terces per day. Additionally, you gain a bonus of one terce for each scale exhumed by Yelleg and Malser, regardless of type. While Yelleg and Malser warm themselves at the fire or take their tea, you yourself are entitled to dive for scales."

"'Dive'?" asked Cugel in perplexity.

"Precisely so, into the pit created by Sadlark's impact with the mire. The work is tedious and one must dive deep. Recently —" here Weamish drank an entire goblet of wine at a gulp "— I scratched into a whole nest of good quality scales, with many 'specials' among them, and the next week, by great good fortune, I did the same. Thus I was able to amortize my account, and I have elected to retire on the instant."

Cugel's meal had suddenly gone tasteless. "And your previous earnings?"

"On good days I might earn as much as Yelleg and Malser."

Cugel turned his eyes to the ceiling. "With an income of twelve terces a day and expenses ten times as much, how does one profit by working?"

"Your question is to the point. First of all, one learns to dine without reference to subtle distinctions. Also, when one sleeps the sleep of exhaustion, he ignores the decor of his chamber."

"As supervisor, I will make changes!" But Cugel spoke with little conviction.

Weamish, now somewhat befuddled, held up a long white

finger. "Still, do not overlook the opportunities! They exist, I assure you, and in unexpected places!" Leaning forward, Weamish showed Cugel a leer of cryptic significance.

"Speak on!" said Cugel. "I am attentive!"

After belching, swallowing another draught of wine, and looking over his shoulder, Weamish said: "I can only emphasize that, to overcome the wiles of such as Twango, the most superb skills are necessary."

"Your remarks are interesting," said Cugel. "May I refill your goblet?"

"With pleasure." Weamish drank with satisfaction, then leaned once more toward Cugel. "Would you care to hear a great joke?"

"I would indeed."

Weamish spoke in a confidential whisper: "Twango considers me already in my dotage!" Leaning back in his chair, Weamish showed Cugel a gap-toothed grin.

Cugel waited, but Weamish's joke had been told. Cugel laughed politely. "What an absurdity!"

"Is it not? When by a most ingenious method I have settled my accounts? Tomorrow I will leave Flutic and spend several years traveling among the fashionable resorts. Then let Twango wonder as to who is in his dotage, he or I."

"I have no doubt as to his verdict. In fact, all is clear except the details of your 'ingenious method'."

Weamish gave a wincing grimace and licked his lips, as vanity and bravado struggled against the last reeling elements of his caution. He opened his mouth to speak. . . . A gong sounded, as someone at the door pulled hard on the bell-rope.

Weamish started to rise, then, with a careless laugh, subsided into his chair. "Cugel, it now becomes your duty to attend to late visitors, and to early visitors as well."

"I am 'supervisor of operations', not general lackey," said Cugel.

"A noble hope," said Weamish wistfully. "First you must cope with Gark and Gookin, who enforce all regulations to the letter."

"They will learn to walk softly in my presence!"

The shadow of a lumpy head and a dapper long-billed cap fell over the table. A voice spoke. "Who will learn to walk softly?"

Cugel looked up to find Gookin peering over the edge of the shelf.

Again the gong sounded. Gookin called out: "Cugel, to your feet! Answer the door! Weamish will instruct you in the routine."

"As supervisor," said Cugel, "I hereby assign you to this task. Be quick!"

In response Gookin flourished a small three-stranded knout, each thong terminating in a yellow sting.

Cugel thrust up on the shelf with such force that Gookin sprawled head over heels through the air to fall into a platter of assorted cheeses which had been set out upon the buffet. Cugel picked up the knout and held it at the ready. "Now then: will you go about your duties? Or must I beat you well, then throw both you and your cap into this pot of tripes?"

Into the refectory came Twango on the run, with Gark sitting bulge-eyed on his shoulder. "What is all this commotion? Gookin, why do you lie among the cheeses?"

Cugel said: "Since I am supervisor, you should properly address me. The facts of the case are these: I ordered Gookin to answer the door. He attempted a flagrant insolence, and I was about to chastise him."

Twango's face became pink with annoyance. "Cugel, this is not our usual routine! Heretofore the supervisor has habitually answered the door."

"We now make an instant change! The supervisor is relieved of menial duties. He will earn triple the previous salary, with lodging and sustenance included at no charge."

Once more the gong sounded. Twango muttered a curse. "Weamish! Answer the door! Weamish? Where are you?"

Weamish had departed the refectory.

Cugel gave a stern order: "Gark! Respond to the gong!"

Gark gave back a surly hiss. Cugel pointed to the door. "Gark, you are hereby discharged, on grounds of insubordination! The same applies to Gookin. Both of you will immediately leave the premises and return to your native swamp."

Gark, now joined by Gookin, responded only with hisses of defiance.

Cugel turned to Twango. "I fear that unless my authority is affirmed I must resign."

Twango threw up his arms in vexation. "Enough of this foolishness! While we stand here the gong rings incessantly!" He marched off down the corridor toward the door, with Gark and Gookin bounding behind him.

Cugel followed at a more leisurely gait. Twango threw open the door, to admit a sturdy man of middle age wearing a hooded brown cloak. Behind him came two others in similar garments.

Twango greeted the visitor with respectful familiarity. "Master Soldinck! The time is late! Why, at this hour, do you fare so far?"

Soldinck spoke in a heavy voice: "I bring serious and urgent news, which could not wait an instant."

Twango stood back aghast. "Mercantides is dead?"

"The tragedy is one of deception and theft!"

"What has been stolen?" asked Twango impatiently. "Who has been deceived?"

"I will recite the facts. Four days ago, at noon precisely, I arrived here with the strong-wagon. I came in company with Rincz and Jornulk, both, as you know, elders and persons of probity."

"Their reputations have never been assailed, to my knowledge. Why now do you bring them into question?"

"Patience; you shall hear!"

"Proceed! Cugel, you are a man of experience; stand by and exercise your judgment. This, incidentally, is Master Soldinck of the firm Soldinck and Mercantides, Shipping Agents."

Cugel stepped forward and Soldinck continued his declaration.

"With Rincz and Jornulk, I entered your workroom. There, in our presence, you counted out and we packed six hundred and eighty scales into four crates."

"Correct. There were four hundred 'ordinarys', two hundred 'specials' and eighty 'premium specials' of unique character."

"Just so. Together, and in the presence of Weamish, we packed the crates, sealed them, affixed bands and plaques. I suggest that Weamish be summoned, that he may put his wisdom to the solution of our mystery."

"Gark! Gookin! Be so good as to summon Weamish. Still, Master Soldinck, you have not defined the mystery itself!"

"I will now do so. With yourself, Weamish, Rincz, Jornulk and myself on hand, the scales were encased as always in your workroom. Weamish then, to our supervision, placed the cases upon the wheeled carrier, and we complimented him both for the nicety in which he had decorated the carrier and his care to ensure that the cases might not fall to the ground. Then, with Rincz and me in the lead, you and Jornulk behind, Weamish carefully rolled the cases down the corridor, pausing, so I recall, only long enough to adjust his shoe and comment to me upon the unseasonable chill."

"Precisely so. Continue."

"Weamish rolled the carrier to the wagon and the cases were transferred into the strong-box, which was immediately locked. I wrote a receipt to you, which Rincz and Jornulk countersigned, and on which Weamish placed his mark as witness. Finally I paid over to you your money, and you gave me the receipted invoice."

"We drove the wagon directly to Saskervoy, where, with all formality, the cases were transferred into a vault, for dispatch to far Almery."

"And then?"

"Today, Mercantides thought to verify the quality of the scales. I opened a case, so carefully certified, to find only lumps of mud and gravel. Thereupon all cases were investigated. Each case contained nothing but worthless soil, and there you have the mystery. We hope that either you or Weamish can help us resolve this shocking affair, or, failing that, refund our money."

"The last possibility is out of the question. I can add nothing to your statement. All went as you have described. Weamish may have noticed some peculiar incident, but surely he would have notified me."

"Still, his testimony may suggest an area of investigation, if only he would present himself."

Gark bounded into the room, eyes bulging in excitement. He called out in a rasping voice: "Weamish is on the roof He is behaving in an unusual manner!"

Twango flourished his arms in distress. "Senile, yes, but foolish so soon? He has only just retired!"

"What?" cried Soldinck. "Weamish retired? A great surprise!"

"For us all! He settled his accounts to the last terce, then declared his retirement."

"Most odd!" said Soldinck. "We must bring Weamish down from the roof and at once!"

With Gark bounding ahead, Twango ran out into the garden, with Soldinck, Rincz, Jornulk and Cugel coming after.

The night was dark, illuminated only by a few sickly constellations. Light from within, striking up through the roof-panes, showed Weamish walking a precarious route along the ridge.

Twango called out: "Weamish, why are you walking on high? Come down at once!"

Weamish looked here and there to discover the source of the call. Observing Twango and Soldinck, he uttered a wild cry in which defiance seemed mingled with mirth.

"That is at best an ambiguous response," said Soldinck.

Twango called again: "Weamish, a number of scales are missing, and we wish to ask a question or two."

"Ask away, wherever you like and all night long — anywhere except only here. I am walking the roof and do not care to be disturbed."

"Ah, but Weamish, it is you of whom we wish to ask the questions! You must come down at once!"

"My accounts are settled! I walk where I will!"

Twango clenched his fists. "Master Soldinck is puzzled and disturbed! The missing scales are irreplaceable!"

"No less am I, as you will learn!" Again Weamish uttered his strange cacchination.

Soldinck spoke sourly: "Weamish has become addled."

"Work gave his life meaning," explained Twango. "He dived deep into the slime and found a whole nest of scales, so he paid off his account. Ever since he has been acting strangely."

Soldinck asked: "When did he find the scales?"

"Only two days ago." Once more Twango raised his voice. "Weamish! Come down at once! We need your help!"

Soldinck asked: "Weamish found his scales after we had accepted the last shipment?"

"Quite true. One day later, as a matter of fact."

"A curious coincidence."

Twango stared at him blankly. "Surely you cannot suspect Weamish!"

"The facts point in his direction."

Twango turned sharply about. "Gark, Gookin, Cugel! Up to the roof! Help Weamish to the ground!"

Cugel spoke haughtily. "Gark and Gookin are my subordinates. Inform me as to your wishes and I will issue the necessary orders."

"Cugel, your attitudes have become intolerable! You are hereby demoted! Now, up on the roof with you! I want Weamish brought down at once!"

"I have no head for heights," said Cugel. "I resign my position."

"Not until your accounts are settled. They include the fine cheeses into which you flung Gookin."

Cugel protested, but Twango turned his attention back to the roof and refused to listen.

Weamish strolled back and forth along the ridge. Gark and Gookin appeared behind him. Twango called up: "Weamish, take all precautions! Gark and Gookin will lead the way!"

Weamish gave a final wild scream, and running along the ridge, hurled himself off into space, to land head-first upon the pavement below. Gark and Gookin crept to the edge of the roof to peer pop-eyed down at the limp figure.

After a brief inspection, Twango turned to Soldinck. "I fear that Weamish is dead."

"What then of the missing scales?"

"You must look elsewhere," said Twango. "The theft could not have occurred at Flutic."

"I am not so sure," said Soldinck. "In fact, I suspect otherwise."

"You are deceived by coincidences," said Twango. "The

night is chill; let us return inside. Cugel, convey the corpse to the gardener's shed in the back garden. Weamish's grave is ready; in the morning you may bury him."

"If you recall," said Cugel, "I have resigned my place. I no longer consider myself employed at Flutic, unless you concede distinctly better terms."

Twango stamped his feet. "Why, at this time of tribulation, must you annoy me with your nonsense? I lack the patience to deal with you! Gark! Gookin! Cugel thinks to shirk his duties!"

Gark and Gookin crept forward. Gookin flung a noose around Cugel's ankles, while Gark threw a net over Cugel's head. Cugel fell heavily to the ground, where Gark and Gookin beat him well with short staves.

After a period Twango came to the door. He cried out: "Stop! The clamor offends our ears! If Cugel has changed his mind, let him go about his work."

Cugel decided to obey Twango's orders. Cursing under his breath, he dragged the corpse to a shed in the back garden. Then he limped to that hut vacated by Weamish, and here he passed a wakeful night, by reason of sprains, bruises, and contusions.

At an early hour Gark and Gookin pounded on the door. "Out and about your work!" called Gookin. "Twango wishes to inspect the interior of this hut."

Cugel, despite his aches, had already made such a search, to no avail. He brushed his clothing, adjusted his hat, sauntered from the hut, and stood aside while Gark and Gookin, under Twango's direction, searched the premises. Soldinck, who apparently had spent the night at Flutic, watched vigilantly from the doorway.

Twango finished the search. "There is nothing here," he told Soldinck. "Weamish is vindicated!"

"He might have secreted the scales elsewhere!"

"Unlikely! The scales were packed while you watched. Under close guard they were taken to the wagon. You yourself, with Rincz and Jornulk, transferred the cases to your wagon. Weamish had no more opportunity to steal the scales than I myself!"

"Then how do you explain Weamish's sudden wealth?"

"He found a nest of scales; is that so bizarre?"

Soldinck had nothing more to say. Departing Flutic, he returned over the hill to Saskervoy.

Twango called a staff meeting in the refectory. The group included Yelleg, Malser, Cugel and Bilberd the feeble-minded gardener. Gark and Gookin crouched on a high shelf, monitoring the conduct of all.

Twango spoke somberly. "I stand here today in sorrow! Poor Weamish, while strolling in the dark, suffered an accident and is no longer with us. Sadly, he did not live to enjoy his retirement. This concept alone must give us all cause for reflection!

"There is other news, no less disturbing. Four cases of scales, representing great value, have somehow been preempted, or stolen. Does anyone here have information, no matter how trivial, concerning this heinous act?" Twango looked from face to face. "No? In that case, I have no more to say. All to their tasks, and let Weamish's lucky find be an inspiration to all!"

"One final word! Since Cugel is unfamiliar with the routines of his work, I ask that all extend to him the hand of cheerful good-fellowship and teach him whatever he needs to know. All to work, then, at speed and efficiency!"

Twango called Cugel aside. "Last night we seem to have had a misunderstanding as to the meaning of the word 'supervisor'. At Flutic, this word denotes a person who supervises the comfort and convenience of his fellow workers, including me, but who by no means controls their conduct."

"That distinction has already been made clear," said Cugel shortly.

"Precisely so. Now, as your first duty, you will bury Weamish. His grave is yonder, behind the bilberry bush. At this time you may select a site and excavate a grave for yourself, in the unhappy event that you should die during your tenure at Flutic."

"This is not to be thought of," said Cugel. "I have far to go before I die."

"Weamish spoke in much the same terms," said Twango. "But he is dead! And his comrades are spared a melancholy task, since he dug, tended and decorated a fine grave." Twango chuckled sadly. Weamish must have felt the flutter of the black bird's wings! Only two days ago I found him cleaning and ordering his grave, and setting all to rights!"

"Two days ago?" Cugel considered. "This was after he had found his scales."

"True! He was a dedicated man! I trust that you, Cugel, as you live and work at Flutic, will be guided by his conduct!"

"I hope to do exactly that," said Cugel.

"Now you may bury Weamish. His carrier is yonder in the shed. He built it himself and it is only fitting that you use it to convey his corpse to the grave."

"That is a kind thought." With no further words Cugel went to the shed and brought out the carrier: a table rolling on four wheels. Impelled, so it would seem, by a desire to beautify his handiwork, Weamish had attached a skirt of dark blue cloth to hang as a fringe below the top surface.

Cugel loaded Weamish's body upon the carrier and rolled it out into the back garden. The carrier functioned well, although the top surface seemed insecurely attached to the frame. Odd, thought Cugel, when the vehicle must carry valuable cases of scales! Making an inspection, Cugel found that a peg secured the top surface to the frame. When he pulled away the peg, the top pivoted and would have spilled the corpse had he not been alert.

Cugel investigated the carrier in some detail, then wheeled the corpse to that secluded area north of the manse which Weamish had selected for his eternal rest.

Cugel took stock of the surroundings. A bank of myrhadion trees dangled long festoons of purple blossoms over the grave. Gaps in the foliage allowed a view along the beach and over the sea. To the left a slope grown over with bitterbush and syrinx descended to the pond of of black slime.

Already Yelleg and Malser were at work. Hunching and shuddering to the chill, they dived from a platform into the slime. Pulling themselves as deep as possible by means of weights and ropes, they groped for scales, and at last emerged panting and gasping and dripping black ooze.

Cugel gave his head a shake of distaste, then uttered a sharp exclamation as something stung his right buttock. Jerking about he discovered Gark watching from under the broad leaf of a madder plant. He carried a small contrivance by which he could launch pebbles, and which he had evidently used upon Cugel. Gark adjusted the bill of his red cap and hopped forward. "Work at speed, Cugel! There is much to be done!"

Cugel deigned no response. With all dignity he unloaded the corpse, and Gark took his leave.

Weamish indeed had maintained his grave with pride. The hole, five feet deep, had been dug square and true, although at the bottom and to the side the dirt seemed loose and friable. Cugel nodded with quiet satisfaction.

"Quite likely," Cugel told himself. "Not at all unlikely."

With spade in hand he jumped into the grave and prodded into the dirt. From the corner of his eye he noticed the approach of a small figure in a red cap. Gark had returned, hoping to catch Cugel unaware, and fair game for another skillfully aimed pebble. Cugel loaded the spade with dirt, swung it high, up and over, and heard a gratifying squawk of surprise.

Cugel climbed from the grave. Gark squatted at a little distance, shaking the dirt from his cap. "You are careless where you throw your dirt!"

Cugel, leaning on his spade, chuckled. "If you skulk through the bushes, how can I see you?"

"The responsibility is yours. It is my duty to inspect your work."

"Jump down into the grave, where you may inspect at close range!"

Gark's eyes bulged in outrage, and he gnashed the chitinous parts of his mouth. "Do you take me for a numbskull? Get on with your work! Twango will not pay good terces for idle hours of dreaming!"

"Gark, you are stern!" said Cugel. "Well, if I must, I must." Without further ceremony he rolled Weamish into his grave, covered him over, and tamped down the mold.

So passed the morning. At noon Cugel made an excellent lunch of braised eel with ramp and turnips, a conserve of exotic fruits and a flask of white wine. Yelleg and Malser, lunching upon coarse bread and pickled acorns, watched sidelong in mingled surprise and envy.

During the late afternoon, Cugel went out to the pond to assist the divers as they finished work for the day. First Malser emerged from the pond, hands like claws, then Yelleg. Cugel flushed away the slime with water piped from a stream, then Yelleg and Malser went to a shed to change clothes, their skin shriveled and lavender from the cold. Since Cugel had neglected to build a fire, their complaints were curtailed only by the chattering of their teeth.

Cugel hastened to repair the lack, while the divers discussed the day's work. Yelleg had gleaned three 'ordinary' scales from under a rock, while Malser, exploring a crevice, had discovered four of the same quality.

Yelleg told Cugel: "Now you may dive if you see fit, though the light fails fast."

"This is the time Weamish dived," said Malser. "He often used the hours of early morning, as well. But no matter what his exertions never did he neglect our warming fire."

"It was an oversight on my part," said Cugel. "I am not yet accustomed to the routine."

Yelleg and Malser grumbled somewhat more, then went to the refectory, where they dined on boiled kelp. For his own meal, Cugel took first a tureen of hunter's goulash, with morels and dumplings. For a second course, he selected a fine cut of roast mutton, with a piquant sauce, assorted side dishes, and a rich red wine; then, for dessert, he devoured a large dish of mungberry trifle.

Yelleg and Malser, on their way from the refectory, stopped to advise Cugel. "You are consuming meals of excellent quality, but the prices are inordinate! Your account with Twango will occupy your efforts for the rest of your life."

Cugel only laughed and made an easy gesture. "Sit down, and allow me to repair my deficiencies of this afternoon. Gark! Two more goblets, another flask of wine and be quick about it!"

Yelleg and Malser willingly seated themselves. Cugel poured wine with a generous hand, and refilled his own goblet as well. He leaned comfortably back in his chair.

"Naturally," said Cugel, "the possibility of exorbitant charges has occurred to me. Since I do not intend to pay, I care not a fig for expense!"

Both Yelleg and Malser murmured in surprise. "That is a remarkably bold attitude!"

"Not altogether. At any instant the sun may lurch into oblivion. At this time, were I to owe Twnago ten thousand terces for a long series of excellent meals, my last thoughts would be happy ones!"

Both Yelleg and Malser were impressed by the logic of the concept, which had not previously occurred to them.

Yelleg mused: "Your point seems to be that if one's debt to Twango hovers always at thirty or forty terces, it might as well be ten thousand!"

Malser said thoughtfully: "Twenty thousand, or even thirty thousand, would seem an even more worthy debt."

"This is an ambition of truly great scope!" declared Yelleg. "As of this moment, I believe that I will try a good slice of that roast mutton!"

"And I as well!" said Malser. "Let Twango worry about the cost! Cugel, I drink to your health!"

Twango jumped from a nearby booth, where he had sat unseen. "I have heard the whole of this base conversation! Cugel, your concepts do you no credit! Gark! Gookin! In the future Cugel must be served only the Grade Five cuisine, similar to that formerly enjoyed by Weamish."

Cugel only shrugged. "If necessary, I will pay my account."

"That is good news!" said Twango. "And what will you use for terces?"

"I have my little secrets," said Cugel. "I will tell you this much: I intend notable innovations in the scale-gathering process."

Twango snorted incredulously. "Please perform these miracles in your spare time. Today you neglected to dust the relics; you neither waxed nor polished the parquetry. You failed to dig your grave, and you neglected to carry out the kitchen wastes."

"Gark and Gookin must carry out the garbage," said Cugel. "While I was still supervisor, I rearranged the work schedule."

Gark and Gookin, on the high shelf, set up a protest.

"The schedule is as before," said Twango. "Cugel, you must observe the regular routine." He departed the room, leaving Cugel, Yelleg and Malser to finish their wine.

Before sunrise Cugel was awake and abroad in the back garden, where the air was damp and chill, and heavy with silence. Bottle-yew and larch imposed silhouettes in a ragged fringe around the mulberry-gray sky; mist lay in low ribbons across the pond.

Cugel went to the gardener's shed, where he secured a stout spade. Somewhat to the side, under a lush growth of pauncewort, he noticed an iron tub, or trough, ten feet long by three feet wide, built to a purpose not now in evidence. Cugel examined the trough with care, then went to the back of the garden. Under the myrhadion tree he started to dig that grave ordained by Twango.

Despite the melancholy nature of the task, Cugel dug with zest.

The work was interrupted by Twango himself, who came carefully across the garden, wearing his black gown and a bicorn hat of black fur to guard his head against the bite of the morning chill.

Twango paused beside the grave. "I see that you have taken my censure to heart. You have worked to good effect, but why, may I ask, have you dug so close to poor Weamish? You will lie essentially side by side."

"Quite so. I feel that Weamish, were he allowed one last glimmer of perception, would take comfort in the fact."

Twango pursed his lips. "That is a nice sentiment, though perhaps a trifle florid." He glanced up toward the sun. "Time passes us by! In your attention to this particular task, you are neglecting routine. At this moment you should be emptying the kitchen waste bins!"

"Those are chores more properly consigned to Gark and Gookin."

"Not so! The handles are too high."

"Let them use smaller bins! I have more urgent work at hand, such as the efficient and rapid recovery of Sadlark's scales."

Twango peered sharply sidewise. "What do you know about such matters?"

"Like Weamish, I bring a fresh viewpoint to bear. As you know, Weamish made a notable success."

"True. . . .Yes, quite so. Still, we cannot turn Flutic topsy-turvy for the sake of possibly impractical speculation."

"Just as you like," said Cugel. He climbed from the grave and for the rest of the morning worked at menial tasks, laughing and singing with such verve that Gark and Gookin made a report to Twango.

At the end of the afternoon Cugel was allowed an hour to his own devices. He laid a spray of lilies on Weamish's grave, then resumed digging in his own grave. . . .After a few moments he noticed Gookin's blue cap, where that grotesque pastiche of homunculus and frog crouched under a mallow leaf.

Cugel pretended not to notice and dug with energy. Before long he encountered the cases which Weamish had secreted to the side of his own grave.

Pretending to rest, Cugel surveyed the landscape. Gookin crouched as before. Cugel returned to his work.

One of the cases had been broken open, presumably by Weamish, and all its contents removed except for a small parcel of twenty low-value 'specials', left behind perhaps by oversight. Cugel tucked the parcel into his pouch, then covered over the case, just as Gookin came hopping across the sward. "Cugel, you have overstayed your time! You must learn precision!"

Cugel responded with dignity. "You will notice that I am digging my grave."

"No matter! Yelleg and Malser are in need of their tea."

"All in good time," said Cugel. He climbed from the grave and went to the gardener's shed where he found Yelleg and Malser standing hunched and numb. Yelleg cried out: "Tea is one of the few free perquisites rendered by Twango! All day we grope through the freezing slime, anticipating the moment when we may drink tea and warm our shriveled skin at the fire!"

Malser chimed in: "There is neither tea nor fire! Weamish was more assiduous!"

"Be calm!" said Cugel. "I still have not mastered the routine."

Cugel set the fire alight and brewed tea; Yelleg and Malser grumbled further but Cugel promised better service in the future and the divers were appeased. They warmed themselves and drank tea, then once more ran down to the pond and plunged into the slime.

Shortly before sunset Gookin summoned Cugel to the pantry. He indicated a tray upon which rested a silver goblet. "This is Twango's tonic which you must serve to him every day at this time."

"What?" cried Cugel. "Is there no end to my duties?"

Gookin responded only with a croak of indifference. Cugel snatched up the tray and carried it to the workroom. He found Twango sorting scales: inspecting each in turn through a lens, then placing it into one of several boxes, his hands encased in soft leather gloves.

Cugel put down the tray. "Twango, a word with you!"

Twango, with lens to his eye, said: "At the moment, Cugel, I am occupied, as you can see."

"I serve this tonic under protest! Once again I cite the terms of our agreement, by which I became 'supervisor of operations' at Flutic. This post does not include the offices of valet, scullion, porter, dogs-body and general roustabout. Had I known the looseness of your categories —"

Twango made an impatient gesture. "Silence, Cugel! Your peevishness grates on the nerves."

"Still, what of our agreement?"

"Your position has been reclassified. The pay remains the same, so you have no cause for dissatisfaction." Twango drank the tonic. "Let us hear no more on the subject. I might also mention that Weamish customarily donned a white coat before serving the tonic. We thought it a nice touch."

Twango went back to his work, referring on occasion to the pages of a large leather-bound book hinged with brass and reinforced with brass filigree. Cugel watched sourly from the side. Presently he asked: "What will you do when the scales run out?"

"I need not concern myself for some time to come," said Twango primly.

"What is that book?"

"It is a work of scholarship and my basic reference: Haruviot's *Intimate Anatomy of Several Overworld Personages*. I use it to identify the scales; it is invaluable in this regard."

"Interesting!" said Cugel. "How many sorts do you find?"

"I cannot specify exactly." Twango indicated a group of unsorted scales. "These gray-green 'ordinaries' are typical of the dorsal areas; the pinks and vermilions are from under the torso. Each has its distinctive chime." Twango held a choice gray-green 'ordinary' to his ear and tapped it with a small metal bar. He listened with eyes half-closed. "The pitch is perfect! It is a pleasure to handle scales such as this."

"Then why do you wear gloves?"

"Aha! Much that we do confuses the layman! Remember, we deal with stuff of the overworld! When wet it is mild, but when dry, it often irks the skin."

Twango looked to his diagram and selected one of the 'specials'. "Hold out your hand. . . . Come, Cugel, do not cringe! You will not suddenly become an overworld imp, I assure you of this!"

Cugel gingerly extended his hand. Twango touched the 'special' to his palm. Cugel felt a puckering of the skin and a stinging as if at the abrasive suck of a lamprey. With alacrity he jerked back his hand.

Twango chuckled and returned the scale to its position. "For this reason I wear gloves when I handle dry scales."

Cugel frowned down at the table. "Are all so acrid?"

"You were stung by a 'Turret Frontal Lapidative', which is quite active. These 'Juncture Spikes' are a somewhat easier. The 'Pectoral Sky-break Spatterlight', so I suspect, will prove to be the most active of all, as it controlled Sadlark's entire web of forces. The 'ordinaries' are mild, except upon long contact."

"Amazing how these forces persist across the aeons!"

"What is 'time' in the overworld? The word may not even enter the parlance. And speaking of time, Weamish customarily devoted this period to diving for scales; often he worked long hours into the night. His example is truly inspiring! Through fortitude, persistence and sheer grit, he paid off his account!"

"My methods are different," said Cugel. "The results may well be the same. Perhaps in times to come you will mention the name 'Cugel' to inspire your staff."

"I suppose that it is not impossible."

Cugel went out into the back garden. The sun had set; in the twilight the pond lay black and lusterless. Cugel went to work with a fervor which might have impressed even Weamish. Down to the shore of the pond he dragged the old iron trough, then brought down several coils of rope.

Daylight had departed, save only for a streak of metallic eggplant along the ocean's horizon. Cugel considered the pond, where at this time Weamish was wont to dive, guided by the flicker of a single candle on the shore.

Cugel gave his head a sardonic shake and sauntered back to the manse.

Early in the morning Cugel returned to the pond. He knotted together several coils of rope to create a single length, which he tied from a stunted juniper on one side of the pond to a bull-thorn bush on the other, so that the rope stretched across the center of the pond.

Cugel brought a bucket and a large wooden tub to the shore. He launched the trough upon the pond, loaded tub and bucket into his makeshift scow, climbed aboard, and then, tugging on the rope, pulled himself out to the middle.

Yelleg and Malser, arriving on the scene, stopped short to stare. Cugel also noted the red and blue caps of Gark and Gookin where they lurked behind a bank of heliotrope.

Cugel dropped the bucket deep into the pond, pulled it up and poured the contents into the tub. Six times he filled and emptied the bucket, then pulled the scow back to shore.

He carried a bucket full of slime to the stream and, using a large sieve, screened the stuff in the bucket.

To Cugel's amazement, when the water flushed away the slime, two scales remained in the sieve: an 'ordinary' and a second scale of remarkable size, with elaborate radiating patterns and a dull red node at the center.

A flicker of movement, a darting little arm: Cugel snatched

at the fine new scale, but too late! Gookin started to bound away. Cugel jumped out like a great cat and bore Gookin to the ground. He seized the scale, kicked Gookin's meager haunches, to project him ten feet through the air. Alighting, Gookin jumped to his feet, brandished his fist, chattered a set of shrill curses. Cugel retaliated with a heavy clod. Gookin dodged, then turned and ran at full speed toward the manse.

Cugel reflected a moment, then scooped a hole in the mold beside a dark blue mitre-bush and buried his fine new scale. The 'ordinary' he tucked into his pouch, then went to fetch another bucket of slime from the scow.

Five minutes later, with stately tread, Twango came across the garden. He halted to watch as Cugel sieved a bucketful of slime.

"An ingenious arrangement," said Twango. "Quite clever — though you might have asked permission before sequestering my goods to your private use."

Cugel said coldly: "My first concern is to gather scales, for our mutual benefit."

"Hmmf. . . .Gookin tells me that already you have recovered a notable 'special'."

"A 'special'? It is no more than an 'ordinary'." Cugel brought the scale from his pouch.

With pursed lips Twango inspected the scale. "Gookin was quite circumstantial in his report."

"Gookin is that individual for whom the word 'mendacity' was coined. He is simply not to be trusted. Now please excuse me, as I wish to return to work. My time is valuable."

Twango stood dubiously aside and watched as Cugel sieved a third bucket-load of slime. "It is very strange about Gookin. How could he imagine the 'Spatterlight' in such vivid detail?"

"Bah!" said Cugel. "I cannot take time to reflect upon Gookin's fantasies."

"That is quite enough, Cugel! I am not interested in your views. In exactly seven minutes you are scheduled to sanitize the laundry."

Halfway through the afternoon Master Soldinck, of the firm

Soldinck and Mercantides, arrived at Flutic. Cugel conducted him to Twango's work-room, then busied himself nearby while Soldinck and Twango discussed the missing scales.

As before, Soldinck asserted that the scales had never truly been given into his custody, and on these grounds demanded a full refund of his payment.

Twango indignantly rejected the proposal. "It is a perplexing affair," he admitted. "In the future we shall use iron-clad formalities."

"All very well, but at this moment I am concerned not with the future but with the past. Where are my missing scales?"

"I can only reiterate that you signed the receipt, made payment, and took them away in your wagon. This is indisputable! Weamish would so testify were he alive!"

"Weamish is dead and his testimony is worth nothing."

"The facts remain. If you wish to make good your loss, then the classical recourse remains to you: raise the price to your ultimate customer. He must bear the brunt."

"There, at least, is is a constructive suggestion," said Soldinck. "I will take it up with Mercandides. In the meantime, we will soon be shipping a mixed cargo south aboard the *Galante*, and we hope to include a parcel of scales. Can you assemble another order of four cases, within a day or so?"

Twango tapped his chin with a plump forefinger. "I will have to work overtime sorting and indexing; still, using all my reserves, I believe that I can put up an order of four cases within a day or two."

"That will be satisfactory, and I will report as much to Mercantides."

Two days later Cugel placed a hundred and ten scales, for the most part 'ordinaries', before Twango where he sat at his ork table.

Twango stared in sheer amazement. "Where did you find these?"

"I seem to have plumbed the pocket from which Weamish took so many scales. These will no doubt balance my account."

Twango frowned down at the scales. "A moment while I

look over the records. . . . Cugel, I find that you still owe fifty-three terces. You spent quite heavily in the refectory and I show extra charges upon which you perhaps failed to reckon."

"Let me see the invoices. . . . I can make nothing of these records."

"Some were prepared by Gark and Gookin. They are perhaps a trifle indistinct."

Cugel threw down the invoices in disgust. "I insist upon a careful, exact and legible account!"

Twango spoke through compressed lips. "Your attitude, Cugel, is both brash and cynical. I am not favorably impressed."

"Let us change the subject," said Cugel. "When next do you expect to see Master Soldinck?"

"Sometime in the near future. Why do you ask?"

"I am curious as to his commercial methods. For instance, what would he charge Iucounu for a truly notable 'special', such as the 'Sky-break Spatterlight'?"

Twango said heavily: "I doubt if Master Soldinck would release this information. What, may I ask, is the basis for your interest?"

"No great matter. During one of our discussions, Weamish theorized that Soldinck might well prefer to buy expensive 'specials' direct from the diver, thus relieving you of considerable detail work."

For a moment Twango moved his lips without being able to produce words. At last he said: "The idea is inept, in all its phases. Master Soldinck would reject any and all scales of such dubious antecedents. The single authorized dealer is myself, and my seal alone guarantees authenticity. Each scale must be accurately identified and correctly indexed."

"And the invoices to your staff: they are also accurate and correctly indexed? Or, from sheer idle curiosity, shall I put the question to Master Soldinck?"

Twango angrily took up Cugel's account once again. "Naturally, there may be small errors, in one or another direction. They tend to balance out in the end. . . . Yes, I see an error here, where Gark misplaced a decimal point. I must counsel him to a greater precision. It is time you were serving tea to

Yelleg and Malser. You must cure this slack behaviour! At Flutic we are brisk!"

Cugel sauntered out to the pond. The time was the middle afternoon of a day extraordinarily crisp, with peculiar black-purple clouds veiling the bloated red sun. A wind from the north creased the surface of the slime; Cugel shivered and pulled his cloak up around his neck.

The surface of the pond broke; Yelleg emerged and with crooked arms pulled himself ashore, to stand in a crouch, dripping ooze. He examined his gleanings but found only pebbles, which he discarded in disgust. Malser, on his hands and knees, clambered ashore and joined Yelleg; the two of them ran to the rest hut, only to emerge a moment later in a fury. "Cugel! Where is our tea? The fire is cold ashes! Have you no mercy?"

Cugel strolled over to the hut, where both Yelleg and Malser advanced upon him in a threatening manner. Yelleg shook his massive fist in Cugel's face. "You have been remiss for the last time! Today we propose to beat you and throw you into the pond!"

"One moment," said Cugel. "Allow me to build a fire, as I myself am cold. Malser, start the tea, if you will."

Speechless with rage, the two divers stood back while Cugel kindled a fire. "Now then," said Cugel, "you will be happy to learn that I have dredged into a rich pocket of scales. I paid off my account and now Bilberd the gardener must serve the tea and build the fire."

Yelleg asked between clenched teeth: "Are you then resigning your post?"

"Not altogether. I will continue, for at least a brief period, in an advisory capacity."

"I am puzzled," said Malser. "How is it that you find so many scales with such little effort?"

Cugel smiled and shrugged. "Ability, and not a little luck."

"But mostly luck, eh? Just as Weamish had luck?"

"Ah, Weamish, poor fellow! He worked hard and long for his luck! Mine came more quickly. I have been fortunate!"

Yelleg spoke thoughtfully: "A curious succession of events! Four cases of scales disappear. Then Weamish pays off his account. Then Gark and Gookin come with their hooks and

Weamish jumps from the roof. Next, honest hard-working Cugel pays off his account, though he dredges but an hour a day."

"Curious indeed!" said Malser. "I wonder where the missing scales could be!"

"And I, no less!" said Yelleg.

Cugel spoke in mild rebuke: "Perhaps you two have time for wool-gathering, but I must troll for scales."

Cugel went to his scow and sieved several buckets of slime. Yelleg and Malser decided to work no more, each having gleaned three scales. After dressing, they stood by the edge of the pond watching Cugel, muttering together in low voices.

During the evening meal Yelleg and Malser continued their conversation, from time to time darting glances toward Cugel. Presently Yelleg struck his fist into the palm of his hand, as if he had been struck by a novel thought, which he immediately communicated to Malser. Then both nodded wisely and glanced again toward Cugel.

The next morning, while Cugel worked his sieve, Yelleg and Malser marched out into the back garden. Each carried a lily which he laid upon Weamish's grave. Cugel watched intently from the side of his eye. Neither Malser nor Yelleg gave his own grave more than cursory attention: so little, in fact, that Malser, in backing away, fell into the excavation. Yelleg helped him up and the two went off about their work.

Cugel ran to the grave and peered down to the bottom. The dirt had broken away from the side wall and the corner of a case might possibly have been evident to a careful inspection.

Cugel pulled thoughtfully at his chin. The case was not conspicuous. Malser, mortified by his clumsy fall, in all probability had failed to notice it. This, at least, was a reasonable theory. Nevertheless, to move the scales might be judicious; he would do so at the first opportunity.

Taking the scow out upon the slime, Cugel filled the tub; then, returning to the shore, he sieved the muck, to discover a pair of 'ordinaries' in the sieve.

Twango summoned Cugel to the work-room. "Cugel, to-morrow we ship four cases of prime scales at precisely noon. Go to the carpenter shop and build four stout cases to proper specifications. Then clean the carrier, lubricate the wheels, and put it generally into tip-top shape; there must be no mishaps on this occasion."

"Have no fear," said Cugel. "We will do the job properly."

At noon Soldinck, with his companions Rincz and Jornulk, halted their wagon before Flutic. Cugel gave them a polite welcome and ushered them into the work-room.

Twango, somewhat nettled by Soldinck's scrutiny of floor, walls and ceiling, spoke crisply. "Gentlemen, on the table you will observe scales to the number of six hundred and twenty, both 'ordinary' and 'special', as specified on this invoice. We shall first inspect, verify and pack the 'specials'."

Soldinck pointed toward Gark and Gookin. "Not while those two subhuman imps stand by! I believe that in some way they cast a spell to befuddle not only poor Weamish but all the rest of us. Then they made free with the scales."

Cugel stated: "Soldinck's point seems valid. Gark, Gookin: begone! Go out and chase frogs from the garden!"

Twango protested: "That is foolishly and unnecessarily harsh! Still, if you must have it so, Gark and Gookin will oblige us by departing."

With red-eyed glares toward Cugel, Gark and Gookin darted from the room.

Twango now counted out the 'special' scales, while Soldinck checked them against an invoice and Cugel packed them one by one into the case under the vigilant scrutiny of Rincz and Jornulk. Then, in the same manner, the 'ordinaries' were packed. Cugel, watched closely by all, fitted covers to the cases, secured them well, and placed them on the carrier.

"Now," said Cugel, "since from this point to the wagon I will be prime custodian of the scales, I must insist that, while all witness, I seal the cases with wax, into which I inscribe my special mark. By this means I and every one else must be assured that the cases we pack and load here arrive securely at the wagon."

"A wise precaution," said Twango. "We will all witness the process."

Cugel sealed the boxes, made his mark into the hardening

wax, then strapped the cases to the carrier. He explained: "We must take care lest a vibration or an unforeseen jar dislodge one of the cases, to the possible damage of the contents."

"Right, Cugel! Are we now prepared?"

"Quite so. Rincz and Jornulk, you will go first, taking care that the way is without hindrance. Soldinck, you will precede the carrier by five paces. I will push the carrier and Twango will follow five paces to the rear. In absolute security we shall thereby bring the scales to the wagon."

"Very good," said Soldinck. "So it shall be. Rincz, Jornulk! You will go first, using all alertness!"

The procession departed the work-room and passed through a dark corridor fifteen yards long, pausing only long enough for Cugel to call ahead to Soldinck: "Is all clear?"

"All is clear," came back Soldinck's reassurance. "You may come forward!"

Without further delay Cugel rolled the carrier out to the wagon. "Notice all! The cases are delivered to the wagon in the number of four, each sealed with my seal. Soldinck, I hereby transfer custody of these valuables to you. I will now apply more wax, upon which you will stamp your own mark. . . . . Very good; my part of the business is done."

Twango congratulated Cugel. "And done well, Cugel! All was proper and efficient. The carrier looked neat and orderly with its fine coat of varnish and the neat apron installed by Weamish. Now then, Soldinck, if you will render me the receipt and my payment in full, the transaction will be complete."

Soldinck, still in a somewhat surly mood, gave over the receipt and counted out terces to the stipulated amount; then, with Rincz and Jornulk, he drove his wagon back to Saskervoy.

Cugel meanwhile wheeled the carrier to the shop. He inverted the top surface on its secret pivot, to bring the four cases into view. He removed the lids, lifted out the packets, put the broken cases into the fire, and poured the scales into a sack.

A flicker of motion caught his attention. Cugel peered sideways and glimpsed a smart red cap disappearing from view at the window.

Cugel stood motionless for ten seconds, then he moved with

haste. He ran outside, but saw neither Gark nor Gookin, nor yet Yelleg nor Malser who presumably were diving in the pond.

Returning into the shop, Cugel took the sack of scales and ran fleet-footed to that hovel inhabited by Bilberd the half-witted gardener. Under a pile of rubbish in the corner of the room he hid the sack, then ran back to the shop. Into another sack he poured an assortment of nails, studs, nuts, bolts and assorted trifles of hardware, and replaced this sack on the shelf. Then, after stirring the fire around the burning cases, he busied himself varnishing the upper surface of the carrier.

Three minutes later Twango arrived with Gark and Gookin at his heels, the latter carrying long-handled man-hooks.

Cugel held up his hand. "Careful, Twango! The varnish is wet!"

Twango called out in a nasal voice: "Cugel, let us have no evasion! Where are the scales?"

"'Scales'? Why do you want them now?"

"Cugel, the scales, if you please!"

Cugel shrugged. "As you like." He brought down a tray. "I have had quite a decent morning. Six 'ordinaries' and a fine 'special'! Notice this extraordinary specimen, if you will!"

"Yes, that is a 'Malar Astrangal', which fits over the elbow part of the third arm. It is an exceedingly fine specimen. Where are the others, which, so I understand, are numbered in the hundreds?"

Cugel looked at him in amazement. "Where have you heard such an extraordinary fantasy?"

"That is a matter of no consequence! Show me the scales or I must ask Gark and Gookin to find them!"

"Do so, by all means," said Cugel with dignity. "But first let me protect my property." He placed the six 'ordinaries' and the 'Malar Astrangal' in his pouch. At this moment, Gark, hopping up on the bench, gave a rasping croak of triumph and pulled down the sack Cugel had so recently placed there. "This is the sack! It is heavy with scales!"

Twango poured out the contents of the sack. "A few minutes ago," said Cugel, "I looked through this sack for a clevis to fit upon the carrier. Gark perhaps mistook these objects for scales." Cugel went to the door. "I will leave you to your search."

The time was now approaching the hour when Yelleg and Malser ordinarily took their tea. Cugel looked into the shed, but the fire was dead and the divers were nowhere to be seen.

Good enough, thought Cugel. Now was the time to remove from his grave those scales originally filched by Weamish.

He went to the back of the garden, where, in the shade of the myrhadian tree he had buried Weamish and dug his own grave.

No unwelcome observers were in evidence. Cugel started to jump down into his grave, but stopped short, deterred by the sight of four broken and empty cases at the bottom of the hole.

Cugel returned to the manse and went to the refectory where he found Bilberd the gardener.

"I am looking for Yelleg and Malser," said Cugel. "Have you seen them recently?"

Bilberd simpered and blinked. "Indeed I have, about two hours ago, when they departed for Saskervoy. They said that they were done diving for scales."

"That is a surprise," said Cugel through a constricted throat.

"True," said Bilberd. "Still, one must make an occasional change, otherwise he risks stagnation. I have gardened at Flutic for twenty-three years and I am starting to lose interest in the job. It is time that I myself considered a new career, perhaps in fashion design, despite the financial risks."

"An excellent idea!" said Cugel. "Were I a wealthy man, I would instantly advance to you the necessary capital!"

"I appreciate the offer!" said Bilberd warmly. "You are a generous man, Cugel!"

The gong sounded, signaling visitors. Cugel started to respond, then settled once more into his seat: let Gark or Gookin or Twango himself answer the door.

The gong sounded, again and again, and finally Cugel, from sheer vexation, went to answer the summons.

At the door stood Soldinck, with Rincz and Jornulk. Soldinck's face was grim. "Where is Twango? I wish to see him at once."

"It might be better if you returned tomorrow," said Cugel. "Twango is taking his afternoon rest."

"No matter! Rouse him out, in double-quick time! The matter is urgent!"

"I doubt if he will wish to see you today. He tells me that his fatigue is extreme."

"What?" roared Soldinck. "He should be dancing for joy! After all, he took my good terces and gave me cases of dried mud in exchange!"

"Impossible," said Cugel. "The precautions were exact."

"Your theories are of no interest to me," declared Soldinck. "Take me to Twango at once!"

"He is unavailable for any but important matters. I wish you a cordial good-day." Cugel started to close the door, but Soldinck set up an outcry, and now Twango himself appeared on the scene. He asked: "What is the reason for this savage uproar? Cugel, you know how sensitive I am to noise!"

"Just so," said Cugel, "but Master Soldinck seems intent upon a demonstration."

Twango turned to Soldinck. "What is the difficulty? We have finished our business for the day."

Cugel did not await Soldinck's reply. As Bilberd had remarked, the time had come for a change. He had lost a goodly number of scales to the dishonesty of Yelleg and Malser, but as many more awaited him in Bilberd's hut, with which he must be content.

Cugel hastened through the manse. He looked into the refectory, where Gark and Gookin worked at the preparation of the evening meal.

Very good, thought Cugel, in fact, excellent! Now he need only avoid Bilberd, take the sack of scales and be away. . . . . He went out into the garden, but Bilberd was not at his work.

Cugel went to Bilberd's hut and put his head through the door. "Bilberd?"

There was no response. A shaft of red light slanting through the door illuminated Bilberd's pallet in full detail. By the diffused light, Cugel saw that the hut was empty.

Cugel glanced over his shoulder, entered the hut and went to the corner where he had hidden the sack.

The rubbish had been disarranged. The sack was gone.

From the manse came the sound of voices. Twango called: "Cugel! Where are you? Come at once!"

Quick and silent as a wraith, Cugel slipped from Bilberd's hut and took cover in a nearby juniper copse. Sidling from shadow to shadow, he circled the manse and came out upon the road. He looked right and left, then, discovering no threat, set off on long loping strides to the west. Through the forest and over the hill marched Cugel, and presently arrived at Saskervoy.

Two days later, while strolling the esplanade, Cugel noticed that ancient tavern known as 'The Iron Cockatrice'. As he drew near, the door opened and two men lurched into the street: one massive, with yellow curls and a heavy jaw; the other lean, with gaunt cheeks, black hair and a hooked nose. Both wore costly garments, with double-tiered hats, red satin sashes and boots of fine leather.

Cugel, looking once, then a second time, recognized Yelleg and Malser. Each had enjoyed at least a bottle of wine and possibly two. Yelleg sang a ballad of the sea and Malser sang "Tirra la lirra, we are off to the land where the daisies grow!" in refrain. Preoccupied with the exact rhythm of their music, they brushed past Cugel, looking neither right nor left, and went off along the esplanade toward another tavern, 'The Star of the North'.

Cugel started to follow, then jumped back at the rumble of approaching wheels. A fine carriage, drawn by a pair of high-stepping perchers, swerved in front of him and rolled off along the esplanade. The driver wore a black velvet suit with silver epaulettes, and a large hat with a curling black plume; beside him sat a buxom lady in an orange gown. Only with difficulty could Cugel identify the driver as Bilberd, former gardener at Flutic. Cugel muttered sourly under his breath: "Bilberd's new career, which I generously offered to finance, has cost me rather more than I expected."

Early the next morning Cugel left Saskervoy by the east

road. He crossed over the hills and came down upon upon Shanglestone Strand.

Nearby, the eccentric towers of Flutic rose into the morning sunlight, sharp against the northern murk.

Cugel approached the manse by a devious route, keeping to the cover of shrubs and hedges, pausing often to listen. He heard nothing; a desolate mood hung in the air.

Cautiously Cugel circled the manse. The pond came into view. Out in the middle Twango sat in the iron scow, shoulders hunched and neck pulled down. As Cugel watched, Twango hauled in a rope; up from the depths came Gark with a small bucket of slime, which Twango emptied into the tub.

Twango returned the bucket to Gark who made a chattering sound and dived again into the depths. Twango pulled on a second rope to bring up Gookin with another bucket.

Cugel retreated to the dark blue mitre-bush. He dug down and, using a folded cloth to protect his hand, retrieved the 'Pectoral Sky-break Spatterlight'.

Cugel went to take a final survey of the pond. The tub was full. Gark and Gookin, two small figures caked with slime, sat at either end of the scow, while Twango heaved at the overhead rope. Cugel watched a moment, then turned and went his way back to Saskervoy.

2
THE INN
OF BLUE LAMPS

WHEN Master Soldinck returned to Flutic in search of his missing scales, Cugel decided not to take part in the inquiry. He imediately departed Flutic by an obscure route and set off to the west toward the town Saskervoy.

After a period Cugel pused to catch his breath. His mood was bitter. Through the duplicity of underlings he carried, not a valuable parcel of scales, but only a handful of 'ordinaries' and a single 'special' of distinction: the 'Malar Astrangal'. The most precious scale of all, the 'Pectoral Sky-break Spatterlight', remained hidden in the back garden at Flutic, but Cugel hoped to retain this scale, if only because it was coveted by Iucounu the Laughing Magician.

Cugel again set off along the road: through a dank forest of thamber oak, yew, mernache and goblin-tree. Wan red sunlight sifted through the foliage; shadows, by some trick of perception, seemed to be stained dark blue.

Cugel maintained an uneasy watch to either side, as was only prudent during these latter times. He saw much that was strange and sometimes beautiful: white blossoms held high on tall tendrils above spangles of low flat leaves; fairy castles of fungus growing in shelves, terraces and turrets over rotting stumps; patterns of black and orange bracken. Once, indistinct at a distance of a hundred yards, Cugel thought to see a tall man-like shape in a lavender jerkin. Cugel carried no weapon, and he breathed easier when the road, mounting a hillside, broke out into the afternoon daylight.

At this moment Cugel heard the sound of Soldinck's wagon returning from Flutic. He stepped off the road and waited in the shadow of a rock. The wagon passed by, and Soldinck's grim expression was a convincing sign that his talks with Twango had not gone well.

The sound of the wagon receded and Cugel resumed his journey. The road crossed over a windy ridge, descended the slope by a series of traverses, then, rounding a bluff, allowed Cugel a view over Saskervoy.

Cugel had thought to find little more than a village. Saskervoy exceeded his expectations, both in size and in its air of ancient respectability. Tall narrow houses stood side by side along the streets, the stone of their structure weathered by ages of lichen, smoke and sea-fog. Windows glistened and brass-work twinkled in the red sunlight; such was the way at Saskervoy.

Cugel followed the road down into the town and proceeded toward the harbor. Strangers were evidently a novelty for the folk of Saskervoy. At Cugel's approach, all stopped to stare, and not a few hurriedly crossed the street. They seemed, thought Cugel, a people of old-fashioned habit, and perhaps conservative in their views. The men wore black swallow-tail coats with voluminous trousers and black buckled shoes, while the women, in their shapeless gowns and round, punch-bowl hats pulled low, were like dumplings.

Cugel arrived at a plaza beside the harbor. Several ships of good proportion lay alongside the dock, any one of which might be sailing south, perhaps as far as Almery.

Cugel went to sit on a bench. He examined the contents of his pouch, discovering sixteen 'ordinaries', two 'specials' of minor value and the 'Malar Astrangal'. Depending upon Soldinck's standards of payment, the scales might or might not cover the costs of a sea voyage.

Almost direcly across the plaza, Cugel noticed a sign affixed to the front of an imposing stone building:

SOLDINCK AND MERCANTIDES
EXPORTERS AND IMPORTERS OF QUALITY PRODUCTS
SHIPPING AGENTS

Cugel considered a range of strategies, each more subtle than the next. All grounded against a crude and basic reality: in order to take lodging at an inn, he must sell scales to pay his account.

Afternoon was waning. Cugel rose to his feet. He crossed the plaza and entered the offices of Soldinck and Mercantides.

The premises were heavy with dignity and tradition; along with the odors of varnish and old wood, the sweet-sour scent of decorum hung in the air. Crossing the hush of a high-ceilinged chamber, Cugel approached a polished brown marble counter. On the other side an old clerk sat frowning into a ledger, and failed to acknowledge Cugel's presence.

Cugel gave a peremptory rap on the counter.

"One moment! Patience, if you please!" said the clerk, and went on with his work, despite Cugel's second irritated rap.

Finally, making the best of circumstances, Cugel set himself to wait upon the clerk's convenience.

The outer door opened; into the chamber came a man of Cugel's own age, wearing a tall-crowned hat of brown felt and a rumpled suit of blue velvet. His face was round and placid; tufts of pale hair like wisps of hay protruded from under his hat. His belly pressed forward the front of his coat, and a pair of broad buttocks rode upon two long spindle-shanked legs.

The newcomer advanced to the counter; the clerk jumped to his feet with alacrity. "Sir, how may I be of assistance?"

Cugel stepped forward in annoyance and raised his finger. "One moment! My business remains to be dealt with!"

The others paid him no heed. The newcomer said: "My name is Bunderwal, and I wish to see Soldinck."

"This way, sir! I am happy to say that Soldinck is at liberty."

The two departed the room, while Cugel fumed with impatience.

The clerk returned. He started to go to his ledger, then noticed Cugel. "Did you want something?"

"I also require a few words with Soldinck," said Cugel haughtily. "Your methods are incorrect. Since I entered the chamber first, you should have dealt first with my affairs."

The clerk blinked. "The idea, I must say, has an innocent simplicity in its favor. What is your business with Soldinck?"

"I want to arrange passage by the quickest and most comfortable means to Almery."

The clerk went to study a wall map. "I see no mention of such a place."

"Almery lies below the bottom edge of the map."

The clerk gave Cugel a wondering glance. "That is a far distance. Well, come along; perhaps Soldinck will see you."

'You need merely announce the name 'Cugel'."

The clerk led the way to the end of a hall and pushed his head through a pair of hangings. "A certain 'Cugel' is here to see you."

There was a moment of strained silence, then Soldinck's voice came in response: "Well then, Diffin: what does he want?"

"Transport to a possibly imaginary land, as best I can make out."

"Hmmf. . . . .Show him in."

Diffin held aside the hangings for Cugel, then shuffled back the way he had come. Cugel entered an octagonal chamber furnished in austere luxury. Soldinck, gray-haired and stern-faced, stood beside an octagonal table while Bunderwal sat on a couch upholstered in maroon plush. Crimson sunlight, entering through high windows, illuminated a pair of barbaric wall-hangings, woven in the backlands of Far Cutz. A heavy black iron chandelier hung by an iron chain from the ceiling.

Cugel rendered Soldinck a formal greeting, which Soldinck acknowledged without warmth. "What is your business, Cugel? I am consulting Bunderwal on matters of importance and I can spare only a moment or two."

"I will be brief," said Cugel coldly. "Am I correct in assuming that you ship scales to Almery at the command of Iucounu the Magician?"

"Not entirely," said Soldinck. "We convey the scales to our factor at Port Perdusz, who then arranges trans-shipment."

"Why, may I ask, do you not ship directly to Almery?"

"It is not practical to venture so far south."

Cugel frowned in annoyance. "When does your next ship leave for Port Perdusz?"

"The *Galante* sails before the week is out."

"And what are the charges for passage to Port Perdusz?"

"We carry only select passengers. The charges, so I believe, are three hundred terces: a sum —" and here Soldinck's voice became somewhat lofty "— perhaps beyond your competence."

"Not at all. I have here a number of scales which should bring considerably more than that amount."

Soldinck showed a flicker of interest. "I will at least look them over."

Cugel displayed his scales. "Notice especiallly this very fine 'Malar Astrangal'!"

"It is a decent specimen, despite the greenish tinge to the marathaxus." Soldinck scanned the scales with a practiced eye. "I value the lot generously at approximately one hundred and eighty-three terces."

The sum was twenty terces more than Cugel had dared hope for. He started to make an automatic protest, then thought better of it. "Very well; the scales are yours."

"Take them to Diffin; he will give you your money." Soldinck gestured toward the hangings.

"Another matter. From curiosity, what will you pay for the 'Pectoral Sky-break Spatterlight'?"

Soldinck looked up sharply. "You have custody of this scale?"

"For the moment let us think in hypothetical cases."

Soldinck raised his eyes to the ceiling. "If it were in prime condition, I might well risk as much as two hundred terces."

Cugel nodded. "And why should you not, since Iucounu will pay two thousand terces or even more?"

"I suggest then that you take this hypothetical item directly to Iucounu. I can even suggest a convenient route. If you return eastward along Shanglestone Strand, you will come to Hag Head and the Castle Cil. Veer south to avoid the Great Erm, which you will find to be infested with erbs and leucomorphs. The Mountains of Magnatz lie ahead of you; they are extremely dangerous, but if you try to bypass them you must risk the Desert of Obelisks. Of the lands beyond I know little."

"I have some acquaintance with these lands," said Cugel. "I prefer passage aboard the *Galante*."

"Mercantides insists that we transport only persons in our own employ. We are chary of well-spoken passengers who, at a given signal, become merciless pirates."

"I will be pleased to accept a position with your firm," said Cugel. "I have capabilities of many sorts; I believe that you will find me useful."

Soldinck smiled a cold brief smile. "Unfortunately, a single post is open at the moment, that of supercargo aboard the *Galante*, for which I already have a qualified applicant, namely Bunderwal."

Cugel gave Bunderwal a careful inspection. "He seems to be a modest, decent and unassuming person, but definitely not a sound choice for the position of supercargo."

"And why do you say that?"

"If you will notice," said Cugel, "Bunderwal shows the drooping nostrils which indicate an infallible tendency toward sea-sickness."

"Cugel is a man of discernment!" declared Bunderwal. "I would rate him an applicant of fair to good quality, and I urge you to ignore his long spatulate fingers which I last noticed on Larkin the baby-stealer. There is a significant difference between the two: Larkin has been hanged and Cugel has not been hanged."

Cugel said: "We are posing problems for poor Soldinck, who already has worries enough. Let us be considerate. I suggest that we trust our fortunes to Mandingo the three-eyed Goddess of Luck." He brought a packet of playing cards from his pouch.

"The idea has merit," said Bunderwal. "But let us use my cards which are newer and easier for the eyes of Soldinck."

Cugel frowned. He gave his head a decisive shake and replaced the cards in his pouch. "As I analyze the situation, I see that despite your inclinations — I am truly sorry to say this, Bunderwal — it is not proper to deal with Soldinck's important affairs in so frivolous a fashion. I suggested it only as a test. A person of the proper qualities would have rejected the idea out of hand!"

Soldinck was favorably impressed. "On the mark, Cugel!"

"Allow me to suggest a comprehensive program," said Cugel. "By reason of my wide experience and better address, I will accept the post of supercargo. Bunderwal, so I believe, will make an excellent understudy to Diffin the clerk."

Soldinck turned to Bunderwal: "What do you say to this?"

"Cugel's qualifications are impressive," Bunderwal admitted.

"Against them I can counterpose only honesty, skill, dedication, and tireless industry. Further, I am a dignified citizen of the area, not a fox-faced vagabond in an over-fancy hat."

Cugel turned to Soldinck: "At last — and we are lucky in this — Bunderwal's style, which consists of slander and vituperation, can be contrasted with my own dignity and restraint. I still must point out his oily skin and over-large buttocks; they indicate a bent for high-living and even a tendency toward peculation. If indeed we hire Bunderwal as under-clerk, I suggest that all locks be reinforced, for the better protection of your valuables."

Bunderwal cleared his throat to speak, but Soldinck held up his hands. "Gentlemen, I have heard enough! I will discuss your qualifications with Mercantides, who may well wish to interview you both. Tomorrow at noon I will have further news for you."

Cugel bowed. "Thank you, sir." He turned to Bunderwal and indicated the hangings. "You may go, Bunderwal. I wish a private word with Soldinck."

Bunderwal started to protest but Cugel said: "I must discuss the sale of valuable scales."

Bunderwal reluctantly departed. Cugel turned to Soldinck. "During our discussion, the 'Spatterlight' was mentioned."

"True. You never defined the exact state of your control over this scale."

"Nor will I do so now, except to emphasize that the scale is safely hidden. If I were attacked by footpads, their efforts would fail. I mention this only to save us both inconvenience."

Soldinck showed a grim smile. "Your claims as to 'comprehensive experience' would seem to be well-founded."

Cugel collected the sum of one hundred and eighty-three terces from Diffin, who counted out the coins three times, and passed them only reluctantly across the brown marble counter. Cugel swept the terces into his pouch, then departed the premises.

Recalling the advice of Weamish, Cugel took lodging at The Inn of Blue Lamps. For his supper he consumed a platter of roasted blowfish, with side dishes of carbade, yams and sluteberry mash. Leaning back over wine and cheese, he surveyed the company.

Across the room, at a table beside the fireplace, two men began to play at cards. The first was tall and thin with a cadaverous complexion, bad teeth in a long jaw, lank black hair and drooping eyelids. The second displayed a powerful physique, a heavy nose and jaw, a top-knot of red hair and a fine glinting red beard.

To augment their game, they cast about for other players. The tall man cried out: "Hoy there, Fursk! What about a round at Skax? No?"

The man with the red beard called: "There's good Sabtile, who never refuses a game! Sabtile, this way with your full purse and bad luck! Excellent."

"Who else? What about you there, with the long nose and fancy hat?"

Cugel diffidently approached the table. "What game do you play? I warn you, at cards I am a hopeless duffer."

"The game is Skax, and we don't care how you play, so long as you cover your bets."

Cugel smiled politely. "If only to be sociable, I will venture a hand or two, but you must teach me the fine points of the game."

The red-bearded man guffawed. "No fear! You will learn them as fast as the hands are dealt! I am Wagmund; this is Sabtile and this saturnine cutthroat is Koyman, embalmer to the town Saskervoy and a most reputable citizen. Now then! The rules for Skax are thus and so." Wagmund went on to explain the mode of play, emphasizing his points by pounding the table with a blunt forefinger. "So then, Cugel, is this all clear? Do you think you will be able to cope with the game? Remember, all bets must be made in solid terces. One may not hold his cards beneath the table or move them back and forth in a suspicious manner."

"I am both inexperienced and cautious," said Cugel. "Still, I think I understand the game and I will risk two, no three, terces, and I hereby bet one discrete, solid and whole terce on the first sally."

"That's the spirit, Cugel!" said Wagmund approvingly.

"Koyman, distribute the cards, if you will!"

"First," Sabtile pointed out, "you must place out your own bet!"

"True," admitted Wagmund. "See that you do the same."

"No fear of that; I am known for my quick and clever style of play."

"Fewer boasts and more money!" called Koyman. "I await your terces!"

"What of your own bet, my good stealer of ornamental gold sphincter-clasps* from the corpses entrusted into your care?"

"An oversight: simply that and no more."

The play proceeded. Cugel lost eleven terces, and drank two mugs of the local beer: a pungent liquid brewed from acorns, bittermoss and black sausage. Presently Cugel was able to introduce his own cards into the game, whereupon his luck changed and he quickly won thirty-eight terces, with Wagmund, Koyman and Sabtile crying out and smiting their foreheads in disbelief at the unfavorable consequences of their play.

Into the common room ambled Bunderwal. He called for beer and for a space stood watching the game, teetering up and down on his toes and smoking dried herbs in a long-stemmed clay pipe. He seemed a skillful analyst of the game, and from time to time called out his approval of good play, while chaffing the losers for their blunders. "Ah then, Koyman, why did you not play down your Double-red and sweep the field before Cugel beat you with his Green Varlets?"

Koyman snapped: "Because the last time I did so, Cugel brought out the Queen of Devils and destroyed my hopes." Koyman rose to his feet. "I am destitute. Cugel, at least tender me a beer from your winnings."

"With pleasure!" Cugel called the serving boy. "Beer for Koyman and also for Bunderwal!"

"Thank you." Koyman signaled Bunderwal to his place. "You may try your luck against Cugel, who plays with uncanny skill."

"I will try him for a terce or two. Ho boy! Bring fresh cards,

---

* An awkward rendering of the more succinct *Anfangel dongobel*.

and throw away these limp old rags! Some are short, some are long; some are stained; others show strange designs."

"New cards by all means," cried Cugel heartily. "Still I will take these old cards and use them for practice. Bunderwal, where is your bet?"

Bunderwal placed out a terce and distributed the new cards with a fluttering agility of the fingers which caused Cugel to blink.

Several sallies were played out, but luck had deserted Cugel. He relinquished his chair to another and went to stand behind Bunderwal, in order to study the manner in which Bunderwal conducted his play.

After winning ten terces, Bunderwal declared that he wanted no more gaming for the evening. He turned to Cugel. "Allow me to invest some of my winnings in a noble purpose: the ingestion of good beer. This way; I see a couple of chairs vacant by the wall. Boy! Two mugs of the best Tatterblass!"

"Right, sir!" The boy saluted and ran down into the still-room.

Bunderwal put away his pipe. "Well, Cugel: what do you think of Saskervoy?"

"It seems a pleasant community, with prospects for the earnest worker."

"Exactly so, and in fact it is to this subject that I address myself. First, I drink to your continued prosperity."

"I will drink to prosperity in the abstract," said Cugel cautiously. "I have had little experience of it."

"What? With your dexterity at Skax? My eyes are crossed from the attempt to follow your flamboyant flourishes."

"A foolish mannerism," said Cugel. "I must learn to play with less display."

"It is no great matter," said Bunderwal. "Of more importance is that employment offered by Soldinck, which already has prompted several regrettable interchanges."

"True," said Cugel. "Let me make a suggestion."

"I am always open to new concepts."

"The supercargo possibly controls other posts aboard the *Galante*. If you will —"

Bunderwal held up his hand. "Let us be realistic. I perceive you to be a man of decision. Let us put our case to the test here and now, and let Mandingo determine who applies for the position and who stands aloof."

Cugel brought out his cards. "Will you play Skax or Rampolio?"

"Neither," said Bunderwal. "We must settle upon on a test where the outcome is not fore-ordained. . . . Notice the glass yonder, where Krasnark the landlord keeps his sphigales." Bunderwal indicated a glass-sided box. Within resided a number of crustaceans, which, when broiled, were considered a notable delicacy. The typical sphigale measured eight inches in length, with a pair of powerful pincer-claws and a whip-tail sting.

"These creatures show different temperaments," said Bunderwal. "Some are fast, some slow. Choose one and I will choose another. We will set our racers upon the floor and the first to reach the opposite wall wins the test."

Cugel studied the sphigales. "They are mettlesome beasts, no question as to this." One of the sphigales, a creature striped red, yellow and an unpleasant chalk-blue, caught his eye. "Very well; I have selected my racer."

"Extract him with the tongs, but take care! They use both pincers and sting with a will."

Working discreetly so as to avoid attention, Cugel seized his racer with the tongs and placed it on the line; Bunderwal did likewise.

Bunderwal addressed his beast: "Good sphigale, run your best; my future hangs on your speed! At the ready! Take position! Go!"

Both men lifted their tongs and discreetly departed the vicinity of the tank. The sphigales ran out across the floor. Bunderwal's racer, noticing the open doorway, turned aside and fled into the night. Cugel's sphigale took refuge in the boot removed by Wagmund that he might warm his feet at the fire.

"I declare both contestants disqualified," said Bunderwal. "We must test our destiny by other means."

Cugel and Bunderwal resumed their seats. After a moment Bunderwal conceived a new scheme. "The still-room is beyond this wall and half a level lower. To avoid collisions, the serving-boys descend by the steps on the right, and come up with their trays by the steps to the left. Each passageway is closed outside of working hours by one of those heavy sliding shutters. As you will observe, the shutters are held up by a chain. Notice further. This chain here to hand controls the shutter to the stairs on the left, up which the serving boys come with their beer and other orders. Thirdly, each of the serving boys wears a round pill-box cap, to keep his hair out of the food. The game we play is this. Each man in turn adjusts the chain, and he is obliged to lower the shutter by one or more links. At length one of the boys will brush off his cap on the bottom bar of the shutter. When this occurs the man last to touch the chain loses the wager and must relinquish all claim to the post of supercargo."

Cugel considered the chain, the shutter which slid up and down to close off the passageway, and appraised the serving boys.

"The boys vary somewhat in height," Bunderwal pointed out, "with perhaps three inches separating the shortest from the most tall. On the other hand, I believe that the tallest boy is inclined to hunch down his head. It makes for an intricate strategy."

Cugel said: "I must stipulate that neither of us may signal, call or cause distractions calculated to upset the pure logic of the game."

"Agreed!" said Bunderwal. "We must play the game like gentlemen. Further, to avoid spurious tactics of delay, let us stipulate that the move must be made before the second boy emerges. For instance, you have lowered the shutter and I have calculated that the tallest boy is next to emerge. I may, or may not, as I choose, wait until one boy has emerged, but then I must slip my chain before the second boy appears."

"A wise regulation, to which I agree. Do you care to go first?"

Bunderwal disclaimed the privilege. "You, in a sense, are our guest here in Saskervoy, and you shall have the honor of the first play."

"Thank you." Cugel lifted the chain from its peg and lowered the shutter by two links. "It is now your turn, Bunderwal."

You may wait until one boy has emerged, if you choose, and indeed I will expedite the process by ordering more beer for ourselves."

"Good. Now, I must bend my keenest faculties to the game. I see that one must develop an exquisite sense of timing. I hereby lower the chain two links."

Cugel waited and the tall boy emerged carrying a tray loaded with four pitchers of beer. By Cugel's estimate, he avoided the shutter by a gap equivalent to thirteen links of the chain. Cugel at once let slip four links.

"Aha!" said Bunderwal. "You play with a flair! I will show that I am no less dashing than you! Another four links!"

Cugel appraised the shutter under narrow lids. A slippage of six more links should strike off the tall boy's cap with smartness and authority. If the boys served regularly in turn, the tall boy should be emerging third in line. Cugel waited until the next boy, of medium stature, passed through, then lowered the chain five full links.

Bunderwal sucked in his breath, then gave a chirrup of triumph. "Clever thinking, Cugel! But now quickly, I lower the chain another two links. So I will avoid the short boy, who even now mounts the stairs."

The short boy passed below with a link or two to spare, and Cugel must now move or forfeit the game. Glumly he let go another link from the chain, and now up from the still-room came the tallest boy. As luck would have it, while mounting the stairs he bobbed his head in order to wipe his nose on his sleeve and so passed under the shutter with cap still in place, and it was Cugel's turn to chortle in triumph. "Move, Bunderwal, if you will, unless you wish to concede."

Bunderwal disconsolately let slip a link in the chain. "Now I can only pray for a miracle."

Up the steps came Krasnark the landlord: a heavy-featured man taller than the tall boy, with massive arms and lowering black eyebrows. He carried a tray loaded with a tureen of soup, a brace of roast fowl and a great hemisphere of sour-wabble pudding. His head struck the bar; he fell over backward and disappeared from view. From the still-room came the crash of broken crockery and almost at once a great outcry.

Bunderwal and Cugel quickly hauled up the shutter to its original position and moved to new seats. Cugel said, "I feel that I must be declared winner of the game, since yours was the last hand to touch the chain."

"By no means!" Bunderwal protested. "The thrust of the game, as stated, was to dislodge a cap from the head of one of three persons. This was not done, since Krasnark chose to interrupt the play."

"Here he is now," said Cugel. "He is examining the shutter with an air of perplexity."

"I see no point in carrying the matter any further," said Bunderwal. "So far as I am concerned, the game is ended."

"Except for the adjudication," said Cugel. "I am clearly the winner, from almost any point of view."

Bunderwal could not be swayed. "Krasnark wore no cap, and there the matter must rest. Let me suggest another test, in which chance plays a more decisive role."

"Here is the boy with our beer, at last. Boy, you are remarkably slow!"

"Sorry, sir. Krasnark fell into the still-room and caused no end of tumult."

"Very well; no more need be said. Bunderwal, explain your game."

"It is so simple as to be embarrassing. The door yonder leads out to the urinal. Look about the room; select a champion. I will do likewise. Whichever champion is last to patronize the urinal wins the game for his sponsor."

"The contest seems fair," said Cugel. "Have you selected a champion?"

"I have indeed. And you?"

"I selected my man on the instant. I believe him to be invincible in a contest of this sort. He is the somewhat elderly man with the thin nose and the pursy mouth sitting directly to my left. He is not large but I am made confident by the abstemious manner in which he holds his glass."

"He is a good choice," Bunderwal admitted. "By coincidence I have selected his companion, the gentleman in the gray robe who sips his beer as if with distaste."

Cugel summoned the serving boy and spoke behind his

hand, out of Bunderwal's hearing. "The two gentlemen to my left — why do they drink so slowly?"

The boy shrugged. "If you want the truth, they hate to part with their coin, although both command ample funds. Still, they sit by the hour nursing a gill of our most acrid brew."

"In that case," said Cugel, "bring the gentleman in the gray cloak a double-quart of your best ale, at my expense, but do not identify me."

"Very good, sir."

The boy turned at a signal from Bunderwal who also initiated a short muttered conversation. The boy bowed and ran down to the still-room. Presently he returned to serve the two champions large double-quart mugs of ale, which, after explanation from the boy, they accepted with gloomy good grace, though clearly they were mystified by the bounty.

Cugel became dissatisfied at the fervent manner in which his champion now drank beer. "I fear that I made a poor selection," he fretted. "He drinks as if he had just come in after a day in the desert."

Bunderwal was equally critical of his own champion. "He is already nose-deep in the double-quart. That trick of yours, Cugel, if I must say so, was definitely underhanded. I was forced to protect my own interests, at consideral expense."

Cugel thought, by conversation, to distract his champion from the beer. He leaned over and said: "Sir, you are a resident of Saskervoy, I take it?"

"I am that," said the gentleman. "We are noted for our reluctance to talk with strangers in outlandish costumes."

"You are also noted for your sobriety," suggested Cugel.

"That is nonsense!" declared the champion. "Observe the folk around this room, all gulping beer by the gallon. Excuse me, I wish to follow their example."

"I must warn you that this local beer is congestive," said Cugel. "With every mouthful you risk a spasmodic disorder."

"Balderdash! Beer purifies the blood! Put aside your own drink, if you are alarmed, but leave me in peace with mine." Raising his mug, the champion drank an impressive draught.

Displeased with Cugel's maneuver, Bunderwal sought to distract his own champion by treading on his toe and causing an altercation, which might have persisted for a goodly period, had not Cugel interceded and pulled Bunderwal back to his chair. "Play the game by sporting standards or I withdraw from the contest!"

"Your own tactics are somewhat sharp," muttered Bunderwal.

"Very well!" said Cugel. "Let us have no more interference, of any sort!"

"I agree, but the point becomes moot as your champion is showing signs of uneasiness. He is about to rise to his feet, in which case I win."

"Not so! The first to use the trough loses the game. Notice! Your own champion is rising to his feet; they are going together."

"Then the first to leave the common room must be deemed loser, since almost certainly he will be first at the trough!"

"With my champion in the lead? Not so! The first actually to use the trough is the loser."

"Come then; there can be no exact judgment from this distance."

Cugel and Bunderwal hastened to follow the two champions: through the yard and out to an illuminated shed where a trough fixed to a masonry wall served the needs of the inn's patrons.

The two champions seemed in no hurry; they paused to comment upon the mildness of the night, then, almost in synchrony, went to the trough. Cugel and Bunderwal followed, one to each side, and made ready to render judgment.

The two champions prepared to relieve themselves. Cugel's champion, glancing to the side, noticed the quality of Cugel's attention, and instantly became indignant. "What are you looking at? Landlord! Out here at once! Call the night-guards!"

Cugel tried to explain. "Sir, the situation is not as you think! Bunderwal will verify the case! Bunderwal?"

Bunderwal, however, had returned into the common room. Krasnark the landlord appeared, a bandage across his forehead. "Please, sirs, a moment of quiet! Master Chernitz, be good enough to compose yourself! What is the difficulty?"

"No difficulty!" sputtered Chernitz. "An outrage, rather!

I came out here to relieve myself, whereupon this person ranged himself beside me and acted most offensively. I raised the alarm at once!"

His friend, Bunderwal's erstwhile champion, spoke through clenched lips: "I stand behind the accusation! This man should be ejected from the premises and warned out of town!"

Krasnark turned to Cugel. "These are serious charges! How do you answer them?"

"Master Chernitz is mistaken! I also came out here to relieve myself. Glancing along the wall I noticed my friend Bunderwal and signaled to him, whereupon Master Chernitz set up an embarrassing outcry, and made infamous hints! Better that you eject these two old tree-weasels!"

"What?" cried Chernitz in a passion. "I am a man of substance!"

Krasnark threw up his arms. "Gentlemen, be reasonable! The matter is essentially trivial. Agreed: Cugel should not make signals and greet his friends at the urinal. Master Chernitz might be more generous in his assumptions. I suggest that Master Chernitz retract the term 'moral leper' and Cugel his 'tree-weasel', and there let the matter rest."

"I am not accustomed to such degradations," said Cugel. "Until Master Chernitz apologizes, the term remains in force."

Cugel returned to the common room and resumed his place beside Bunderwal. "You left the urinal quite abruptly," said Cugel. "I waited to verify the results of the contest. Your champion was defeated by several seconds."

"Only after you distracted your own champion. The contest is void."

Master Chernitz and his friend returned to their seats. After a single cold glance toward Cugel, they turned away and spoke in low voices.

At Cugel's signal the serving boy brought full mugs of Tatterblass beer and both he and Bunderwal refreshed themselves. After a few moments Bunderwal said: "Despite our best efforts, we still have not settled our little problem."

"And why? Because contests of this sort abandon all to chance! As such, they are incompatible with my personal temperament. I am not one to crouch passively with my hindquarters raised, awaiting either the kick or the caress of Destiny! I am Cugel! Fearless and indomitable, I confront every adversity! Through the force of sheer will I —"

Bunderwal made an impatient gesture. "Silence, Cugel! I have heard enough of your braggadocio. You have taken too much beer, and I believe you to be drunk."

Cugel stared at Bunderwal in disbelief. "Drunk? On three draughts of this pallid Tatterblass? I have swallowed rain-water of greater force. Boy! Bring more beer! Bunderwal, what of you?"

"I will join you, with pleasure. Now then, since you reject a further test, are you willing, then, to concede defeat?"

"Never! Let us drink beer, quart for quart, while we dance the double coppola! The first to fall flat is the loser."

Bunderwal shook his head. "Our capacities are both noble and the stuff of which myths are made. We might dance all night, to a state of mutual exhaustion and enrich only Krasnark."

"Well then: do you have a better idea?"

"I do indeed! If you will glance to your left, you will see that both Chernitz and his friend are dozing. Notice how their beards jut out! Here is a swange for cutting kelp. Cut off one beard or the other, and I concede you victory."

Cugel looked askance toward the dozing men. "They are not soundly asleep. I challenge Destiny, yes, but I do not leap off cliffs."

"Very well," said Bunderwal. "Give me the swange. If I cut a beard, then you must allow me the victory."

The serving-boy brought fresh beer. Cugel drank a deep and thoughtful draught. He said in a subdued voice: "The feat is not as easy as it might appear. Suppose I decided upon Chernitz. He need only open his eyes and say: 'Cugel, why are you cutting my beard?' Whereupon, I would suffer whatever penalty the law of Saskervoy prescribes for this offense."

"The same applies to me," said Bunderwal. "But I have carried my thinking a step farther. Consider this: could either Chernitz or the other see your face, or my face, if the lights were out?"

"If the lights were out, the project becomes feasible," said

Cugel. "Three steps across the floor, seizure of the beard, a strike of the swange, three steps back and the deed is done, and yonder I see the valve which controls the lucifer."

"This is my own thinking," said Bunderwal. "Well then: who will make the trial, you or I? The choice is yours."

The better to order his faculties, Cugel took a long draught of beer. "Let me feel the swange. . . . It is adequately sharp. Well then, a job of this sort must be done while the mood is on one."

"I will control the lucifer valve," said Bunderwal. "As soon as the lights go out, leap to the business at hand."

"Wait," said Cugel. "I must select a beard. That of Chernitz is tempting, but the other projects at a better angle. Ah. . . . Very well; I am ready."

Bunderwal rose to his feet and sauntered to the valve. He looked toward Cugel and nodded.

Cugel prepared himself.

The lights went out. The room was dark but for the glimmer of firelight. Cugel strode on long legs across the floor, seized his chosen beard and skillfully wielded the swange. . . . For an instant the valve slipped in Bunderwal's grip, or perhaps a bubble of lucifer remained in the tubes. In any event, for a fraction of a second the lights flashed bright and the now beardless gentleman, staring up in startlement, looked for a frozen instant eye to eye with Cugel. Then the lights once more went out, and the gentleman was left with the image of a dark long-nosed visage with lank black hair hanging from under a stylish hat.

The gentleman cried out in confusion: "Ho! Krasnark! Rascals and knaves are on us! Where is my beard?"

One of the serving boys, groping through the dark, turned the valve and light once more emanated from the lamps.

Krasnark, bandage askew, rushed forth to investigate the confusion. The beardless gentleman pointed to Cugel, now leaning back in his chair with mug in hand, as if somnolent. "There sits the rogue! I saw him as he cut my beard, grinning like a wolf!"

Cugel called out: "He is raving; pay no heed! I sat here

steadfast as a rock while the beard was being cut. This man is the worse for drink."

"Not so! With both my eyes I saw you!"

Cugel spoke in long-suffering tones. "Why should I take your beard? Does it have value? Search me if you choose! You will find not a hair!"

Krasnark said in a puzzled voice: "Cugel's remarks are logical! Why, after all, should he cut your beard?"

The gentleman, now purple with rage, cried out: "Why should anyone cut my beard? Someone did so; look for yourself!"

Krasnark shook his head and turned away. "It is beyond my imagination! Boy, bring Master Mercantides a mug of good Tatterblass at no charge, to soothe his nerves."

Cugel turned to Bunderwal. "The deed is done."

"The deed has been done, and well," said Bunderwal generously. "The victory is yours! Tomorrow at noon we shall go together to the offices of Soldinck and Mercantides, where I will recommend you for the post of supercargo."

"'Mercantides'," mused Cugel. "Was not that the name by which Krasnark addressed the gentleman whose beard I just cut?"

"Now that you mention it, I believe that he did so indeed," said Bunderwal.

Across the room Wagmund gave a great yawn. "I have had enough excitement for one evening! I am both tired and torpid. My feet are warm and my boots are dry; it is time I departed. First, my boots."

At noon Cugel met Bunderwal in the plaza. They proceeded to the offices of Soldinck and Mercantides, and entered the outer office.

Diffin the clerk ushered them into the presence of Soldinck, who indicated a couch of maroon plush. "Please be seated. Mercantides will be with us shortly and then we will take up our business."

Five minutes later Mercantides entered the room. Looking neither right nor left he joined Soldinck at the octagonal table.

Then, looking up, he noticed Cugel and Buderwal. He spoke sharply: "What are you two doing here?"

Cugel spoke in a careful voice: "Yesterday Bunderwal and I applied for the post of supercargo aboard the *Galante*. Bunderwal has withdrawn his application; therefore —"

Mercantides thrust his head forward. "Cugel, your application is rejected, on several grounds. Bunderwal, can you reconsider your decision?"

"Certainly, if Cugel is no longer under consideration."

"He is not. You are hereby appointed to the position. Soldinck, do you endorse my decision?"

"I am well-pleased with Bunderwal's credentials."

"Then that is all there is to it," said Mercantides. "Soldinck, I have a head-ache. If you need me, I will be at home."

Mercantides departed the room, almost as Wagmund entered, supporting the weight of his right foot on a crutch.

Soldinck looked him up and down. "Well then, Wagmund? What has happened to you?"

"Sir, I suffered an accident last night. I regret that I cannot make this next voyage aboard the *Galante*."

Soldinck sat back in his chair. "That is bad news for all of us! Wormingers are hard to come by, especially Wormingers of quality!"

Bunderwal rose to his feet. "As newly-appointed supercargo of the *Galante*, allow me to make a reommendation. I propose that Cugel be hired to fill the vacant position."

Without enthusiasm Soldinck looked toward Cugel: "You have had experience in this line of work?"

"Not in recent years," said Cugel. "I will, however, consult with Wagmund in regard to modern trends."

"Very well; we cannot be too choosy, since the *Galante* sails in three days. Bunderwal, you will report at once to the ship. Cargo and supplies must be stowed, and properly! Wagmund, perhaps you will show Cugel your worms and explain their little quirks. Are there any questions? If not, all to their duties!. The *Galante* sails in three days!"

CHAPTER
II

FROM SASKERVOY TO TUSTVOLD

1
ABOARD
THE *GALANTE*

CUGEL'S first impression of the *Galante* was, on the whole, favorable. The hull was generously proportioned and floated in a buoyant and upright manner. The careful joinery and the lavish use of ornamental detail implied an equal concern for luxury and comfort below-decks. A single mast supported a yard to which was attached a sail of dark blue silk. From a swan's-neck stanchion at the bow swung an iron lantern; another even more massive lantern hung from a pedestal on the quarter-deck.

To these appurtenances Cugel gave his approval; they contributed to the forward motion of the ship and served the convenience of the crew. On the other hand, he could not automatically endorse a pair of ungainly outboard walkways, or sponsons, which ran the length of the hull, both port and starboard, only inches above the waterline. What could be their function? Cugel stepped a few paces along the dock, to secure a better view of the odd constructions. Were they promenade decks for the passengers' exercise? They seemed too narrow and too precarious, and too rudely exposed to wave and spray. Might they be platforms from which passengers and crew might conveniently bathe and launder their clothes while the ship lay becalmed? Or vantages from which the crew might repair the hull?

Cugel put the problem aside. So long as the *Galante* carried him in comfort to Port Perdusz, why cavil at details? Of more immediate concern were his duties as "worminger': an occupation of which he knew nothing.

Wagmund, the previous worminger, suffered a sore leg and had refused to help Cugel. In a gruff voice Wagmund said: "First things first! Go aboard the ship, make sure of your quarters and stow your gear; Captain Baunt is a martinet and will not tolerate clutter. When you are properly squared away, search out Drofo, the Chief Worminger; let him provide you instruction. Luckily for you, the worms are in prime condition."

Cugel owned only the clothes on his back; this was his 'gear', although in his pouch he carried an article of great value: the 'Pectoral Sky-break Spatterlight' from the turret of the demiurge Sadlark. Now, as Cugel stood on the dock, he conceived a cunning scheme to safeguard 'Spatterlight' from pilferage.

In a secluded area behind a pile of crates, Cugel doffed his fine triple-tiered hat. He removed the rather garish ornament which clipped up the side-brim, then, using great care to avoid 'Spatterlight's' avid bite, he wired the scale to his hat, where now it seemed only a hat-clasp. The erstwhile ornament he tucked into his pouch.

Cugel returned along the dock to the *Galante*. He climbed the gangway and stepped down upon the midship deck. To his right was the after-house, with a companion-way leading up to the quarter-deck. Forward, tucked into the bluff bows, was the forepeak, with the galley and crew's mess-hall; and below, the crew's quarters.

Three persons stood within range of Cugel's vision. The first was the cook, who had stepped out on deck in order to spit over the side. The second, a person tall and gaunt with the long sallow face of a tragic poet, stood by the rail, brooding over the sea. A sparse beard the color of dark mahogany straggled across his chin; his hair, of the same dark roan-russet color, was bound in a black kerchief. With gnarled white hands he gripped the rail and turned not so much as a glance toward Cugel.

The third man carried a bucket whose contents he tossed over the side. His hair was thick, white and close-cropped; his mouth was a thin slash in a ruddy square-jawed face. This would be the cabin steward, thought Cugel: a post for which the man's brisk and even truculent demeanor seemed unsuitable.

Of the three, only the man with the bucket chose to notice Cugel. He called out sharply: "Hoy, you skew-faced vagabond!

Be off with you! We need no salves nor talismans nor prayers nor erotic adjuncts!"

Cugel responded coldly: "You would do well to moderate your tone. I am Cugel, and I am here at the express solicitation of Soldinck! You may now show me to my quarters, and with a civil tongue in your head!" The other heaved a heavy sigh, as of infinite patience put to the test. He called down a passageway: "Bork! On deck!"

A short fat man with a round red face bounded up from below. "Aye, sir; what needs to be done?"

"Show this fellow to his quarters; he says he is Soldinck's guest. I forget his name: Fugle or Kungle or something of the sort."

Bork scratched his nose in puzzlement. "I have had no notice of him. With Master Soldinck and all his family aboard, where will I find accommodation? Not unless this gentleman uses your own cabin, while you go forward to double up with Drofo."

"That idea is not to my liking!"

Bork spoke plaintively: "Have you a better suggestion?"

The other threw up his arms and stalked off up the deck. Cugel looked after him. "And who is that surly fellow?"

"That is Captain Baunt. He is irritated because you will be occupying his cabin."

Cugel rubbed his chin. "All taken with all, I would prefer to use a cabin ordinarily assigned to single gentlemen."

"Not possible on this voyage, sir. Master Soldinck is accompanied by Madame Soldinck and their three daughters, and space is at a premium."

"I hesitate to inconvenience Captain Baunt," said Cugel. "Perhaps I should —"

"Say no more, sir! Drofo's snores will not trouble Captain Baunt, and I daresay we will all manage very well. This way, sir; I will show you to your cabin."

The steward led Cugel to the commodious chamber formerly occupied by Captain Baunt. Cugel looked approvingly here and there. "This will do quite nicely. I particularly like the view from these windows."

Captain Baunt appeared in the doorway. "I trust that all is to your satisfaction?"

"Eminently so. I will be very comfortable here." To Bork Cugel said: "You may serve me a light collation, if you will, as I breakfasted early."

"Certainly, sir; by all means."

Captain Baunt said gruffly: "I ask only that you do not disarrange the shelves. My collection of water-moth shells is irreplaceable and I do not wish my antique books to be disturbed."

"Have no fear! Your belongings are as secure as if they were my own. And now, if you will excuse me, I wish to rest a few hours before inquiring into my duties."

"'Duties'?" Captain Baunt frowned in puzzlement. "What might they be?"

Cugel spoke with dignity. "Soldinck has asked me to undertake a few simple tasks during the voyage."

"Odd. He said nothing about this to me. Bunderwal is the new supercargo and I understand that some weird lank-limbed outlander is to serve as under-worminger."

"I have accepted the post of worminger," said Cugel in austere tones.

Captain Baunt stared at Cugel slack-jawed. "You are the under-worminger?"

"That is my understanding," said Cugel.

Cugel's new quarters were located far forward in the bilges, where the stem-piece met the keel. The furnishings were simple: a narrow bunk with a sackful of dried reeds and a case where hung a few rancid garments abandoned by Wagmund.

By the light of a candle Cugel assessed his contusions. None seemed of a dangerous or disfiguring nature, even though Captain Baunt's conduct had exceeded all restraint.

A nasal voice reached his ears: "Cugel, where are you? On deck, at the double!"

Cugel groaned and limped up to the deck. Awaiting him was a tall fleshy young man with a thick cluster of black curls and small close-set black eyes. This person inspected Cugel with frank curiosity. "I am Lankwiler, worminger full and able, and hence your superior, though both of us serve under Chief Worminger Drofo. He now wishes to deliver an inspirational lecture. Listen carefully, if you know what is good for you. Come this way."

Beside the mast stood Drofo: the gaunt man with dark mahogany beard whom Cugel had noticed on his arrival aboard ship.

Drofo pointed toward the hatch. "Sit."

Cugel and Lankwiler seated themselves and waited with polite attention.

With head bent forward and hands clasped behind his back Drofo surveyed his underlings. After a moment he spoke, in a deep and passionless voice. "I can tell you much! Listen, and you will gain wisdom to surpass the scholars at the Institute, with their concords and paradigms! But do not mistake me! The weight of my words is no more than the weight of a single rain-drop! To know, you must do! After a hundred worms and ten thousand leagues, then with justice you may say, 'I am wise!' or, to precisely the same effect: 'I am a worminger!' At this time, because you are wise and because you are a worminger, you will not wish to utter vainglories. You will choose reticence, since your worth will speak for itself!" Drofo looked from face to face. "Am I clear?"

Lankwiler spoke in puzzlement: "Not entirely. The scholars at the Institute routinely calculate the weight of single raindrops. Is this to be considered good or bad?"

Drofo responded politely: "We are not adjudging the research of scholars at the Institute. We are discussing, rather, the work of the worminger."

"Ah! All is now clear!"

"Precisely so!" said Cugel. "Proceed, Drofo, with your interesting remarks!"

With arms behind his back, Drofo took a step to port, then a step to starboard. "Our calling is starkly noble! The dilettante, the weakling, the fool: all reveal themselves in their true colors. When the voyage goes well, then any mooncalf is bright and merry; he dances a jig and plays the concertina, and everyone thinks: 'Oh, for the life of the worminger!' But then hardship attacks! Black pust rages without remorse; impactions come like the gongs of Fate; the worm takes to rearing and plunging:

then the popinjay is revealed, or, more likely, is discovered hiding in the darkest corner of the hold!"

Cugel and Lankwiler mulled over the remarks, while Drofo paced to port, then to starboard.

Drofo pointed a long pale fore-finger toward the sea. "Yonder we go, halfway between the sky and the ocean floor, where the secrets of every age are concealed in a darkness which will grow absolute when the sun goes out."

As if to emphasize Drofo's remarks, the face of the sun momentarily glazed over with a dark film, similar to a rheum in an old man's eye. After a flutter and a wink, the light of day returned, to the obvious relief of Lankwiler, although Drofo ignored the incident. He held his finger in the air.

"The worm is a familiar of the sea! It is wise, though it uses six concepts only: sun, wave, wind, horizon, dark deep, faithful direction, hunger, and satiation. . . . Yes, Lankwiler? Why are you counting on your fingers?"

"Sir, it is no great matter."

"The worms are not clever," said Drofo. "They perform no tricks and they know no jokes. The good worminger, like his worms, is a man of simplicity. He cares little for what he eats and is indifferent as to whether he sleeps wet or dry, or even if he sleeps at all. When his worms drive straight, when the wake lies true, when ingestion is sharp and voidure is proper: then the worminger is serene. He craves no more from the world, neither wealth nor ease nor the sensuous caress of languid females nor trinkets like that foppish bedazzlement Cugel wears in his hat. His way is the watery void!"

"Most inspiring!" cried Lankwiler. "I am proud to be a worminger! Cugel, what of you?

"I no less!" declared Cugel. "It is a worthy calling, and the hat ornament, while of no intrinsic value, is an heirloom."

Drofo gave an indifferent nod. "Now I will divulge the first axiom of our trade, which indeed can be expanded to a universal application. Thus: 'A man may show himself to you and say, "I am a Master Worminger!" Or a Master Worminger may stand to the side and speak no word. How is truth to be known? It is told by the worms.'

"I will particularize. Should you see a yellow bilious creature with bloated fausicles, gills crusted with gangue, an impacted clote, who is thereby at fault? The worm, who knows only water and space? Or he who should tend it? Can we call him a worminger? Form your own opinion. But here is another worm, strong, steadfast in direction, pink as the sunrise! This worm testifies to the faith of its worminger, who tirelessly burnishes its linctures, disimpedes its clote, scrapes and combs the gills until they shine like silver! He is in mystical communion with surge and sea, and knows the serenity only the worminger can know!

"I will say little more. Cugel, you have small acquaintance with the trade, but I take it as a good sign that you have come to me for training, since my methods are not soft. You will learn or you will drown, or suffer a blow of the flukes, or worse, incur my displeasure. But you have started well and I will teach you well. Never think me harsh, or over-bearing; you will be in self-defeating error! I am stern, yes, even severe, but in the end, when I acknowledge you a worminger, you will thank me."

"Good news indeed," muttered Cugel.

Drofo paid him no heed. "Lankwiler, you perhaps lack something of Cugel's intensity, but you have the advantage of a voyage beside Wagmund, who suffers a sore leg. I have pointed out to you certain errors and laxities, and my remarks are surely fresh in your mind; am I correct?"

"Absolutely!" said Lankwiler with a bland smile.

"Good. You will show Cugel the bins and sacks, and fit him out with a good reamer and pincts. Cugel, does your equipment include a pair of sound straddlers?"

Cugel made a negative sign. "I neglected them in my haste."

"A pity. . . . Well, you may use Wagmund's excellent equipment, but you must see to its care."

"I shall do so."

"Then make ready your gear. It is almost time to fetch the worms; the *Galante* sails directly upon Soldinck's order."

Lankwiler took Cugel forward to the locker under the forepeak, where he sorted through the gear, putting aside the best articles for his own use and tossing Cugel a casual selection from what remained.

Lankwiler advised Cugel: "Pay no great heed to old Drofo. He has inhaled too much salt-spray and I suspect that he uses the worms' ear-tonic as a tipple, for he is often queer."

Emboldened by Lankwiler's affability Cugel put a cautious question: "If we are dealing only with worms, why do we need such crude and heavy gear?"

Lankwiler looked up blankly, and Cugel hastened to add: "I assume that we work with our worms at a table, or perhaps a bench; therefore I wonder why Drofo glorifies deprivation and exposure to the elements. Are we required to rinse the worms in salt water, or dig them from the mire by night?"

Lankwiler chuckled. "You have never wormed before?"

"Very little, certainly."

"All will be made clear; let us not gossip and theorize, or waste time in idle verbalizing; like Drofo, I am a man of deeds, not rhetoric."

"Just so," said Cugel coldly.

With a twitch of sly mockery on his lips, Lankwiler said: "From the peculiar style of your hat I deduce that you derive from a far and exotic region."

"True," said Cugel.

"And how do you find the Land of Cutz?"

"It has interesting aspects; still I am anxious to return to civilization."

Lankwiler sniffed. "I am from Tugersbir sixty miles to the north, where civilization is also rife. Now then: here are Wagmund's straddles. I think that I will borrow this set with the silver conches; you may choose from among the others. Be careful; Wagmund, like a bald-headed man in a fur hat, is proud and vain, and childishly meticulous with his gear. Briskly now, unless you are ready for another barrage of Drofo's dogma." The two took their gear to the deck. With Drofo in the lead they disembarked from the *Galante* and marched north along the dock to a long pen where a number of enormous tubular creatures, seven to nine feet in diameter and almost as long as the *Galante* itself, lay placidly afloat.

Drofo pointed. "Yonder with the yellow knobs, Lankwiler, are the beasts which were assigned into your care. As you see, they are in need of attention. Cugel, the two beasts at the extreme left, with the blue knobs, are Wagmund's fine worms which now come under your supervision."

Lankwiler made a thoughtful suggestion. "Why not let Cugel supervise the worms with the yellow knobs, while I command the Blues? This scheme has the advantage of affording Cugel valuable training in basic procedures at a formative time in his career."

Drofo ruminated a moment. "Possibly so, possibly so. But we lack time to analyze the matter in all its aspects; therefore we will abide by the original plan."

"This is correct thinking," said Cugel. "It conforms with the Second Axiom of our trade: 'If Worminger A despoils his beasts, then Worminger A must restore them to health, not blameless hard-working Worminger B'.

Lankwiler was discomfited. "Cugel may have learned thirty different axioms from a book, but, as Drofo himself pointed out, these are no substitute for experience."

"The original plan will hold," said Drofo. "Now then: bring your beasts to the ship and clamp them into their cinctures: Cugel to port, Lankwiler to starboard."

Lankwiler quickly recovered his composure. "Aye, aye, sir," he cried heartily. "Come along, Cugel; shake a leg, now! We'll have those worms clamped up in jig-time, Tugersbir-style!"

"So long as you tie none of your peculiar Tugersbir knots," said Drofo. "Last trip Captain Baunt and I pondered the complications of your easy-off hitch for half an hour."

Lankwiler and Cugel descended to the pens where a dozen worms idled at the surface of the water, or moved slowly to the thrust of their caudal flukes. Some were pink or even scarlet-rose; others were pale ivory or a sour and sulfurous yellow. The head parts were complicated: a short thick proboscis, an optical bump with a single small eye and immediately behind, a pair of knobs on short stalks. These knobs, painted in different colors, denoted ownership, and functioned as directional apparatus.

"Smartly now, Cugel!" called Lankwiler. "Use all your theorems! Old Drofo likes to see our coat-tails fluttering in the wind! Get into your straddles and mount one of your worms!"

"In all candour," said Cugel nervously, "I have forgotten many of my skills."

"Little skill is needed," said Lankwiler. "Watch me! I jump on the beast, I throw the hood over its eye. I seize its knobs and the worm carries me where I wish to go. Watch! You will see!"

Lankwiler jumped out on one of the worms, ran along its length, jumped to another, and then another and at last straddled a worm with yellow knobs. He threw a hood over its eye and seized the knobs. The worm swung its flukes and carried him out the water-gate, which Drofo had opened, and across the water to the *Galante*.

Cugel gingerly sought to achieve the same result, but his worm, when finally he straddled it and grasped its knobs, promptly dived deep. Cugel, in despair, pulled back on the knobs and the worm rushed to the surface, flung itself fifteen feet into the air and sent Cugel flying across the pen.

Cugel struggled ashore. By the gate stood Drofo, his brooding gaze directed toward Cugel.

The worms floated as placidly as before. Cugel heaved a deep sigh, once again jumped down upon the worm, and again straddled it. He hooded the eye and with cautious fingers tweaked the blue knobs. The creature paid no heed. Cugel delicately twisted the organ, which startled the worm so that it moved forward. Cugel continued to experiment, and by spasms and jerks the worm approached the end of the pen, where Drofo waited. Through chance, or perversity, the worm swam for the gate; Drofo pulled it ajar, and the worm slid past, with Cugel, head on high, feigning a confident and easy control.

"Now then!" said Cugel. To the *Galante*!"

The worm, despite Cugel's wishes, veered toward the open sea. Standing by the gate, Drofo gave a sad nod, as if in verification of some inner conviction. He brought from his waistcoat a silver whistle and blew three shrill tones. The worm swung in a circle and drove up beside the water-gate. Drofo jumped down upon the ridged pink back, and kicked negligently at the knobs. "Observe! The knobs are played thus and so. Right, left. Shallow, deep. Halt, start. Is this clear?"

"Once more, if you will," said Cugel. "I am anxious to learn your technique."

Drofo repeated the procedure, then, urging the worm toward the *Galante*, stood in melancholy reflection while the worm drove through the water and ranged itself beside the ship, and at last Cugel apprehended the purpose of the walkways which had so perplexed him: they allowed swift and ready access to the worms.

"Observe," said Drofo. "I will demonstrate how the beast is clamped. So, and so, and so. Unction is applied here and here, to prevent the formation of galls. Are you clear on this?"

"Absolutely!"

"Then bring the second worm."

Profiting by the instruction, Cugel guided the second worm to its place and clamped it properly. Then, as Drofo had instructed, Cugel applied unction. A few minutes later, to his gratification, he heard Drofo chiding Lankwiler for neglecting the unction. Lankkwiler's explanation, that he disliked the odor of the substance, found no favor with Drofo.

A few minutes later, Drofo stood both Lankwiler and Cugel at attention while he again made the two under-wormingers aware of his expectations.

"On the last voyage Wagmund and Lankwiler were the wormingers. I was not aboard; Gieselman was Chief Worminger. I see that he was far too slack. While Wagmund dealt most professionally with his worms, Lankwiler, through ignorance and sloth, allowed his worms to deteriorate. Examine these beasts. They are yellow as quince. Their gills are black with gangue. You may be sure that in the future Lankwiler will deal more faithfully with his worms. As for Cugel, his training has definitely been sub-standard. Aboard the *Galante* his deficiency will almost magically be corrected, as will Lankwiler's turpitude.

"Now heed! We depart Saskervoy for the wide sea in two hour's time. You will now feed your beasts a half-measure of victual, and make ready your baits. Cugel, you will then groom your beasts and inspect for timp. Lankwiler, you will immediately begin to chip gangue. You will also inspect for timp, pust and fluke-mites. Your off-beast shows signs of impaction; you must give it a drench."

"Wormingers, to your beasts!"

With brush, scraper, gouge and reamer, with pots of salve, toner and unction, Cugel groomed his worms to Drofo's instruction. From time to time a wave washed over the worms, and across the walkway. Drofo, leaning over the rail, advised Cugel from above: "Ignore the wet! It is an artificial and factitious sensation. You are constantly wet on the inside of your skin from all manner of fluids, many of a vulgar nature; why shrink from good salt brine on the outside? Ignore wetness of all sorts; it is a worminger's natural state."

Halfway into the afternoon Master Soldinck and his party arrived at the dock. Captain Baunt mustered all hands on the midship deck to welcome the group aboard ship.

First to step from the gangplank was Soldinck, with Madame Soldinck on his arm, followed by Soldinck's daughters Meadhre, Salasser and Tabazinth.

Captain Baunt, taut and immaculate in his dress uniform, delivered a short speech. "Soldinck, we of the *Galante* welcome you and your admirable family aboard! Since we will live in proximity for several weeks, or even months, allow me to perform introductions.

"I am Captain Baunt; this is our supercargo, Bunderwal. Beside him stands Sparvin, our redoubtable boatswain, who commands Tilitz — see him yonder with the blond beard — and Parmele. Our cook is Angshott and the carpenter is Kinnolde.

"Here stand the stewards. They are trusty Bork, who is learned in the identification of sea-birds and water-moths. He is assisted by Claudio and Vilip, and occasionally, when he can be found, and when the mood is on him, by Codniks the deck-boy.

"By the rail, aloof from the society of ordinary mortals, we find our wormingers! Conspicuous in any company is Chief Worminger Drofo, who deals with the profundities of nature as casually as Angshott the cook juggles his broad-beans and garlic. At his back, fierce and ready, stand Lankwiler and Cugel. Agreed, they seem sodden and dispirited, and smell somewhat of worm, but this is as it should be. To quote Drofo's favorite dictum: 'A dry sweet-smelling worminger is a lazy worminger'. So never be deceived; these are hardy men of the sea, and ready for anything!

"And there you have it: a fine ship, a strong crew and now,

by some miracle, a bevy of beautiful girls to enhance the sea-scape! The presages are good, though our voyage is long! Our course is south by east across the Ocean of Sighs. In due course we will raise the estuary of the Great Chaing River which opens into the Land of the Falling Wall, and there, at Port Per-dusz, we will make our arrival. So now: the moment of depar-ture is at hand! Master Soldinck, what is your word?"

"I find all in order. Give the command at discretion."

"Very good, sir. Tillitz, Parmele! Cast off the lines, fore and aft! Drofo, ready with your worms! Sparvin, steer slantwise past the old sun's azimuth, until we clear Bracknock Shoal! The sea is calm, the wind is slack. Tonight we shall dine by lantern-light on the quarter-deck, while our great worms, tended by Cugel and Lankwiler, drive us through the dark!"

Three days passed, during which Cugel acquired a sound foundation in the worminger's trade.

Drofo, in his commentaries, provided a number of valuable theoretical insights. "For the worminger," said Drofo, "day and night, water, air and foam are but slightly different aspects of a larger environment, whose parameters are defined by the gran-deur of the sea and the tempo of the worm."

"Allow me this question," said Cugel. "When do I sleep?"

"'Sleep'? When you are dead, then you shall sleep long and sound. Until that mournful event, guard each iota of awareness; it is the only treasure worthy of the name. Who knows when fire will leave the sun? Even the worms, which are ordinarily fatalistic and inscrutable, give uneasy signs. This very morning at dawn I saw the sun falter at the horizon and sag backward as if in debility. Only after a great sick pulse could it swing itself into the sky. One morning we will look to the east and wait, but the sun will fail to appear. Then you may sleep."

Cugel learned the use of sixteen implements and discovered much in regard to the worms' physiology. Timp, fluke-mites, gangue and pust became his hated enemies; impactions of the clote were a major annoyance, requiring the sub-surface use of reamer, drench-bar and hose, in a position which, when the im-

paction was eased, became subject to the full force of the efflux-
ion.

Drofo spent much of his time at the bow, brooding over the
sea. Occasionally Soldinck, or Madame Soldinck, strolled forward to speak with him; at other times Meadhre, Salasser and
Tabazinth, alone or in concert, joined Drofo at the bow and listened respectfully to his opinions. At Captain Baunt's sly
suggestion, they prevailed upon Drofo to play the flute. "False
modesty is not befitting to a worminger," said Drofo. He
played and simultaneously danced three hornpipes and a sal-
tarello.

Drofo seemed inattentive to either worms or wormingers,
but this negligence was illusory. One afternoon Lankwiler neglected fully to bait the baskets which hung eight inches in front
of his worms; as a result they slackened their effort, while
Cugel's worms, properly baited, swam with zeal, so that the
Galante began to swing westward in a great slow curve, despite
the helmsman's correction.

Drofo, summoned from the bow, instantly diagnosed the difficulty and, further, discovered Lankwiler asleep in a warm
nook beside the galley.

Drofo nudged Lankwiler with his toe. "Be good enough to
arouse yourself. You have not baited your worms; as a result
the ship is off course."

Lankwiler stared up in confusion, his black curls matted and
his eyes looking in different directions. "Ah yes," mumbled
Lankwiler. "The bait! It slipped my mind and I fear that I dozed
off."

"I am surprised that you could sleep so soundly while your
worms went slack!" said Drofo. "A skilled worminger is constantly keen. He learns to sense the least irregularity, and instantly divines its source."

"Yes, yes," muttered Lankwiler. "I now understand my mistake. 'Sense irregularity', 'divine source'. I will make a
memorandum."

"Furthermore," said Drofo, "I notice a virulent case of timp
on your off-worm, which you must take pains to abate."

"Absolutely, sir! At once, if not sooner!" Lankwiler struggled to his feet, hid a cavernous yawn behind his hand while Drofo watched impassively, then lurched off to his worms.

Later in the day Cugel chanced to overhear a conversation between Drofo and Captain Baunt. "Tomorrow afternoon," said Drofo, "we shall have a taste of wind. It will be good for the worms. They are not yet at full vigor, and I see no reason to push them."

"True, true," said the captain. "How do you fancy your wormingers?"

"At this time neither enjoys a rating of 'excellent,'" said Drofo. "Lankwiler is obtuse and somewhat sluggish. Cugel lacks experience and wastes energy preening in front of the girls. He works to an absolute minimum, and detests water with the fervor of a hydrophobic cat."

"His worms appear sound."

Drofo gave his head a disparaging shake. "Cugel does the right things for the wrong reasons. Through sloth he neither overfeeds nor overbaits; his worms suffer little bloat. He despises the work of dealing with timp and gangue so fiercely that he obliterates its first appearance."

"In that case, his work would seem satisfactory."

"Only to a layman! For a worminger, style and harmony of purpose are everything!"

"You have your problems; I have mine."

"How so? I thought that all went smoothly."

"To a certain extent. As you may be aware, Madame Soldinck is a woman of strong and immutable purposes."

"I divined something along those lines."

"At lunch today I mentioned that our position was two or three days sail north-east of Lausicaa."

"That would be my own reckoning, by the lay of the sea," said Drofo. "It is an interesting island. Pulk the worminger lives at Pompodouros."

"Are you acquainted with the Paphnissian Baths?"

"Not of my own experience. I believe that women bathe in these springs hoping to regain youth and beauty."

"Just so. Madame Soldinck, we will agree, is an estimable woman."

"In every respect. She is stern in her principles, unyielding in her rectitude, and she will not submit to injustice."

"Yes. Bork calls her opinionated, obstinate and cantankerous, but this is not quite the same thing."

"Bork's language at least has the merit of economy," said Drofo.

"In any event, Madame Soldinck is neither young nor beautiful. Indeed, she is plump and squat. Her face is prognathous and she wears a faint black mustache. She is definitely genteel and her character is strong, so that Soldinck is guided by her suggestions. So now, since Madame Soldinck wishes to bathe in the Paphnissian Springs, we must perforce put in to Lausicaa."

"The event will serve my own interests very well," said Drofo. "At Pompodouros I will hire the worminger Pulk and discharge either Cugel or Lankwiler, who can then find his own way back to the mainland."

"Not a bad idea, if Pulk still resides at Pompodouros."

"He does indeed and will gladly return to the sea."

"In that case, half your problems are solved. Which will you put ashore: Cugel or Lankwiler?"

"I have not yet decided. It will depend on the worms."

The two men moved away and Cugel was left to ponder the conversation. It seemed that, at least until the *Galante* departed Lausicaa, he must work with vigor, and diminish his attentions to Soldinck's daughters.

Cugel at once found his scrapers and removed all traces of gangue from his worms, then combed gills till they shone silver-pink.

Lankwiler meanwhile had inspected the advanced infestation of timp on his off-worm. During the night he painted the knobs of this worm blue and then, while Cugel drowsed, he drove his off-worm around the vessel and exchanged it for Cugel's excellent off-worm, which he clamped into place on his own side. He painted the knobs yellow and congratulated himself that he had avoided a tedious task.

In the morning Cugel was startled to discover the deterioration of his off-worm.

Drofo came past and called down to Cugel: "That infestation of timp is an abomination. Also, unless I am much mistaken, that swelling indicates a severe impaction which must be relieved at once."

Cugel, recalling the overheard conversation, went to work with a will. While towed underwater he plied reamer, drench-hoses and gant-hook, and after three hours exertion, dislodged the impaction. At once the worm lost something of its bilious color and strained for its bait with renewed zest.

When Cugel finally returned to the deck he heard Drofo call down to Lankwiler: "Your off-worm has improved noticeably! Keep up the good work!"

Cugel went to look down at Lankwiler's off-worm. . . Strange that overnight Lankwiler's impacted yellow beast with its crawling infestation of timp should become so notably sound, while, during the same interval, Cugel's healthy pink worm had suffered so profound a disaster!

Cugel pondered the circumstances with care. He climbed down on the sponson and scraped at the off-worm's knobs, to discover under the blue paint, the gleam of yellow.

Cugel ruminated further, then transferred his worms, placing the healthy worm in the 'off' position.

While Cugel and Lankwiler took their evening meal, Cugel spoke of his trials. "Amazing how quickly they take up a case of timp, or an impaction! All day I worked on the beast, and tonight I moved it inboard where I can tend it more conveniently."

"A sound idea," said Lankwiler. "At last I have cured one of my beasts, and the other shows signs of improvement. Have you heard? We are putting into Lausicaa, so that Madame Soldinck can dive into the Paphnissian waters and emerge a virgin."

"I will tell you something in absolute confidence," said Cugel. "The deck boy tells me that Drofo plans to hire a veteran worminger by the name of Pulk at Pompodouros."

Lankwiler chewed his lips. "Why should he do that? He already has two expert wormingers."

"I can hardly believe that he plans to discharge you or yet me," said Cugel. "Still, that would seem the only possibility."

Lankwiler frowned and finished his meal in silence.

Cugel waited until Lankwiler went off for his evening nap,

then stole down to the starboard sponson and cut deeply into the knobs of Lankwiler's sick beast; then, returning to his own sponson, he made a great show of attacking the timp.

From the corner of his eye he saw Drofo come to the rail, pause a moment, then continue on his way.

At midnight the baits were removed so that the worms might rest. The *Galante* floated quietly on the calm sea. The helmsman lashed the wheel; the deck boy drowsed under the great forward lantern where he was supposed to keep sharp lookout. Overhead glimmered those stars yet surviving including Achernar, Algol, Canopus and Cansaspara.

From his cranny crept Lankwiler. He slipped across the deck like a great black rat, and swung down to the starboard sponson. He unclamped the sick worm and urged it from its traces.

The worm floated free. Lankwiler sat in the straddles and pulled at the knobs but the nerves had been severed and the signal caused only pain. The worm beat its flukes and surged away to the northwest, with Lankwiler sitting a-straddle and frantically tugging at the knobs.

In the morning Lankwiler's disappearance dominated all conversations. Chief Worminger Drofo, Captain Baunt and Soldinck met in the grand saloon to discuss the affair, and presently Cugel was called before the group.

Soldinck, sitting on a tall-backed chair of carved skeel, cleared his throat. "Cugel, as you know, Lankwiler has gone off with a valuable worm. Can you shed any light on the affair?"

"Like everyone else, I can only theorize."

"We would be pleased to hear your ideas," said Soldinck.

Cugel spoke in a judicious voice: "I believe that Lankwiler despaired of becoming a competent worminger. His worms went sick, and Lankwiler could not face up to the challenge. I tried to help him; I let him take one of my sound worms so that I might bring his sickly creature back to health, as Drofo must surely have noticed, although he was unusually reticent in this regard."

Soldinck turned to Drofo. "Is this true? If so, it reflects great credit upon Cugel."

Drofo spoke in a subdued voice: "Yesterday morning I counseled Cugel in this regard."

Soldinck turned back to Cugel. "Continue, if you will."

"I can only surmise that dejection urged Lankwiler to perform a final despairing act."

Captain Baunt cried out: "That is unreasonable! If he felt dejection, why not simply jump into the sea? Why suborn our valuable worm to his personal and private uses?"

Cugel reflected a moment. "I suppose that he wanted to make a ceremony of the occasion."

Soldinck blew out his cheeks. "All this to the side, Lankwiler's act is a great inconvenience. Drofo, how will we fare with only three worms?"

"We shall have no great difficulty. Cugel can readily manage both sponsons. To ease the helmsman we will use double bait to starboard and half-bait to port, and so without difficulty we will arrive at Lausicaa, and there make adjustments."

Captain Baunt had already altered course toward Lausicaa, so that Madame Soldinck might bathe in the Paphnissian Springs. Baunt, who had hoped to make a quick passage, was not happy with the delay, and watched Cugel closely, to make sure that the worms were used to the maximum efficiency. "Cugel!" called Captain Baunt. "Adjust the lead on that off-worm; it is pulling us broadside!"

"Aye, sir."

And presently: "Cugel! Your starboard worm is listless; it merely slaps the water. Freshen its bait!"

"I am already at double-bait," grumbled Cugel. "It was fresh an hour ago."

"Then use half a gill of Heidinger's Allure, and be quick about it! I wish to make Pompodouros before sunset tomorrow!"

During the night the starboard worm, becoming fretful, began to slap at the water with its flukes. Drofo, aroused by the splashing, came up from his cabin. Leaning on the rail he watched as Cugel ran back and forth along the sponson, trying to throw a check-line over the mischievous worm's flukes.

After a few moments observation, Drofo diagnosed the problem. He called out in a nasal voice: "Always lift the bait before throwing a check-line. . . Now then, what is happening down there?"

Cugel responded sullenly: "The worm wants to swim up, down and sideways."

"What did you feed?"

"The usual: half Chalcorex and half Illem's Best."

"You might use a bit less Chalcorex for the next day or so. That lump of tissue behind the turret is usually a dependable signal. How did you bait?"

"Double-bait, as I was instructed. The captain ordered a further half-gill of Heidinger's Allure."

"There is your problem. You have over-baited, which is an act of folly."

"At Captain Baunt's orders!"

"That excuse is worse than none. Who is the worminger, you or Captain Baunt? You know your worms; you must work them by the dictates of your experience and good judgment. If Baunt interferes, ask him to come down and advise you in regard to an infestation of gangue. That is the way of the worminger! Change bait at once and drench the worm with a seep of Blagin's Mulcent."

"Very good, sir," said Cugel between his teeth.

Drofo made a brief survey of sky and horizon, then returned to his cabin and Cugel busied himself with the drench.

Captain Baunt had ordered the sail set, hoping to catch a waft of favorable air. Two hours after midnight a cross-wind arose, causing the sail to flap against the mast, creating a dismal sound which aroused Captain Baunt from his slumber. Baunt lurched out on deck. "Where is the watch? Hoy! Worminger! You there! Is no one about?"

Cugel, clambering up to the deck from the sponson, replied: "Only the lookout, who is asleep under the lantern."

"Well then, what of you? Why have you not silenced that sail? Are you deaf?"

"No sir. I have been under-water, drenching with Blagin's Mulcent."

"Well then, heave aft on the leach-line, and abate that cursed slatting!"

Cugel hastened to obey, while Captain Baunt went to the starboard rail. Here he discovered new cause for dissatisfaction. "Worminger, where is your bait? I ordered double-bait, with aroma of Allure!"

"Sir, one cannot drench while the worm exerts itself for bait."

"Why then did you drench? I ordered no Mulcent!"

Cugel drew himself up. "Sir, I drenched that worm according to the dictates of my best judgment and experience."

Captain Baunt stared blankly, threw his arms in the air, turned and went back to his bed.

2
LAUSICAA

THE SUN, dropping down the sky, passed behind a ledge of low clouds and twilight came early. The air was still; the ocean lay flat, with a surface like heavy satin, exactly reflecting the sky, so that the *Galante* seemed to float through a void of marvellous lavender luminosity. Only the bow waves, spreading away at V-angles in rolling black and lavender ripples, defined the surface of the sea.

An hour before sunset Lausicaa appeared on the horizon: a shadow almost lost in the plum-colored murk.

As darkness fell, a dozen lights flickered from the town Pompodouros, reflecting across the opening into the harbor and easing the approach for Captain Baunt.

A wharf fronting the town showed as a heavy mark, blacker than black, across the reflections. In unfamiliar waters and in the dark, Captain Baunt prudently elected to drop anchor rather than attempt mooring at the dock.

From the quarter-deck Captain Baunt called forward: "Drofo! Bring up your baits!"

"Up baits!" came back Drofo's acknowledgment, then, in a different voice: "Cugel! Debait all worms!"

Cugel snatched bait from the two port worms, scrambled across the deck, jumped down upon the starboard sponson and debaited the starboard worm. The *Galante* barely drifted through the water, to idle motions of the worms' flukes.

Captain Baunt called out again: "Drofo, muffle your worms!"

"Muffle worms!" came Drofo's response, and then: "Cugel, muffles all around! Quick now!"

Cugel muffled the starboard worm, but fell into the water and was slow with the port muffles, prompting a complaint

98

from Captain Baunt. "Drofo, hurry the muffles! Are you conducting a rite for the dead? Boatswain, ready the anchor!"

"Muffles going on!" sang out Drofo. "Look sharp, Cugel!"

"Anchor at the ready, sir."

The worms were muffled at last, and the *Galante* barely drifted through the water.

"Let go the anchor!" called Captain Baunt.

"Anchor in the water, sir! Bottom at six fathoms."

The *Galante* lay placidly to anchor. Cugel eased the worms in their cinctures, applied unguent and fed each worm a measure of victual.

After the evening meal Captain Baunt assembled the ship's company on the midship deck. Standing halfway up the companionway ladder he spoke a few words in regard to Lausicaa and the town Pompodouros.

"Those of you who have visited this place before, I doubt if there are many, will understand why I must issue warnings. In a nut-shell, you will find certain customs which guide the folk of this island to be at variance with our own. They may impress you as strange, grotesque, laughable, disgraceful, picturesque or commendable, depending upon your point of view. Whatever the case, we must take note of these customs and abide by them, since the folk of Lausicaa will definitely not alter their ways in favor of ours."

Captain Baunt smilingly acknowledged the presence of Madame Soldinck and her three daughters. "My remarks apply almost exclusively to the gentlemen aboard, and if I touch upon topics which might be considered tasteless, I can only plead necessity; so I beg your indulgence!"

Soldinck cried out bluffly: "Enough of your breast-beating, Baunt! Speak up! We are all reasonable people aboard, Madame Soldinck included!"

Captain Baunt waited until the laughter had died down. "Very well then! Look along the dock yonder; you will notice three persons standing under the street-lamp. All are men. The faces of each are hidden behind hoods and veils. For this precaution there is reason: the ebullience of the local females. So vivacious is their nature that men dare not display their faces for fear of provoking ungovernable impulses. Female voyeurs go so far as to peek through windows of the clubhouse where the men gather to drink beer, sometimes with their faces partially exposed."

At this information Madame Soldinck and her daughters laughed nervously. "Extraordinary!" said Madame Soldinck. "And women of every social class act in this fashion?"

"Absolutely!"

Meadhre asked diffidently: "Do the men propose marriage with their faces concealed?"

Captain Baunt reflected. "So far as I know, the idea never enters anyone's head."

"It does not seem a wholesome atmosphere in which to bring up children," said Madame Soldinck.

"Apparently the children are not seriously affected," said Captain Baunt. "Until the age of ten boys may sometimes be seen bare-faced, but even during these tender years they are protected from adventurous young females. At the age of ten they 'go under the veil', to use the local idiom."

"How tiresome for the girls!" sighed Salasser.

"And also undignified!" said Tabazinth with emphasis. "Suppose I noticed what appeared to be a handsome young man, and ran after him and finally subdued him, and then, when I pulled away his hood, I found protruding yellow teeth, a big nose and a narrow receding forehead. What next? I would feel a fool simply getting up and walking away."

Meadhre suggested: "You could tell the gentleman that you merely wanted directions back to the ship."

"Whatever the case," Captain Baunt went on, "the women of Lausicaa have evolved techniques to restore the equilibrium. After this fashion:

"The men are partial to spraling, which are small delicate bidechtils. They swim at the surface of the sea in the early morning. The women, therefore, arise in the pre-dawn hours, wade out into the sea, where they capture as much spraling as possible, then return to their huts.

"Those women with a good catch set their fires going and hang out signs, such as: FINE SPRALING TODAY, or TASTY SPRALING TO YOUR ORDER."

"The men arise in due course and stroll about the town. When at last they work up an appetite, they stop by a hut where the sign offers refreshment to their taste. Often, if the spraling is fresh and the company good, they may stay for dinner as well."

Madame Soldinck sniffed and murmured aside to her daughters, who merely shrugged and shook their heads.

Soldinck climbed two steps up the companionway ladder. "Captain Baunt's remarks are not be taken lightly! When you go ashore, wear a robe or a loose gown and by some means muffle your face so as to avoid any unseemly or improper incident! Am I clear?"

Captain Baunt said: "In the morning we will moor at the dock and attend to our various items of business. Drofo, I suggest that you put this interval to good purpose. Anoint your animals well and cure all chafes, galls and cankers. Exercise them daily about the harbor, since idleness brings on impaction. Cure all your infestations; trim all gills. These hours in port are precious; each must be used to the fullest, without regard for day or night."

"This echoes my own thinking," said Drofo. "I will immediately give the necessary orders to Cugel."

Soldinck called out: "A final word! Lankwiler's departure with the starboard off-worm might have caused us enormous inconvenience were it not for the wise tactics of our Chief Worminger. I propose a cheer for the estimable Drofo!"

Drofo acknowledged the acclamation with a curt jerk of the head, then turned away to instuct Cugel, after which he went forward to lean on the rail and brood across the waters of the harbor.

Cugel worked until midnight with his cutters, burnishing irons and reamer, then treated pust, gangue, and timp. Drofo had long since vacated his place on the bow and Captain Baunt had retired early. Cugel stealthily abandoned his work and went below to his bunk.

Almost immediately, or so it seemed, he was aroused by Codnicks the deck-boy. Blinking and yawning Cugel stumbled up to the deck, to find the sun rising and Captain Baunt impatiently pacing back and forth.

At the sight of Cugel Captain Baunt stopped short. "Hurrah! You have finally decided to honor us with your presence! Naturally our important business ashore can wait until you have drowsed and dozed to your heart's content. Are you finally able to face the day?"

"Aye, sir!"

"Thank you, Cugel. Drofo, here, at long last, is your worminger!"

"Very good, Captain. Cugel, you must learn to be on hand when you are needed. Now return your worms into cincture. We are ready to work our way into the dock. Keep your muffles ready to hand. Use no bait."

With Captain Baunt on the quarter-deck, Drofo alert at the bow and Cugel tending worms to port and starboard, the *Galante* eased across the harbor to the dock. Longshoremen, wearing long black gowns, tall hats with veils shrouding their faces, took mooring-lines and made the ship fast to bollards. Cugel muffled the worms, eased cinctures and fed victual all around.

Captain Baunt assigned Cugel and the deck-boy to gangplank watch; every one else, suitably dressed and veiled, went ashore. Cugel immediately concealed his features behind a makeshift veil, donned a cloak and likewise went ashore, followed in short order by Codnicks the deck-boy.

Many years before, Cugel had passed through the old city Kaiin in Ascolais, north of Almery. In the decayed grandeur of Pompodouros he discovered haunting recollections of Kaiin, conveyed principally by the fallen and ruined palaces along the hillside, now overgrown with foxglove and stone-weed and a few small pencil cypresses.

Pompodouros occupied a barren hollow surrounded by low hills. The present inhabitants had put the mouldering stones from the ruins to their own purposes: huts, the men's club-house, the market-dome, a sick-house for men and another for women, one slaughter-house, two schools, four taverns, six temples, a number of small work-shops and the brewery. In the plaza a dozen white dolomite statues, now more or less dilapi-

dated, cast stark black shadows away from the wan red sunlight.

There seemed no streets to Pompodouros, only open areas
and cleared spaces through the rubble which served as avenues.
Along these by-ways the men and women of the town moved
about their business. The men, by virtue of their long gowns
and black veils hanging below their hats, seemed tall and spare.
The women wore skirts of furze dyed dark green, dark red,
gray or violet-gray, tasseled shawls and beaded caps, into which
the more coquettish inserted the plumes of sea-birds.

A number of small carriages, drawn by those squat heavy-
legged creatures known as 'droggers', moved through the
places of Pompodouros; others, awaiting hire, ranged in a line
before the men's club-house.

Bunderwal had been delegated to escort Madame Soldinck
and her daughters on a tour of nearby places of interest; they
hired a carriage and set off about their sight-seeing. Captain
Baunt and Soldinck were met by several local dignitaries and
conducted into the men's club-house.

With his face concealed behind the veil, Cugel also entered
the club-house. At a counter he bought a pewter jug of beer
and took it to a booth close beside that where Captain Baunt,
Soldinck, and some others drank beer and discussed business of
the voyage.

By pressing his ear against the back of the booth and listening with care, Cugel was able to capture the gist of the conversation. "— most extraordinary flavor to this beer," came Soldinck's voice. "It tastes of tar."

"I believe that it is brewed from tarweed and other such con-
stituents," replied Captain Baunt. "It is said to be nutritious but
it slides down the gullet as if it had claws. . . . Aha! Here is
Drofo."

Soldinck lifted his veil to look. "How can you tell, with his
face concealed?"

"Easily. He wears the yellow boots of a worminger."

"That is clear enough. Who is the other person?"

"I suspect the gentleman to be his friend Pulk. Hoy, Drofo!
Over here!"

The newcomers joined Captain Baunt and Soldinck. Drofo said: "I hereby introduce the worminger Pulk, of whom you have heard me speak. I have hinted of our needs and Pulk has been kind enough to give the matter his attention."

"Good!" said Captain Baunt. "I hope that you also mentioned our need for a worm, preferably a 'Motilator' or a 'Magna-fluke'?"

"Well, Pulk," asked Drofo, "what of it?"

Pulk spoke in a measured voice. "I believe that a worm of the requisite quality might be available from my nephew Fuscule, especially if he were signed aboard the *Galante* as a worminger."

Soldinck looked from one to the other. "Then we would have three wormingers aboard ship, in addition to Drofo. That is impractical."

"Quite so," said Drofo. "Ranked in order of indispensability, the wormingers would be first, myself, then Pulk, then Fuscule, and finally —" Drofo paused.

"Cugel?"

"Just so."

"You are suggesting that we discharge Cugel upon this bleak and miserable island?"

"It is one of our options."

"But how will Cugel return to the mainland?"

"No doubt some means will suggest itself."

Pulk said: "Lausicaa, after all, is not the worst place in the world. The spraling is excellent."

"Ah yes, the spraling!" Soldinck spoke with warmth in his voice. "How does one sample this delicacy?"

"Nothing could be easier," said Pulk. "One merely walks along the streets of the female quarter until he sees a sign which meets his fancy. He thereupon reaches out, detaches the sign and carries it into the house."

"Does he knock?" Soldinck inquired cautiously.

"Sometimes. Knocking is considered a mark of gentility."

"Another matter. How does one discover the attributes of his hostess before he, let us say, commits himself?"

"Several tactics exist. The casual visitor, such as yourself, is well-advised to act upon local advice, since once the door opens and the visitor enters the house, he will find it difficult if not impossible to make a graceful exit. If you like, I will ask Fuscule to advise you."

"Discreetly, of course. Madame Soldinck would not care to learn of my interest in the local cuisine."

"You will find Fuscule accomodating in all respects."

"Another matter: Madame Soldinck wants to visit the Paphnissian Baths, of which she has heard many remarkable reports."

Pulk made a courteous gesture. "I myself would be happy to escort Madame Soldinck; unfortunately I will be more than busy during the next few days. I suggest that we assign Fuscule to this duty as well."

"Madame Soldinck will be happy with this plan. Well, Drofo, shall we hazard another goblet of this phenolic seepage? It is at least not deficient in authority."

"Sir, my tastes are austere."

"Captain, what of you?"

Captain Baunt made a negative indication. "I must now return to the ship and discharge Cugel from his post, since this has been your disposition of the case." He arose to his feet and departed the clubhouse, followed by Drofo.

Soldinck drank from the pewter goblet and made a wry face. "Conceivably, this brew might be painted upon the ship's bottom, to discourage the growth of marine pests. Still, we must make do." He tilted the goblet on high, and set it down with a thud. "Pulk, perhaps now is as good a time as any to taste the local spraling. Is Fuscule at liberty?"

"He might be resting, or perhaps burnishing his worm, but in any case he will happy to assist you. Boy! Run to Fuscule's house and ask him to meet Master Soldinck here at once. Explain that I, Pulk, sent the message and pronounced it urgent. And now, sir —" Pulk rose to his feet "— I will leave you in the care of Fuscule, who will be along shortly."

Cugel jumped up from the booth, hastened outdoors and waited in the shadow beside the club-house. Pulk and the serving-boy emerged and went off in different directions. Cugel ran after the boy and called him to a halt. "One moment! Soldinck has altered his plans. Here is a florin for your trouble."

"Thank you, sir." The boy turned back toward the club-house. Cugel once again engaged his attention. "No doubt you are acquainted with the women of Pompodouros?"

"Only by sight. They will serve me no spraling; in fact they are quite vulgar in their taunts."

"A pity! But no doubt your time will come. Tell me, of all the women, which might be considered the most formidable and awesome?"

The boy reflected. "That is a very hard choice to make. Krislen? Ottleia? Terlulia? In all justice, I must select Terlulia. There is a joke to the effect that when she goes to catch spraling, the sea-birds fly to the other side of the island. She is tall and portly, with red spots on her arms and large teeth. Her manner is commanding and it is said that she insists on a good bargain for her spraling."

"And where does this person make her home?"

The boy pointed. "See yonder the hut with the two windows? That is the place."

"And where will I find Fuscule?"

"Farther along this very avenue, at the worm-pen."

"Good. Here is another florin for you. When you return to the club-house, tell Master Soldinck only that Fuscule will be along shortly."

"As you say, sir."

Cugel proceeded along the road at best speed, and in short order arrived at the house of Fuscule, hard beside a worm-pen built of stones piled out into the sea. At a work-bench, repairing a burnishing tool, stood Fuscule: a tall man, very thin, all elbows, knees and long spare shanks.

Cugel put on a haughty manner and approached. "You, my good fellow, I assume to be Fuscule?"

"What of it?" demanded Fuscule in a sour voice, barely looking up from his work. "Who are you?"

"You may call me Master Soldinck, of the ship *Galante*. I understand that you consider yourself a worminger of sorts."

Fuscule looked briefly up from his work. "Understand as you like."

"Come, fellow! Do not take that tone with me! I am a man

of importance! I have come to buy your worm if you are willing to sell cheap."

Fuscule put down his tools and gave Cugel a stony inspection from under his veil. "Certainly I will sell my worm. No doubt you are in dire need, or you would not come to Lausicaa to buy a worm. My price, under the circumstances and in view of your gracious personality, is five thousand terces. Take it or leave it."

Cugel gave a rasping cry of outrage. "Only a villain could make such avaricious demands! I have traveled far across this dying world; never have I encountered such cruel rapacity! Fuscule, you are a larcenous scoundrel, and physically repulsive as well!"

Fuscule's stony grin shifted the fabric of his veil. "This sort of abuse will never persuade me to lower my prices."

"It is tragic, but I have no choice but to submit," lamented Cugel. "Fuscule, you drive a hard bargain!"

Fuscule shrugged. "I am not interested in your opinions. Where is the money? Pay it over, every terce in cold hard coin! Then take the worm and our transaction is complete."

"Patience!" said Cugel sternly. "Do you think I carry such sums on my person? I must fetch the money from the ship. Will you wait here?"

"Be quick! Though in all candour —" Fuscule gave voice to a harsh chuckle "— for five thousand terces I will wait an appreciable time."

Cugel picked up one of Fuscule's tools and carelessly tossed it into the worm-pen. In slack-jawed amazement Fuscule ran to look down after the tool. Stepping forward, Cugel pushed him into the water, then stood watching as Fuscule floundered about the pen. "That is punishment for your insolence," said Cugel. "Remember, I am Master Soldinck and an important person. I will be back in due course with the money."

With long strides Cugel returned to the club-house and went to the booth where Soldinck waited. "I am Fuscule," said Cugel, disguising his voice. "I understand that you have worked up an appetite for some good spraling."

"True!" Soldinck peered up into Cugel's veil and winked in

sly cameraderie. "But we must be discreet! That is of the essence!"

"Just so! I understand completely!"

Cugel and Soldinck departed the club-house and stood in the plaza. Soldinck said: "I must admit that I am somewhat fastidious, perhaps to a fault. Pulk has eulogized you as a man of rare discrimination in these matters."

Cugel nodded sagely. "It can justly be said that I know my left foot from my right."

Soldinck spoke on in a pensive voice. "I like to dine in pleasant surroundings, to which the charm of the hostess makes an important contribution. She should be a person of excellent or even exquisite appearance, neither portly nor emaciated. She should be flat in the belly, round in the haunch and fine in the shank like a swift racing animal. She should be reasonably clean and not smell of fish, and if she had a poetic soul and a romantic disposition, it would not come amiss."

"This is a select category," said Cugel. "It would include Krislen, Ottleia and most certainly Terlulia."

"Why waste time, then? You may take me to the hut of Terlulia, but by carriage if you please. I am almost foundered under the cargo of beer I have taken aboard."

"It shall be as you say or my name is not Fuscule." Cugel signaled for a carriage. After assisting Soldinck into the passenger space, Cugel went to confer with the driver. "Do you know the house of Terlulia?"

The driver looked around in evident curiosity, but the veil concealed his expression. "Certainly, sir."

"You may take us to a place nearby." Cugel climbed to a seat beside Soldinck. The driver kicked down a pedal connected to a lever, which in turn drove a flexible rod smartly against the drogger's rump. The animal trotted across the plaza, the driver steering by a wheel which, when rotated, pulled at cords connected to the drogger's long slender ears.

As they rode, Soldinck spoke of the *Galante* and affairs of the voyage. "Wormingers are a temperamental lot. This has been made clear to me by Lankwiler who leapt on a worm and rode off to the north, and Cugel, whose conduct is barely less eccentric. Cugel of course will be put ashore here at Pompodouros, and you, so I hope, will assume his duties — especially, my dear fellow, if you will sell me your good worm at a price fair to us both."

"No difficulty whatever," said Cugel. "What price did you have in mind?"

Under his veil Soldinck frowned thoughtfully. "At Saskervoy such a worm as yours might well sell for as high as seven hundred or even eight hundred terces. Applying the proper discounts, we arrive at a rough but generous sum of six hundred terces."

"The figure seems somewhat low," said Cugel dubiously. "I had hoped for at least a hundred terces more."

Soldinck reached into his pouch and counted forth six golden centums. "I fear that this is all I am now able to pay."

Cugel accepted the money. "The worm is yours."

"That is the way I like to do business," said Soldinck. "Briskly and with minimal haggling. Fuscule, you are a clever fellow and a hard bargainer! You will go far in this world."

"I am happy to hear your good opinion," said Cugel. "Now see yonder: that is the house of Terlulia. Driver, stop the carriage!"

The driver, pulling back a long lever, constricted brackets against the legs of the drogger, and so brought the beast to a stand-still.

Soldinck alighted and considered the structure which Cugel had pointed out. "That is the house of Terlulia?"

"Exactly so. You will notice her sign."

Soldinck dubiously surveyed the placard which Terlulia had affixed to her door. "With the red paint and flashing orange lights it is hardly demure."

"That is the basic nature of camouflage," said Cugel. "Go to the door, detach the sign and carry it into the hut."

Soldinck drew a deep breath. "So be it! Mind you now, not so much as a hint to Madame Soldinck! In fact, now would be an excellent time to show her the Paphnissian Baths if Bunderwal has brought her back to the ship."

Cugel bowed politely. "I shall see to it at once. Driver, take me to the ship *Galante*."

The carriage returned toward the harbor. Looking over his

shoulder, Cugel saw Soldinck approach Terlulia's hut. The door opened to his coming; Soldinck seemed to freeze in his tracks and then to sag somewhat on limp legs. By a means invisible to Cugel, he was snatched forward and into the house.

As the carriage approached the harbor, Cugel spoke to the driver: "Tell me something of the Paphnissian Baths. Do they confer any palpable benefits?"

"I have heard conflicting reports," said the driver. "We are told that Paphnis, then Goddess of Beauty and Gynodyne of the Century, paused on the summit of Mount Dein to rest. Nearby she found a spring where she laved her feet, thus charging the water with virtue. Sometime later the Pandalect Cosmei founded a nympharium on the site and built a splendid balneario of green glass and nacre, and so the legends were proliferated."

"And now?"

"The spring flows as before. On certain nights the ghost of Cosmei wanders among the ruins. At other times one may hear the faint sound of singing, no more than a whisper, apparently echoes of songs sung by the nymphs."

"If there were indeed efficacy to the waters," mused Cugel, "one would think that Krisler and Ottleia and even the redoubtable Terlulia would make use of the magic. Why do they not do so?"

"They claim that they want the men of Pompodouros to love them for their spiritual qualities. It may be sheer obstinacy, or perhaps they have all tested the springs, without effect. It is one of the great female mysteries."

"What of the spraling?"

"Everyone must eat."

The carriage entered the plaza and Cugel called the driver to a halt. "Which of these avenues leads up to the Paphnissian Baths?"

The driver pointed. "Just along there and then five miles up the mountainside."

"And what is your fee for the trip?"

"Ordinarily I charge three terces, but for persons of importance the fee is occasionally somewhat higher."

"Well then, Soldinck has required me to escort Madame Soldinck to the Baths and she prefers that we go alone, to minimize her embarrassment. I will therefore hire the use of your carriage for ten terces, plus an additional five terces to buy your beer during my absence. Soldinck will disburse this sum upon his return from the hut of Terlulia."

"If he has the strength to lift his hand," grumbled the driver. "All fees should be paid in advance."

"Here is your beer money, at least," said Cugel. "The rest must be collected from Soldinck."

"It is irregular, but I suppose it will do. Observe then. This pedal accelerates the vehicle. This lever brings it to a halt. Turn this wheel to direct the vehicle in the way you wish to go. If the drogger squats to the ground this lever drives a spur into its groin and it will leap forward with renewed vigor."

"Clarity itself," said Cugel. "I will return your carriage to the rank in front of the club-house."

Cugel drove the carriage to the wharf and halted beside the *Galante*. Madame Soldinck and her daughters sat in lounging-chairs on the quarter-deck looking across the plaza and commenting upon the curious sights of the town.

"Madame Soldinck!" called Cugel. "It is I, Fuscule, who have come to escort you to the Baths of Paphnis. Are you ready? We must make haste, since the day is drawing on!"

"I am quite ready. Is there room for all of us?"

"I am afraid not. The beast could not pull us up the mountain. Your daughters must remain behind."

Madame Soldinck descended the gangplank and Cugel jumped to the ground. "'Fuscule'?" mused Madame Soldinck. "I have heard your name but I cannot place you."

"I am the nephew of Pulk the worminger. I am selling a worm to Master Soldinck and I hope to become worminger aboard your ship."

"I see. Whatever the case, it is kind of you to take me on this excursion. Will I need special bathing clothes?"

"None are necessary. There is adequate seclusion, and garments diminish the effect of the waters."

"Yes, that seems reasonable."

Cugel assisted Madame Soldinck into the carriage, then climbed into the driver's seat. He thrust down the accelerator pedal and the carriage rolled off across the plaza.

Cugel followed the road up the mountainside. Pompodouros fell below, then disappeared among the stony hills. Thick black sedge to either side gave off a sharp aromatic odor and it became clear to Cugel where the folk of the island derived the raw material for their beer.

The road at last turned off into a dreary little meadow. Cugel halted the carriage to rest the drogger. Madame Soldinck called out in a reedy voice: "Are we almost to the fountain? Where is the temple which shelters the baths?"

"There is still some distance to go,' said Cugel.

"Truly? Fuscule, you should have provided a more comfortable carriage. This vehicle bounces and jounces as if I were riding a board being dragged over the rocks, nor is there protection from the dust."

Swinging around in his seat, Cugel spoke severely: "Madame Soldinck, please put aside your complaints, as they grate on the nerves. In fact, there is more to be said, and I will use the even-handed candour of a worminger. For all your estimable qualities, you have been spoiled and pampered by too much luxury, and, of course, over-eating. You are living a decadent dream! In reference to the carriage: enjoy the comfort while it is available to you, since, when the way becomes steep, you will be obliged to walk."

Madame Soldinck stared up speechless.

"Furthermore, this is the place where I customarily collect my fee," said Cugel. "How much money do you carry on your person?"

Madame Soldinck at last found her tongue. She spoke icily: "Surely you can wait until we return to Pompodouros. Master Soldinck will deal justly with you at the proper time."

"I prefer hard terces now to justice then. Here I can maximize my fee. In Pompodouros I must compromise with Soldinck's avarice."

"That is a callous point of view."

"It is the voice of classical logic, as we are taught at wormingers' school. You may pay over at least forty-five terces."

"Absurd! I carry no such sum on my person!"

"Then you may give me that fine opal you wear at your shoulder."

"Never! That is a valuable gem! Here is eighteen terces; it is all I have with me. Now take me at once to the baths and without further insolence."

"You are starting out on the wrong foot, Madame Soldinck! I plan to sign upon the *Galante* as worminger, no matter what the inconvenience to Cugel. He can be marooned here forever, for all I care. In any case you will be seeing much of me, and cordiality will be returned in kind, and you may also introduce me to your toothsome daughters."

Again Madame Soldinck found herself at a loss for words. Finally she said: "Take me to the baths."

"It is time to proceed," said Cugel. "I suspect that the drogger, if consulted, would claim already to have expended eighteen terces worth of effort. On Lausicaa we are not grossly overweight like you outlanders."

Madame Soldinck said with flinty control: "Your remarks, Fuscule, are extraordinary."

"Save your breath, as you may need it when the drogger begins to flag."

Once again Madame Soldinck sat silent.

The hillside indeed became more steep and the road traversed back and forth until, breasting a little ridge, it dipped into a glade shaded under yellow-green gingerberry trees, and a single tall lancelade, with a glossy dark red trunk and feathery black foliage, standing like a king.

Cugel halted the carriage beside a stream which trickled across the glade. "Here we are, Madame Soldinck. You may bathe in the water and I will take note of the results."

Madame Soldinck surveyed the stream without enthusiasm. "Can this be the site of the baths? Where is the temple? And the fallen statue? Where is Cosmei's bower?"

"The baths proper are farther up the mountain," said Cugel in a languid voice. "This is the identical water, which in any event works to small effect, especially in exaggerated cases."

Madame Soldinck grew red in the face. "You may drive me down the hill at once. Master Soldinck will make other arrangements for me."

"As you like. However, I will take my gratuity now, if you please."

"You may refer to Master Soldinck for your gratuity. I am sure that he will have something to say to you."

Cugel turned the carriage about and started back down-hill, saying: "Never will I understand the ways of women."

Madame Soldinck sat in frigid silence and in due course the carriage came down into Pompodouros. Cugel took Madame Soldinck to the *Galante*; without a backward glance she stalked up the gangplank.

Cugel returned the carriage to the rank, then entered the club-house and seated himself in an inconspicuous booth. He rearranged his veil, draping it from inside the brim of his hat, that he might no longer be mistaken for Fuscule.

An hour passed. Captain Baunt and Chief Worminger Drofo, having completed various errands, strolled across the plaza to stand in conversation in front of the club-house, where they were presently joined by Pulk.

"And where is Soldinck?" asked Pulk. "Surely by now he has consumed all the spraling good for him."

"So I would think," said Captain Baunt. "He could hardly have come to any mishap."

"Not with Fuscule in charge," said Pulk. "No doubt they are standing by the pen, discussing Fuscule's worm."

Captain Baunt pointed up the hill. "Here comes Soldinck now! He seems in a bad way, as if he can hardly put one foot in front of another!"

Hunched forward and walking with exaggerated care, Soldinck crossed the plaza by an indirect route and at last joined the group in front of the club-house. Captain Baunt stepped forward to meet him. "Are you well? Has something gone wrong?"

Soldinck spoke in a voice thin and husky: "I have had an awful experience."

"What happened? At least you are alive!"

"Only barely. These last few hours will haunt me forever. I

blame Fuscule, in all respects. I name him a demon of perversity! I bought his worm; at least that is ours. Drofo, go fetch it to the ship; we will leave this sink-hole at once."

Pulk put a tentative question: "Will Fuscule still be our worminger?"

"Ha!" declared Soldinck savagely. "He will not tend worms on my ship! Cugel commands the position."

Madame Soldinck, having observed Soldinck as he crossed the plaza, could restrain her rage no longer. She descended to the dock and approached the club-house. As soon as she came within ear-shot of Soldinck she cried out: "So there you are at last! Where were you while I was suffering insolence and ridicule at the hands of that vicious Fuscule? The instant he puts his foot aboard our ship I leave! Compared to Fuscule, Cugel is a blessed angel of light! Cugel must remain the worminger!"

"That, my dear, is exactly my own opinion."

Pulk tried to insert a soothing word. "I cannot believe that Fuscule would act other than correctly! Surely there has been a mistake or a misunderstanding of some sort —"

"A misunderstanding, when he demanded forty-five terces and took eighteen only because I had no more; and wanted my precious opal in the bargain, then visited upon me ignominies I cannot bear to think upon? And he boasted, if you can believe it, of how he intended to worm aboard the *Galante*! That will never be, if I myself must stand guard at the gang-plank!"

Captain Baunt said: "The decision is definite in this regard. Fuscule must be a madman!"

"A madman or worse! It is hard to describe the scope of his evil! And yet, all the while, I sensed familiarity, as if somewhere, in a previous existence, or a nightmare, I had known him!"

"The mind plays strange tricks," observed Captain Baunt. "I am anxious to meet this remarkable individual."

Pulk called out: "Here he comes now, with Drofo! At last we shall have an explanation, and perhaps a suitable apology."

"I want neither!" cried Madame Soldinck. "I want only to see the last of this dismal island!" Turning on her heel, she swept off across the plaza and back aboard the *Galante*.

Marching with vigorous steps, Fuscule approached the

group, with Drofo strolling a pace or two behind. Fuscule
halted, and raising his veil, surveyed the group. "Where is Soldinck?"

Keeping a tight grip on his temper, Soldinck said coldly:
"You know very well who I am! I know you as well, for a
scoundrel and a blackguard. I will not comment upon the poor
taste of your prank, nor your insufferable conduct toward
Madame Soldinck. I prefer that we conclude our business on
the basis of absolute formality. Drofo, why are you not taking
our worm to the *Galante*?"

"I will respond to that question," said Fuscule. "Drofo will
be allowed the worm after you have paid me my five thousand
terces, plus eleven terces for my double-cambered fluke-chister
which you discarded with such cavalier ease, together with
another twenty terces for your attack upon my person. Your
account therefore stands at a total of five thousand and thirty-
one terces. You may pay me on this instant."

Cugel, mingling with a group of others, came from the
club-house and stood watching the altercation from a little distance.

Soldinck advanced two pugnacious steps toward Fuscule.
"Are you mad? I bought your worm for a fair sum and paid
you cash on the spot. Let us have no more dancing and dodging! Deliver the worm to Drofo at once, or we will take immediate and drastic measures!"

"Needless to say, you have forfeited your post as worminger
aboard the *Galante*", Captain Baunt pointed out. "So deliver the
worm and let us have an end to the business."

"Pah!" cried Fuscule in a passion. "You shall not have my
worm, not for five thousand terces nor yet ten! And as for the
other items on the account —" stepping forward he struck Soldinck smartly on the side of the head "— that will pay for the
chister and this —" he dealt Soldinck another blow "— must settle for the remainder."

Soldinck rushed forward to settle his own accounts; Captain
Baunt attempted to intervene but his intent was misunderstood
by Pulk, who with one mighty heave threw him to the ground.

The confusion was eventually controlled by Drofo, who put

himelf between the opposing parties and held out his arms to
induce restraint. "Peace, every one! There are peculiar aspects
to this situaltion which must be analyzed. Fuscule, you claim
that Soldinck offered you five thousand terces for your worm,
then threw your chister into the water?"

"That indeed is my claim!" cried Fuscule furiously.

"Are those likely events? Soldinck is notorious for his par-
simony! Never would he offer five thousand terces for a worm
worth at best two thousand! How do you explain such a
paradox?"

"I am a worminger, not a student of weird psychological
mysteries," grumbled Fuscule. "Still, now that I reflect on it,
the man who called himself Soldinck stood a head taller than
this little toad. He also wore an unusual hat of several folds, and
walked with his legs bent at the knees."

Soldinck spoke excitedly: "The description mignt well fit
the villain who recommended me to the hut of Terlulia! He
walked with a stealthy gait, and called himself Fuscule."

"Aha!" said Pulk. "Affairs are starting to sort themselves
out. Let us find a booth in the club-house and approach our inquiry properly, over a jug of good black beer!"

"The concept is sound but in this case unnecessary," said
Drofo. "I can already put a name to the individual at fault."

Captain Baunt said: "I also have an intuition in this regard."

Soldinck looked resentfully from face to face. "Am I then so
dense? Who is this person?"

"Can there be any more doubt?" asked Drofo. "His name is
Cugel."

Soldinck blinked, then clapped his hands together. "That is a
reasonable deduction!"

Pulk spoke in gentle admonition: "Now that the guilty person has been identified, it appears that you owe Fuscule an
apology."

The memory of Fuscule's blows still rankled with Soldinck.
"I will feel more generous when he returns the five hundred
terces I paid him for his worm. And never forget: it was he
who accused me of throwing away his chister. Apologies are
due from the other direction."

"You are still confused," said Pulk. "The five hundred terces were paid to Cugel."

"Possibly so. Still, I feel that careful inquiries are in order."

Captain Baunt turned to look around the bystanders. "I thought that I saw him a few minutes ago. . . . He seems to have slipped away."

For a fact, as soon as he had seen which way the wind was blowing, Cugel had taken himself in haste to the *Galante*. Madame Soldinck was in the cabin, acquainting her daughters with the events of the day. No one was on hand to interfere as Cugel ran here and there about the ship. He dropped the gang-plank, threw off the mooring-lines, pulled hoods from the worms and placed triple bait in the hoppers, then ran up to the quarter-deck and threw the wheel hard over.

At the club-house Soldinck was saying: "I distrusted him from the start! Still, who could imagine such protean depravity?"

Bunderwal, the supercargo, concurred. "Cugel, while plausible, is nonetheless a bit of a scoundrel."

"He must now be summoned to an accounting," said Captain Baunt. "It is always an unpleasant task."

"Not all that unpleasant," muttered Fuscule.

"We must give him a fair hearing, and the sooner the better. I fancy the club-house will serve as well as any for our forum."

"First we must find him," said Soldinck. "I wonder where the rascal has taken cover? Drofo, you and Pulk look aboard the *Galante*. Fuscule, glance inside the club-house. Do or say nothing to alarm him; merely indicate that I want to put a few general questions. . . . Yes, Drofo? Why are you not off about your errand?"

Drofo pointed toward the sea. He spoke in his usual pensive voice: "Sir, you may look for yourself."

3

THE OCEAN
OF SIGHS

THE RED morning sun reflected from the dark sea in exact replica.

The worms idled effortlessly at half-bait; the *Galante* drifted through the water as softly as a boat sliding through a dream.

Cugel slept somewhat later than usual, in that bed formerly enjoyed by Soldinck.

The crew of the *Galante* worked quietly and efficiently at their appointed tasks.

A tap at the door aroused Cugel from his rest. After stretching and yawning Cugel called out in a melodious voice: "Enter!"

The door opened; into the cabin came Tabazinth, the youngest and perhaps the most winsome of Madame Soldinck's daughters, though Cugel, had he been pressed for judgment, would have stoutly defended the special merits of each.

Tabazinth, who was gifted with a buxom chest and robust little haunches while still retaining a slender and flexible waist, showed to the world a round face, a mop of dark curls and a pink mouth chronically pursed as if in restraint of a smile. She carried a tray which she set on the bedside table. With a demure glance over her shoulder she started to leave the chamber. Cugel called her back.

"Tabazinth, my dear! The morning is fine; I will take my breakfast on the quarter-deck. You may instruct Madame Soldinck to lash the wheel and take her relief." "As you like, sir." Tabazinth picked up the tray and left the cabin.

Cugel arose from the bed, applied a scented lotion to his face, rinsed his mouth with one of Soldinck's select balsams, then wrapped himself in an easy gown of pale blue silk. He listened. . . . Down the companion-way ladder came the thud of

119

Madame Soldinck's steps. Through the forward port-hole
Cugel watched as she marched forward to that cabin formerly
occupied by Chief Worminger Drofo. As soon as she had disappeared from view, Cugel stepped out upon the midship deck.
He inhaled and exhaled deep breaths of the cool morning air,
then climbed to the quarter-deck.

Before sitting down to his breakfast Cugel went to the taff-
rail, to survey the state of the sea and assess the progress of the
ship. From horizon to horizon the water lay flat, with nothing
to be seen but the image of the sun. The wake astern seemed
adequately straight — a testimony as to the quality of Madame
Soldinck's steering — while the claw of the escalabra pointed
due south.

Cugel gave a nod of approval; Madame Soldinck might well
become a competent helmswoman. On the other hand, she
showed small skill as a worminger, and her daughters here were
marginal at best.

Cugel seated himself to his breakfast. One by one he raised
the silver covers to peer into the platters. He discovered a com-
pote of spiced fruit, poached sea-bird livers, porridge of drist
and raisins, a pickle of lily-bulbs and small black fungus-balls
with several different kinds of pastry: a breakfast more than
adequate in which he recognized the work of Meadhre, oldest
and most conscientious of the daughters. Madame Soldinck, on
the single time she had been pressed into service, had prepared a
meal so quietly unappetizing that Cugel had refrained from
again assigning her to the galley.

Cugel ate at leisure. A most pleasant harmony existed between himself and the world: an interlude to be prolonged,
cherished and savored to the utmost. To memorialize this
special condition Cugel lifted his exquisitely delicate
tea-cup and sipped the limpid nectar brewed from Soldinck's
choicest blend of herbs.

"Just so!" said Cugel. The past was gone; the future might
end tomorrow, should the sun go dark. Now was now, to be
dealt with on its own terms.

"Precisely so!" said Cugel.

And yet. . . . Cugel glanced uneasily over his shoulder. It was
right and proper to exploit the excellences of the moment, but

still, when conditions reached an apex, there was nowhere to go but down.

Even now, without tangible reason, Cugel felt an eery strain in the atmosphere, as if, just past the edge of his awareness, something had gone askew.

Cugel jumped to his feet and looked over the port rail. The worms, on half-bait, worked without strain. Everything seemed in order. Likewise with the starboard worm. Cugel slowly went back to his breakfast.

Cugel applied the full force of his intellect to the problem: what had aroused his uneasiness? The ship was sound; food and drink were ample; Madame Soldinck and her daughters had apparently come to terms with their new careers; and Cugel congratulated himself upon his wise, kindly but firm administration.

For a period immediately after departure Madame Soldinck produced a furious torrent of abuse, which Cugel finally decided to abate, if only in the interests of ship-board morale. "Madame," said Cugel, "your outcries disturb us all. They must cease."

"I name you an oppressor! A monster of evil! A laharq, or a keak * !"

Cugel replied: "Unless you desist I will order you confined in the hold."

"Bah!" said Madame Soldinck. "Who will carry out your orders?"

"If necesuary I will implement them myself! Ship's discipline must be maintained. I am now captain of this vessel, and these are my commands. First, you are to hold your tongue. Second, you will assemble aft on the midship deck to hear the address I am about to deliver."

With poor grace Madame Soldinck and her daughters gathered at the spot which Cugel had designated.

Cugel climbed halfway up the companionway ladder. "Ladies! I will be grateful for your complete attention!" Cugel looked smilingly from face to face. "Now then! I am aware that

*laharq: a creature of vicious habits, native to the tundras north of Saskervoy.
 keak: a horrid hybrid of demon and deep-sea fanged eel.

today has not yielded optimum rewards to us all. Still, now is now, and we must come to terms with circumstance. In this regard I can offer a word or two of advice.

"Our first concern is for marine regulation, which stipulates quick and exact obedience to the captain's orders. Shipboard work will be shared. I have already accepted the duties of command. From you, my crew, I will expect good will, cooperation and zest, whereupon you will find me lenient, understanding and even affectionate."

Madame Soldinck called out sharply: "We want neither you nor your lenience! Take us back to Pompodouros!"

Meadhre, the oldest daughter, said in a melancholy voice: "Hush, Mama! Be realistic! Cugel does not dare return to Pompodouros, so let us find where in fact he plans to take us."

"I will now provide that information," said Cugel. "Our port of destination is Val Ombrio on the coast of Almery, a goodly sail to the south."

Madame Soldinck cried out in shock: "You cannot be serious! In between lie waters of deadly peril! This is common knowledge!"

Cugel said coldly: "I suggest, Madame, that you place your faith in someone like myself, rather than the housewives of your social circle."

Salasser advised her mother: "Cugel will do as he likes in any case; why oppose his wishes? It will only make him angry."

"Sound thinking!" declared Cugel. "Now, as to the work of the ship: each of you must become a competent worminger, at my instruction. Since we have ample time we will drive the worms at half-bait only, which will be to their advantage. We also lack the services of Angshott the cook; still, we have ample stores and I see no reason to stint ourselves. I encourage all of you to give full scope to your culinary skills."

"Today I will prepare a tentative work-schedule. During the day I will maintain the look-out and supervise ship-board processes. Perhaps here I should mention that Madame Soldinck, by virtue of her years and social position, will not be required to act as 'night-steward'. Now then, in regard to —"

Madame Soldinck took a quick step forward. "One moment! The 'night-steward' — what are her duties and why should I be disqualified?"

Cugel looked off across the sea. "The duties of the 'night-steward' are more or less self-explanatory. She is assigned to the aft-cabin, where she looks to the convenience of the captain. There is prestige to the post; it is only fair that it should be shared among Meadhre, Salasser and Tabazinth."

Again Madame Soldinck became agitated. "It is as I feared! I, Cugel, will be 'night-steward'! Do not attempt to dissuade me!"

"All very well, madame, but your skills are needed at the helm."

Meadhre said: "Come, Mama, we are not so frail and pathetic as you fear."

Tabazinth said with a laugh: "Mama, it is you who deserves special consideration and not we. We can cope with Cugel very well."

Salasser said: "We must let Cugel make the decisions, since the responsibilities are his."

Cugel spoke. "There I suggest we let the matter rest. Now I must deal, once and once only, with a somewhat macabre concept. Let us assume that someone aboard this ship — let us call her Zita, after the Goddess of Unknowable Things — let us assume that Zita has decided to remove Cugel from the realm of the living. She considers poison in his food, a knife in his gullet, a blow and a push so that Cugel falls into the sea."

"Genteel persons are not likely to consider such conduct," said Cugel. "Still, I have evolved a plan to reduce this likelihood to nothing. Deep in the forward hold I will install a destructive device, using a quantity of explosive, a candle, and a fuse. Every day I will unlock an impregnable iron-bound door and replace the candle. If I neglect to do so, the candle will burn down and ignite the wick. The explosive will blow a hole in the hull and the ship will sink like a stone. Madame Soldinck, you appear distrait; did you hear me properly?"

"I heard you all too well."

"Then this completes my remarks for the moment. Madame Soldinck, you may report to the wheel, where I will demonstrate the basic principles of steering. Girls, you will first prepare our lunch, then see to the comfort of our various cabins."

At the wheel Madame Soldinck continued to warn of dangers to the south. "The pirates are blood-thirsty! There are sea-monsters: the blue codorfins, the thryfwyd, the forty-foot water-shadow! Storms strike from all directions; they toss ships about like corks!"

"How do the pirates survive amid such dangers?"

"Who cares how they survive? Our fervent hope is that they perish."

Cugel laughed. "Your warnings fly in the face of facts! We carry goods for Iucounu which must be delivered by way of Val Ombrio, on the coast of Almery."

"It is you who are ignorant of facts! The goods are transshipped through Port Perdusz, where our factors make special arrangements. To Port Perdusz we must go."

Cugel laughed once again. "Do you take me for a fool? On the instant the ship touched dock you would be bawling in all directions for the thief-takers. As before: steer south." Cugel went off to his lunch, leaving Madame Soldinck glowering at the escalabra.

On the morning of the next day Cugel felt the first intimation that something had gone askew at the edges of reality. Try as he might, the exact discrepancy, or slippage, or unconformity evaded his grasp. The ship functioned properly, although the worms, on half-bait, seemed a trifle sluggish, as if after a hard stint, and Cugel made a mental note to dose them with a tonic.

A covey of high clouds in the western sky presaged wind, which, if favorable, would further rest the worms. . . . Cugel frowned in perplexity. Drofo had made him aware as to variations in the ocean's color, texture and clarity. Now it seemed as if this were the identical ocean they had crossed the day before. Ridiculous, Cugel told himself; he must keep a grip upon his imagination.

Late in the afternoon Cugel, looking astern, noticed a portly little cog approaching at its best speed. Cugel took up his lens and studied the ship, which was propelled by four splashing and inefficient worms being driven to their utmost. On the deck Cugel thought to recognize Soldinck, Captain Baunt, Pulk and others, while a tall pensive figure, surely Drofo, stood at the bow contemplating the sea.

Cugel looked around the sky. Night was two hours distant. Without urgency he ordered double-bait for all worms and a half-gill each of Rouse's Tonic. The *Galante* moved easily away from the pursuing ship.

Madame Soldinck had watched all with interest. She asked at last: "Who sailed that ship?"

"They seemed to be Sarpent Island traders," said Cugel. "A rough lot, by all accounts. In the future give such ships a wide berth."

Madame Soldinck made no comment, and Cugel went off to ponder a new mystery: how had Soldinck come at him so swiftly?

With the coming of darkness, Cugel changed course and the pursuing ship was lost astern. Cugel told Madame Soldinck: "In the morning they'll be ten leagues off our course." He turned to go below. . . . A gleam of light, from the black iron stern lantern, caught his eye.

Cugel uttered a cry of vexation and extinguished the light. He turned angrily to Madame Soldinck: "Why did you not tell me that you had lit up the lantern?"

Madame Soldinck gave an indifferent shrug. "In the first place, you never asked."

"And in the second place?"

"It is prudent to show a light while at sea. That is the rule of the cautious mariner."

"Aboard the *Galante* it is unnecessary to light lights except upon my orders."

"Just as you like."

Cugel tapped the escalabra. "Keep to the present course for one hour, then turn south."

"Unwise! Tragically unwise!"

Cugel descended to the midship deck and stood leaning on the rail until the soft chime of silver bells summoned him to his

dinner, which tonight was served in the aft cabin on a table
spread with white linen.

The meal was adequate to Cugel's expectations and he so in-
formed Tabazinth who tonight was on duty as 'night-steward'.
"There was perhaps a trace too much fennel in the fish sauce,"
he noted, "and the second service of wine — I refer to the Pale
Montrachio — was clearly taken up a year before its fullest
bounty. Still, all in all, there was little to be faulted and I hope
you will so inform the kitchen."

"Now?" asked Tabazinth demurely.

"Not necessarily," said Cugel. "Why not tomorrow?"

"Soon enough, I should think."

"Exactly so. We have our own business to discuss. But
first —" Cugel glanced out the stern window "— as I half-
expected, that crafty old woman has again put light to the stern
lantern. I cannot imagine what she has in her mind. What good
is a great flare of light astern? She is not steering backward."

"She probably wishes to warn off that other ship which was
following so close on our heels."

"The chances of collision are small. I want to avoid attention, not attract it."

"All is well, Cugel. You must not fret." Tabazinth approached and placed her hands on his shoulders. "Do you like
the way I dress my hair? I have put on a special scent; it is called
'Tanjence', who was a beautiful woman of fable."

"Your hair is charming to the point of distraction; the scent
is sublime; but I must go up and set things right with your
mother."

With pouts and smiles Tabazinth tried to restrain him. "Ah,
Cugel, how can I put faith in your flattery if at the first pretext
you run off helter-skelter? Stay with me now; show me the full
measure of your interest! Leave the poor old woman to her
steering."

Cugel put her aside. "Control your amiability, my bountiful
little poppet! I will be gone no more than an instant, and then
you shall see!"

Cugel ran from the cabin, climbed to the quarter-deck. As he
had feared, the lantern burned with a blatant glare. Without

pausing to chide Madame Soldinck, Cugel not only extinguished the light, but removed glow-box, spurts and lumenex,
and threw them into the sea.

Cugel addressed Madame Soldinck: "You have seen the last
of my kindly forbearance. If lights again show from this ship,
you will not enjoy the aftermath."

Madame Soldinck haughtily held her tongue, and after a
final inspection of the escalabra, Cugel returned to his cabin.
After more wine and several hours of frolicking with
Tabazinth, he fell soundly asleep and did not return to the
quarter-deck that night.

In the morning, as Cugel sat blinking in the sunlight, he
again felt that strange sense of displacement which had troubled
him on other occasions. He climbed to the quarter-deck, where
Salasser stood at the wheel. Cugel went to look at the escalabra;
the claw pointed directly to the south.

Cugel returned to the midship deck and inspected the
worms; they eased and lolled through the water on half-bait,
apparently healthy save for what seemed to be fatigue and a
touch of timp on the port outboard beast.

Today there would be wet work along the sponsons, from
which only the 'night-steward' might hope to be excused.

A day passed, and another: for Cugel a halcyon time of ease,
zestful refreshment in the sea air, splendid cuisine, and the un-
stinting attention of his 'night-stewards'. A single source of
disturbance were those strange displacements in time and space
which he now thought to be no more than episodes of déjà
vu.

On the morning that Tabazinth served him breakfast on the
quarter-deck, his meal was interrupted by the sighting of a
small fishing vessel. Beyond, to the south-west, Cugel made
out the dim outline of an island, which he studied in perplexity.
Déjà vu, once again?

Cugel took the wheel and steered so as to pass close by the
fishing-boat, which was worked by a man and two boys. As he
passed abeam, Cugel went to the rail and hailed the fisherman:
"Halloo! What island lies yonder?"

The fisherman looked at Cugel as if he lacked intelligence. "It is Lausicaa, as you should well know. If I were in your shoes, I would give this region a wide berth."

Cugel gaped toward the island. Lausicaa? How could it be, unless magic were at work?

Cugel went in confusion to the escalabra; all seemed in order. Amazing! He had depa ted toward the south; now he returned from the north, and must change course or run aground upon the place from which he had started!

Cugel swung the ship to the east and Lausicaa faded over the horizon. He then changed course again, and steered once more to the south.

Madame Soldinck, standing by, curled her lip in disgust. "South again? Have I not warned of dangers to the south?"

"Steer south! Not an iota east, not the fraction of an iota west! South is our desired direction! Put north astern and steer south!"

"Insanity!" muttered Madame Soldinck.

"Insanity, not at all! I am as sane as yourself! Admittedly this voyage has given me several queasy moments. I am unable to explain our approach to Lausicaa from the north. It is as if we had completed a circumnavigation!"

"Iucounu the Magician has put a spell on the ship to safeguard his shipment. This is the most reasonable hypothesis and yet another reason to make for Port Perdusz."

"Out of the question," said Cugel. "I am now going below to think. Report all extraordinary circumstances."

"The wind is coming up," said Madame Soldinck. "We may even have a storm."

Cugel went to the rail, and indeed cat's-paws from the northwest roughened the glossy black surface of the sea. "Wind will rest the worms," said Cugel. "I cannot imagine why they are so spiritless! Drofo would insist that they have been overworked, but I know better."

Descending to the midship deck, Cugel dropped the blue silk mainsail from its brails and sheeted home the clews. The sail bellied to the breeze and water tinkled under the hull.

Cugel arranged a comfortable chair where he could prop his feet on the rail and, with a bottle of Rozpagnola Amber at his elbow, settled himself to watch Meadhre and Tabazinth as they dealt with an incipient case of gangue on the port inboard worm.

The afternoon passed and Cugel drowsed to the gentle motion of the ship. He awoke to find that the cat's-paws had become a soft breeze, so that there was a surging motion to the ship, a modest bow wave and a gurgle of wake at the stern.

Salasser, the 'night-steward', served tea in a silver pot and a selection of small pastries, which Cugel consumed in an unusually abstracted mood.

Rising from his chair, Cugel climbed to the quarter-deck. He found Madame Soldinck in a testy mood. "The wind is not good," she told him. "Better that you pull in the sail."

Cugel rejected her advice. "The wind blows us nicely along our course and the worms are able to rest."

"The worms need no rest," snapped Madame Soldinck. "With the sails pulling the ship, I cannot steer where I want to steer."

Cugel indicated the escalabra. "Steer south! That is the way you want to steer! The claw shows the way!"

Madame Soldinck had no more to say, and Cugel left the quarter-deck.

The time was sunset. Cugel went forward to the bow and stood under the lantern, as Drofo was wont to do. Tonight the western sky was dramatic with a high array of cirrus wisps scarlet on the dark blue sky. At the horizon the sun lingered and hesitated, as if reluctant to leave the world of daylight. A sour blue-green corona rimmed the edge of the globe: a phenomenon which Cugel had never noticed before. A purple bruise on the sun's surface seemed to pulse, like the orifice of a polyp: a portent? . . . . Cugel started to turn away, then, struck by a sudden thought, looked up into the lantern. The glow-box, spurts and lumenex, which Cugel had removed from the stern lantern, were not to be seen here either.

It seemed, thought Cugel, as if fertile minds worked hard aboard the *Galante*. "Nonetheless," Cugel told himself, "it is with me whom they deal, and I am not known as Cugel the Clever for nothing."

For still a few minutes Cugel stood at the bow. On the

quarter-deck the three girls and Madame Soldinck drank tea and watched Cugel sidelong. Cugel put an arm to the lantern-post, creating a gallant silhouette against the sky of sunset. The high clouds now showed the color of old blood, and were clearly the precursors of wind. It might be wise to tuck a reef into the sail.

The light of sunset died. Cugel pondered the strange events of the voyage. To sail south all day and wake up the next morning in waters farther north than the starting point of the day before: this was an unnatural sequence. . . . What sensible explanation, other than magic, existed? An ocean swirl? A retrograde escalabra?

One conjecture followed another across Cugel's mind, each more unlikely than the last. At one especially preposterous notion he paused to voice a sardonic chuckle before rejecting it along with other more plausible theories. . . . He stopped short and returned to review the idea, since, oddly enough, the theory fitted precisely to all the facts.

Except in a single crucial aspect.

The theory rested on the premise that Cugel's mental capacity was of a low order. Cugel chuckled once again, but less comfortably, and presently he stopped chuckling.

The mysteries and paradoxes of the voyage were now illuminated. It seemed that Cugel's innate chivalry and sense of decency had been exploited and his easy trustfulness had been turned against him. But now the game would change!

A tinkle of silver bells announced the service of his dinner. Cugel delayed a moment for a last look around the horizon. The breeze was blowing with greater force and piling up small waves which slapped against the *Galante's* bluff bows.

Cugel walked slowly aft. He climbed to the quarter-deck where Madame Soldinck had only just come on watch. Cugel gave her a crisp nod which she ignored. He looked at the escalabra; the claw indicated 'South'. Cugel went to the taff-rail and casually glanced up into the lantern. The glow-box was not in place, which proved nothing. Cugel said to Madame Soldinck: "A nice breeze will rest the worms."

"That may well be."

"The course is south, fair and true."

Madame Soldinck deigned no response. Cugel descended to a dinner which in all respects met his critical standards. The meal was served by the 'night-steward' Salasser, whom Cugel found no less charming than her sisters. Tonight she had dressed her hair in the style of the Spanssian Corybants, and wore a simple white gown belted at the waist with a golden rope — a costume which nicely set off her slender figure. Of the three girls, Salasser possessed possibly the most refined intelligence, and her conversation, while sometimes quaint, impressed Cugel by reason of its freshness and subtlety.

Salasser served Cugel his dessert: a torte of five flavors, and while Cugel consumed the delicacy, Salasser began to remove his shoes.

Cugel drew his feet back. "For a time I will wear my shoes."

Salasser raised her eyebrows in surprise. Cugel was usually ready enough to seek the comforts of the couch as soon as he had finished his dessert.

Tonight Cugel put aside the torte half-finished. He jumped to his feet, ran from the cabin and climbed to the quarter-deck where he found Madame Soldinck in the act of putting light to the lantern.

Cugel spoke angrily: "I believe that I have made myself clear on this subject!" He reached into the lantern and despite Madame Soldinck's cry of protest removed the functioning parts and threw them far into the dark.

He descended to the cabin. "Now," he told Salasser, "you may remove my shoes."

An hour later Cugel jumped from the couch and wrapped himself in his gown. Salasser raised to her knees. "Where are you going? I have thought of somethihg innovative."

"I will be back at once."

On the quarter-deck Cugel once again discovered Madame Soldinck as she put fire to several candles which she had placed into the lantern. Cugel snatched away the candles and threw them into the sea.

Madame Soldinck protested: "What are you doing? I need the light for steering purposes!"

"You must steer by the glim in the escalabra! You have heard my last warning!"

Madame Soldinck, muttering under her breath, hunched over the wheel. Cugel returned to the cabin. "Now," he told Salasser, "to your innovation! Although I suspect that, after twenty aeons, few stones have been left unturned."

"So it may be," said Salasser with charming simplicity. "But are we then to be deterred from a new trial?"

"Naturally not," said Cugel.

The innovation was tested, and Cugel suggested a variation which also proved successful. Cugel then jumped to feet and started to run from the room, but Salasser caught him and drew him back to the couch. "You are as restless as a tonquil! What has vexed you so?"

"The wind is rising! Listen how the sail flaps! I must make an inspection."

"Why irk yourself?" coaxed Salasser. "Let Mama deal with such things."

"If she trims the sail, she must leave the wheel. And who is tending the worms?"

"The worms are resting. . . . Cugel! Where are you going?"

Cugel had already run out upon the midship-deck, to find the sail back-winded and furiously flogging at the sheets. He climbed to the quarter-deck, where he discovered that Madame Soldinck, becoming discouraged, had abandoned her post and gone to her quarters.

Cugel checked the escalabra. The claw indicated a northerly direction, with the ship ducking and yawing and sidling astern. Cugel spun the wheel; the bow fell off; the wind caught the sail with a great clap of sound, so that Cugel feared for the sheets. Irritated by the jerking, the worms swung up from the water, plunged, broke their cinctures and swam away.

Cugel called out: "All hands on deck!" but no-one responded. He lashed the wheel and working in the dark brailed up the sail, suffering several sharp blows from the flailing sheets.

The ship now blew directly down-wind, in an easterly direction. Cugel went in search of his crew, to discover that all had locked themselves in their cabins, from which they silently ignored his orders.

Cugel kicked furiously at the doors, but only bruised his

foot. He limped back amidships and made all as secure as possible.

The wind howled through the rigging and the ship began to show an inclination to broach. Cugel once more ran forward and roared orders to his crew. He elicited a response only from Madame Soldinck: "Go away, and leave us to die in peace! We are all sick."

Cugel gave a final kick to the door and, limping, made his way to the wheel, where with great exertion he managed to keep the ship tracking steady before the wind.

All night Cugel stood at the wheel while the wind keened and shrieked and the waves reared ever higher, sometimes to break against the transom in surging white foam. On one such occasion Cugel looked over his shoulder, to discover a glare of reflected light.

Light? From where?

The source must be the windows of the aft cabin. Cugel had set no lamps aglow — which implied that someone else had done so, in defiance of his explicit orders.

Cugel dared not leave the wheel to extinguish the light. . . . Small matter, Cugel told himself; tonight he could shine a beacon across the ocean and there would be none to see.

Hours went by and the ship rushed eastward before the gale, with Cugel a barely animate hulk at the wheel. After an interminable period the night came to an end and a dull purple blush entered the sky. At last the sun rose to reveal an ocean of rolling black waves tumbled with white froth.

The wind abated. Cugel found that once again the ship would hold its own course. Painfully he straightened his body, stretched his arms, and worked his numb fingers. He descended to the aft-cabin, and discovered that someone had arranged two lamps in the stern window.

Cugel extinguished the lights and changed from the gown of pale blue silk to his own clothes. He pulled the three-tiered hat clasped with 'Spatterlight' upon his head, adjusted the tilt to best effect and marched forward. He found Madame Soldinck and her daughters in the galley, sitting at the table over a breakfast of tea and sweet-cakes. None displayed the ravages of sea-sickness; indeed all seemed well-rested and serene.

Madame Soldinck, turning her head, looked Cugel up and down. "Well then, what do you want here?"

Cugel spoke with icy formality. "Madame, be advised that all your schemes are known."

"Indeed? You know them all?"

"I know all those I care to know. They add no luster to your reputation."

"Which schemes are these? Inform me, if you please."

"As you wish," said Cugel. "I will agree that your plot, to a certain degree, was ingenious. At your request we sailed south during the day on half-bait, that we might rest the worms. At night, when I had gone to take my rest, you veered course to the north."

"More accurately, north by east."

Cugel made a gesture to indicate that it was all one. "Then, driving the worms on tonics and double-bait, you tried to keep the ship in the neighborhood of Lausicaa. But I caught you out."

Madame Soldinck gave a scornful chuckle. "We wanted no more sea-voyage; we were returning to Saskervoy."

Cugel was momentarily taken aback. The plan had been insolent beyond his suspicions. He feigned easy carelessness of manner. "No great difference. From the first I sensed that we were not sailing new water, and indeed it caused me a moment or two of bafflement — until I noticed the sorry state of the worms, and all became clear. Still, I tolerated your mischief; such melodramatic efforts amused me! And meanwhile I enjoyed my rest, the ocean air, meals of fine quality —"

Meadhre interjected a comment. "I, Tabazinth, Salasser — we spat in every dish. Mama sometimes stepped into the galley. I do not know what she did."

With an effort Cugel retained his aplomb. "At night I was entertained by games and antics, and here at least I have no complaint."

Salasser said: "The reverse is not true. Your fumbling and groping with cold hands has bored us all."

Tabazinth said, "I am not naturally unkind but the truth must be told. Your natural characteristics are really inadequate and, also, your habit of whistling between your teeth should be corrected."

Meadhre began to giggle. "Cugel is innocently proud of his innovations, but I have heard small children exchanging theories of more compelling interest."

Cugel said stiffly: "Your remarks add nothing to the discussion. On occasions to come, you may be assured that —"

"What occasions?" asked Madame Soldinck. "There will be no others. Your foolishness has run its course."

"The voyage is not over," said Cugel haughtily. "When the wind moderates, we will resume our course to the south."

Madame Soldinck laughed aloud. "The wind is not just wind. It is the monsoon. It will shift in three months. When I decided that Saskervoy was impractical, I steered to where the wind will blow us into the estuary of the Great Chaing River. I have signaled Master Soldinck and Captain Baunt that all was in order, and to keep clear until I bring us in to Port Perdusz."

Cugel laughed airily. "It is a pity, Madame, that a plot of such intricacy must come to naught." He bowed stiffly amd departed the galley.

Cugel took himself aft to the chart-room and consulted the portfolio. The estuary of the Great Chaing cut a long cleft into that region known as the Land of the Falling Wall. To the north a blunt peninsula marked 'Gador Porrada' shouldered into the ocean, apparently uninhabited save for the village 'Tustvold'. South of the Chaing, another peninsula: 'The Dragon's Neck', longer and narrower than Gador Porrada, thrust a considerable distance into the ocean, to terminate in a scatter of rocks, reefs and small islands: 'The Dragon-Fangs'. Cugel studied the chart in detail, then closed the portfolio with a fateful thud. "So be it!" said Cugel. "How long, oh how long, must I entertain false hopes and fond dreams? Still, all will be well. . . .Let us see how the land lays."

Cugel climbed to the quarter-deck. At the horizon he noted a ship which under the lens proved to be that lubberly little cog he had evaded several days before. Even without worms, using clever tactics, he could easily evade so clumsy a craft!

Cugel sheeted the sail hard back to the starboard, then jumping up to the quarter-deck, he swung the wheel to bring the ship around on a port tack, steering as close to north as the ship would point.

The crew of the cog, noting his tactic, veered to cut him off and drive him back south into the estuary, but Cugel refused to be intimidated and held his course.

To the right the low coast of Gador Porrada was now visible; to the left, the cog blundered importantly through the water.

Using the lens Cugel discerned the gaunt form of Drofo on the bow, signaling triple-bait for the worms.

Madame Soldinck and the three girls came from the galley to stare across the water at the cog, and Madame Soldinck screamed officious instructions to Cugel which were blown away on the wind.

The *Galante*, with a hull ill-adapted to sailing, made a great deal of leeway. For best speed Cugel fell away several points to the east, in the process veering closer upon the low-lying coast, while the cog pressed relentlessly down upon him. Cugel desperately swung the wheel, thinking to achieve a remarkable down-wind jibe which would totally discomfit those persons aboard the cog, not to mention Madame Soldinck. For best effect he sprang down upon the deck to trim the sheets, but before he could return to the wheel, the ship rushed off downwind.

Cugel climbed back to the quarter-deck and spun the wheel, hoping to bring the ship back on a starboard reach. Glancing toward the near shore of Gador Porrada, Cugel saw a curious sight: a group of sea-birds walking on what appeared to be the surface of the water. Cugel stared in wonder, as the sea-birds walked this way and that, occasionally lowering their heads to peck at the surface.

The *Galante* came to slow sliding halt. Cugel decided that he had run aground on the Tustvold mud-flats.

So much for birds who walked on water.

A quarter-mile to sea the cog dropped anchor and began to lower a boat. Madame Soldinck and the girls waved their arms in excitement. Cugel wasted no time in farewells. He lowered himself over the side and floundered toward the shore.

The mud was deep, viscous, and smelled most unpleasantly. A heavy ribbed stalk terminating in a globular eye reared from the mud to peer at him, and twice he was attacked by pincer-lizards, which luckily he was able to out-distance.

Finally Cugel arrived at the shore. Rising to his feet, he found that a contingent from the cog had already arrived aboard the *Galante*. One of the forms Cugel saw to be Soldinck, who pointed toward Cugel and shook his fist. At this same moment Cugel discovered that he had left the total sum of his terces aboard the *Galante*, including the six golden centums received from Soldinck in the sale of Fuscule's worm.

This was a bitter blow. Soldinck was joined at the rail by Madame Soldinck, who made insulting signals of her own.

Disdaining response, Cugel turned and trudged off along the shore.

CHAPTER III

FROM TUSTVOLD TO PORT PERDUSZ

1
THE COLUMNS

CUGEL marched along the foreshore, shivering to the bite of the wind. The landscape was barren and dreary; to the left, black waves broke over the mud-flats; to the right, a line of low hills barred access to inland regions.

Cugel's mood was bleak. He carried neither terces nor so much as a sharp stick to protect himself against footpads. Slime from the mud-flats squelched in his boots and his sodden garments smelled of marine decay.

At a tidal pool Cugel rinsed out his boots and thereafter walked more comfortably, though the slime still made a mockery of style and dignity. Hunching along the shore Cugel resembled a great bedraggled bird.

Where a sluggish river seeped into the sea, Cugel came upon an old road, which might well lead to the village Tustvold, and the possibility of food and shelter. Cugel turned inland, away from the shore.

To keep himself warm Cugel began to trot and jog, with knees jerking high. So passed a mile or two, and the hills gave way to a curious landscape of cultivated fields mingled with areas of wasteland. In the distance steep-sided knolls rose at irregular intervals, like islands in a sea of air.

No human habitation could be seen, but in the fields groups of women tended broad-beans and millet. As Cugel jogged past, they raised from their work to stare. Cugel found their attention offensive, and ran proudly past, looking neither right nor left.

Clouds sliding over the hills from the west cooled the air and seemed to presage rain. Cugel searched ahead for the village Tustvold, without success. The clouds drifted across the sun, darkening the already wan light, and the landscape took on the semblance of an ancient sepia painting, with flat perspectives and the pungko trees superimposed like scratchings of black ink.

A shaft of sunlight struck through the clouds, to play upon a cluster of white columns, at a distance of something over a mile.

Cugel stopped short to stare at the odd array. A temple? A mausoleum? The ruins of an enormous palace? Cugel continued along the road, and presently stopped again. The columns varied in height, from almost nothing to over a hundred feet, and seemed about ten feet in girth.

Once more Cugel proceeded. As he drew near he saw that the tops of the columns were occupied by men, reclining and basking in what remained of the sunlight.

The rent in the clouds sealed shut and the sunlight faded with finality. The men sat up and called back and forth, and at last descended the columns by ladders attached to the stone. Once on the ground, they trooped off toward a village half-hidden under a grove of shrack-trees. This village, about a mile from the columns, Cugel assumed to be Tustvold.

At the back of the columns a quarry cut into one of the steep-sided knolls Cugel had noted before. From this quarry emerged a white-haired old man with stooping shoulders, sinewy arms and the slow gait of one who precisely gauges each movement. He wore a white smock, loose gray t ousers and well-used boots of strong leather. From a braided leather cord around his neck hung an amulet of five facets. Spying Cugel he halted, and waited as Cugel approached.

Cugel used his most cultivated voice: "Sir, jump to no conclusions! I am neither a vagabond nor a mendicant, but rather a seafarer who arrived on shore by way of the mud-flats."

"That is not the ordinary route," said the old man. "Practised men of the sea most often use the docks at Port Perdusz."

"Quite so. The village yonder is Tustvold?"

"Properly speaking, Tustvold is that mound of ruins yonder which I quarry for white-stone. The local folk use the name for the village as well, and no great harm is done. What do you seek from Tustvold?"

"Food and shelter for the night. However, I cannot pay a groat, since my belongings remain aboard the ship."

The old man gave his head a disparaging shake. "In Tustvold you will get only what you pay for. They are a parsimonious lot, and spend only for advancement. If you will be satisfied with a pallet and a bowl of soup for your supper, I can gratify your needs, and you may dismiss all thought of payment."

"That is a generous offer," said Cugel. "I accept with pleasure. May I introduce myself? I am Cugel."

The old man bowed. "I am Nisbet, the son of Nisvangel, who quarried here before me and the grandson of Rounce, who was also a quarry-man. But come! Why stand here shivering when a warm fire awaits inside?"

The two walked toward Nisbet's abode: a huddle of ramshackle sheds leaning one on the other, built of planks and stone: the accretion of many years, perhaps centuries. Conditions within, while comfortable, were no less undisciplined. Each chamber was cluttered with curios and antiques collected by Nisbet and his predecessors while quarrying the ruins of Old Tustvold and elsewhere.

Nisbet poured a bath for Cugel and provided a musty old gown which Cugel might wear until his own clothes were clean. "That is a task better left to the women of the village," said Nisbet.

"If you recall, I lack all funds," said Cugel. "I accept your hospitality with pleasure but I refuse to impose a financial burden upon you."

"No burden whatever," said Nisbet. "The women are anxious to do me favors, so that I will give them priorities in the work."

"In that case, I accept the favor with thanks."

Cugel gratefully bathed and wrapped himself in the old gown, then sat down to a hearty meal of candle-fish soup, bread and pickled ramp, which Nisbet recommmended as a specialty of the region. They ate from antique dishes of many sorts and used utensils no two alike, even to the material from which they were fabricated: silver, glossold, black iron, gold, a green alloy of copper, arsenic and other substances. Nisbet identified these objects in an off-hand manner. "Each of the mounds you see rising from the plain represents an ancient city, now in ruins and covered over with the sift of time. When I am allowed an hour or two of leisure, I often go out to mine another of the mounds, and often I find objects of interest. That salver, for instance, was taken from the eleventh phase of the city Chelopsik, and is fashioned from corfume inlaid with petrified fire-flies. The characters are beyond my skill to read, but would seem to recite a children's song. This knife is even older; I found it in the crypts below the city I call Arad, though its real name is no longer known."

"Interesting!" said Cugel. "Do you ever find treasure or valuable gems?"

Nisbet shrugged. "Each of these articles is priceless: a unique memorial. But now, with the sun about to go dark, who would pay good terces to buy them? More useful is a bottle of good wine. In this connection, I suggest that, like grandees of high degree, we repair to the parlor where I will broach a bottle of well-aged wine, and we will warm our shins before the fire."

"A sound notion!" declared Cugel. He followed Nisbet into a chamber furnished with an over-sufficiency of chairs, settees, tables, and cushions of many kinds, together with a hundred curios.

Nisbet poured wine from a stoneware bottle of great age, to judge from the iridescent oxides which encrusted the surface. Cugel tasted the wine with caution, to find a liquor heavy and strong, and redolent of strange fragrances.

"A noble vintage," pronounced Cugel.

"Your taste is sound," said Nisbet. "I took it from the store-room of a wine-merchant on the fourth level of Xei Cambael. Drink heartily; a thousand bottles still moulder in the dark."

"My best regards!" Cugel tilted his goblet. "Your work lacks nothing for perquisites; this is clear. You have no sons to carry on the traditions?"

"None. My spouse died long years ago by the sting of a blue fanticule, and I lacked all taste for someone new." With a grunt Nisbet heaved himself to his feet and fed wood to the fire. He lurched back into his chair and gazed into the flames. "Yet often I sit here of nights, thinking of how it will be when I am gone."

"Perhaps you should take an apprentice."

Nisbet uttered a short hollow laugh. "It is not all so easy. Boys of the town think of tall columns even before they learn to spit properly. I would prefer the company of a man who knows something of the world. What, by the way, is your own trade?"

Cugel made a deprecatory gesture. "I am not yet settled upon a career. I have worked as worminger and recently I commanded a sea-going vessel."

"That is a post of high prestige!"

"True enough, but the the malice of subordinates forced me to vacate the position."

"By way of the mud-flats?"

"Precisely so."

"Such are the ways of the world," said Nisbet. "Still, you have much of your life ahead, with many great deeds to do, while I look back on life with my deeds already done, and none of them greatly significant."

Cugel said: "When the sun goes out, all deeds, significant or not, will be forgotten together."

Nisbet rose to his feet and broached another jug of wine. He refilled the goblets, then returned to his chair. "Two hours of loose philosophizing will never tilt the scale against the worth of one sound belch. For the nonce I am Nisbet the quarryman, with far too many columns to raise and far too much work on order. Sometimes I wish that I too might climb a column and bask away the hours."

The two sat in silence, looking into the flames. Nisbet finally said: "I see that you are tired. No doubt you have had a tedious day." He pulled himself to his feet and pointed. "You may sleep on yonder couch."

In the morning Nisbet and Cugel breakfasted upon griddle-cakes with a conserve of fruits prepared by women of the village; then Nisbet took Cugel out to the quarry. He pointed to his excavation which had opened a great cleft in the side of the mound.

"Old Tustvold was a city of thirteen phases, as you can see

with your own eyes. The people of the fourth level built a temple to Miamatta, their Ultimate God of Gods. These ruins supply white-stone to my needs. . . . The sun is aloft. Soon the men from the village will be coming out to use their columns; indeed, here they come now."

The men arrived, by the twos and threes. Cugel watched as they climbed their columns and composed themselves in the sunlight.

In puzzlement Cugel turned to Nisbet. "Why do they sit so diligently on their columns?"

"They absorb a healthful flux from the sunlight," said Nisbet. "The higher the column the more pure and rich is the flux, as well as the prestige of place. The women, especially, are consumed with ambition for the altitude of their husbands. When they bring in the terces for a new segment, they want it at once, and hector me unmercifully until I achieve the work, and if I must put off one of their rivals, so much the better."

"Odd that you have no competitors, in what must be a profitable business."

"It is not so odd when you consider the work involved. The stone must be brought down from the temple, sized, polished, cleaned of old inscriptions, given a new number and lifted to the top of a column. This entails considerable work, which would be impossible without this." Nisbet touched the five-faceted amulet that he wore around his neck. "A touch of this object negates the suction of gravity, and the heaviest object rises into the air."

"Amazing!" said Cugel. "The amulet is a valuable adjunct to your trade."

"'Indispensable' is the word. . . . Ha! Here comes Dame Croulsx to chide me for my lack of diligence."

A portly middle-aged woman with the flat round face and russet hair typical of the village folk approached. Nisbet greeted her with all courtesy, which she dismissed with a curt gesture. "Nisbet, again I must protest! Since I paid my terces, you have raised first a segment to Tobersc and another to Cillincx. Now my husband sits in their shadow, and their wives gloat together at my discomfiture. What is wrong with my money? Have you forgotten the gifts of bread and cheese I sent out by my daughter Turgola? What is your answer?"

"Dame Croulsx, give me only a moment to speak! Your 'Twenty' is ready for the raising and I was so about to inform your husband."

"Ah! That is good news! You will understand my concern."

"Certainly, but to avoid future misunderstanding, I must inform you that both Dame Tobersc and Dame Cillincx have placed orders for their 'Twenty-ones'."

Dame Croulsx's jaw dropped. "So soon, the andelwipes? In that case I too will have my 'Twenty-one', and you must start on it first."

Nisbet gave a piteous groan and clawed at his white beard. "Dame Croulsx, be reasonable! I can work only to the limit of these old hands, and my legs no longer propel me at nimble speed. I will do all possible; I can promise no more."

Dame Croulsx argued another five minutes, then started to march away in a huff, but Nisbet called her back. "Dame Croulsx, a small service you can do for me. My friend Cugel needs his garments expertly washed, cleaned, mended and returned to prime condition. Can I impose this task upon you?"

"Of course! You need only ask! Where are the garments?"

Cugel brought out the soiled clothes and Dame Croulsx returned to the village. "That is the way it goes," said Nisbet with a sad smile. "Strong new hands are needed to carry on the trade. What is your opinion in the matter?"

"The trade has much in its favor," said Cugel. "Let me ask this: Dame Croulsx mentioned her daughter Turgola; is she appreciably more comely than Dame Croulsx? And also: are daughters as anxious to oblige the quarryman as their mothers?"

Nisbet replied in a ponderous voice: "As to your first question: the folk of the village are Keramian stock, fugitives from the Rhab Faag and none are notable for a splendid appearance. Turgola, for instance, is squat, underslung, and shows protruding teeth. As for your second question, perhaps I have misread the signs. Dame Petishko has often offered to massage my back, though I have never complained of pain. Dame Gezx is at times strangely over-familiar. . . . Ha hm. Well, no matter. If, as I hope, you become 'associate quarryman,' you must make your own interpretation of these little cordialities, though I trust that you will not bring scandal to an enterprise which, to now, has been based upon probity."

Cugel laughingly dismissed the possibility of scandal. "I am favorably inclined to your offer; for a fact I lack the means to travel onward. I will therefore undertake at least a temporary commitment, at whatever wage you consider proper."

"Excellent!" said Nisbet. "We will arrange such details later. Now to work! We must raise the Croulsx 'Twenty'."

Nisbet led the way to the work-shop on the quarry floor, where the 'Twenty' stood ready on a pallet: a dolomite cylinder five feet tall and ten feet in diameter.

Nisbet tied several long ropes to the segment. After looking here and there, Cugel put a perplexed question: "I see neither rollers nor hoists nor cranes; how do you, one man alone, move such great masses of stone?"

"Have you forgotten my amulet? Observe! I touch the stone with the amulet and the stone becomes charged with revulsion for its native stuff. If I kick it lightly — so! no more than a tap! — the magic is fugitive and will last only long enough to bring the segment to its place. If I were to kick with force, the stone might stay repulsive to the land for a month, or even longer."

Cugel examined the amulet with respect. "How did you gain such sleight?"

Nisbet took Cugel outside and pointed to a bluff overlooking the plain. "See where the trees hang past the cliff? At that place a great magician named Makke the Maugifer built a manse and ruled the land with his mauging magic. He mauged east and he mauged west, north and south; persons could lift their eyes to his face once, or with effort twice, but never three times, so strong was his maugery.

"Makke planted a square garden with magic trees at the four corners; the ossip tree survives to this day, and there is no better boot-dressing than wax of the ossip berries. I dress my boots with ossip wax and they are proof against the rocks of the quarry: so I was taught by my father, who learned from his father, and so back through time to a certain Nisvaunt, who first went to Makke's garden for ossip berries. There he discovered the amulet and its strength.

"Nisvaunt first established himself in the porterage trade and moved goods great distances with ease. He became weary of the dust and dangers of travel and settled on this spot to become a quarryman, and I am the last of the line."

The two men returned to the work-shed. Under Nisbet's direction, Cugel took up the ropes and pulled at the 'Twenty', so that it slid slowly though the air and out toward the columns.

Nisbet halted at the base of a column marked with a plaque reading:

THE LOFTY MONUMENT OF

CROULSX

"WE EXULT ONLY IN THE UPPER ALTITUDES!"

Nisbet raised his head and called: "Croulsx! Come down from your coluumn! Your segment is ready to mount."

Croulsx's head, as he peered over the side of the column, was silhouetted against the sky. Satisfied that the calls were intended for himself, he descended to the ground. "Your work has not been swift," he told Nisbet gruffly. "Too long have I been forced to use an inferior flux."

Nisbet made light of the complaints. "'Now' is 'now', and at that instant known as 'now' your segment is ready and 'now' you can enjoy the upper radiances."

"All very well with your 'nows'!" grumbled Croulsx. "You ignore the deterioration of my health."

"I can only work to my best speed," said Nisbet. "In this regard, allow me to introduce my new associate, Cugel. I fancy that work will now go with a fling, owing to Cugel's experience and energy."

"If such is the case I will now place my order for five new segments. Dame Croulsx will validate the order with a deposit."

"I cannot acknowledge your order at this moment," said Nisbet. "However, I will keep your needs in mind. Cugel, are you ready? Then climb, if you will, to the top of Xippin's column and haul the segment gently on high. Croulsx and I will guide it from below."

The segment was efficiently set in place and Croulsx immediately climbed to the top, and arranged himself to best advantage in the red sunlight. Nisbet and Cugel returned to the shed and Cugel was instructed in the techniques of shaping, rounding and smoothing the white-stone.

Cugel soon understood why Nisbet was delinquent in his deliveries. First, age had slowed his movements to a degree for which his efficiency could not compensate. Secondly, Nisbet was almost hourly interrupted by visitors: women of the village with orders, demands, complaints, gifts and persuasions.

On Cugel's third day of employment, a group of merchant traders stopped by Nisbet's abode. They were members of a dark-skinned race notable for amber eyes, aquiline features and proudly erect posture. Their garments were no less distinctive: pantaloons bound with sashes, shirts with wing collars, underjackets and cut-away tabards, in the colors of black, tan, fusk and umber. They wore wide-brimmed black hats with slouch crowns, which Cugel considered of excellent address. They had brought with them a great high-wheeled wagon loaded with objects concealed under a tarpaulin. As the elder of the group conferred with Nisbet, the others removed the cloth, to reveal what appeared to be a large number of stacked corpses.

Nisbet and the elder came to an agreement and the four Maots — so Nisbet identified them to Cugel — began to unload the wagon. Nisbet took Cugel somewhat aside and pointed to a far mound. "That is Old QaHr which once held sway from the Falling Wall to the Silkal Strakes. During their high age the folk of QaHr practiced a unique religion, which, I suppose, is no more preposterous than any other. They believed that a man or woman upon dying entered afterlife using that bodily condition in which he or she had died, thereupon to pass eternity amid feasting, revelry and other pleasures regarding which propriety forbids mention. Hence it became the better part of wisdom to die in the full flower of life, since, for example, a rachitic old man, toothless, short-winded and dyspeptic, could never fully enjoy the banquets, songs and nymphs of paradise. The folk of QaHr therefore arranged to die at an early age, and they were embalmed with such skill that their corpses even today seem fresh with life. The Maots quarry the QaHr mausoleum for these corpses and convey them across the Wild Waste to the Thuniac Conservatory at Noval, where, as I understand it, they are put to some sort of ceremonial use."

While he spoke the Maot traders had unloaded the corpses, laid them in a row, and roped them together. The elder signaled Nisbet who walked along the line of corpses, touching each with his amulet. He then walked back along the line and delivered to each corpse the activating kick. The Maot elder paid Nisbet his fee; there was an interchange of gracious small talk and then the Maots set off to the northeast, the corpses drifting behind at an altitude of fifty feet.

Such interludes, while entertaining and instructive, tended to delay the orders whose delivery was ever more urgently demanded, both by the men, who were invigorated by the upper-air radiance, and by the women, who funded the raising of a column both in the interests of their husbands' health and also to enhance the prestige of the family.

To speed the work, Cugel initiated several labor-saving short-cuts, thereby arousing Nisbet's high approval. "Cugel, you will go far in this business! These are clever innovations!"

"I am pondering others even more novel," said Cugel. "Clearly, we must keep abreast of demand if only to maximize our own profits."

"No doubt, but how?"

"I will give the matter my best attention."

"Excellent! The problem is as good as solved." So declared Nisbet who then went off to prepare a gala supper, which included three bottles of sumptuous green wine from the stores of the Xei Cambael wine-seller. Nisbet indulged himself to such an extent that he fell asleep on a couch in the parlour.

Cugel seized the opportunity to conduct an experiment. From the chain around Nisbet's neck he unclasped the five-sided amulet and rubbed it along the arms of a heavy chair. Then, as he had seen Nisbet do, he gave the chair an activating kick.

The chair remained as heavy as before.

Cugel stood back in perplexity. In some manner he had misapplied the power of the amulet. Or might the magic be immanent in Nisbet and no other?

Unlikely. An amulet was an amulet.

Where then did Nisbet's act differ from his own?

Nisbet, the better to warm his feet before the fire, had removed his boots. Cugel removed his own shoes, which were worn almost to shreds, and slipped his feet into Nisbet's boots.

He rubbed the chair with the five-sided amulet and kicked it with Nisbet's boots. The chair instantly rebuffed gravity, to float in the air.

Most interesting, thought Cugel. He returned the amulet to Nisbet's neck and the boots to where he had found them.

On the morrow Cugel told Nisbet: "I discover that I need boots of strong leather, like yours, proof against the rocks of the quarry. Where can I obtain such boots?"

"Such items are included among our perquisites," said Nisbet. "Today I will send a messenger into the village and call for Dame Tadouc the cobbler-woman." Nisbet laid his finger alongside his crooked old nose and turned Cugel a mischievous leer. "I have learned how to control the women of Tustvold Village, or, for that matter, women in general! Never give them all they want! That is the secret of my success! In this present case, Dame Tadouc's husband sits on a column of only fourteen segments, making do with shadows and low-quality flux, while Dame Tadouc endures the condescension of her peers. For this reason, there is no harder-working woman in the village, save possibly Dame Kylas, who fells trees and shapes the natural wood into timber of specified size. In any event, you will be fitted for boots within the hour and I daresay that you will be wearing them tomorrow."

As Nisbet had predicted, Dame Tadouc came out from the village on the run and asked of Nisbet his requirements. "Meanwhile, Sir Nisbet, I trust that you will give earnest attention to my order for three new segments. Poor Tadouc has developed a cough and needs more intense radiation for his health."

"Dame Tadouc, the boots are needed by my associate Cugel,

whose present shoes are all shreds and holes, so that his toes scratch the ground."

"A pity, a pity!"

"In regard to your segments, I believe that the first of the three is scheduled for delivery in perhaps a week, and the others soon after."

"That is good news indeed! Now, Sir Cugel, as to your boots?"

"I have long admired those worn by Nisbet. Please make me exact duplicates."

Dame Tadouc looked at him in bafflement. "But Sir Nisbet's feet are two inches longer than yours, and somewhat more narrow, and as flat as halibuts!"

Cugel paused to think. The dilemma was real. If the magic resided in Nisbet's boots, then only exact replicas would seem to serve the purpose.

Nisbet dissolved the quandary. "Naturally, Dame Tadouc, cobble the boots to fit! Why would Cugel place an order specifically for ill-fitting boots?"

"For a moment I was perplexed," said Dame Tadouc. "Now I must run home to cut leather. I have a hide taken from the back of an old bull bauk and I will make you boots to last your life's span or until the sun goes out, whichever is the sooner. In either case, you will lack all further need for boots. Well then, to work."

On the following day the boots were delivered, and, in response to Cugel's specifications, they matched Nisbet's boots in every particular save size.

Nisbet examined the boots with approval. "Dame Tadouc has applied a dressing which is good enough for common folk, but as soon as it wears off and the leather acquires a thirst, we shall apply ossip wax and your boots will then be as strong as my own."

Cugel enthusiastically clapped his hands together. "To celebrate the arrival of these boots I suggest another gala evening!"

"Why not? A fine pair of boots is something to celebrate!"

The two dined on broad-beans and bacon, marsh-hens stuffed with mushrooms, sour-grass and olives and a hunch of cheese. With these dishes they consumed three bottles of that Xei Cambael wine known as 'Silver Hyssop'. Such was the information supplied by Nisbet, who, as an antiquarian, had studied many of the ancient scripts. As they drank, they toasted not only Dame Tadouc, but also that long-dead wine-merchant whose bounty they now enjoyed, though indeed the wine seemed perhaps a trifle past its prime.

As before, Nisbet became fuddled and lay down on the couch for a nap. Cugel unclasped the five-sided amulet and returned to his experiments.

His new boots, despite their similarity to those of Nisbet, lacked all useful effect, save that for which they were intended, while Nisbet's boots, alone or in conjunction with the amulet, defeated gravity with ease.

Most peculiar! thought Cugel, as he replaced the amulet on Nisbet's chain. "The only difference between the two pairs of boots was the dressing of ossip wax — from berries gathered in the garden of Makke the Maugifer.

To ransack the clutter of generations in search of a pot of boot-dressing was not a task to be undertaken lightly. Cugel went off to his own couch.

In the morning Cugel told Nisbet: "We have been working hard, and it is time for a little holiday. I suggest that we stroll over to yonder bluff and there survey the gardens of Makke the Maugifer. We can also pick ossip berries for boot-dressing, and — who knows? — we might come upon another amulet."

"A sound idea," said Nisbet. "Today I too lack zest for work."

The two set off across the plain toward the bluff: a distance of a mile. Cugel towed a sack containing their needs which Nisbet had touched with his amulet and kicked, in order to negate the weight.

By an easy route they climbed the bluff and approached Makke's garden.

"Nothing is left," said Nisbet sadly. "Save only the ossip tree, which seems to flourish despite neglect. That heap of rubble is all that remains of Makke's manse, which was built five-sided like the amulet."

Cugel approached the heap of stones, and thought to notice

a wisp of vapor rising through the cracks. He went close and dropping to his knees moved several of the stones. To his ears came the sound of a voice, and then another, engaged in what seemed an excited dialogue. So faint and elusive were the voices that words could not be distinguished and Nisbet, when Cugel summoned him to the crevice, could hear no sounds whatever.

Cugel drew back from the mound. To move the rocks might yield magical treasures, or, more likely, some unimaginable woe. Nisbet was of a like mind and the two moved somewhat back from the ruined manse. Sitting on a slab of mouldering stone, they ate a lunch of bread, cheese, spiced sausage and onions, washed down with pots of village-brewed beer.

A few yards away the ossip tree extended heavy branches from a gnarled silver-gray trunk five feet in diameter. Silver-green berries hung in clusters from the end of every twig, each berry a waxy sphere half an inch in diameter.

After Cugel and Nisbet had finished their lunch, they plucked berries sufficient to fill four sacks, which Nisbet caused to float in the air. Trailing their harvest behind them, the two returned to the quarry.

Nisbet brought out a great cauldron and set water to boiing, then added berries. Presently a scum formed on the surface. "There is the wax," said Nisbet, and skimmed it off into a basin. Four times the process was repeated, until all the berries had been boiled and the basin was filled with wax.

"We have done a good days work," announced Nisbet. "I see no reason why we should not dine accordingly. There are a pair of excellent fillets in the larder, provided by Dame Petish who is butcher to the town. If you will kindly lay a fire I will look through the closet for appropriate wine."

Once again Cugel and Nisbet sat down to a repast of heartening proportions, but as Nisbet worked to open a second flask of wine, the sound of slamming doors and the thud of heavy footsteps reached their ears.

An instant later a woman tall and portly, massive in arm and leg, with a bony jaw, a broken nose and coarse red hair, entered the room.

Nisbet laboriously heaved himself to his feet. "Dame Sequorce! I am surprised to see you here this time of night."

Dame Sequorce surveyed the table with disapproval. "Why are you not out shaping my segments which are long overdue?"

Nisbet spoke with cool hauteur: "Today Cugel and I attended to important business, and now, as is our habit, we dine. You may return in the morning."

Dame Sequorce paid no heed. "You take your morning meal far too late and your evening meal far too early, and you drink overmuch wine. Meanwhile my husband huddles well below the husbands of Dame Petish, Dame Haxel, Dame Croulsx and others. Since kindliness has no effect, I have decided to try a new tactic, for which I use the term 'fear'. In three words: if you do not gratify my needs in short order, I will bring my sisters here and perform a serious mischief."

Nisbet employed the gentle voice of pure reason: "If I acceded to your request —" "Not a request; a threat!" "— the other women of the town might also try to intimidate me, to the detriment of orderly business."

"I care nothing for your problems! Provide my segments, at once!"

Cugel rose to his feet. "Dame Sequorce, your conduct is singularly gross. Once and for all, Nisbet will not be coerced! He will provide you your segments in his own good time. He now demands that you leave the premises, and on quiet feet!"

"Nisbet now makes demands, does he?" Striding forward, Dame Sequorce seized Nisbet's beard. "I did not come to listen to your braggadocio!" She gave the beard a sharp tweak, then stepped back. "I am going, but only because I have delivered my message, which I hope you will take seriously!"

Dame Sequorce departed, leaving behind a heavy silence. At last Nisbet spoke in falsely hearty tones: "A dramatic incursion, to be sure! I must have Dame Wyxsco look to the locks. Come, Cugel! Return to your supper!"

The two continued with their meal, but the festive mood could not be recaptured. Cugel at last said: "What we need is a stock, or repository, of segments ready for raising, so that we can gratify these prideful women on demand."

"No doubt," said Nisbet. "But how is this to be done?"

Cugel tilted his head cautiously sidewise. "Are you ready for unorthodox procedures?"

With a bravado conferred partly by wine and partly by Dame Sequorce's rude handling of his beard, Nisbet declared: "I am a man to stop at nothing when circumstances cry out for deeds!"

"In that case, let us get to work," said Cugel. "The whole night lies before us! We shall demolish our problems once and for all! Bring lamps."

Despite his brave words Nisbet followed Cugel with hesitant steps. "Exactly what do you have in mind?"

Cugel refused to discuss his plan until they reached the columns. Here he signaled the laggard Nisbet to greater speed. "Time is of the essence! Bring the lamp to this first column."

"That is the column of Fidix."

"No matter. Put down the lamp, then touch the column with your amulet and kick it very gently: no more than a brush. First, let me secure the column with this rope. . . . Good. Now, apply amulet and kick!"

Nisbet obeyed; the column momentarily became weightless, during which interval Cugel extricated the 'One' segment and pushed it aside. After a few seconds the magic dissipated and the column returned to its former position.

"Observe!" cried Cugel. "A segment which we shall renumber and sell to Dame Sequorce, and a fig for her nuisances!"

Nisbet uttered a protest: "Fidix will surely notice the deduction!"

Cugel smilingly shook his head. "Improbable. I have watched the men climbing their columns. They come out blinking and half asleep. They trouble to look at nothing but the state of the weather and the rungs of their ladders."

Nisbet pulled dubiously at his beard. "Tomorrow, when Fidix climbs his column, he will find himself unaccountably lower by a segment."

"That is why we must remove the 'One' from every column. So now to work! There are many segments to move."

With dawn lightening the sky Cugel and Nisbet towed the last of the segments to a hiding place behind a pile of rocks on the floor of the quarry. Nisbet now affected a tremulous joy. "For the first time a sufficiency of segments is conveniently to hand. Our lives shall now flow more smoothly. Cugel, you have a fine and resourceful mind!"

"Today we must work as usual. Then, in the unlikely event that the subtractions are noticed, we shall merely disclaim all knowledge of the affair, or blame it on the Maots."

"Or we could claim that the weight of the columns had pushed the 'Ones' into the ground."

"True. Nisbet, we have done a good night's work!"

The sun moved into the sky, and the first contingent of men straggled out from the village. As Cugel had predicted, each climbed to the top of his column and arranged himself without any display of doubt or perplexity, and Nisbet uttered a hollow laugh of relief.

Over the next few weeks Cugel and Nisbet satisfied a large number of orders, though never in such profusion as to arouse comment. Dame Sequorce was allowed two segments, rather than the three she had demanded, but she was not displeased. "I knew I could get what I wanted! To gain the satisfaction of one's wishes one needs only to propose unpleasant alternatives. I will order two more segments shortly when I can afford your exorbitant prices; in fact, you may begin work on them now, so that I need not wait. Eh, Nisbet? Do you remember how I pulled your beard?"

Nisbet responded with formal politeness. "I will make a note of your order, and it will be fulfilled in its proper sequence."

Dame Sequorce responded only with a coarse laugh and went her way.

Nisbet gave a despondent sigh. "I had hoped that a flow of segments would glut our customers, but, if anything, we seem to have stimulated demand. Dame Petish, for instance, is annoyed that Dame Gillincx's husband now sits on the same level as Petish himself. Dame Viberl fancies herself the leader of society, and insists that two segments separate Viberl from his social inferiors."

Cugel shrugged. "We can only do what is possible."

In unexpectedly short order the segments of the stockpile were distributed, and the women of the town once again became importunate. Cugel and Nisbet discussed the situation at length, and decided to meet excessive demands with absolute obduracy.

Certain of the women, however, taking note of Dame Sequorce's success, began to make ever more categorical threats. Cugel and Nisbet at last accepted the inevitable and one night went out to the columns and removed all the 'Twos'. As before, the men noticed nothing. Cugel and Nisbet attempted to fill the backlog of orders, and the antique urn in which Nisbet stored his terces filled to overflowing.

One day a young woman came to confer with Nisbet. "I am Dame Mupo; I have been wed only a week, but it is time to start a column for Mupo, who is somewhat delicate and in need of upper level flux. I have inspected the area and selected a site, but as I walked among the columns I noted an odd circumstance. The bottom segments are numbered 'Three' rather than 'One', which would seem to be more usual. What is the reason for this?"

Nisbet started to stammer, and Cugel quickly entered the conversation. "This is an innovation designed to help young families such as your own. For instance, Viberl enjoys pure and undiluted radiance on his 'Twenty four'. By starting you off with a 'Three' instead of a 'One', you are only twenty one blocks below him, rather than twenty three."

Dame Mupo nodded her comprehension. "That is helpful indeed!"

Cugel went on to say: "We do not publicize the matter, since we cannot be all things to all people. Just regard this service as Nisbet's kindly assistance to you personally, and since poor Mupo is not in the best of health, we will provide you not only your 'Three' but your 'Four' as well. But you must say nothing of this to anyone, not even Mupo, as we cannot extend these favors everywhere."

"I understand completely! No one shall know!"

On the next day Dame Petish appeared at the quarry. "Nisbet, my niece has just married Mupo and brings me a peculiar and garbled story about 'Threes' and 'Fours' which, frankly, I cannot understand. She claims that your man Cugel promised her a segment at no charge, as a service to young families. I am interested because next week another niece is marrying, and if you are giving two segments for the price of one it is only fair that you deal in the same manner with an old and valued customer such as myself."

Cugel said smoothly: "My explanation confused Dame Mupo. Recently we have noticed vagrants and vagabonds among the columns. We warned them off, and then, to confuse would-be thieves, we altered our numerative system. In practice, nothing is changed; you need not concern yourself."

Dame Petish departed, dubiously shaking her head. She paused by the columns and looked them up and down for several minutes, then returned to the village.

Nisbet said nervously: "I hope no one else comes asking questions. Your answers are remarkable and confuse even me, but others may be more incisive."

"I imagine that we have heard the last of the matter," said Cugel, and the two returned to work.

During the early afternoon Dame Sequorce came out from the village with several of her sisters. They paused several minutes by the columns, then continued to the quarry.

Nisbet said in a quavering voice: "Cugel, I appoint you spokesman for the concern. Be good enough to mollify these ladies."

"I will do my best," said Cugel. He went out to confront Dame Sequorce. "Your segments are not yet ready. You may return in a week."

Dame Sequorce seemed not to hear. She turned her pale blue eyes around the quarry. "Where is Nisbet?"

"Nisbet is indisposed. Our delivery time is once again a month or more, since we must quarry more white-stone. I am sorry, but we cannot oblige you any sooner."

Dame Sequorce fixed her gaze full upon Cugel. "Where are the 'Ones' and 'Twos'? Why are they gone so that the 'Threes' rest on the ground?"

Cugel feigned surprise. "Is this really the case? Very odd. Still, nothing is permanent and the 'Ones' and 'Twos' may have crumbled into dust."

"There is no evidence of such dust around the base of the columns."

Cugel shrugged. "Since the columns remain at their relative

elevations, no great damage has been done."

From the back of the quarry one of Dame Sequorce's sisters came running. "We have found a pile of segments hidden behind some rocks, and all are 'Twos'!"

Dame Sequorce gave Cugel a brief side-glance, then turned and strode back to the village, followed by her sisters.

Cugel went glumly into Nisbet's abode. Nisbet had been listening from behind the door. "All things change," said Cugel. "It is now time to leave."

Nisbet jumped back in shock. "'Leave'? My wonderful house? My antiques and famous bibelots? That is unthinkable!"

"I fear That Dame Sequorce will not stop with simple criticism. Remember her dealings with your beard?"

"I do indeed, and this time I will defend myself!" Nisbet went to a cabinet and selected a sword. "Here is the finest steel of Old Kharai! Here, Cugel! Another blade of equal worth in a splendid harness! Wear it with pride!"

Cugel buckled the ancient sword about his waist. "Defiance is all very well but a whole skin is better. I suggest that we prepare for all eventualities."

"Never!" cried Nisbet in a passion. "I will stand in the doorway of my house and the first to attack shall feel the edge of my sword!"

"They will stand back and throw rocks," said Cugel.

Nisbet paid no heed and went to the doorway. Cugel reflected a moment, then carried various goods to the wagon left by the Maot traders: food, wine, rugs, garments. In his pouch he placed a pot of ossip boot-dressing, after first anointing his boots, and two handfuls of terces from Nisbet's urn. A second pot of boot dressing he tossed upon the wagon.

Cugel was interrupted in his work by an excited call from Nisbet. "Cugel! They are coming, at speed! They are like an army of raging beasts!"

Cugel went to the door and surveyed the oncoming women. "You and your valiant sword may deter this horde from the front door, but they will merely enter from the back. I suggest withdrawal. The wagon is ready."

Reluctantly Nisbet went to the wagon. He looked over Cugel's preparations. "Where are my terces? You load boot dressing but no terces! Is that sensible?"

"The boot dressing, and not your amulet, defies gravity. The urn was too heavy to carry."

Nisbet nevertheless ran inside and staggered out with his urn, spilling terces behind him.

The women were now close at hand. Observing the wagon they emitted a great roar of wrath. "Villains, halt!" cried Dame Sequorce. Neither Cugel nor Nisbet heeded her command.

Nisbet brought his urn to the wagon and loaded it with the other goods but when he tried to climb to the seat he fell, and Cugel had to lift him aboard. Cugel kicked the wagon and gave it a great push so that it floated away into the air, but when Cugel tried to jump upon the wagon, he lost his footing and fell to the ground.

There was no time for a second attempt; the women were upon him. Holding sword and pouch so that they did not impede his running, Cugel took to his heels, with the fastest of the women in pursuit.

After half a mile the women gave up the chase and Cugel paused to catch his breath. Already smoke was rising from Nisbet's abode, as the mob wreaked vicarious vengeance on Nisbet. On top of their columns the men stood up, the better to observe events. High in the sky the wagon drifted eastward on the wind, with Nisbet peering over the side.

Cugel heaved a sigh. Slinging the pouch over his shoulder, he set off to the south toward Port Perdusz.

2
FAUCELME

SETTING his course by the bloated red sun, Cugel journeyed south across an arid wasteland. Small boulders cast black shadows; an occasional stand-back bush, with leaves like fleshy pink ear-lobes, thrust thorns toward Cugel as he passed.

The horizons were blurred behind haze the color of watered carmine. No human artifact could be seen, nor any living creature, except on a single occasion when, far to the south, Cugel noted a pelgrane of impressive wingspan flying lazily from west to east. Cugel flung himself flat and lay motionless until the creature had disappeared into the eastern haze. Cugel then picked himself up, dusted off his garments and proceeded south.

The pallid soil reflected heat. Cugel paused to fan his face with his hat. In so doing he brushed his wrist lightly across 'Spatterlight', the sky-breaker scale which Cugel now used as a hat ornament. The contact caused an instant searing pain and a sucking sensation as if 'Spatterlight' were anxious to engulf the whole of Cugel's arm and perhaps more. Cugel looked askance at the ornament: his wrist had barely made contact! 'Spatterlight' was not an object to be dealt with casually.

Cugel gingerly replaced the hat on his head and continued south at speed, hoping to come upon shelter before nightfall. He moved at so hasty a gait that he almost blundered over the brink of a sink-hole fifty yards wide. He stopped short with one leg poised over the abyss, with a black tarn a hundred feet below. For a few breathless seconds Cugel tottered in a state of disequilibrium, then lurched back to safety.

After catching his breath, Cugel proceeded with greater caution. The sink-hole, he soon discovered, was not an isolated case. Over the next few miles he came upon others of greater or less dimension and few gave warning of their presence; there was only an instant brink and a far drop into dark water.

At larger sink-holes dark blue weeping-willow trees hung over the edge, half-concealing rows of peculiar habitations. These were narrow and tall, like boxes piled one on the other. There seemed no concern for precision and parts of the structures rested on the branches of the weeping-willows.

The folk who had built the tree-towers were difficult to see among the shadows of the foliage; Cugel glimpsed them as they darted across their queer little windows, and several times he thought to see them slipping into the sink-hole on slides polished from the native limestone. Their stature was that of a small human being or a boy, though their countenances suggested a peculiar hybridization of reptile, stalking bang-nose beetle and miniature gid. To cover their gray-green pelts they wore flounced belly-guards of pale fiber, and caps with black ear-flaps, apparently fabricated from human skulls.

The aspect of these folk gave Cugel little hope of obtaining hospitality, and indeed prompted him to slip away before they decided to pursue him.

As the sun sank low, Cugel became ever more nervous. If he tried to travel by night, he would certainly blunder into a sink-hole. If he thought to wrap himself in his cloak and sleep in the open, he thereupon became prey for visps, which stood nine feet tall and looked across the night through luminous pink eyes, and traced the scent of flesh by means of two flexible proboscises growing from each side of their scalp-crest.

The lower limb of the sun touched the horizon. In desperation Cugel tore up branches of brittlebush, whose wood made excellent torches. He approached a sink-hole fringed with weeping-willows and selected a tree-tower somewhat isolated from the others. As he drew near, he glimpsed weasel-like shapes darting back and forth in front of the windows.

Cugel drew his sword and pounded on the planked wall. "It is I, Cugel!" he roared. "I am king of this wretched wasteland! How is it that none of you have paid your fees?"

From within came a chorus of howling high-pitched invective, and filth was flung from the windows. Cugel drew back and set one of the branches afire. From the windows came piercing cries of outrage, and certain residents of the tree-tower ran out into the branches of the weeping-willow and slid down into the water of the sink-hole.

Cugel kept a wary eye to the rear, so that none of the tree-tower folk should creep up from behind to jump on his back. He pounded again on the walls. "Enough of your slops and filth! Pay over a thousand terces at once, or vacate the premises!"

From within nothing could be heard but hisses and whispers. Watching in all directions, Cugel circled the structure. He found a door and thrust in the torch, to discover a work-room, with a polished limestone bench across one wall, on which rested several alabaster ewers, cups and trenchers. There was neither hearth nor stove; evidently the tree-tower folk shunned the use of fire; nor was there communication with the upper levels, by means of ladders, traps or stairs.

Cugel left his branches of brittlebush and his burning torch on the dirt floor and went to gather more fuel. In the plum-colored afterglow he collected four armloads of branches and brought them to the tree-tower; during the final load he heard at frighteningly close hand the melancholy call of a visp.

Cugel hurriedly returned to the tree-tower. Once again the residents issued furious protests, and strident screams echoed back and forth across the sink-hole.

"Vermin, settle down!" called Cugel. "I am about to take my rest."

His commands went unheeded. Cugel brought his torch from the work-room and flourished it in all directions. The tumult instantly died.

Cugel returned into the work-room and blocked the door with the limestone slab, which he propped into place with a pole. He lay his fire so that it would burn slowly, one brand at a time. Wrapping himself in his cloak, he composed himself to sleep.

During the night he awoke at intervals to tend his fire, to listen and to peer through a crack out across the sink-hole, but all was quiet save for the calls of wandering visps.

In the morning Cugel aroused himself with the coming of sunlight. Through cracks he scrutinized the area outside the tree-tower, but nothing seemed amiss, and no sound could be heard.

Cugel pursed his lips in dubious reflection. He would have been reassured by some more or less overt demonstration of hostility. The quiet was over-innocent.

Cugel asked himself: "How, in similar case, would I punish an interloper as bold as myself?"

And next: "Why risk fire or sword?"

Then: "I would plan a horrid surprise."

Finally: "Logic leads to the concept of a snare. So then: let us see what there is to be seen." Cugel removed the limestone slab from the door. All was quiet: even more quiet than before. The entire sink-hole held its breath. Cugel studied the ground before the tree-tower. He looked right and left, to discover cords dangling from the branches of the tree. The ground before the door had been sprinkled with a suspicious amount of soil, which failed to conceal altogether the outlines of a net.

Cugel picked up the limestone slab and thrust it at the back wall. The planks, secured with pegs and withes, broke loose; Cugel jumped through the hole and was away, with cries of outrage and disappointment ringing after him.

Cugel continued to march south, toward far hills which showed as shadows behind the haze. At noon he came upon an abandoned farmstead beside a small river, where he gratefully sated his thirst. In an old orchard he found an ancient crab-apple tree heavy with fruit. He ate to satiation and filled his pouch.

As Cugel set off on his way he noticed a stone tablet with a weathered inscription:

EVIL DEEDS WERE DONE AT THIS PLACE

* * *

MAY FAUCELME KNOW PAIN UNTIL THE SUN GOES OUT

* * *

AND AFTER

A cold draught seemed to touch the back of Cugel's neck, and he looked uneasily over his shoulder. "Here is a place to be avoided," he told himself, and set off at full stride of his long legs.

An hour later Cugel passed beside a forest where he discovered a small octagonal chapel with the roof collapsed. Cugel cautiously peered within, to find the air heavy with the reek of visp. As he backed away, a bronze plaque, green with the corrosion of centuries, caught his eye. The characters read:

MAY THE GODS OF GNIENNE WORK BESIDE

— ∗ —

THE DEVILS OF GNARRE TO WARD US

— ∗ —

FROM THE FURY OF FAUCELME

Cugel suspired a quiet breath, and backed away from the chapel. Both past and present oppressed the region; with the utmost relief would Cugel arrive at Port Perdusz!

Cugel set off to the south at a pace even faster than before.

As the afternoon waned, the land began to swell in hillocks and swales: precursors to the first rise of the hills which now bulked high to the south. Trees straggled down from the upper-level forests: mylax with black bark and broad pink leaves; barrel-cypress, dense and impenetrable; pale gray parments, dangling strings of spherical black nuts; graveyard oak, thick and gnarled with crooked sprawling branches.

As on the previous evening, Cugel saw the day grow old with foreboding. As the sun dropped upon the far hills he broke out into a road running roughly parallel to the hills, which presumably must connect by one means or another with Port Perdusz.

Stepping out upon the road, Cugel looked right and left, and to his great interest saw a farmer's wain halted about half a mile to the east, with three men standing by the back end.

To avoid projecting an impression of urgency, Cugel composed his stride to an easy saunter, in the manner of a casual traveler, but at the wain no one seemed either to notice or to care.

As Cugel drew near, he saw that the wain, which was drawn by four mermelants, had suffered a breakdown at one of its tall rear wheels. The mermelants feigned disinterest in the matter and averted their eyes from the three farmers whom the mermelants liked to consider their servants. The wain was loaded high with faggots from the forest, and at each corner thrust high a three-pronged harpoon intended as a deterrent to the sudden swoop of a pelgrane.

As Cugel approached, the farmers, who seemed to be brothers, glanced over their shoulders, then returned unsmilingly to their contemplation of the broken wheel.

Cugel strolled up to the wagon. The farmers watched him sidelong, with such disinterest that Cugel's affability congealed on his face.

Cugel cleared his throat. "What seems to be wrong with your wheel?"

The oldest of the brothers responded in a series of surly grunts: "Nothing 'seems' to be wrong with the wheel. Do you take us for fools? Something is definitely and factually wrong. The retainer ring has been lost; the bearings have dropped out. It is a serious matter, so go your way and do not disturb our thinking." Cugel held up a finger in arch reproach. "One should never be too cock-sure! Perhaps I can help you."

"Bah! What do you know of such things?"

The second brother said: "Where did you get that odd hat?"

The youngest of the three attempted a thrust of heavy humor. "If you can carry the load on the axle while we roll the wheel, then you can be of help. Otherwise, be off with you."

"You may joke, but perhaps I can indeed do something along these lines," said Cugel. He appraised the wain, which weighed far less than one of Nisbet's columns. His boots had been anointed with ossip wax and all was in order. He stepped forward and gave the wheel a kick. "You will now discover both wheel and wagon to be weightless. Lift, and discover for yourselves."

The youngest of the brothers seized the wheel and lifted,

exerting such strength that the weightless wheel slipped from his grasp and rose high into the air, where it was caught in the wind and blown away to the east. The wagon, with a block under the axle, had taken no effect from the magic and remained as before.

The wheel rolled away down the sky. From nowhere, or so it seemed, a pelgrane swung down and, seizing the wheel, carried it off.

Cugel and the three farmers watched the pelgrane and the wheel disappear over the mountains.

"Well then," said the oldest. "What now?"

Cugel gave his head a rueful shake. "I hesitate to make further suggestions."

"Ten terces is the value of a new wheel," said the oldest brother. "Pay over that sum at once. Since I never threaten I will not mention the alternatives."

Cugel drew himself up. "I am not one to be impressed by bluster!"

"What of cudgels and pitchforks?"

Cugel took a step back and dropped a hand to his sword. "If blood runs along the road, it will be yours, not mine!"

The farmers stood back, collecting their wits. Cugel moderated his his voice. "A wheel such as yours, damaged, broken, and worn almost through to the spokes, might fairly be valued at two terces. To demand more is unrealistic."

The oldest brother declared in grandiose tones: "We will compromise! I mentioned ten terces, you spoke of two. Subtracting two from ten leaves eight; therefore pay us eight terces and everyone will be satisfied."

Cugel still hesitated. "Somewhere I sense a fallacy. Eight terces is still too much! Remember, I acted from altruism! Must I pay for good deeds?"

"Is it a good deed to send our wheel whirling through the air? If this is your kindness, spare us anything worse."

"Let us approach the matter from a new direction," said Cugel. "I need lodging for the night. How far is your farmstead?"

"Four miles, but we shall not sleep in our beds tonight; we must stay to guard our property."

"There is another way," said Cugel. "I can make the whole wagon weightless —"

"What?" cried the first brother. "So that we lose wagon as well as wheel?"

"We are not the dunderheads you take us for!" exclaimed the second brother.

"Give us our money and go your way!" cried the youngest. "If you need lodging, apply to the manse of Faucelme a mile along the road."

"Excellent notion!" declared the first brother with a broad grin. "Why did not I think of it? But first: our ten terces."

"Ten terces? Your jokes are lame. Before I part with a single groat I want to learn where I can securely pass the night."

"Did we not tell you? Apply to Faucelme! Like you he is an altruist and welcomes passing vagabonds to his manse."

"Remarkable hats or none," chuckled the youngest.

"During the olden times a 'Faucelme' seems to have despoiled the region," said Cugel. "Is the 'Faucelme' yonder a namesake? Does he follow in the foot-steps of the original?"

"I know nothing of Faucelme nor his forbears," said the oldest brother.

"His manse is large," said the second brother. "He never turns anyone from his door."

"You can see the smoke from his chimney even now," said the youngest. "Give us our money and be off with you. Night is coming on and we must prepare against the visps."

Cugel rummaged among the crab-apples and brought out five terces. "I give up this money not to please you but to punish myself for trying to improve a group of primitive peasants."

There was another spate of bitter words, but at last the five terces were accepted, and Cugel departed. As soon as he had passed around the wagon he heard the brothers give vent to guffaws of coarse laughter.

The mermelants lay sprawled untidily in the dirt, probing the roadside weeds for sweet-grass with their long tongues. As Cugel passed, the lead animal spoke in a voice barely comprehensible through a mouthful of fodder. "Why are the lumpkins laughing?"

Cugel shrugged. "I helped them with magic and their wheel flew away, so I gave them five terces to stifle their outcries."

"Tricks, full and bold!" said the mermelant. "An hour ago they sent the boy to the farm for a new wheel. They were ready to roll the old wheel into the ditch when they saw you."

"I ignore such paltriness," said Cugel. "They recommended that I lodge tonight at the manse of Faucelme. Again I doubt their good faith."

"Ah, those treacherous grooms * ! They think they can trick anyone! So they send you to a sorcerer of questionable repute."

Cugel anxiously searched the landscape ahead. "Is no other shelter at hand?"

"Our grooms formerly took in wayfarers and murdered them in their beds, but no one wanted to bury the corpses so they gave up the trade. The next lodging is twenty miles."

"That is bad news," said Cugel. "How does one deal with Faucelme?"

The mermelants munched at the sweet-grass. One said: "Do you carry beer? We are beer-drinkers of noble repute and show our bellies to all."

"I have only crab-apples, to which you are welcome."

"Yes, those are good," said the mermelant, and Cugel distributed what fruit he carried.

"If you go to Faucelme, be wary of his tricks! A fat merchant survived by singing lewd songs the whole night long and never turning his back on Faucelme."

One of the farmers came around the wagon, to halt in annoyance at the sight of Cugel. "What are you doing here? Be off with you and stop annoying the mermelants."

Deigning no reply, Cugel set off along the road. With the sun scraping along the forested sky-line, he came to Faucelme's manse: a rambling timber structure of several levels, with a profusion of bays, low square towers with windows all around,

---

*The mermelants, to sustain vanity, refer to their masters as 'grooms' and 'teders'. Ordinarily amiable, they are fond of beer, and when drunk rear high on their splayed rear legs to show their ribbed white bellies. At this juncture any slight provocation sends them into paroxysms of rage, and they exercise their great strength for destruction.

balconies, decks, high gables and a dozen tall thin chimneys.

Concealing himself behind a tree, Cugel studied the house. Several of the windows glowed with light, but Cugel noted no movement within. It was, he thought, a house of pleasant aspect, where one would not expect to find a monster of trickery in residcence.

Crouching, keeping to the cover of trees and shrubbery, Cugel approached the manse. With cat-like stealth he sidled to a window and peered within.

At a table, reading from a yellow-leafed book, sat a man of indeterminate age, stoop-shouldered and bald except for a fringe of brown-gray hair. A long nose hooked from his rather squat head, with protuberant milky golden eyes close-set to either side. His arms and legs were long and angular; he wore a black velvet suit and rings on every finger, save the forefingers where he wore three. In repose his face seemed calm and easy, and Cugel looked in vain for what he considered the signals of depravity.

Cugel surveyed the room and its contents. On a sideboard rested a miscellany of curios and oddments: a pyramid of black stone, a coil of rope, glass bottles, small masks hanging on a board, stacked books, a zither, a brass instrument of many arcs and beams, a bouquet of flowers carved from stone.

Cugel ran light-footed to the front door, where he discovered a heavy brass knocker in the form of a tongue dangling from the mouth of a gargoyle. He let the knocker drop and called out: "Open within! An honest wayfarer needs lodging and will pay a fee!"

Cugel ran back to the window. He watched Faucelme rise to his feet, stand a moment with head cocked sidewise, then walk from the room. Cugel instantly opened the window and climbed within. He closed the window, took the rope from the sideboard and went to stand in the shadows.

Faucelme returned, shaking his head in puzzlement. He seated himself in his chair and resumed his reading. Cugel came up behind him, looped the rope around his chest, again and again, and it seemed as if the rope would never exhaust the coil. Faucelme was presently trussed up in a cocoon of rope.

At last Cugel revealed himself. Faucelme looked him up and

down, in curiosity rather than rancor, then asked: "May I inquire the reason for this visit?"

"It is simple stark fear," said Cugel. "I dare not pass the night out of doors, so I have come to your house for shelter."

"And the ropes?" Faucelme looked down at the web of strands which bound him into the chair.

"I would not care to offend you with the explanation," said Cugel.

"Would the explanation offend me more than the ropes?"

Cugel frowned and tapped his chin. "Your question is more profound than it might seem, and verges into the ancient analyses of the Ideal versus the Real."

Faucelme sighed. "Tonight I have no zest for philosophy. You may answer my question in terms which proximate the Real."

"In all candour, I have forgotten the question," said Cugel.

"I will re-phrase it in words of simple structure. Why have you tied me to my chair, rather than entering by the door?"

"At your urging then, I will reveal an unpleasant truth. Your reputation is that of a sly and unpredictable villain with a penchant for morbid tricks."

Faucelme gave a sad grimace. "In such a case my bare denial carries no great weight. Who are my detractors?"

Cugel smilingly shook his head. "As a gentleman of honour I must reserve this information."

"Aha indeed!" said Faucelme, and became reflectively silent.

Cugel, with half an eye always for Faucelme, took occasion to inspect the room. In addition to the side-board, the furnishings included a rug woven in tones of dark red, blue and black, an open cabinet of books and librams, and a tabouret.

A small insect which had been flying around the room alighted on Faucelme's forehead. Faucelme reached up a hand through the bonds and brushed away the insect, then returned his arm into the coil of ropes.

Cugel turned to look in slack-jawed wonder. Had he tied the ropes improperly? Faucelme seemed bound as tightly as a fly in a spider-web.

Cugel's attention was attracted by a stuffed bird, standing four feet high, with a woman's face under a coarse mop of black hair. A two-inch crest of transparent film rose at the back of the forehead. A voice sounded over his shoulder. "That is a harpy from the Xardoon Sea. Very few remain. They are partial to the flesh of drowned sailors, and when a ship is doomed they come to keep vigil. Notice the ears —" Faucelme's finger reached over Cugel's shoulder and lifted aside the hair "— which are similar to those of a mermaid. Be careful with the crest!" The finger tapped the base of the prongs. "The points are barbed."

Cugel looked around in amazement, to see the finger retreating, pausing to scratch Faucelme's nose before disappearing into the ropes.

Cugel quickly crossed the room and tested the bonds, which seemed at adequate tension. Faucelme at close range took note of Cugel's hat ornament and made a faint hissing sound between his teeth.

"Your hat is a most elaborate confection," said Faucelme. "The style is striking, though in regions such as this you might as effectively wear a leather stocking over your head." So saying, he glanced down at his book.

"It well may be," replied Cugel. "And when the sun goes out a single loose smock will fulfill every demand of modesty."

"Ha ha! Fashions will then be meaningless! That is a droll notion!" Faucelme stole a glance at his book. "And that handsome bauble: where did you secure so showy a piece?" Again Faucelme swept his eyes across the pages of his book.

"It is a bit of brummagem I picked up along the way," said Cugel carelessly. "What are you reading with such avidity?" He picked up the book. "Hm. . . .'Madame Milgrim's Dainty Recipes'."

"Indeed, and I am reminded that the carrot pudding wants a stir. Perhaps you will join me for a meal?" He spoke over his shoulder: "*Tzat!*" The ropes fell away to a small loose coil and Faucelme rose to his feet. "I was not expecting guests, so tonight we will dine in the kitchen. But I must hurry, before the pudding scorches."

He stalked on long knob-kneed legs into the kitchen with Cugel coming doubtfully after. Faucelme motioned to a chair. "Sit down and I will find us a nice little morsel or two: nothing high nor heavy, mind you, no meats nor wines as they inflame the blood and according to Madame Milgrim give rise to flactomies. Here is some splendid gingle-berry juice which I recommend heartily. Then we shall have a nice stew of herbs and our carrot pudding."

Cugel seated himself at the table and watched with single-minded vigilance as Faucelme moved here and there, collecting small dishes of cakes, preserves, compotes and vegetable pastes. "We shall have a veritable feast! Seldom do I indulge myself, but tonight, with a distinguished guest, all discipline goes by the boards!" He paused in his work. "Have you told me your name? As the years advance, I find myself ever more absent-minded."

"I am Cugel, and originally of Almery, where I am now returning."

"Almery! A far way to go, with curious sights at every step, and many a danger as well. I envy you your confidence! Shall we dine?"

Cugel ate only from the dishes which Faucelme himself ate, and thought to feel no ill effects. Faucelme spoke discursively as he ate from this or that plate with prim little nips: ". . . . name has unfortunate antecedents in the region. Apparently the nineteenth aeon knew a 'Faucelme' of violent habit indeed, and there may have been another 'Faucelme' a hundred years later, though at that distance in time lifetimes blur together. I shudder to think of their deeds. . . . Our local villains now are a clan of farmers: angels of mercy by comparison, nevertheless with certain nasty habits. They give their mermelants beer to drink, then send them out to intimidate travellers. They dared to come up here one day, stamping up and down the porch and showing their bellies. 'Beer!' they shouted. 'Give us good beer!' Naturally I keep no such stuff on hand. I took pity on them and explained at length the vulgar qualities of inebriation, but they refused to listen, and used offensive language. Can you believe it? 'You double-tongued old wowser, we have listened long enough to your cackle and now we want beer in return!' These were their very words! So I said: 'Very well; you shall have beer.' I prepared a tea of bitter belch-wort and nuxium; I chilled it and caused it to fume, in the manner of beer. I called out:

'Here is my only beer!' and served it in ewers. They slapped down their noses and sucked it up in a trice. Immediately they curled up like sow-bugs and lay as if dead for a day and a half. Finally they uncoiled, rose to their feet, befouled the yard in a most lavish manner, and skulked away. They have never returned, and perhaps my little homily has brought them to sobriety."

Cugel tilted his head sidewise and pursed his lips. "An interesting story."

"Thank you." Faucelme nodded and smiled as if musing over pleasant memories. "Cugel, you are a good listener; also you do not swill down your food with chin in plate, then look hungrily here and there for more. I appreciate delicacy and a sense of style. In fact, Cugel, I have taken a fancy to you. Let us see what we can do to help you along the road of life. We shall take our tea in the parlour: the finest Amber Moth-wing for an honoured guest! Will you go ahead?"

"I will wait and keep you company," said Cugel. "It would be rude to do otherwise."

Faucelme spoke heartily: "Your manners are those of an earlier generation. One does not see their like among the young folk of today, who think of nothing but self-indulgence."

Under Cugel's watchful eye Faucelme prepared tea and poured it into cups of egg-shell porcelain. He bowed and gestured to Cugel. "Now to the parlour."

"Lead the way, if you will."

Faucelme showed a face of whimsical surprise, then shrugged and preceded Cugel into the parlour. "Seat yourself, Cugel. The green velour chair is most comfortable."

"I am restless," said Cugel. "I prefer to stand."

"Then at least take off your hat," said Faucelme with a trace of petulance.

"Certainly," said Cugel.

Faucelme watched him with bird-like curiosity. "What are you doing?"

"I am removing the ornament." Protecting his hands with a folded kerchief, Cugel slipped the object into his pouch. "It is hard and sharp and I fear that it might mar your fine furniture."

"You are most considerate and deserve a little gift. This rope for instance: it was walked by Lazhnascenthe the Lemurian, and is imbued with magical properties. For instance, it responds to commands; it is extensible and stretches without loss of strength as far as you require. I see that you carry a fine antique sword. The filigree of the pommel suggests Kharay of the eighteenth aeon. The steel should be of excellent quality, but is it sharp?"

"Naturally," said Cugel. "I could shave with the edge, were I of a mind to do so."

"Then cut yourself a convenient length of the rope: let us say ten feet. It will tuck neatly into your pouch, yet it will stretch ten miles at your command."

"This is true generosity!" declared Cugel, and measured off the stipulated length. Flourishing his sword, he cut at the rope, without effect. "Most peculiar," said Cugel.

"Tut, and all the time you thought your sword to be sharp!" Faucelme touched two fingers to a mischievous grin. "Perhaps we can repair the deficiency." From a cabinet he brought a long box, which, when opened, proved to contain a shining silver powder.

"Thrust your blade into the glimmister," said Faucelme. "Let none touch your fingers, or they will become rigid silver bars."

Cugel followed the instructions. When he withdrew the sword, it trailed a fine sift of spangling glimmister. "Shake it well," said Faucelme. "An excess only mars the scabbard."

Cugel shook the blade clean. The edge of the sword twinkled with small coruscations, and the blade itself seemed luminous.

"Now!" said Faucelme. "Cut the rope."

The sword cut through the rope as if it were a strand of kelp.

Cugel gingerly coiled the rope. "And what are the commands?"

Faucelme picked up the loose rope. "Should I wish to seize upon something, I toss it high and use the cantrap 'Tzip!', in this fashion —"

"Halt!" cried Cugel, raising his sword. "I want no demonstrations!"

Faucelme chuckled. "Cugel, you are as brisk as a tittle-bird. Still, I think none the less of you. In this sickly world, the rash die young. Do not be frightened of the rope; I will be mild. Observe, if you will! To disengage the rope, call the order '*Tzat*', and the rope returns to hand. So then!" Faucelme stood back and held up his hands in the manner of one who dissembles nothing. "Is this the conduct of a 'sly and unpredictable villain'?"

"Decidedly so, if the villain, for the purposes of his joke, thinks to simulate the altruist."

"Then how will you know villain from altruist?"

Cugel shrugged. "It is not an important distinction."

Faucelme seemed to pay no heed; his mercurial intellect was already exploring a new topic. "I was trained in the old tradition! We found our strength in the basic verities, to which you, as a patrician, must surely subscribe. Am I right in this?"

"Absolutely, and in all respects!" declared Cugel. "Recognizing, of course, that these fundamental verities vary from region to region, and even from person to person."

"Still, certain truths are universal," argued Faucelme. "For instance, the ancient rite of gift exchange between host and guest. As an altruist I have given you a fine and nutritious meal, a length of magic rope and perduration of the sword. You will demand with full vigor what you may give me in return, and I will ask only for your good regard —"

Cugel said with generous spontaneity: "It is yours, freely and without stint, and the basic verities have been fulfilled. Now, Faucelme, I find myself somewhat fatigued and so —"

"Cugel, you are generous! Occasionally, as we toil along our lonely path through life we encounter one who instantly, or so it seems, becomes a dear and trusted friend. I shall be sorry to see you depart! You must leave me some little memento, and in fact I will refuse to take anything other than that bit of tinsel you wear on your hat. A trifle, a token, no more, but it will keep your memory green, until the happy day of your return! You may now give over the ornament."

"With pleasure," said Cugel. Using great care he reached

into his pouch and withdrew the ornament which had originally clasped his hat. "With my warmest regards, I present you
with my hat ornament."

Faucelme studied the ornament a moment, then looked up
and turned the full gaze of his milky golden eyes upon Cugel.
He pushed back the ornament. "Cugel, you have given me too
much! This is an article of value — no, do not protest! — and I
want only that rather vulgar object with the spurious red gem
at the center which I noticed before. Come, I insist! It will hang
always in a place of honour here in my parlour!"

Cugel showed a sour smile. "In Almery lives Iucounu the
Laughing Magician."

Faucelme gave a small involuntary grimace.

Cugel continued. "When I see him he will ask: 'Cugel,
where is my 'Pectoral Sky-break Spatterlight' which was entrusted into your care?' What can I tell him? That a certain
Faucelme in the Land of the Falling Wall would not be denied?"

"This matter bears looking into," muttered Faucelme. "One
solution suggests itself. If, for instance, you decided not to return to Almery, then Iucounu would not learn the news. Or if,
for instance —" Faucelme became suddenly silent.

A moment passed. Faucelme spoke in a voice of affability:
"You must be fatigued and ready for your rest. First then: a
taste of my aromatic bitters, which calm the stomach and refresh the nerves!"

Cugel tried to decline but Faucelme refused to listen. He
brought out a small black bottle and two crystal cups. Into
Cugel's cup he poured a half-inch of pale liquid. "This is my
own distillation," said Faucelme. "See if it is to your taste."

A small moth fluttered close to Cugel's cup and instantly fell
dead to the table.

Cugel rose to his feet. "I need no such tonic tonight," said
Cugel. "Where shall I sleep?"

"Come." Faucelme led Cugel up the stairs and opened the
door into a room. "A fine cozy little nook, where you will rest
well indeed."

Cugel drew back. "There are no windows! I should feel
stifled."

"Oh? Very well, let us look into another chamber. . . . What of this? The bed is soft and fine."

Cugel voiced a question: "What is the reason for the massive iron gridwork above the bed? What if it fell during the night?"

"Cugel, this is sheer pessimism! You must always look for the glad things of life! Have you noticed, for instance, the vase of flowers beside the bed!"

"Charming! Let us look at another room."

"Sleep is sleep!" said Faucelme peevishly. "Are you always so captious? . . . . Well then, what of this fine chamber? The bed is good; the windows are wide. I can only hope that the height does not affect you with vertigo."

"This will suit me well," said Cugel. "Faucelme, I bid you good night."

Faucelme stalked off down the hall. Cugel closed the door and opened wide the window. Against the stars he could see tall thin chimneys and a single cypress rearing above the house.

Cugel tied an end of his rope to the bed-post, then kicked the bed, which at once knew revulsion for the suction of gravity and lifted into the air. Cugel guided it to the window, pushed it through and out into the night. He darkened the lamp, climbed aboard the bed and thrust away from the manse toward the cypress tree, to which he tied the other end of the rope. He gave a command: "Rope, stretch long."

The rope stretched and Cugel floated up into the night. The manse showed as an irregular bulk below, blacker than black, with yellow quadrangles to mark the illuminated rooms.

Cugel let the rope stretch a hundred yards. "Rope, stretch no more!"

The bed stopped with a soft jerk. Cugel made himself comfortable and watched the manse.

Half an hour passed. The bed swayed to the vagrant airs of the night and under the eiderdown Cugel became drowsy. His eyelids became heavy. . . . An effulgence burst soundlessly from the window of the room to which he had been assigned. Cugel blinked and sat upright, and watched a bubble of luminous pale gas billow from the window.

The room went dark, as before. A moment later the window flickered to the light of a lamp, and Faucelme's angular figure, with elbows akimbo, showed black upon the yellow rectangle. The head jerked this way and that as Faucelme looked out into the night.

At last he withdrew and the window went dark.

Cugel bcame uneasy with his proximity to the manse. He took hold of the rope and said: "*Tzat!*"

The rope came loose in his hand.

Cugel said: "Rope, shrink!"

The rope became once more ten feet long.

Cugel looked back toward the manse. "Faucelme, whatever your deeds or misdeeds, I am grateful to you for this rope, and also your bed, even though, through fear, I must sleep in the open."

He looked over the side of the bed and by starlight saw the glimmer of the road. The night was dead calm. He drifted, if at all, to the west.

Cugel hung his hat on the bed-post. He lay back, pulled the eiderdown over his head and went to sleep.

The night passed. Stars moved across the sky. From the waste came the melancholy call of the visp: once, twice, then silence.

Cugel awoke to the rising of the sun, and for an appreciable interval could not define his whereabouts. He started to throw a leg over the side of the bed, then pulled it back with a startled jerk.

A black shadow fluttered across the sun; a heavy black object swooped down to alight at the foot of Cugel's bed: a pelgrane of middle years, to judge by the silky gray hair of its globular abdomen. Its head, two feet long, was carved of black horn, like that of a stag-beetle and white fangs curled up past its snout. Perching on the bedstead it regarded Cugel with both avidity and amusement.

"Today I shall breakfast in bed," said the pelgrane. "Not often do I so indulge myself."

It reached out and seized Cugel's ankle, but Cugel jerked back. He groped for his sword but could not draw it from the scabbard. In his frantic effort he caught his hat with the tip of his scabbard; the pelgrane, attracted by the red glint, reached for the hat. Cugel thrust 'Spatterlight' into its face.

The wide brim and Cugel's own terror confused the flow of events. The bed bounded as if relieved of weight; the pelgrane was gone.

Cugel looked to all sides in puzzlement.

The pelgrane had disappeared.

Cugel looked at 'Spatterlight', which seemed to shine with perhaps a somewhat more vivacious glow.

With great caution Cugel arranged the hat upon his head. He looked over the side and noticed approaching in the road a small two-wheeled cart pushed by a fat boy of twelve or thirteen years.

Cugel threw down his rope to fix upon a stump and drew himself to the surface. When the boy rolled the push-cart past, Cugel sprang out upon the road. "Hold up! What have we here?"

The boy jumped back in fright. "It is a new wheel for the wain and breakfast for my brothers: a pot of good stew, a round of bread and a jug of wine. If you are a robber there is nothing here for you."

"I will be the judge of that," said Cugel. He kicked the wheel to render it weightless, and heaved it spinning away through the sky while the boy watched in open-mouthed wonder. Cugel then took the pot of stew, the bread and the wine from the cart. "You now may proceed," he told the boy. "If your brothers inquire for the wheel and the breakfast, you may mention the name 'Cugel' and the sum 'five terces'."

The boy trundled the cart away at a run. Cugel took the pot, bread and wine to his bed and, loosing the rope, drifted high into the air.

Along the road at a run came the three farmers, followed by the boy. They halted and shouted: "Cugel! Where are you? We want a word or two with you." And one added ingenuously: "We wish to return your five terces!"

Cugel deigned no response. The boy, searching around the sky for the wheel, noticed the bed and pointed, and the farmers, red-faced with fury, shook their fists and bawled curses.

Cugel listened with impassive amusement for a few minutes, until the breeze, freshening, swept him off toward the hills and Port Perdusz.

CHAPTER
IV

FROM
PORT PERDUSZ
TO
KASPARA VITATUS

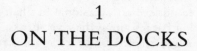

1
ON THE DOCKS

A FAVORABLE wind blew Cugel and his bed over the hills in comfort and convenience. As he drifted over the last ridge, the landscape dissolved into far distances, and before him, from east to west, spread the estuary of the River Chaing, in a great sweep of liquid gunmetal.

Westward along the shore Cugel noticed a scatter of mouldering gray structures: Port Perdusz. A half-dozen vessels were tied up at the docks; at so great a distance Cugel could not distinguish one from the other.

Cugel caused the bed to descend by dangling his sword and boots over either side, so that they were seized by the forces of gravity. Driven by capricious gusts of wind, the bed dropped in directions beyond Cugel's control and eventually fell into a thicket of tulsifer reeds only a few yards inland from the river.

Reluctantly abandoning the bed, Cugel picked his way toward the river road, across soggy turf rampant with a dozen species of more or less noxious plants: russet and black burdock, blister-bush, brown-flowered hurse, sensitive vine which jumped back in distaste as Cugel approached. Blue lizards hissed angrily and Cugel, already in poor humour owing to contact with the blister-bush, reviled them in return: "Hiss away, vermin! I expect nothing better from such low-caste beasts!"

The lizards, divining the gist of Cugel's rebuke, ran at him by jerks and bounds, hissing and spitting, until Cugel picked up a dead branch, and by beating at the ground kept them at bay.

Cugel finally gained the road. He brushed off his clothes, slapped his hat against his leg, taking care to avoid contact with 'Spatterlight'. Then, shifting his sword so that it swung at its most jaunty angle, he set off toward Port Perdusz.

The time was middle afternoon. A line of tall deodars bordered the road; Cugel walked in and out of black shadow and red sunlight. He noticed an occasional hut halfway up the hillside and decaying barges along the river-bank. The road passed an ancient cemetery shaded under straggling rows of cypress, then swung toward the river to avoid a bluff on which perched a ruined palace.

Entering the town proper, the road swung around the back of a central plaza, where it passed in front of a large semicircular building, at one time a theater or concert hall, but now an inn. The road then returned to the waterfront and led past those vessels which Cugel had noticed from the air. A question hung heavy in Cugel's mind: might the *Galante* still lie in port?

Unlikely, but not impossible.

Cugel would find most embarrassing a chance confrontation with Captain Baunt, or Drofo, or Madame Soldinck, or even Soldinck himself.

Halting in the roadway, Cugel rehearsed a number of conversational gambits which might be used to ease the tensions. At length he admitted to himself that, realistically, none could be expected to succeed, and that a formal bow, or a simple and noncommittal nod of the head, would serve equally well.

Maintaining a watch in all directions, Cugel sauntered out on the decaying old wharf. He discovered three ships and two small coastwise vessels, as well as a ferry to the opposite shore.

None was the *Galante*, to Cugel's great relief.

The first vessel, and farthest downstream from the plaza, was a heavy and nameless barge, evidently intended for the river trade. The second, a large carrack named *Leucidion* had been discharged of cargo and now appeared to be undergoing repairs. The third, and closest to the plaza, was the *Avventura*, a trim little ship, somewhat smaller than the others, and now in the process of taking on cargo and provisions for a voyage.

The docks were comparatively animated, with the passage of drays, the shouting and cursing of porters, the gay music of concertinas from aboard the barge.

A small man, portly and florid, wearing the uniform of a minor official, paused to inspect Cugel with a calculating eye, then turned away and entered one of the nearby warehouses.

Over the rail of the *Leucidion* leaned a burly man wearing a striped shirt of indigo blue and white, a conical black hat with a golden chain dangling beside his right ear, and a spigoted golden boss in his left cheek: the costume of the Castillion Shorelanders *.

Cugel confidently approached the *Leucidion* and, assuming a jovial expression, waved his hand in greeting.

The ship-master watched impassively, making no response.

Cugel called out: "A fine ship! I see that she has been somewhat disabled."

The ship-master at last responded: "I already have been notified in this regard."

"Where will you sail when the damage is repaired?"

"Our usual run."

"Which is?"

"To Latticut and The Three Sisters, or to Woy if cargo offers."

"I am looking for passage to Almery," said Cugel.

"You will not find it here," said the ship-master with a grim smile. "I am brave but not rash."

In a somewhat peevish voice Cugel protested: "Surely someone must sail south out of Port Perdusz! It is only logical!"

The ship-master shrugged and looked toward the sky. "If this is your reasoned opinion, then no doubt it is so."

Cugel pushed impatiently down at the pommel of his sword. "How do you suggest that I make my journey south?"

"By sea?" The ship-master jerked his thumb toward the *Avventura*. "Talk to Wiskich; he is a Dilk and a madman, with the seamanship of a Blue Mountain sheep. Pay him terces enough

---

*At Castillion banquets a cask is placed on a balcony over the refection hall. Flexible pipes lead down to each place. The diner seats himself, fixes a pipe to the spigot in his cheek, so that he may drink continously as he dines, so avoiding the drudgery of opening flasks, pouring out mugs or goblets, raising, tilting and setting down the mug or goblet, with the consequent danger of breakage or waste. By this process he both eats and drinks more efficiently, and thus gains time for song.

and he will sail to Jehane itself."

"This I know for a fact," said Cugel. "Certain cargoes of value arrive at Port Perdusz from Saskervoy, and are then trans-shipped to Almery."

The ship-master listened with little interest. "Most likely they move by caravan, such as Yadcomo's or Varmous'. Or, for all I know, Wiskich sails them south in the *Avventura*. All Dilks are mad. They think they will live forever and ignore danger. Their ships carry mast-head lamps so that, when the sun goes out, they can light their way back across the sea to Dilclusa."

Cugel started to put another question, but the ship-master had retreated into his cabin.

During the conversation, the small portly man in the uniform had emerged from the warehouse. He listened a moment to the conversation, then went at a brisk pace to the *Avventura*. He ran up the gangplank and disappeared into the cabin. Almost at once he returned down the gangplank where he halted a moment, then, ignoring Cugel, he returned at a placid and dignified gait into the warehouse.

Cugel proceeded to the *Avventura*, hoping at least to learn the itinerary proposed by Wiskich for his ship. At the foot of the gangplank a sign had been posted which Cugel read with great interest:

PASSENGERS FOR THE VOYAGE SOUTH, TAKE NOTE!

PORTS OF CALL ARE NOW DEFINITE. THEY ARE:

MAHAZE AND THE MISTY ISLES

LAVRRAKI REAL, OCTORUS, KAIIN

VARIOUS PORTS OF ALMERY.

DO NOT BOARD SHIP WITHOUT TICKET!

SECURE TICKET FROM TICKET AGENT

IN GRAY WAREHOUSE ACROSS WHARF

With long strides Cugel crossed the wharf and entered the warehouse. An office to the side was identified by an old sign:

OFFICE OF THE TICKET AGENT

Cugel stepped into the office where, sitting behind a disreputable desk, he discovered the small portly man in the dark uniform, now making entries into a ledger.

The official looked up from his work. "Sir, your orders?"

"I wish to take passage aboard the *Avventura* for Almery. You may prepare me a ticket."

The agent turned a page in the ledger and squinted dubiously at a set of entries. "I am sorry to say that the voyage is fully booked. A pity . . . . Just a moment! There may be a cancellation! If so, you are in luck, as there will be no other voyage this year. . . . Let me see. Yes! The Hierarch Hopple has taken ill."

"Excellent! What is the fare?"

"The available billet is for first class accomodation and victualling, at two hundred terces."

"What?" cried Cugel in anguish. "That is an outrageous fee! I have but forty-five terces to my pouch, and not a groat more!"

The agent nodded placidly. "Again you are in luck. The Hierarch placed a deposit of one hundred and fifty terces upon the ticket, which sum has been forfeited. I see no reason why we should not add your forty-five terces to this amount and even though it totals to only one hundred and ninety-five, you shall have your ticket, and I will make certain book-keeping adjustments."

"That is most kind of you!" said Cugel. He brought the terces from his pouch, and paid them over to the agent, who returned him a slip of paper marked with characters strange to Cugel. "And here is your ticket."

Cugel reverently folded the ticket and placed it in his pouch. He said: "I hope that I may go aboard the ship at once, as now I lack the means to pay for either food or shelter elsewhere."

"I am sure that there will be no problem," said the ticket agent. "But if you will wait here a moment I will run over to the ship and say a word to the captain."

"That is good of you," said Cugel, and composed himself in a chair. The agent departed the office.

Ten minutes passed, then twenty minutes, and half an hour.

Cugel became restless and, going to the door, looked up and down the wharf, but the ticket agent was nowhere to be seen.

"Odd," said Cugel. He noticed that the sign which had hung by the *Avventura's* gangplank had disappeared. "Naturally!" Cugel told himself. "There is now a full complement of passengers, and no need for further advertisement."

As Cugel watched, a tall red-haired man with muscular arms and legs came unsteadily along the dock, apparently having taken a drop too many at the inn. He lurched up the *Avventura's* gang-plank and stumbled into the cabin.

"Ah!" said Cugel. "The explanation is clear. That is Captain Wiskich, and the agent has been awaiting his return. He will be coming down the gang-plank any moment now."

Another ten minutes passed. The sun was now sinking low into the estuary and a dark pink gloom had descended upon Port Perdusz.

The captain appeared on the deck to supervise the loading of supplies from a dray. Cugel decided to wait no longer. He adjusted his hat to a proper angle, strode across the avenue, up the gangplank and presented himself to Captain Wiskich. "Sir, I am Cugel, one of your first-class passengers."

"All my passengers are first-class!" declared Captain Wiskich. "You will find no pettifoggery aboard the *Avventura!*"

Cugel opened his mouth to stipulate the terms of his ticket, then closed it again; to remonstrate would seem an argument in favor of pettifoggery. He observed the provisions now being loaded aboard, which seemed of excellent quality. Cugel spoke approvingly: "The viands appear more than adequate. It would seem that you set a good table for your passengers!"

Captain Wiskich uttered a yelp of coarse laughter. "First things come first aboard the *Avventura!* The viands are choice indeed; they are for the table of myself and the crew. Passengers eat flat beans and semola, unless they pay a surcharge, for which they are allowed a supplement of kangol."

Cugel heaved a deep sigh. "May I ask the length of the passage between here and Almery?"

Captain Wiskich looked at Cugel in drunken wonder. "Almery? Why should anyone sail to Almery? First one mires his ship in a morass of foul-smelling weeds a hundred miles across. The weeds grow over the ship and multitudes of insects crawl aboard. Beyond is the Gulf of Swirls, then the Serene Sea, now bedeviled by pirates of the Jhardine Coast. Then, unless one detours far west around the Isles of Cloud, he must pass through the Seleune and a whole carnival of dangers."

Cugel became outraged. "Am I to understand that you are not sailing south to Almery?"

Captain Wiskich slapped his chest with a huge red hand. "I am a Dilk and know nothing of fear. Still, when Death enters the room by the door, I leave through the window. My ship will sail a placid course to Latticut, thence to Al-Halambar, thence to Witches Nose and The Three Sisters, and so back to Port Perdusz. If you wish to make the passage, pay me your fare and find a hammock in the hold." "I have already bought my ticket!" stormed Cugel. "For the passage south to Almery, by way of Mahaze!"

"That pest-hole? Never. Let me see your ticket."

Cugel presented that document afforded him by the purported ticket-agent. Captain Wiskich looked at it first from one angle, then another. "I know nothing of this. I cannot even read it. Can you?"

"That is inconsequential. You must take me to Almery or return my money, to the sum of forty-five terces."

Captain Wiskich shook his head in wonder. "Port Perdusz is full of touts and swindlers; still, yours is a most imaginative and original scheme! But it falls short. Get off my ship at once."

"Not until you pay me my forty-five terces!" And Cugel laid his hand suggestively on the pommel of his sword.

Captain Wiskich seized Cugel by the collar and seat of the trousers, frog-marched him along the deck, and heaved him down the gang-plank. "Don't come back aboard; I am a busy man. Ahoy, dray-master! You still must bring me another load! I am in haste to make sail!"

"All in good time. I still must despatch a load to Varmous for his caravan. Now pay me for the present consignment; that is how I do business, on a cash basis only."

"Then bring up your invoice and we will check off the items."

"That is not necessary. The items are all on board."

"The items are on board when I say they are on board. You will take none of my terces until that moment."

"You only delay your last consignment, and I have Varmous' delivery to make."

"Then I will make my own tally and pay by this reckoning."

"Never!" Grumbling for the delay, the dray-master went aboard the *Avventura*.

Cugel went across the wharf and accosted a porter. "A moment of your time, if you please! This afternoon I had dealings with a small fat man in a dark uniform. Where can I find him at this moment?"

"You would seem to speak of poor old Master Sabbas, whose case is tragic. At one time owned and managed the draying business. But he went senile and now he calls himself 'Sab the Swindler' to every one's amusement. That is his son Master Yoder aboard the *Avventura* with Captain Wiskich. If you were foolish enough to give him your terces, you must now think of the act as a kindly charity, for you have brightened the day of poor feeble-minded old Master Sabbas."

"Perhaps so, but I gave over the terces in jest, and now I want them back."

The porter shook his head. "They are gone with the moons of ancient Earth."

"But surely Master Yoder reimburses the victims of his father's delusions!"

The porter merely laughed and went off about his duties.

Yoder presently descended the gang-plank. Cugel stepped forward. "Sir, I must complain of your father's actions. He sold me passage for a fictitious voyage aboard the *Avventura* and now —"

"Aboard the *Avventura*, you say?" asked Yoder.

"Precisely so, and therefore —"

"In that case, Captain Wiskich is your man!" So saying, Yoder went off about his business.

Cugel glumly walked back to the central plaza. In a yard beside the inn Varmous prepared his caravan for its journey. Cugel noticed three carriages, each seating a dozen passengers, and four wagons loaded with cargo, equipment and supplies. Varmous was immediately evident: a large man, bulky of shoulder, arm, leg and thigh, with ringlets of yellow hair, mild blue eyes and an expression of earnest determination.

Cugel watched Varmous for a few moments, then stepped forward and introduced himself. "Sir, I am Cugel. You would seem to be Varmous, director of the caravan."

"That is correct, sir."

"When, may I ask, does your caravan leave Port Perdusz?"

"Tomorrow, in the event that I receive all my stores from the indolent dray-master."

"May I ask your itinerary?"

"Certainly. Our destination is Torqual, where we will arrive in time for the Festival of Ennoblements. We travel by way of Kaspara Vitatus, which is a junction point for travel in several directions. However, I am obliged to notify you that our roster is complete. We can accept no more applications for travel."

"Perhaps you wish to employ another driver, or attendant, or guard?"

"I have ample personnel," said Varmous. "Still, I thank you for your interest."

Cugel disconsolately entered the inn, which, so he found, had been converted from a theater. The stage now served as a first-class dining hall for persons of fastidious taste, while the pit served as a common room. Sleeping chambers had been built along the balcony and sojourners could overlook both the first-class dining hall and the common room below merely by glancing from their doors.

Cugel presented himself to the office beside the entrance, where a stout woman sat behind a wicket.

"I have just arrived in town," said Cugel in a formal voice. "Important business will occupy me for the better part of a week. I will require food and lodging of excellent quality for the duration of my visit."

"Very good, sir! We will be happy to oblige. Your name?"

"I am Cugel."

"You may now pay over a deposit of fifty terces against charges."

Cugel spoke stiffly: "I prefer to pay at the end of my visit, when I can examine the bill in detail."

"Sir, this is our invariable rule. You would be astonished to learn of the scurrilous vagabonds who try every conceivable trick upon us."

"Then I must go find my servant, who carries the money."

Cugel departed the inn. Thinking that by chance he might come upon Master Sabbas, Cugel returned to the wharves.

The sun had set; Port Perdusz was bathed in wine-colored gloom. Activity had diminished somewhat, but drays still carried goods here and there among the warehouses.

Sab the Swindler was nowhere to be seen, but Cugel had already put him aside in favor of a new and more positive concept. He went to that warehouse where Yoder stored his victuals and stood waiting in the shadows.

From the warehouse came a dray driven not by Yoder but by a man with a ruff of ginger-colored hair and long bristling mustaches with waxed points. He was a person of style who wore a wide-brimmed hat with a tall green plume, double-toed boots and a mauve knee-length coat embroidered with yellow birds. Cugel removed his own hat, the most notable element of his costume, and tucked it into his waist-band.

As soon as the dray had moved a few yards along the wharf Cugel ran forward and accosted the driver. He spoke briskly: "Is this last load for the *Avventura*? If so, Captain Wiskich does not appreciate so much unnecessary delay."

The driver spoke with unexpected spirit: "I am indeed loaded for the *Avventura*. As for delay, I know of none! These are choice viands and careful selection is of the essence."

"True enough; no need to belabor the point. You have the invoice?"

"I do indeed! Captain Wiskich must pay to the last terce before I unload so much as an anchovy. Those are my strict instructions."

Cugel held up his hand. "Be easy! All will go smoothly. Captain Wiskich is conducting business over here in the warehouse. Come; bring your invoice."

Cugel led the way into the old gray warehouse, now dim with dusk, and signaled the driver into the office marked *Ticket Agent*.

The driver peered into the office. "Captain Wiskich? Why do you sit in the dark?"

Cugel threw his cloak over the driver's head and tied him well with the wonderful extensible rope, then gagged him with his own kerchief.

Cugel took the invoice and the fine wide-brimmed hat. "I will be back shortly; in the meantime, enjoy your rest."

Cugel drove the dray to the *Avventura* and drew up to a halt. He heard Captain Wiskich bawling to someone in the forecastle. Cugel shook his head regretfully. The risks were disproportionate to the gain; let Captain Wiskich wait.

Cugel continued along the wharf, and across the plaza to where Varmous worked among the wagons of his caravan.

Cugel pulled the driver's wide-brimmed hat low over his face and hid the sword under his cloak. With the invoice in hand he sought out Varmous. "Sir, I have delivered your load of victual, and this is the invoice, now due and payable."

Varmous, taking the invoice, read down the billing. "Three hundred and thirty terces? These are high-quality viands! My order was far more modest, and was quoted to me at two hundred terces!"

Cugel made a debonair gesture. "In that case, you need only pay two hundred terces," he said grandly. "We are interested only in the satisfaction of our customers."

Varmous glanced once more at the invoice. "It is a rare bargain! But why should I argue with you?" He handed Cugel a purse. "Count it, if you like, but I assure you that it contains the proper amount."

"That is adequate assurance," said Cugel. "I will leave the dray here and you may unload it at your convenience." He bowed and departed.

Returning to the warehouse Cugel found the driver as he had left him. Cugel said: "*Tzat!*" to loosen the bonds and placed the wide-brimmed hat upon the driver's head. "Do not stir for five minutes! I will be waiting just outside the door and if you stick out your head I will lop it off with my sword. Is that clear?"

"Quite clear," muttered the driver.

"In that case, farewell." Cugel departed and returned to the inn where he placed down a deposit and was assigned a chamber on the balcony.

Cugel dined upon bread and sausages, then strolled out to the front of the inn. His attention was attracted by an altercation near Varmous' caravan. Looking more closely, Cugel found Varmous in angry confrontation with Captain Wiskich and Yoder. Varmous refused to surrender his victuals until Captain Wiskich paid him two hundred terces plus a handling charge of fifty terces. Captain Wiskich, in a rage, aimed a blow at Varmous, who stepped aside, then struck Captain Wiskich with such force that he tumbled over backwards. The crew of the *Avventura* was on hand and rushed forward, only to be met by Varmous' caravan personnel carrying staves, and the seamen were soundly thrashed.

Captain Wiskich, with his crew, retired into the inn to plan new strategies, but instead they drank great quantities of wine and committed such nuisances that they were taken by the town constables and immured in an old fortress half-way up the hill, where they were sentenced to three days of confinement.

When Captain Wiskich and his crew were dragged away, Cugel thought long and carefully, then went out and once more conferred with Varmous.

"Earlier today, if you recall, I requested a place in your caravan."

"Conditions have not changed," said Varmous shortly. "Every place is taken."

"Let us suppose," said Cugel, "that you commanded another large and luxurious carriage, capable of carrying twelve in comfort — could you find enough custom to fill these places?"

"Without doubt! They now must wait for the next caravan and so will miss the Festival. But I leave in the morning and there would be no time to secure the supplies."

"That too can be effected, if we are able to arrive at a compact."

"What do you suggest?"

"I provide the carriage and the supplies. You recruit twelve more travelers and charge them premium prices. I pay nothing. We divide the net profits."

Varmous pursed his lips. "I see nothing wrong with this. Where is your carriage?"

"Come; we shall get it now."

Without enthusiasm Varmous followed Cugel out along the dock where finally all was quiet. Cugel boarded the *Avventura* and tied his rope to a ring under the bow and threw the end to Varmous. He kicked the hull with his ossip-charged boots and the vessel at once became revulsive of gravity. Debarking, Cugel untied the mooring lines and the vessel drifted up into the air, to the amazement of Varmous.

"Stretch, line, stretch!" called Cugel and the *Avventura* rose up into the darkness.

Together Varmous and Cugel towed the ship along the road and somewhat out of town and concealed it behind the cypress trees of the graveyard; the two then returned to the inn.

Cugel clapped Varmous on the shoulder. "We have done a good night's work, to our mutual profit!"

"I am not apt for magic," muttered Varmous. "Weirdness makes me eery."

Cugel waved aside his apprehensions. "Now: for a final goblet of wine to seal our compact, then a good night's sleep, and tomorrow, we set off on our journey!"

2
THE CARAVAN

DURING the pre-dawn stillness Varmous marshaled his caravan, ordering wagons and carriages, guiding passengers to their allotted places, quieting complaints with mild comments and an ingenuous gaze. He seemed to be everywhere at once: a massive figure in black boots, a peasant's blouse and baggy pantaloons, his blond curls confined under a flat wide-brimmed hat.

Occasionally he brought one of his passengers over to Cugel, saying: "Another person for the 'premier' class!"

One by one these passengers accumulated until there were six, including two women, Ermaulde and Nissifer, both of middle years, or apparently so, since Nissifer shrouded herself from head to toe in a gown of rusty brown satin and wore a clump hat with a heavy veil. Where Nissifer was dry and taciturn, and seemed to creak as she walked, Ermaulde was plump and voluble, with large moist features and a thousand copper-colored ringlets.

In addition to Nissifer and Ermaulde, four men had decided to enjoy the privileges of the 'premier' class: a varied group ranging from Gaulph Rabi, an ecclesiarch and pantologist, through Clissum and Perruquil, to Ivanello, a handsome young man who wore his rich garments with enviable flair and whose manner ranged that somewhat limited gamut between easy condescension and amused disdain.

Last to join the group was Clissum, a portly gentleman of good stature and the ineffable airs of a trained aesthete. Cugel acknowledged the introduction, then took Varmous aside.

"We now have assigned six passengers to the 'premier' category," said Cugel. "Cabins 1, 2, 3, and 4 are those designated for passenger use. We can also take over that double cabin

200

formerly shared by the cook and the steward, which means that
our own cook and steward must go to the forecastle. I, as captain of the vessel, will naturally use the after cabin. In short, we
are now booked to capacity."

Varmous scratched his cheek and showed Cugel a face of
bovine incomprehension. "Surely not yet! The vessel is larger
than three carriages together!"

"Possibly true, but the cargo hold claims much of the
space."

Varmous gave a dubious grunt. "We must manage better."

"I see no flaws in the existing situation," said Cugel. "If you
yourself wish to ride aboard, you can arrange a berth in the
forepeak."

Varmous shook his head. "That is not the problem. We must
make room for more passengers. Indeed, I intended the after
cabin, not for the use of either you or me — after all, we are
veterans of the trail and demand no languid comforts —"

Cugel held up his hand. "Not so! It is because I have known
hardship that I now so greatly enjoy comfort. The *Avventura* is
full. We can offer no further 'premier' accommodation."

Varmous showed a streak of mulish obstinacy. "In the first
place, I cannot spare a cook and a steward for the delectation of
six passengers and yourself. I counted upon you to fulfill this
duty."

"What!" cried Cugel. "Review, if you will, the terms of our
compact! I am captain, and no more!"

Varmous heaved a sigh. "Further, I have already sold four
other 'premiers' — aha! Here they are now! Doctor Lalanke and
his party."

Turning about, Cugel observed a tall gentleman, somewhat
sallow and saturnine of countenance, with dense black hair,
quizzically arched black eyebrows and a pointed black beard.

Varmous performed the introductions. "Cugel, here is Doctor Lalanke, a savant of remark and renown."

"Tush," said Lalanke. "You are positively effusive!"

Behind, walking in a row with long slow steps and arms
hanging straight down to narrow hips, like mechanical dolls, or
persons sleep-walking, came three maidens even paler than
Doctor Lalanke, with short hair loose and intensely black.

Cugel looked from one to the other; they were much alike, if not identical, with the same large gray eyes, high cheekbones and flat cheeks slanting down to small pointed chins. White trousers fitted snugly to their legs and hips, which were only just perceptibly feminine; soft pale green jackets were belted to their waists. They halted behind Doctor Lalanke and stood looking toward the river, neither speaking nor displaying interest in the folk around them.

Fascinating creatures, thought Cugel.

Doctor Lalanke spoke to Varmous. "These are the component members of my little tableaux: mimes, if you will. They are Sush, Skasja and Rlys, though which name applies to which I do not know and they do not seem to care. I look upon them as my wards. They are shy and sensitive, and will be happy in the privacy of the large cabin you have mentioned."

Cugel instantly stepped forward. "One moment! The after cabin aboard the *Avventura* is occupied by the captain, which is to say myself. There is accomodation for six in the 'premier' category. Ten persons are present. Varmous, you must repair your mistake and at once!"

Varmous rubbed his chin and looked up into the sky. "The day is well underway and we must arrive at Fierkle's Fountain before dark. I suppose we had better inspect the 'premier' categories and see what can be done."

The group walked to the grove of cypress trees which concealed the *Avventura*. Along the way, Varmous spoke persuasively to Cugel: "In a business such as ours, one must occasionally make a small sacrifice for the general advantage. Hence —"

Cugel spoke with emphasis: "No more wheedling! I am adamant!"

Varmous shook his head sadly. "Cugel, I am disappointed in you. Do not forget that I helped acquire the vessel, at some risk to my reputation!"

"My planning and my magic were decisive! You only pulled on a rope. Remember also that at Kaspara Vitatus we part company. You will continue to Torqual while I fare south in my vessel."

Varmous shrugged. "I expect no difficulties except those of the next few minutes. We must discover which among our 'premier' passengers are truly strident and which can be induced to ride the carriages."

"That is reasonable," said Cugel. "I see that there are tricks to the trade, which I will be at pains to learn."

"Just so. Now, as to tactics, we must always seem of the same mind; otherwise the passengers will play us one against the other, and all control is lost. Since we cannot confer on each case, let us signal our opinions in this fashion: a cough for the boat and a sniff for the carriage."

"Agreed!"

Arriving at the boat the passengers stood back in skepticism. Perruquil, who was small, thin, hot-eyed, and seemed to be constructed only of nerves knotted around bones, went so far as to suggest duplicity. "Varmous, what is your plot? You take our terces, put us in the cabins of this ruined vessel, then go quietly off with your caravan: is that the way of it? Be warned: I was not born yesterday!"

"Boats do not ordinarily sail on the dry land," murmured the aesthete Clissum.

"Quite true," said Varmous. "By Cugel's magic, this vessel will fly safely and smoothly through the air."

Cugel spoke in a serious voice: "Because of a regrettable oversight, too many passengers have been booked aboard the *Avventura*, and four persons will be required to ride in our 'premier' carriage, at the head of the column where they can enjoy an intimate view of the nearby landscape. In this connection let me ask: who among you suffers either vertigo or an obsessive fear of heights?"

Perruquil fairly danced to the spasmodic forces of his emotion. "I shall not change to inferior accomodations! I was first to pay over my terces and Varmous guaranteed me a top priority! If necessary, I can bring the constable, who witnessed the transaction; he will support my case."

Varmous coughed significantly and Cugel coughed as well.

Ermaulde took Varmous aside and spoke a few urgent words in his ear, whereupon Varmous raised his hands to the sides of his head and pulled at his golden curls. He looked at Cugel and coughed sharply.

Clissum said: "For me there is no choice, only stark necessity! I cannot tolerate the road-side dust; I would wheeze and gasp and go into asthmatic convulsions."

Perruquil seemed to find Clissum's sonorous diction and epicurean mannerisms offensive. He snapped: "If indeed you are so asthenic, are you not rash to venture so far out along the caravan trails?"

Clissum, rolling his eyes to the sky, spoke in his richest tones: "As I spend the seconds of my life on this dying world, I am never dismal nor sodden with woe! There is too much glory, too much wonder! I am a pilgrim on a life-long quest; I search here, there, everywhere, for that elusive quality —"

Perruquil said impatiently: "How does this bear upon your asthma?"

"The connection is both implicit and explicit. I vowed that, come what may, I would sing my odes at the Festival, even if contorted in the face from an asthmatic fit. When I found that I might journey in the clean upper air, my rapture knew no bounds!"

"Bah," muttered Perruquil. "Perhaps we all are asthmatic; Varmous has never troubled to ask."

During the discussion, Varmous whispered into Cugel's ear. "Ermaulde reveals that she is pregnant with child! She fears that, if subjected to the jolts and jars of the carriage, an untoward event might occur. There is no help for it: she must ride in cushioned ease aboard the *Avventura*."

"I agree, in all respects," said Cugel.

Their attention was attracted by Ivanello's merry laugh. "I have full faith in Varmous! Why? Because I paid double-fare for the best possible accommodation which, so he assured me, I could choose myself. I therefore select the after cabin. Cugel can bed himself down with the other teamsters."

Cugel gave a distinct sniff, and spoke sharply: "In this case, Varmous referred only to the carriages. A lad like you will enjoy jumping on and off and gathering berries along the way. The *Avventura* has been reserved for persons of taste and breeding, such as Clissum and Ermaulde."

"What of me?" cried the ecclesiarch Gaulph Rabi. "I am studied in four infinities and I sit as a full member of the Collegium. I am accustomed to special treatment. In order to perform my meditations I need a quiet place, such as the cabin."

Nissifer, with a rustling and a sour smell, took two steps forward. She spoke in a curious husky whisper. "I will ride the ship. Whoever interferes will be tainted."

Ivanello threw his head back and looked at the woman through half-closed lids. "'Tainted'? How do you mean 'tainted'?

"Do you truly care to learn?" came the husky whisper.

Cugel, suddenly alert, looked around the group. Where were Doctor Lalanke and his wards? In sudden apprehension he ran around to the gangplank and bounded aboard.

His fears were well realized. The three mimes had secluded themselves in the after cabin. Doctor Lalanke stood in the doorway making signals. At the sight of Cugel he cried out in vexation: "Irritating little creatures! Once they decide upon a whim they are beyond control. Sometimes I am beside myself with frustration; I admit it freely!"

"Nevertheless, they must leave my cabin!"

Lalanke showed a wan smile. "I can do nothing. Persuade them to leave however you like."

Cugel went into the cabin. The three maidens sat on the bunk watching him through large gray eyes. Cugel pointed to the door. "Out with you! This is the captain's cabin, and I am the captain."

The maidens with one accord drew up their legs and folded their arms around their knees. "Yes, yes, charming indeed," said Cugel. "I am not sure whether or not I have the taste for such epicene little creatures. Under proper circumstances I am willing to experiment, but not in a group of three which would be distracting. So come now: remove your fragile little bodies, or I must eject you."

The maidens sat still as owls.

Cugel heaved a sigh. "So it must be." He started toward the bed but was interrupted by the impatient voice of Varmous. "Cugel? Where are you? We need to make decisions."

Cugel went out on deck to find that all the 'premier' passengers had climbed the gangplank and were disputing possession of the cabins. Varmous told Cugel: "We can delay no longer! I will bring up the caravan and we will tow the boat behind the first carriage."

Cugel cried out in fury: "There are too many passengers aboard! Four must take to the carriages! Meanwhile Doctor Lalanke and his troupe have taken my cabin!"

Varmous shrugged his ponderous shoulders. "Since you are captain, you need only issue the appropriate order. Meanwhile, remove the mooring lines all but one and prepare your magic."

Varmous descended to the ground. "Wait!" cried Cugel. "Where is the steward to cook and serve our meals?"

"All in good time," said Varmous. "You will prepare the noon lunch, as you have nothing better to do. Now pull up your gangplank! Make ready for departure!"

Seething with annoyance, Cugel tied his rope from the stem— head ring to the trunk of a cypress, then drew aboard the other lines. With the help of Doctor Lalanke and Clissum he pulled aboard the gangplank.

The caravan came along the road. Varmous loosened the rope from the cypress and the boat floated into the air. Varmous tied the rope to the back of the first carriage which was pulled by two farlocks of the bulky Black Ganghorn breed. Without further ado Varmous climbed aboard the carriage and the caravan set off along the river road.

Cugel looked about the deck. The passengers lined the rails, looking out over the countryside and congratulating themselves upon their mode of transport. A semblance of cameraderie had already come into being, affecting all save Nissifer who sat huddled in a rather peculiar posture beside the hold. Doctor Lalanke also stood somewhat apart. Cugel joined him by the rail. "Have you removed your wards from my cabin?"

Doctor Lalanke gravely shook his head. "They are curious little creatures, innocent and without guile, motivated only by the force of their own needs."

"Surely they must obey your commands!"

Through some extraordinary flexibility of feature, Doctor Lalanke managed to seem both apologetic and amused. "So one would think. I often wonder how they regard me: certainly not as their master."

"Most singular! How did they come into your custody?"

"I must inform you that I am a man of great wealth. I live beside the Szonglei River not far from Old Romarth. My manse is built of rare woods: tirrinch, gauze difono, skeel, purple trank, camfer and a dozen others. My life might well be one of ease and splendor, but, to validate the fact of my existence, I annotate the lives and works of the great magicians. My collection of memorabilia and curious adjuncts is remarkable." As he spoke his eyes rested upon the scale 'Spatterlight', which Cugel used for a hat ornament.

Cugel asked cautiously: "And you yourself are a magician?"

"Alas! I lack the strength. I can grasp a trifling spell against stinging insects, and another to quiet howling dogs, but magic like yours, which wafts a ship through the air, is beyond my capacity. And while we are on the subject, what of the object you wear on your hat: it exhales an unmistakable flux!"

"The object has a curious history, which I will relate at a more convenient time," said Cugel. "At this moment —"

"Of course! You are more interested in the 'mimes', as I call them, and this may well be the function for which they were contrived."

"I am mostly interested in ejecting them from my cabin."

"I will be brief, though I must revert to Grand Motholam of the late eighteenth aeon. The arch-magician Moel Lel Laio lived in a palace cut from a single moonstone. Even today, if you walk the Plain of Gray Shades, you may find a shard or two. When I excavated the old crypts I found a cambent box containing three figurines, of cracked and discolored ivory, each no larger than my finger. I took these objects to my manse and thought to wash away the grime, but they absorbed water as fast as I applied it, and I finally put them into basins to soak overnight. In the morning I found the three as you see them now. I used the names Sush, Skasja and Rlys after the Tracynthian Graces and tried to give them speech. Never have they uttered a sound, not even one to the other.

"They are strange creatures, oddly sweet, and I could detail their conduct for hours. I call them 'mimes' because when the mood comes on them they will posture and preen and simulate a hundred situations, none of which I understand. I have learned to let them to do as they will; in return they allow me to care for them."

"All very well," said Cugel. "Now the mimes of the late eighteenth aeon must discover the reality of today, as embodied in the person of Cugel. I warn you, I may be forced to eject them bodily!"

Doctor Lalanke shrugged sadly. "I am sure that you will be as gentle as possible. What are your plans?"

"The time for planning is over!" Cugel marched to the door of the cabin and flung it wide. The three sat as before, staring at Cugel with wondering eyes.

Cugel stood to the side and pointed to the door. "Out! Go! Depart! Be off with you! I am ready to lie down on my bunk and take my rest."

None of the three twitched so much as a muscle. Cugel stepped forward and took the arm of the maiden facing him on his right. Instantly the room fluttered with motion and before Cugel understood what was happening he was propelled from the cabin.

Cugel angrily ran back within and tried to seize the nearest of the mimes. She slipped sober-faced from his grasp, and again the room seemed full of fluttering figures: up, down, and around like moths. Finally Cugel managed to seize one from behind and, carrying her to the door, thrust her out on deck. At the same time he was thrust forward and instantly the ejected maiden returned into the cabin.

The other passengers had come to watch. All laughed and called out jocular remarks, save only Nissifer who paid no heed. Doctor Lalanke spoke as if in vindication: "You see how it goes? The more abrupt your conduct, the more determined their response."

Cugel said through gritted teeth: "They will come out to eat; then we shall see."

Doctor Lalanke shook his head. "That is an unreliable hope. Their appetites are slight; now and then they will take a bit of fruit, or a sweet-cake, or a sip of wine."

"Shame, Cugel!" said Ermaulde. "Would you starve three poor girls already so pale and peaked?"

"If they dislike starvation they can leave my cabin!"

The ecclesiarch lifted high a remarkably long white forefinger, with knobbed knuckles and a yellow fingernail. "Cugel, you cultivate your senses as if they were hot-house plants. Why not, once and for all, break the tyranny of your internal organs? I will give you a tract to study."

Clissum spoke: "In the last analysis the comfort of your passengers must supersede your own. Another matter! Varmous guaranteed a gracious cuisine of five or six courses. The sun has risen high and it is time that you set about your preparations for lunch."

Cugel said at last: "If Varmous made this guarantee, let Varmous do the cooking."

Perruquil set up an outcry, but Cugel would not relent. "My own problems are paramount!"

"Then what is our recourse?" demanded Perruquil.

Cugel pointed to the gunwale. "Slide down the rope and complain to Varmous! In any case, do not trouble me."

Perruquil marched to the gunwhale and raised a great shout. Varmous turned up his broad face. "What is the difficulty?"

"It lies with Cugel. You must attend to the matter at once."

Varmous patiently halted the caravan, pulled down the boat and climbed aboard. "Well then, what now?"

Perruquil, Clissum and Cugel spoke together, until Varmous held up his hands. "One at a time, if you please. Perruquil, what is your complaint?"

Perruquil pointed a trembling finger at Cugel. "He is like a stone! He shrugs off our demands for food and will not relinquish accommodations to those who paid dearly for them!"

With a sigh Varmous said: "Well then, Cugel? How do you account for your conduct?"

"In no way whatever. Evict those insane maidens from my cabin, or the *Avventura* no longer follows the caravan, but sails to best advantage on the wind."

Varmous turned to Doctor Lalanke. "There is no help for it. We must submit to Cugel's demand. Call them out."

"But where then will we sleep?"

"There are three bunks in the crew's forecastle for the maidens. There is another bunk in the forepeak carpenter shop, which is quiet and which will suit His Reverence Gaulph Rabi very well. We will put Ermaulde and Nissifer in the port cabins, Perruquil and Ivanello in the starboard cabins, while you and Clissum will share the double cabin. All problems are thereby solved, so let the maidens come forth."

Doctor Lalanke said dubiously: "That is the nub of the matter! They will not come! Cugel tried twice to put them out; twice they ejected him instead."

Ivanello, lounging to the side, said: "And a most entertaining spectacle it was! Cugel came flying out as if he were trying to leap a wide ditch."

Doctor Lalanke said: "They probably misunderstood Cugel's intentions. I suggest that the three of us enter together. Varmous, you may go first, then I will follow and Cugel can bring up the rear. Allow me to make the signs."

The three entered the cabin to find the maidens seated demurely on the bunk. Doctor Lalanke made a series of signs; with every show of docility the three filed from the cabin.

Varmous shook his head in bewilderment. "I cannot understand the furore! Cugel, is this the extent of your complaint?"

"I will say this: the *Avventura* will continue to sail with the caravan."

Clissum pulled at his plump chin. "Since Cugel refuses to cook, where and how do we partake of the fine cuisine you advertised?"

In a spiteful voice Perruquil said: "Cugel suggested that you yourself should do the cooking."

"I have more serious responsibilities, as Cugel well knows," said Varmous stiffly. "It seems that I must assign a steward to the ship." Leaning over the gunwhale he called: "Send Porraig aboard!"

The three maidens suddenly performed a giddy gyration, then a leaping, crouching ballet of postures, which they accented with mocking glances and flippant gestures toward Cugel. Doctor Lalanke interpreted the movements. "They are expressing an emotion or, better, an attitude. I would not dare attempt a translation."

Cugel turned away indignantly, in time to glimpse a flutter of fusty brown satin and the closing of the door to his cabin.

In a fury Cugel called out to Varmous: "Now the woman Nissifer has taken over my cabin!"

"This fol-de-rol must stop!" said Varmous. He knocked on the door. "Madame Nissifer, you must remove to your own quarters!"

From within came a husky whisper, barely audible. "I will stay here, since I must have the dark."

"That is impossible! We have already allotted this cabin to Cugel!"

"Cugel must go elsewhere."

"Madame, I regret that Cugel and I must enter the cabin and conduct you to your proper berth."

"I will place a taint."

Varmous looked toward Cugel with puzzled blue eyes. "What does she mean by that?"

"I am not quite clear," said Cugel. "But no matter! Caravan regulations must be enforced. This is our first concern."

"Quite so! Otherwise we invite chaos."

"Here, at least, we are agreed! Enter the cabin; I stand resolutely at your back!"

Varmous settled his blouse, squared the hat upon his golden curls, pushed the door ajar and stepped into the cabin, with Cugel on his heels. . . . Varmous uttered a strangled cry and lurched back into Cugel, but not before Cugel discovered an acrid stench so vile and incisive that his teeth felt tender in their sockets.

Varmous stumbled to the rail, leaned back on his elbows and looked blearily across the deck. Then, with an air of great fatigue, he climbed over the gunwhale and lowered himself to the ground. He spoke a few words to Porraig the steward, who thereupon boarded the vessel. Varmous slackened the rope and the *Avventura* once more floated high.

Cugel, after a moment's reflection, approached Doctor Lalanke. "I am impressed by your gentility and in turn I will be generous. You and your wards are now assigned to the captain's cabin."

Doctor Lalanke became more saturnine than ever. "My wards would be confused. For all their frivolity, they are deeply sensitive and easily disturbed. The forecastle, as it turns out, is quite comfortable."

"Just as you like." Cugel sauntered forward, to find that the cabin formerly allotted to Nissifer had been taken by the ecclesiarch Gaulph Rabi, while Porraig the steward had settled into the carpenter shop.

Cugel made a hissing sound between his teeth. Finding an old cushion and a ragged tarpaulin, he contrived a tent on the foredeck, and there took up residence.

The river Chaing meandered down a wide valley demarcated into fields and folds by ancient stone walls, with groups of stone farmsteads huddling under black feather trees and indigo oaks. At the side, weather-worn hills basking in the red sunlight trapped lunes of black shadow in their hollow places.

All day the caravan followed the banks of the river, passing through the villages Goulyard, Trunash and Sklieve. At sundown camp was made in a meadow beside the river.

When the sun lurched low behind the hills, a great fire was built and the travelers gathered in a circle to warm themselves against the evening chill.

The 'premier' passengers dined together on coarse but hearty fare which even Clissum found acceptable — all except Nissifer, who kept to her cabin, and the mimes, who sat cross-legged beside the hull of the *Avventura* staring fascinated into the flames. Ivanello appeared in a costume of the richest quality: loose breeches of a gold, amber and black corduroy twill, fitted black boots, a loose fusk-ivory shirt embroidered with gold floriations. From his right ear, on three inches of chain, dangled a milk-opal sphere almost an inch in diameter: a gem which fascinated the three mimes to the edge of entrancement.

Varmous poured wine with a generous hand and the company became convivial. One of the ordinary passengers, a certain Ansk-Daveska called out: "Here we sit, strangers cast willy-nilly into each other's company! I suggest that each of us in turn introduces himself and tells his story, of whom he is and something of his achievements."

Varmous clapped his hands together. "Why not? I will start off. Madlick, serve more wine. . . .My story is essentially simple. My father kept a fowl-run at Waterwan across the estuary and produced fine fowl for the tables of the locality. I thought to follow in his footsteps, until he took a new spouse who could not abide the odor of burning feathers. To please this woman my father gave up the fowl and thought to cultivate lirkfish in shallow ponds, which I excavated from the ground. But owls gathered in the trees and so annoyed the spouse that she went off with a dealer in rare incenses. We then operated a ferry service from Waterwan to Port Perdusz, until my father took too much wine and, falling asleep in the ferry, drifted out to sea. I then became involved in the caravan trade and you know all the rest."

Gaulph Rabi spoke: "I hope that my life, in contrast to that of Varmous, will prove inspiring, especially to the younger persons present, or even to such marginal personalities as Cugel and Ivanello."

Ivanello had gone to sit beside the mimes. He called out: "Now then! Insult me as you will, but do not pair me off with Cugel!"

Cugel refused to dignify the comment with his attention.

Gaulph Rabi showed only a faint cold smile. "I have lived a life of rigid discipline, and the benefits of my regimen must be clear to all. While still a catechumen at the Obtrank Normalcy I made a mark with the purity of my logic. As First Fellow of the Collegium, I composed a tract demonstrating that succulent gluttony sickens the spirit like dry rot in wood. Even now, when I drink wine I mix therein three drops of aspergantium which brings about a bitter taste. I now sit on the Council and I am a Pantologist of the Final Revelation."

"An enviable achievement!" declared Varmous. "I drink to your continued success, and here is a goblet of wine without aspergantium, that you may join us in the toast without distraction from the vile flavors."

"Thank you," said Gaulph Rabi. "This is a legitimate usage."

Cugel now addressed the group: "I am a grandee of Almery, where I am heir to an ancient estate. While striving against injustice I ran afoul of an evil magician who sent me north to die. Little did he realize that submission is foreign to my nature —"

Cugel looked around the group. Ivanello tickled the mimes with a long straw. Clissum and Gaulph Rabi argued Vodel's Doctrine of Isoptogenesis in a quiet undertone. Doctor Lalanke and Perruquil discussed the hostelries of Torqual.

Somewhat sulkily Cugel returned to his seat. Varmous, who had been planning the route with Ansk-Daveska, finally noticed and called out: "Well done, Cugel! Most interesting indeed! Madlick, I believe that two more jugs of the economy-grade wine are in order. It is not often that we celebrate such festivals along the trail! Lalanke, do you plan to present one of your tableaus?"

Doctor Lalanke made signals; the maidens, preoccupied with Ivanello's nonsense, at last noticed the gesticulations. They leapt to their feet and for a few moments performed a set of dizzying saltations.

Ivanello came over to Doctor Lalanke and whispered a question into his ear.

Doctor Lalanke frowned. "The question is indelicate, or at least over-explicit, but the answer is 'yes'."

Ivanello put another discreet question, to which Doctor Lalanke's response was definitely frosty. "I doubt if such ideas even enter their heads." He turned away and resumed his conversation with Perruquil.

Ansk-Daveska brought out his concertina and played a merry tune. Ermaulde, despite Varmous' horrified expostulations, jumped to her feet and danced a spirited jig.

When Ermaulde had finished dancing, she took Varmous aside: "My symptoms were gas pains only; I should have reassured you but the matter slipped my mind."

"I am much relieved," said Varmous. "Cugel will also be pleased, since, as captain of the *Avventura*, he would have been forced to serve as obstetrician."

The evening proceeded. Each of the group had a story to tell or a concept to impart, and all sat while the fire burned down to embers.

Clissum, so it developed, had composed several odes and upon urging from Ermaulde recited six stanzas from an extended work entitled: *O Time, Be Thou the Sorry Dastard?* in dramatic fashion, with vocal cadenzas between each stanza.

Cugel brought out his packet of cards and offered to teach Varmous and Ansk-Daveska Skax, which Cugel defined as a game of pure chance. Both preferred to listen as Gaulph Rabi responded to the indolent questions of Ivanello: ". . . . no confusion whatever! The Collegium is often known as 'the Convergence', or even as 'the Hub', in a jocular sense, of course. But the essence is identical."

"I fear that you have the better of me," said Ivanello. "I am lost in a jungle of terminology."

"Aha! There speaks the voice of the layman! I will simplify!"

"Please do."

"Think of a set of imaginary spokes, representing between twenty and thirty infinities — the exact number is still uncertain. They converge in a focus of pure sentience; they intermingle then diverge in the opposite direction. The location of this 'Hub' is precisely known; it is within the precincts of the Collegium."

Varmous called out a question: "What does it look like?"

Gaulph Rabi gazed a long moment into the dying fire. "I think that I will not answer that question," he said at last. "I would create as many false images as there were ears to hear me."

"Half as many," Clissum pointed out delicately.

Ivanello smiled lazily up toward the night sky, where Alphard the Lonely stood in the ascendant. "It would seem that a single infinity would suffice for your studies. Is it not grandiose to preempt so many?"

Gaulph Rabi thrust forward his great narrow face. "Why not study for a term or two at the Collegium and discover for yourself?"

"I will give thought to the matter."

The second day was much like the first. The farlocks ambled steadily along the road and a breeze from the west pushed the *Avventura* slightly ahead of the foremost carriage.

Porraig the steward prepared an ample breakfast of poached oysters, sugar-glazed kumquats and scones sprinkled with the scarlet roe of land-crabs.

Nissifer remained immured in her cabin. Porraig brought a

tray to the door and knocked. "Your breakfast, Madame Nissifer!"

"Take it away," came a hoarse whisper from within. "I want
no breakfast."

Porraig shrugged and removed both the tray and himself as
rapidly as possible, since the fetor of Nissifer's 'taint' had not
yet departed the area.

At lunch matters went in the same style and Cugel instructed Porraig to serve Nissifer no more meals until she appeared in the dining saloon.

During the afternoon Ivanello brought out a long-necked
lute tied with a pale blue ribbon, and sang sentimental ballads
to gentle chords from the lute. The mimes came to watch in
wonder, and it became a topic of general discussion as to
whether or not they heard the music, or even grasped the meaning of Ivanello's activities. In any event, they lay on their bellies, chins resting on their folded fingers, watching Ivanello
with grave gray eyes and, so it might seem, dumb adoration.
Ivanello was emboldened to stroke Skasja's short black hair. Instantly Sush and Rlys crowded close and Ivanello had to caress
them as well.

Smiling and pleased with his success, Ivanello played and
sang another ballad, while Cugel watched sourly from the
foredeck.

Today the caravan passed only a single village, Port Titus,
and the landscape seemed perceptibly wilder. Ahead rose a massive stone scarp through which the river had carved a narrow
gorge, with the road running close alongside.

Halfway through the afternoon the caravan came upon a
crew of timber-cutters, loading their timber aboard a barge.
Varmous brought the caravan to a halt. Jumping down from the
carriage he went to make inquiries and received unsettling
news: a section of mountain had collapsed into the gorge, rendering the river road impassable.

The timber-cutters came out into the road and pointed north
toward the hills. "A mile ahead you will come upon a side-
road. It leads up through Tuner's Gap and off across Ildish
Waste. After two miles the road forks and you must veer to the

right, around the gorge and in due course down to Lake Zaol and Kaspara Vitatus."

Varmous turned to look up toward the gap. "And the road: is it safe or dangerous?"

The oldest timber-cutter said: "We have no exact knowledge, since no one has recently come down through Tuner's Gap. This in itself may be a negative sign."

Another timber-cutter spoke. "At the Waterman's Inn I have heard rumors of a nomad band down from the Karst. They are said to be stealthy and savage, but since they fear the dark they will not attack by night. You are a strong company and should be safe unless they take you from ambush. An alert watch should be maintained."

The youngest of the timber-cutters said: "What of the rock goblins? Are they not a serious menace?"

"Bah!" said the old man. "Such things are boogerboos, on the order of wind-stick devils, by which to frighten saucy children."

"Still, they exist!" declared the young timber-cutter. "That, at least, is my best information."

"Bah!" said the old cutter a scond time. "At the Waterman's Inn they drink beer by the gallon, and on their way home they see goblins and devils behind every bush."

The second cutter said thoughtfully: "I will reveal my philosophy. It is better to keep watch for rock-goblins and wind-stick devils and never see them, than not to keep watch so that they leap upon you unawares."

The old cutter made a peremptory sign. "Return to work! Your gossip is delaying this important caravan!" And to Varmous: "Proceed by Tuner's Gap. A week and a day should bring you into Kaspara Vitatus."

Varmous returned to the carriage. The caravan moved forward. After a mile a side-road turned off toward Tuner's Gap, and Varmous reluctantly departed the river-road.

The side-road wound back and forth up over the hills to Tuner's Gap, then turned out across a flat plain.

The time was now almost sunset. Varmous elected to halt for the night where a stream issued from a copse of black deodars. He arranged the wagons and carriages with care, and set out a guard-fence of metal strands which, when activated, would discharge streamers of purple lightning toward hostile intruders, thus securing the caravan against night-wandering hoons, erbs and grues.

Once again a great fire was built, with wood broken from the deodars. The 'premier' passengers partook of three preliminary courses served by Porraig aboard the *Avventura*, then joined the 'ordinaries' for bread, stew and sour greens around the fire.

Varmous served wine, but with a hand less lavish than on the previous evening.

After supper Varmous addressed the group. "As everyone knows, we have made a detour, which should cause us neither inconvenience nor, so I trust, delay. However, we now travel the Ildish Waste, a land which is strange to me. I feel compelled to take special safeguards. You will notice the guard-fence, which is intended to deter intruders."

Ivanello lounging to the side, could not restrain a facetious remark: "What if intruders leap the fence?"

Varmous paid him no heed. "The fence is dangerous! Do not approach it. Doctor Lalanke, you must instruct your wards as best you can of this danger."

"I will do so."

"The Ildish Waste is a wild territory. We may encounter nomads down from the Karst or even the Great Erm itself. These folk, either men or half-men, are unpredictable. Therefore I am setting up a system of vigilant look-outs. Cugel, who rides the *Avventura* and makes his headquarters at the bow, shall be our chief look-out. He is keen, sharp-eyed and suspicious; also he has nothing better to do. I will watch from my place on the forward carriage, and Slavoy, who rides the last wagon, shall be the rear-guard. But it is Cugel, with his commanding view across the landscape, to whom we shall look for protection. That is all I wish to say. Let the festivities proceed."

Clissum cleared his throat and stepped forward, but before he could recite so much as a syllable, Ivanello took up his lute and, banging lustily at the strings, sang a rather vulgar ballad.

Clissum stood with a pained smile frozen on his face, then turned away and resumed his seat.

A wind blew down from the north, causing the flames to leap and the smoke to billow. Ivanello cried out a light-hearted curse. He put down his lute and began to toy with the mimes, whom, as before, he had hypnotized with his music. Tonight he became bolder in his caresses, and encountered no protest so long as he evenly shared his attentions.

Cugel watched with disapproval. He muttered to Doctor Lalanke: "Ivanello is persuading your wards to laxity."

"That may well be his intent," agreed Doctor Lalanke.

"And you are not concerned?"

"Not in the least."

Clissum once again came forward, and holding high a scroll of manuscript, looked smilingly around the group.

Ivanello, leaning back into the arms of Sush, with Rlys pressed against him on one side and Skasja on the other, bent his head over his lute and drew forth a series of plangent chords.

Clissum seemed on the verge of calling out a quizzical complaint when the wind rolled a cloud of smoke into his face and he retreated coughing. Ivanello, head bent so that his chestnut curls glinted in the firelight, smiled and played glissandos on his lute.

Ermaulde indignantly marched around the fire, to stand looking down at Ivanello. In a brittle voice she said: "Clissum is about to chant one of his odes. I suggest that you put aside your lute and listen."

"I will do so with pleasure," said Ivanello.

Ermaulde turned and marched back the way she had come. The three mimes jumped to their feet and strutted behind her, cheeks puffed out, elbows outspread, bellies thrust forward and knees jerking high. Ermaulde, becoming aware of the activity, turned, and the mimes capered away, to dance for five seconds with furious energy, like maenads, before they once again flung themselves down beside Ivanello.

Ermaulde, smiling a fixed smile, went off to converse with Clissum, and both sent scathing glances toward Ivanello, who, putting aside his lute, now gave free rein to his fondling of the mimes. Far from resenting his touch, they pressed ever more closely upon him. Ivanello bent his head and kissed Rlys full on the mouth; instantly both Sush and Skasja thrust forward their faces for like treatment.

Cugel gave a croak of disgust. "The man is insufferable!"

Doctor Lalanke shook his head. "Candidly, I am surprised by their complaisance. They have never allowed me to touch them. Ah well, I see that Varmous has become restless; the evening draws to a close."

Varmous, who had risen to his feet, stood listening to the sounds of night. He went to inspect the guard fence, then addressed the travellers. "Do not become absent-minded! Do not walk in your sleep! Make no rendezvous in the forest! I am now going to my bed and I suggest the same for all of you, since tomorrow we travel long and far across the Ildish Waste."

Clissum would not be denied. Summoning all his dignity, he stepped forward. "I have heard several requests for another of my pieces, to which I shall now respond."

Ermaulde clapped her hands, but many of the others had gone off to their beds.

Clissum pursed his mouth against vexation. "I will now recite my Thirteenth Ode, subtitled: *Gaunt Are the Towers of My Mind*." He arranged himself in a suitable posture, but the wind came in a great gust, causing the fire to wallow and flare. Clouds of smoke roiled around the area and those still present hurried away. Clissum threw his hands high in despair and retired from the scene.

Cugel spent a restless night. Several times he heard a distant cry expressing dejection, and once he heard a chuckling hooting conversation from the direction of the forest.

Varmous aroused the caravan at an early hour, while the pre-dawn sky still glowed purple. Porraig the steward served a breakfast of tea, scones and a savory mince of clams, barley, kangol and pennywort. As usual, Nissifer failed to make an appearance and this morning Ivanello was missing as well.

Porraig called down to Varmous, suggesting that he send Ivanello aboard for his breakfast, but a survey of the camp yielded nothing. Ivanello's possessions occupied their ordinary places; nothing seemed to be missing except Ivanello himself.

Varmous, sitting at a table, made a ponderous investigation, but no one could supply any information whatever. Varmous examined the ground near the guard fence, but discovered no signs of disturbance. He finally made an announcement. "Ivanello for all practical purposes has vanished into thin air. I discover no hint of foul play; still I cannot believe that he disappeared voluntarily. The only explanation would seem to be baneful magic. In truth, I am at a loss for any better explanation. Should anyone entertain theories, or even suspicions, please communicate them to me. Meanwhile, there is no point remaining here. We must keep to our schedule, and the caravan will now get under way. Drivers, bring up your farlocks! Cugel, to your post at the bow!"

The caravan moved out upon Ildish Waste, and the fate of Ivanello remained obscure.

The road, now little more than a track, led north to a fork; here the caravan veered eastward and proceeded beside the hills which rolled away as far as the eye could reach. The landscape was bleak and dry, supporting only a few stunted gong-trees, an occasional tumble of cactus, an isolated dendron, black or purple or red.

Halfway through the morning Varmous called up to the ship: "Cugel, are you keeping a sharp watch?"

Cugel looked down over the gunwale. "I could watch with more purpose if I knew what I was watching for."

"You are looking for hostile nomads, especially those hidden in ambush."

Cugel scanned the countryside. "I see nothing answering to this description: only hills and waste, although far ahead I notice the dark line of a forest, or maybe it is only a river fringed with trees."

"Very good, Cugel. Maintain your look-out."

The day passed and the line of dark trees seemed to recede before them, and at sundown camp was made on a sandy area open to the sky.

As usual, a fire was built, but the disappearance of Ivanello weighed heavy, and though Varmous served out wine, no one drank with cheer, and conversation was pitched in low tones.

As before Varmous arranged his guard-fence. He spoke again to the company. "The mystery remains profound! Since we are without a clue, I recommend everyone to extreme caution. Certainly, do not so much as approach the guard-fence!"

The night passed without incident. In the morning the caravan got under way in good time, with Cugel once more serving as look-out.

As the day went by, the countryside became somewhat less arid. The line of trees now could be seen to mark the course of a river wandering down from the hills and out across the waste.

Arriving at the riverbank the road turned abruptly south and followed the river to a stone bridge of five arches, where Varmous called a halt to allow the teamsters to water their farlocks. Cugel ordered the rope to shorten itself and so drew the *Avventura* down to the road. The 'premier' passengers alighted and wandered here and there to stretch their legs.

At the entrance to the bridge stood a monument ten feet tall, holding a bronze plaque to the attention of those who passed. The characters were illegible to Cugel. Gaulph Rabi thrust close his long nose, then shrugged and turned away. Doctor Lalanke, however, declared the script to be a version of Sarsounian, an influential dialect of the nineteenth aeon, in common use for more than four thousand years.

"The text is purely ceremonial," said Doctor Lalanke. "It reads:

TRAVELERS! AS DRY SHOD YOU CROSS

THE THUNDERING TURMOIL OF THE RIVER SYK,

BE ADVISED THAT YOU HAVE BEEN ASSISTED

BY THE BENEFICENCE OF

KHAIVE, LORD-RULER OF KHARAD

AND

GUARDIAN OF THE UNIVERSE

As we can see, the River Syk no longer thunders a turmoil, but we can still acknowledge the generosity of King Khaive; indeed, it is wise to do so." And Doctor Lalanke performed a polite genuflection to the monument.

"Superstition!" scoffed Gaulph Rabi. "At the Collegium we turn down our ears in reverence only to the Nameless Syncresis at the core of the Hub."

"So it may be," said Doctor Lalanke indifferently and moved away. Cugel looked from Gaulph Rabi to Doctor Lalanke, then quickly performed a genuflection before the monument.

"What?" cried the gaunt ecclesiarch. "You too, Cugel? I took you for a man of judgment!"

"That is precisely why I gave honor to the monument. I judged that the rite could do no harm and cost very little."

Varmous dubiously rubbed his nose, then made a ponderous salute of his own, to the patent disgust of Gaulph Rabi.

The farlocks were brought back to their traces; Cugel caused the *Avventura* to rise high in the air and the caravan proceeded across the bridge.

During the middle afternoon Cugel became drowsy and dropping his head upon his arms, dozed off into a light slumber. . . .Time passed and Cugel became uncomfortable. Blinking and yawning, he surveyed the countryside, and his attention was caught by stealthy movements behind a thicket of smoke-berry bushes which lined the road. Cugel leaned forward and perceived several dozen short swarthy men wearing baggy pantaloons, dirty vests of various colors and black kerchiefs tied around their heads. They carried spears and battle-hooks, and clearly intended harm upon the caravan.

Cugel shouted down to Varmous: "Halt! Prepare your weapons! Bandits hide in ambush behind yonder thicket!"

Varmous pulled up the caravan and blew a blast on his signal horn. The teamsters took up weapons as did many of the passengers and prepared to face an onslaught. Cugel brought the boat down so that the 'premier' passengers might also join the fight.

Varmous came over to the boat. "Exactly where is the ambush? How many lie in wait?"

Cugel pointed toward the ticket. "They crouch behind the smoke-berry bushes, to the number of about twenty-three.

They carry spears and snaffle-irons."

"Well done, Cugel! You have saved the caravan!" Varmous studied the terrain, then, taking ten men armed with swords, dart-guns and poison go-thithers, went out to reconnoiter.

Half an hour passed. Varmous, hot, dusty and irritated, returned with his squad. He spoke to Cugel: "Again, where did you think to observe this ambush?"

"As I told you: behind the thicket yonder."

"We combed the area and found neither bandits nor any sign of their presence."

Cugel looked frowningly toward the thicket. "They slipped away when they saw that we were forewarned."

"Leaving no traces? Are you sure of what you saw? Or were you having hallucinations?"

"Naturally I am sure of what I saw!" declared Cugel indignantly. "Do you take me for a fool?"

"Of course not," said Varmous soothingly. "Keep up the good work! Even if your savages were but phantasms, it is better to be safe than sorry. But next time look twice and verify before you cry out the alarm."

Cugel had no choice but to agree, and returned aboard the *Avventura*.

The caravan proceeded, past the now-tranquil thicket and Cugel once again kept an alert look-out.

The night passed without incident, but in the morning, when breakfast was served, Ermaulde failed to make an appearance.

As before Varmous searched the ship and the area enclosed by the guard-fence, but, like Ivanello, Ermaulde had disappeared as if into thin air. Varmous went so far as to knock on the door of Nissifer's cabin, to assure himself that she was still aboard.

"Who is it?" came the husky whisper.

"It is Varmous. Are you well?"

"I am well. I need nothing."

Varmous turned to Cugel, his broad face creased with worry. "I have never known such dreadful events! What is happening?"

Cugel spoke thoughtfully: "Neither Ivanello nor Ermaulde went off by choice: this is clear. They both rode the *Avventura*, which seems to indicate that the bane also resides aboard the ship."

"What! In the 'premier' class?"

"Such are the probabilities."

Varmous clenched his massive fist. "This harm must be learned and nailed to the counter!"

"Agreed! But how?"

"Through vigilance and care! "At night no one must venture from his quarters, except to answer the call of nature."

"To find the evil-doer waiting in the privy? That is not the answer."

"Meanwhile, we cannot delay the caravan," muttered Varmous. "Cugel, to your post! Watch with care and discrimination."

The caravan once again set off to the east. The road skirted close under the hills, which now showed harsh outcrops of rock and occasional growths of gnarled acacia.

Doctor Lalanke sauntered forward and joined Cugel at the bow, and their conversation turned to the strange disappearances. Doctor Lalanke declared himself as mystified as everyone else. "There are endless possibilities, though none carry conviction. For instance, I could suggest that the ship itself is a harmful entity which during the night opens up its hold and ingests a careless passenger."

"We have searched the hold," said Cugel. "We found only stores, baggage and cockroaches."

"I hardly intended that you take the theory seriously. Still, if we contrived ten thousand theories, all apparently absurd, one among them almost certainly would be correct."

The three mimes came up to the bow and amused themselves by strutting back and forth with long loping bent-kneed strides. Cugel looked at them with disfavor. "What nonsense are they up to now?"

The three mimes wrinkled their noses, crossed their eyes and rounded their mouths into pursy circles, as if in soundless chortling, and looked toward Cugel sidelong as they pranced back and forth.

Doctor Lalanke chuckled. "It is their little joke; they think that they are imitating you, or so I believe."

Cugel turned coldly away, and the three mimes ran back down the deck. Doctor Lalanke pointed ahead to a billow of clouds hanging above the horizon. "They rise from Lake Zaol, beside Kaspara Vitatus, where the road turns north to Torqual."

"It is not my road! I journey south to Almery."

"Just so." Doctor Lalanke turned away and Cugel was left alone at his vigil. He looked around for the mimes, half-wishing that they would return and enliven the tedium, but they were engaged in a new and amusing game, tossing small objects down at the farlocks, which, when so struck, whisked high their tails.

Cugel resumed his watch. To the south, the rocky hillside, ever more steep. To the north, the Ildish Waste, an expanse streaked in subtle colors: dark pink, hazy black-gray, maroon, touched here and there with the faintest possible bloom of dark blue and green.

Time passed. The mimes continued their game, which the teamsters and even the passengers also seemed to enjoy; as the mimes tossed down bits of stuff, the teamsters and passengers jumped down to retrieve the objects.

Odd, thought Cugel. Why was every one so enthusiastic over a game so trifling? . . . . One of the objects glinted of metal as it fell. It was, thought Cugel, about the size and shape of a terce. Surely the mimes would not be tossing terces to the teamsters? Where would they have obtained such wealth?

The mimes finished their game. The teamsters called up from below: "More! Continue the game! Why stop now?" The mimes performed a crazy gesticulation and tossed down an empty pouch, then went off to rest.

Peculiar! thought Cugel. The pouch in some respects resembled his own, which of course was safely tucked away in his tent. He glanced down casually, then looked once again more sharply.

The pouch was nowhere to be seen.

Cugel ran raging to Doctor Lalanke, where he sat on the hold conversing with Clissum. Cugel cried out: "Your wards made off with my pouch! They threw my terces down to the teamsters, and my other adjuncts as well, including a valuable pot of boot dressing, and finally the pouch itself!"

Doctor Lalanke raised his black eyebrows. "Indeed? The rascals! I wondered what could hold their attention so long."

"Please take this matter seriously! I hold you personally responsible! You must redress my losses."

Doctor Lalanke smilingly shook his head. "I regret your misfortune, Cugel, but I cannot repair all the wrongs of the world."

"Are they not your wards?"

"In a casual sense only. They are listed on the caravan manifest in their own names, which puts the onus for their acts upon Varmous. You may discuss the matter with him, or even the mimes themselves. If they took the pouch, let them repay the terces."

"These are not practical ideas!"

"Here is one which is most practical: return forward before we plunge headlong into danger!" Doctor Lalanke turned away and resumed his conversation with Clissum.

Cugel returned to the bow. He stared ahead, across the dismal landscape, considering how best to recover his losses. . . . A sinister flurry of movement caught his eye. Cugel jerked forward and focussed his gaze on the hillside, where a number of squat gray beings worked to pile heavy boulders where the hillside beetled over the road.

Cugel looked with care for several seconds. The creatures were plain in his vision: distorted half-human amloids with peaking scalps and neckless heads, so that their mouths opened directly into their upper torsos.

Cugel made a final inspection and at last called down the alarm: "Varmous! Rock-goblins on the hillside! Grave danger! Halt the caravan and sound the horn!"

Varmous pulled up his carriage and returned the hail. "What do you see? Where is the danger?"

Cugel waved his arms and pointed. "On that high bluff I see mountain goblins! They are piling rocks to tumble down upon the caravan!"

Varmous craned his neck and looked where Cugel had pointed. "I can see nothing."

"They are gray, like the rocks! They sidle askew and run crouching this way and that!"

Varmous rose in his seat and gave emergency signals to his teamsters. He pulled the ship down to the road. "We will give them a great surprise," he told Cugel, and called to the passengers. "Alight, if you please! I intend to attack the goblins from the air."

Varmous brought ten men armed with arrow-guns and fire-darts aboard the *Avventura*. He tied the mooring-line to a strong farlock. "Now, Cugel, let the rope extend so that we rise above the bluff and we will send down our compliments from above."

Cugel obeyed the order; the ship with its complement of armed men rose high into the air and drifted over the bluff.

Varmous stood in the bow. "Now: to the exact site of the ambush."

Cugel pointed. "Precisely there, in that tumble of rocks!"

Varmous inspected the hillside. "At the moment I see no goblins."

Cugel scanned the bluff with care, but the goblins had disappeared. "All to the good! They saw our preparations and abandoned their plans."

Varmous gave a surly grunt. "Are you certain of your facts? You are sure that you saw rock goblins?"

"Of course! I am not given to hysterics."

"Perhaps you were deceived by shadows among the rocks."

"Absolutely not! I saw them as clearly as I see you!"

Varmous looked at Cugel with thoughtful blue eyes. "Do not feel that I am chiding you. You apprehended danger and, quite properly, cried out the alarm, though apparently in error. I will not belabor the matter, except to point out that this lack of judiciousness wastes valuable time."

Cugel could find no answer to the imputations. Varmous went to the gunwhale and called down to the driver of the lead carriage. "Bring the caravan forward and past the bluff! We will mount guard to ensure absolute security."

The caravan moved past the bluff without untoward circumstance, whereupon the *Avventura* was lowered so that the 'premier' passengers might re-embark.

Varmous took Cugel aside. "Your work is beyond reproach; still, I have decided to augment the watch. Shilko, whom you see yonder, is a man of seasoned judgment. He will stand by your side, and each will validate the findings of the other. Shilko, step over here, if you please. You and Cugel must now work in tandem."

"That will be my pleasure," said Shilko, a round-faced stocky man with sand-colored hair and a fringe of curling whiskers. "I look forward to the association."

Cugel glumly took him aboard the ship, and, as the caravan moved ahead, the two went forward to the bow and took up their posts. Shilko, a man of affable volubility, spoke of everything imaginable in definitive detail. Cugel's responses were curt, which puzzled Shilko. In an aggrieved voice he explained: "When I am engaged in this kind of work, I like a bit of conversation to while away the time. Otherwise it is a bore to stand here looking out at nothing in particular. After awhile, one begins to observe mental figments and regard them as reality." He winked and grinned. "Eh, Cugel?"

Cugel thought Shilko's joke in poor taste and looked away.

"Ah well," said Shilko. "So goes the world."

At noon, Shilko went off to the mess-hall to take his lunch. He over-indulged himself both in food and wine, so that during the afternoon he became drowsy. He surveyed the landscape and told Cugel: "There is nothing out there but a lizard or two: this is my considered judgement, and now I propose to take a short nap. If you see anything, be sure to arouse me." He crawled into Cugel's tent and made himself comfortable, and Cugel was left to think bitter thoughts of his lost terces and discarded boot-dressing.

When the caravan halted for the night, Cugel went directly to Varmous. He cited the frivolous conduct of the mimes and complained of the losses he had suffered.

Varmous listened with a mild but somewhat detached interest. "Surely Doctor Lalanke intends a settlement?"

"This is the point at issue! He disclaims responsibility in part and in sum! He declares that you, as master of the caravan, must discharge all damages."

Varmous, whose attention had been wandering, became instantly alert. "He called on me to pay the losses?"

"Exactly so. I now present to you this bill of accounting."

Varmous folded his arms and took a quick step backward. "Doctor Lalanke's thinking is inept."

Cugel indignantly shook the accounting under Varmous' nose. "Are you telling me that you refuse to settle this obligation?"

"It has nothing to do with me! The deed occurred aboard your vessel the *Avventura*."

Cugel again thrust the bill upon Varmous. "Then at least you must serve this accounting upon Doctor Lalanke and levy the payment."

Varmous pulled at his chin. "That is not the correct procedure. You are master of the *Avventura*. Hence, in your official capacity, you must summon Doctor Lalanke to a hearing and there levy whatever charges you think proper."

Cugel looked dubiously toward Doctor Lalanke, where he stood in conversation with Clissum. "I suggest that we approach Doctor Lalanke together, and join our mutual authorities the better to compel justice."

Varmous backed away another step. "Do not involve me! I am only Varmous the wagoneer, who rolls innocently along the ground."

Cugel proposed further arguments, but Varmous put on a face of crafty obstinacy and would not be moved. Cugel finally went to a table where he drank wine and stared glumly into the fire.

The evening passed slowly. A somber mood oppressed the entire camp; tonight there were neither recitations, songs nor jokes, and the company sat around the fire, conversing in desultory undertones. An unspoken question occupied all minds: "Who will be the next to disappear?"

The fire burned low, and the company reluctantly went off to their beds, with many a glance over their shoulders and an exchange of nervous comments.

So the night passed. The star Achernar moved up the eastern quadrant and declined into the west. The farlocks grunted and snuffled as they slept. Far out on the waste a blue light flickered into existence for a few seconds, then died and was seen no more. The rim of the east flushed first purple, then the red of dark blood. After several vain attempts, the sun broke free of the horizon and floated into the sky.

With the rebuilding of the fire the caravan came to life. Breakfast was set out; farlocks were brought to their traces and preparations were made for departure.

Aboard the *Avventura* the passengers made their appearance. Each in turn looked from face to face as if half-expecting another disappearance. Porraig the steward served breakfast to all hands, and carried a tray to the aft cabin. He knocked. "Madame Nissifer, I have brought your breakfast. We are worried as to your health."

"I am well," came the whisper. "I wish nothing. You may go away."

After breakfast Cugel took Doctor Lalanke aside. "I have taken counsel with Varmous," said Cugel. "He assures me that, as master of the *Avventura*, I may make a demand on you for damages suffered as a result of your negligence. Here is the bill of account. You must pay over this sum at once."

Doctor Lalanke gave the bill a brief inspection. His black eyebrows peaked even higher than ever. "This item: amazing! 'Boot dressing, one pot. Value: one thousand terces.' Are you serious?"

"Naturally! The boot dressing contained a rare wax."

Doctor Lalanke returned the bill. "You must present this bill to the persons at fault: namely, Sush, Skasja and Rlys."

"What good will that do?"

Doctor Lalanke shrugged. "I could not hazard a guess. Still, I disassociate myself from the entire affair." He bowed and strolled off to join Clissum, in whom he found qualities compatible with his own.

Cugel went forward to the bow, where Shilko was already on duty. Shilko again showed a voluble tendency; Cugel, as before, replied in terse terms, and Shilko at last fell silent. The caravan meanwhile had moved into a region where hills rose to either side, with the road following the course of the valley between.

Shilko looked along the barren hillsides. "I see nothing in these parts to worry us. What of you, Cugel?"

"At the moment, I see nothing."

Shilko took a last look around the landscape. "Excuse me a moment; I have a message for Porraig." He departed and soon, from the galley, Cugel heard sounds of conviviality.

Somewhat later, Shilko returned, lurching to the wine he had consumed. He called out in a hearty voice: "Ahoy there, Captain Cugel! How go the hallucinations?"

"I do not understand your allusion," said Cugel frigidly.

"No matter! Such things can happen to anyone." Shilko scanned the hillsides. "Have you anything to report?"

"Nothing."

"Very good! That's the way to handle this job! A quick look here and a sharp glance there, then down to the galley for a taste of wine."

Cugel made no comment and Shilko, from boredom, took to cracking his knuckles.

At the noon meal Shilko again consumed more than was perhaps advisable, and during the afternoon became drowsy. "I will just catch forty winks to calm my nerves," he told Cugel. "Keep a close watch on the lizards and call me if anything more important appears." He crawled into Cugel's tent and presently began to snore.

Cugel leaned on the gunwale, formulating schemes to repair his fortunes. None seemed feasible, especially since Doctor Lalanke knew a few spells of elementary magic. . . . Peculiar, those dark shapes along the ridge! What could cause them to jerk and jump in such a fashion? As if tall black shadows were thrusting quickly high to peer down at the caravan, then dodging back down out of sight.

Cugel reached down and pulled at Shilko's leg. "Rouse yourself!"

Shilko emerged from the tent blinking and scratching his head. "What now? Has Porraig brought my afternoon wine?"

Cugel indicated the ridge. "What do you see?"

Shilko looked with red-rimmed eyes along the sky-line, but the shadows were now crouched behind the hills. He turned a quizzical gaze upon Cugel. "What do you perceive? Goblins disguised as pink rats? Or centipedes dancing the kazatska?"

"Neither," said Cugel shortly. "I saw what I believe be a band of wind-stick devils. They are now in hiding on the far side of the hill."

Shilko peered cautiously at Cugel and moved a step away. "Most interesting! How many did you see?"

"I could make no count, but we had best call out the alarm to Varmous."

Shilko looked again along the sky-line. "I see nothing. Might your nerves once more be playing you tricks?"

"Absolutely not!"

"Well, please make certain before you call me again." Shilko dropped to his hands and knees and crawled into the tent. Cugel looked down to Varmous, riding placidly on the lead carriage. He opened his mouth to call down the alarm, then gloomily thought better of it and resumed his vigil.

Minutes passed, and Cugel himself began to doubt the sightings.

The road passed beside a long narrow pond of alkali-green water which nourished several thickets of bristling salt-bush. Cugel leaned forward and focused his gaze upon the bushes, but their spindly stalks provided no cover. What of the lake itself? It seemed too shallow to hide any consequential danger.

Cugel straightened himself with a sense of work well done. He glanced up to the ridge, to discover that the wind-stick devils had reappeared in greater number than before, craning high to peer down at the caravan, then ducking quickly from view.

Cugel pulled at Shilko's leg. "The wind-stick devils have returned in force!"

Shilko backed from the tent and heaved himself erect. "What is it this time?"

Cugel indicated the ridge. "Look for yourself!"

The wind-stick devils, however, had completed their survey, and Shilko saw nothing. This time he merely shrugged wearily and prepared to resume his rest. Cugel however went to the gunwale and shouted down to Varmous: "Wind-stick devils, by the dozen! They gather on the other side of the ridge!"

Varmous halted his carriage. "Wind-stick devils? Where is Shilko?"

"I am here, naturally, keeping a keen look-out."

"What of these 'wind-stick devils'? Have you noticed them?"

"In all candour, and with due respect to Cugel, I must say that I have not seen them."

Varmous chose his words carefully. "Cugel, I am obliged to you for your alert warning, but this time I think that we will go forward. Shilko, continue the good work!"

The caravan proceeded along the road. Shilko yawned and prepared to resume his rest. "Wait!" cried Cugel in frustration. "Notice that gap in the hills yonder? If the devils choose to follow us, they must jump across the gap, and you will be sure to see them."

Shilko grudgingly resigned himself to the wait. "These fancies, Cugel, are a most unhealthy sign. Consider to what sorry extremes they may lead! For your own sake you must curb the affliction. . . . Now: there is the gap! We are coming abreast. Look with great attention and tell me when you see devils jumping across."

The caravan drew abreast of the gap. In a flurry of great smoky shapes, the wind-stick devils leapt over the hill and down upon the caravan.

"Now!" said Cugel.

For a frozen instant Shilko stood with a trembling jaw, then he bawled down to Varmous: "Beware! Wind-stick devils are on the attack!"

Varmous failed to hear properly and looked up toward the boat. He discovered a blur of hurtling dark shapes, but now defense was impossible. The devils tramped back and forth among the wagons while teamsters and passengers fled into the chilly waters of the pond.

The devils wreaked all convenient damage upon the caravan, overturning wagons and carriages, kicking off wheels, scattering stores and baggage. Next, they turned their attention to the *Avventura*, but Cugel caused the rope to lengthen and the vessel floated high. The devils jumped up and clawed at the hull, but fell short by fifty feet. Giving up the attack, they seized all the farlocks, tucking them one under each arm, then jumped over the hill and were gone.

Cugel lowered the boat, while teamsters and passengers emerged from the pond. Varmous had been trapped under his overturned carriage and all hands were required to extricate him.

With difficulty Varmous raised himself to stand upon his bruised legs. He surveyed the damage and gave a despondent groan. "This is beyond understanding! Why are we so cursed?" He looked around the bedraggled company. "Where are the look-outs? . . . .Cugel? Shilko? Be good enough to stand forward!"

Cugel and Shilko diffidently showed themselves. Shilko licked his lips and spoke earnestly: "I called out the alarm; all can testify to this! Otherwise the disaster might have been far worse!"

"You were dilatory; the devils were already upon us! What is your explanation?"

Shilko looked all around the sky. "It may sound strange but Cugel wanted to wait until the devils jumped across the gap."

Varmous turned to Cugel. "I am absolutely bewildered! Why would you not warn us of the danger?"

"I did so, if you will recall! When I first saw the devils, I considered calling the alarm, but —"

"This is most confusing," said Varmous. "You saw the devils previous to the occasion of your warning?"

"Certainly, but —"

Varmous, grimacing in pain, held up his hand. "I have heard enough. Cugel, your conduct has been unwise, to say the very least."

"That is not a sound judgment!" cried Cugel hotly.

Varmous made a weary gesture. "Is it not immaterial? The caravan is destroyed! We are left helpless out on the Ildish Waste! In another month the wind will blow sand over our bones."

Cugel looked down to his boots. They were scuffed and dull, but magic might still reside in them. He pitched his voice in tones of dignity. "The caravan can still proceed, through the courtesy of the excoriated and savagely denounced Cugel."

Varmous spoke sharply: "Please convey your exact meaning!"

"It is possible that magic still remains in my boots. Make ready your wagons and carriages. I will raise them into the air and we will continue as before."

Varmous at once became energetic. He instructed his teamsters, who brought as much order as possible to their wagons and carriages. Ropes were tied to each and the passengers took their places. Cugel, walking from vehicle to vehicle, kicked to apply that levitational force still clinging to his boots. The wagons and carriages drifted into the air; the teamsters took the ropes and waited for the signal. Varmous, whose bruised muscles and sprained joints prevented him from walking, elected to ride aboard the *Avventura*. Cugel started to follow, but Varmous stopped him.

"We need only a single look-out, a man of proved judgment, who will be Shilko. If I were not crippled, I would gladly tow the ship, but that duty must now devolve upon you. Take up the rope, Cugel, and lead the caravan along the road at your best speed."

Recognizing the futility of protest, Cugel seized the rope and marched off down the road, towing the *Avventura* behind him.

At sunset, the wagons and carriages were brought down and camp was made for the night. Slavoy, the chief teamster, under the supervision of Varmous, set out the guard-fence; a fire was built and wine was served to defeat the gloom of the company.

Varmous made a terse address. "We have suffered a serious set-back and much damage has been done. Still, it serves no purpose to point the finger of blame. I have made calculations and taken advice from Doctor Lalanke, and I believe that four days of travel will bring us to Kaspara Vitatus, where repairs can be made. Until then, I hope that no one suffers undue inconvenience. A final remark! The events of today are now in the past, but two mysteries still oppress us: the disappearances of Ivanello and Ermaulde. Until these matters are clarified, all must be careful! Wander nowhere alone! At any suspicious circumstance, be sure to notify me."

The evening meal was served and a mood of almost frenetic gaiety overcame the company. Sush, Skasja and Rlys performed a set of bounding, hopping exercises and presently it became clear that they were mimicking the wind-stick devils.

Clissum became elevated by wine. "Is it not wonderful?" he cried out. "This excellent vintage has stimulated all three segments of my mind, so that while one observes this fire and the Ildish Waste beyond, another composes exquisitely beautiful odes, while the third weaves festoons of imaginary flowers to cover the nudity of passing nymphs, also imaginary!"

The ecclesiarch Gaulph Rabi listened to Clissum with disapproval and put four drops of aspergantium, rather than the customary three, into his own wine. "Is it necessary to go to such inordinate extremes?"

Clissum raised a wavering finger. "For the freshest flowers and the most supple nymphs, the answer is: emphatically yes!"

Gaulph Rabi spoke severely: "At the Collegium we feel that contemplation of even a few infinities is stimulation enough, at least for persons of taste and culture." He turned away to continue a conversation with Perruquil. Clissum mischievously sprinkled the back of Gaulph Rabi's gown with a pervasively odorous sachet, which caused the the austere ecclesiarch great perplexity to the end of the evening.

With the dying of the embers, the mood of the company again became subdued, and only reluctantly did they go off to their beds.

Aboard the *Avventura* Varmous and Shilko now occupied the berths which had been those of Ivanello and Ermaulde, while Cugel kept to his tent on the bow.

The night was quiet. Cugel, for all his fatigue, was unable to sleep. Midnight was marked by a muffled chime of the ship's clock.

Cugel dozed. An unknown period of time went by.

A small sound aroused Cugel to full alertness. For a moment he lay staring up into the dark; then, groping for his sword, he crawled to the opening of the tent.

The mast-head light cast a pale illumination along the deck. Cugel saw nothing unusual. No sound could be heard. What had aroused him?

For ten minutes Cugel crouched by the opening, then slowly returned to his cushion.

Cugel lay awake. . . . The faintest of sounds reached his ears:

a click, a creak, a scrape. . . .Cugel again crawled to the opening of his tent.

The mast-head lamp cast as many shadows as puddles of light. One of the shadows moved and sidled out across the deck. It seemed to carry a parcel.

Cugel watched with an eery prickling at the back of his neck. The shadow jerked to the rail and with a most peculiar motion tossed its burden over the side. Cugel groped back into his tent for his sword, then crawled out upon the fore-deck.

He heard a scrape. The shadow had merged with other shadows, and could no longer be seen.

Cugel crouched in the dark and presently thought to hear a faint squealing sound, abruptly stilled.

The sound was not repeated.

After a time Cugel hunched back into the tent, and there kept vigil, cramped and cold. . . . With eyes open, he slept. A maroon beam from the rising sun glinted into his open eyes, startling him into full awareness.

With groans for twinges and aches, Cugel hauled himself erect. He donned his cloak and hat, buckled the sword around his waist and limped down to the main deck.

Varmous was only just emerging from his berth when Cugel peered in through the doorway. "What do you want?" growled Varmous. "Am I not even allowed time to adjust my garments?"

Cugel said: "Last night I saw sights and I heard sounds. I fear that we may discover another disappearance."

Varmous uttered a groan and a curse. "Who?"

"I do not know."

Varmous pulled on his boots. "What did you see and what did you hear?"

"I saw a shadow. It threw a parcel into the thicket. I heard a clicking sound, and then the scrape of a door. Later I heard a cry."

Varmous donned his rough cape, then pulled the flat broad-brimmed hat down over his golden curls. He limped out on deck. "I suppose that first of all we should count noses."

"All in good time," said Cugel. "First let us look into the parcel, which may tell us much or nothing."

"As you wish." The two descended to the ground. "Now then: where is the thicket?"

"Over here, behind the hull. If I had not been witness, we would never have known."

They circled the ship and Cugel clambered into the black fronds of the thicket. Almost at once he discovered the parcel and gingerly pulled it out into the open. The two stood looking down at the object, which was wrapped in soft blue fabric. Cugel touched it with his toe. "Do you recognize the stuff?"

"Yes. It is the cloak favored by Perruquil."

They looked down at the parcel in silence. Cugel said: "We now can guess the identity of the missing person."

Varmous grunted. "Open the parcel."

"You may do so if you like," said Cugel.

"Come now, Cugel!" protested Varmous. "You know that my legs cause me pain when I stoop!"

Cugel grimaced. Crouching, he twitched at the binding. The folds of the cloak fell back, to reveal two bundles of human bones, cleverly interlocked to occupy a minimum volume. "Amazing!" whispered Varmous. "Here is either magic or sheer paradox! How else can skull and pelvis be interlocked in such intricate fashion?"

Cugel was somewhat more critical. "The arrangement is not altogether elegant. Notice: Ivanello's skull is nested into Ermaulde's pelvis; similarly with Ermaulde's skull and Ivanello's pelvis. Ivanello especially would be annoyed by the carelessness."

Varmous muttered: "Now we know the worst. We must take action."

With one accord the two looked up to the hull of the ship. At the port-hole giving into the aft cabin there was movement as the hanging was drawn aside, and for an instant a luminous eye looked down at them. Then the curtain dropped and all was as before.

Varmous and Cugel returned around the ship. Varmous spoke in a heavy voice. "You, as master of the *Avventura*, will wish to lead the decisive action. I will of course cooperate in every respect."

Cugel pondered. "First we must remove the passengers from

the ship. Then you must bring up a squad of armed men and lead them to the door, where you will issue an ultimatum. I will stand steadfast nearby, and —"

Varmous held up his hand. "By reason of sore legs I cannot issue such an ultimatum."

"Well then, what do you suggest?"

Varmous considered a moment or two, then proposed a plan which required, in essence, that Cugel, using the full authority of his rank, should advance upon the door and, if need be, force an entrance — a plan which Cugel rejected for technical reasons.

At last the two formulated a program which both considered feasible. Cugel went to order the ship's passengers to the ground. As he had expected, Perruquil was not among their number.

Varmous assembled and instructed his crew. Shilko, armed with a sword, was posted as guard before the door, while Cugel mounted to the after-deck. A pair of trained carpenters climbed upon tables and boarded over the portholes, while others nailed planks across the door, barring egress.

From the lake buckets of water were transferred along a human chain and passed up to the afterdeck, where the water was poured into the cabin through a vent.

From within the cabin an angry silence prevailed. Then presently, as water continued to pour in through the vent, a soft hissing and clicking began to be heard, and then a furious whisper: "I declare a nuisance! Let the water abate!"

Shilko, before mounting guard, had stepped into the galley for a few swallows of wine to warm his blood. Posturing and waving his sword before the door, he cried out: "Black hag, your time has come! You shall drown like a rat in a sack!"

For a period the sounds within were stilled, and nothing could be heard but the splash of water into water. Then once again: a hissing and clicking, at an ominous pitch, and a set of rasping vocables.

Shilko, emboldened both by wine and the planks across the door, called out: "Odorous witch! Drown more quietly, or I, Shilko, will cut out both your tongues!" He flourished his sword and cut a caper, and all the while the buckets were busy.

From within the cabin something pressed at the door, but

the planks held secure. Again from within came a heavy thrust; the planks groaned and water spurted through cracks. Then a third impact, and the planks burst apart. Foul-smelling water washed out upon the deck; behind came Nissifer. Clothed in neither gown, hat nor veil, she stood revealed as a burly black creature of hybrid character, half sime and half bazil, with a bristle of black fur between the eyes. From a rusty black thorax depended the segmented abdomen of a wasp; down the back hung sheaths of black chitin-like wing-cases. Four thin black arms ended in long thin human hands; thin shanks of black chitin and peculiar padded feet supported the thorax with the abdomen hanging between.

The creature took a step forward. Shilko emitted a strangled yell and, stumbling backwards, fell to the deck. The creature jumped forward to stand on his arms, then, squatting, drove its sting into his chest. Shilko uttered a shrill cry, rolled clear, turned several frantic somersaults, fell to the ground, bounded blindly to the lake and thrashed here and there in the water, and at last became still. Almost at once the corpse began to bloat.

Aboard the *Avventura*, the creature named Nissifer turned and started to re-enter the cabin, as if satisfied that it had rebuffed its enemies. Cugel, on the afterdeck, slashed down with his sword and the blade, trailing a thousand sparkling motes, cut through Nissifer's left eye and into the thorax. Nissifer whistled in pain and surprise, and stood back the better to identify its assailant. It croaked: "Ah Cugel! You have hurt me; you shall die by a stench."

With a great pounding flutter of wing-cases, Nissifer sprang up to the afterdeck. In a panic Cugel retreated behind the binnacle. Nissifer advanced, the segmented abdomen squirming up and forward between the thin black legs, revealing the long yellow sting.

Cugel picked up one of the empty buckets and flung it into Nissifer's face; then, while Nissifer fought away the bucket, Cugel jumped forward and with a great sweep, cut the vincus, so as to separate abdomen from thorax.

The abdomen, falling to the deck, writhed and worked and presently rolled down the companion-way to the deck.

Nissifer ignored the mutilation and came forward, dripping

a thick yellow liquid from its vincus. It lurched toward the binnacle and thrust out its long black arms. Cugel backed away, hacking at the arms. Nissifer shrieked and lunging forward, swept the sword from Cugel's grasp.

Nissifer stepped forward with clicking wing-cases, and seizing Cugel, drew him close. "Now, Cugel, you will learn the meaning of fetor."

Cugel bent his head and thrust 'Spatterlight' against Nissifer's thorax.

When Varmous, sword in hand, climbed the companionway, he found Cugel leaning limp-legged against the taff-rail.

Varmous looked around the afterdeck. "Where is Nissifer?"

"Nissifer is gone."

Four days later the caravan came down from the hills to the shores of Lake Zaol. Across the glimmering water eight white towers half-hidden in pink haze marked the site of Kaspara Vitatus, sometimes known as 'The City of Monuments.'

The caravan circled the lake and approached the city by the Avenue of the Dynasties. After passing under a hundred or more of the famous monuments, the caravan arrived at the center of town. Varmous led the way to his usual resort, the Kanbaw Inn, and the weary travelers prepared to refresh themselves.

While ordering the cabin occupied by Nissifer, Cugel had come upon a leather sack containing over a hundred terces, which he took into his private possession. Varmous, however, insisted upon helping Cugel explore the effects of Ivanello, Ermaulde, and Perruquil. They discovered another three hundred terces which they shared in equal parts. Varmous took possession of Ivanello's wardrobe, while Cugel was allowed to keep the milk-opal ear-bangle, which he had coveted from the first.

Cugel also offered Varmous full title to the *Avventura* for five hundred terces. "The price is an absolute bargain! Where else will you find a sound vessel, fully outfitted and well-found, for such a price?"

Varmous only chuckled. "If you offered to provide me a goiter of superlative size for ten terces, would I buy, bargain or not?"

"We have here a distinctly different proposition," Cugel pointed out.

"Bah! The magic is failing. Every day the ship sags more heavily to the ground. In the middle of the wilderness what good is a ship which will neither float in the air nor sail in the sand? In a foolhardy spirit, I will offer you a hundred terces, no more."

"Absurd!" scoffed Cugel, and there the matter rested.

Varmous went out to see to the repair of his wagons and discovered a pair of lake fishermen inspecting the *Avventura* with interest. In due course Varmous succeeded in obtaining a firm offer for the vessel, to the amount of six hundred and twenty-five terces.

Cugel, meanwhile, drank beer at the Kanbaw Inn. As he sat musing, into the common room strode a band of seven men with harsh features and rough voices. Cugel looked twice at the leader, then a third time, and finally recognized Captain Wiskich, one-time owner of the *Avventura*. Captain Wiskich evidently had picked up the trail of the vessel and had come in hot pursuit to recover his property.

Cugel quietly departed the common room and went in search of Varmous, who, as it happened, was also on the look-out for Cugel. They met in front of the inn. Varmous wanted to drink beer in the common room, but Cugel led him across the avenue to a bench from which they could watch the sun set into Lake Zaol.

Presently the *Avventura* was mentioned and with surprising ease agreement was reached. Varmous paid over two hundred and fifty terces for full title to the vessel.

The two parted on the best of terms. Varmous went off to locate the fishermen, while Cugel, disguising himself in a hooded cloak and a false beard, took lodging at the Green Star Inn, using the identity Tichenor, a purveyor of antique grave-markers.

During the evening a great tumult was heard, first from the neighborhood of the docks and then at the Kanbaw Inn, and persons coming into the Green Star common room identified the rioters as a group of local fishermen in conflict with a band of newly arrived travelers, with the eventual involvement of Varmous and his teamsters.

Order was restored at last. Not long after, two men looked into the Green Star common room. One called out in a rough voice: "Is there anyone here named Cugel?"

The other spoke with more restraint: "Cugel is urgently needed. If he is here, let him step forward."

When no one responded the two men departed and Cugel retired to his room.

In the morning Cugel went to a nearby hostlery where he purchased a steed for his journey south. The ostler's boy then conducted him to a shop where Cugel bought a new pouch, a pair of saddle-bags into which he packed necessities for his journey. His hat had become shabby and also carried a stench where it had pressed against Nissifer. Cugel removed 'Spatter-light', wrapped it in heavy cloth and tucked it into his new pouch. He bought a short-billed cap of dark green velvet, which, while far from ostentatious, pleased Cugel with its air of restrained elegance.

Cugel paid his account from the terces in the leather sack from Nissifer's cabin; it also exhaled a stench. Cugel started to buy a new sack but was dissuaded by the ostler's boy. "Why waste your terces? I have a sack much like this one which you may have free of charge."

"That is generous of you," said Cugel, and the two returned to the hostlery, where Cugel transferred his terces into the new sack.

The steed was brought forth. Cugel mounted and the boy adjusted the saddle-bags in place. At this moment two men of harsh appearance entered the hostlery, and approached with quick strides. "Is your name Cugel?"

"Definitely not!" declared Cugel. "By no means! I am Tichenor! What do you want with this Cugel?"

"None of your affair. Come along with us; you have an un-convincing manner."

"I have no time for pranks," said Cugel. "Boy, you may hand me up my leather sack." The boy obeyed and Cugel sec-ured the sack to his saddle. He started to ride away but the men interfered. "You must come with us."

"Impossible," said Cugel. "I am on my way to Torqual." He kicked one in the nose and the other in the belly and rode at speed down the Avenue of the Dynasties and so departed Kaspara Vitatus.

After a period he halted, to learn what pursuit, if any, had been offered.

An unpleasant odor reached his nostrils, emanating from the leather sack. To his perplexity, it proved to be the same sack he had taken from Nissifer's cabin.

Cugel anxiously looked within, to find, not terces, but small objects of corroded metal.

Cugel uttered a groan of dismay and, turning his steed, started to return to Kaspara Vitatus, but now he noticed a dozen men crouched low in their saddles coming after him in hot pursuit.

Cugel uttered another wild cry of fury and frustration. He cast the leather sack into the ditch and turning his steed once more rode south at full speed.

CHAPTER
V

FROM
KASPARA VITATUS
TO
CUIRNIF

1
THE
SEVENTEEN
VIRGINS

THE CHASE went far and long, and led into that dismal tract of bone-colored hills known as the Pale Rugates. Cugel finally used a clever trick to baffle pursuit, sliding from his steed and hiding among the rocks while his enemies pounded past in chase of the riderless mount.

Cugel lay in hiding until the angry band returned toward Kaspara Vitatus, bickering among themselves. He emerged into the open; then, after shaking his fist and shouting curses after the now distant figures, he turned and continued south through the Pale Rugates.

The region was as stark and grim as the surface of a dead sun, and thus avoided by such creatures as sindics, shambs, erbs and visps, for Cugel a single and melancholy source of satisfaction.

Step after step marched Cugel, one leg in front of the other: up slope to overlook an endless succession of barren swells, down again into the hollow where at rare intervals a seep of water nourished a sickly vegetation. Here Cugel found ramp, burdock, squallix and an occasional newt, which sufficed against starvation.

Day followed day. The sun rising cool and dim swam up into the dark-blue sky, from time to time seeming to flicker with a film of blue-black luster, finally to settle like an enormous purple pearl into the west. When dark made further progress impractical, Cugel wrapped himself in his cloak and slept as best he could.

On the afternoon of the seventh day Cugel limped down a slope into an ancient orchard. Cugel found and devoured a few withered hag-apples, then set off along the trace of an old road.

The track proceeded a mile, to lead out upon a bluff overlooking a broad plain. Directly below a river skirted a small town, curved away to the southwest and finally disappeared into the haze.

Cugel surveyed the landscape with keen attention. Out upon the plain he saw carefully tended garden plots, each precisely square and of identical size; along the river drifted a fisherman's punt. A placid scene, thought Cugel. On the other hand, the town was built to a strange and archaic architecture, and the scrupulous precision with which the houses surrounded the square suggested a like inflexibility in the inhabitants. The houses themselves were no less uniform, each a construction of two, or three, or even four squat bulbs of diminishing size, one on the other, the lowest always painted blue, the second dark red, the third and fourth respectively a dull mustard ocher and black; and each house terminated in a spire of fancifully twisted iron rods, of greater or lesser height. An inn on the riverbank showed a style somewhat looser and easier, with a pleasant garden surrounding. Along the river road to the east Cugel now noticed the approach of a caravan of six high-wheeled wagons, and his uncertainty dissolved; the town was evidently tolerant of strangers, and Cugel confidently set off down the hill.

At the outskirts to town he halted and drew forth his old purse, which he yet retained though it hung loose and limp. Cugel examined the contents: five terces, a sum hardly adequate to his needs. Cugel reflected a moment, then collected a handful of pebbles which he dropped into the purse, to create a reassuring rotundity. He dusted his breeches, adjusted his green hunter's cap, and proceeded.

He entered the town without challenge or even attention. Crossing the square, he halted to inspect a contrivance even more peculiar than the quaint architecture: a stone fire-pit in which several logs blazed high, rimmed by five lamps on iron stands, each with five wicks, and above an intricate linkage of mirrors and lenses, the purpose of which surpassed Cugel's comprehension. Two young men tended the device with diligence, trimming the twenty-five wicks, prodding the fire, adjusting screws and levers which in turn controlled the mirrors and lenses. They wore what appeared to be the local costume: voluminous blue knee-length breeches, red shirts, brass-

buttoned black vests and broad-brimmed hats; after disinterested glances they paid Cugel no heed, and he continued to
the inn.

In the adjacent garden two dozen folk of the town sat at tables, eating and drinking with great gusto. Cugel watched them
a moment or two; their punctilio and elegant gestures
suggested the manners of an age far past. Like their houses,
they were a sort unique to Cugel's experience, pale and thin,
with egg-shaped heads, long noses, dark expressive eyes and
ears cropped in various styles. The men were uniformly bald
and their pates glistened in the red sunlight. The women parted
their black hair in the middle, then cut it abruptly short a half-
inch above the ears: a style which Cugel considered unbecom-
ing. Watching the folk eat and drink, Cugel was unfavorably
reminded of the fare which had sustained him across the Pale
Rugates, and he gave no further thought to his terces. He strode
into the garden and seated himself at a table. A portly man in a
blue apron approached, frowning somewhat at Cugel's dis-
heveled appearance. Cugel immediately brought forth two
terces which he handed to the man. "This is for yourself, my
good fellow, to insure expeditious service. I have just completed
an arduous journey; I am famished with hunger. You may
bring me a platter identical to that which the gentleman yonder
is enjoying, together with a selection of side-dishes and a bottle
of wine. Then be so good as to ask the innkeeper to prepare me
a comfortable chamber." Cugel carelessly brought forth his
purse and dropped it upon the table where its weight produced
an impressive implication. "I will also require a bath, fresh linen
and a barber."

"I myself am Maier the innkeeper," said the portly man in a
gracious voice. "I will see to your wishes immediately."

"Excellent," said Cugel. "I am favorably impressed with your
establishment, and perhaps will remain several days."

The innkeeper bowed in gratification and hurried off to
supervise the preparation of Cugel's dinner.

Cugel made an excellent meal, though the second course, a
dish of crayfish stuffed with mince and slivers of scarlet man-
goneel, he found a trifle too rich. The roast fowl however could

not be faulted and the wine pleased Cugel to such an extent that he ordered a second flask. Maier the innkeeper served the bottle himself and accepted Cugel's compliments with a trace of complacency. "There is no better wine in Gundar! It is admittedly expensive, but you are a person who appreciates the best."

"Precisely true," said Cugel. "Sit down and take a glass with me. I confess to curiosity in regard to this remarkable town."

The innkeeper willingly followed Cugel's suggestion. "I am puzzled that you find Gundar remarkable. I have lived here all my life and it seems ordinary enough to me."

"I will cite three circumstances which I consider worthy of note," said Cugel, now somewhat expansive by reason of the wine. "First: the bulbous construction of your buildings. Secondly: the contrivance of lenses above the fire, which at the very least must stimulate a stranger's interest. Thirdly: the fact that the men of Gundar are all stark bald."

The innkeeper nodded thoughtfully. "The architecture at least is quickly explained. The ancient Gunds lived in enormous gourds. When a section of the wall became weak it was replaced with a board, until in due course the folk found themselves living in houses fashioned completely of wood, and the style has persisted. As for the fire and the projectors, do you not know the world-wide Order of Solar Emosynaries? We stimulate the vitality of the sun; so long as our beam of sympathetic vibration regulates solar combustion, it will never expire. Similar stations exist at other locations: at Blue Azor; on the Isle of Brazel; at the walled city Munt; and in the observatory of the Grand Starkeeper at Vir Vassilis."

Cugel shook his head sadly. "I hear that conditions have changed. Brazel has long since sunk beneath the waves. Munt was destroyed a thousand years ago by Dystropes. I have never heard of either Blue Azor or Vir Vassilis, though I am widely traveled. Possibly, here at Gundar, you are the solitary Solar Emosynaries yet in existence."

"This is dismal news," declared Maier. "The noticeable enfeeblement of the sun is hereby explained. Perhaps we had best double the fire under our regulator."

Cugel poured more wine. "A question leaps to mind. If, as I suspect, this is the single Solar Emosynary station yet in operation, who or what regulates the sun when it has passed below the horizon?"

The innkeeper shook his head. "I can offer no explanation. It may be that during the hours of night the sun itself relaxes and, as it were, sleeps, although this is of course sheerest speculation."

"Allow me to offer another hypothesis," said Cugel. "Conceivably the waning of the sun has advanced beyond all possibility of regulation, so that your efforts, though formerly useful, are now ineffective."

Maier threw up his hands in perplexity. "These complications surpass my scope, but yonder stands the Nolde Huruska." He directed Cugel's attention to a large man with a deep chest and bristling black beard, who stood at the entrance. "Excuse me a moment." He rose to his feet and approaching the Nolde spoke for several minutes, indicating Cugel from time to time. The Nolde finally made a brusque gesture and marched across the garden to confront Cugel. He spoke in a heavy voice: "I understand you to assert that no Emosynaries exist other than ourselves?"

"I stated nothing so definitely," said Cugel, somewhat on the defensive. "I remarked that I had traveled widely and that no other such 'Emosynary' agency has come to my attention; and I innocently speculated that possibly none now operate."

"At Gundar we conceive 'innocence' as a positive quality, not merely an insipid absence of guilt," stated the Nolde. "We are not the fools that certain untidy ruffians might suppose."

Cugel suppressed the hot remark which rose to his lips, and contented himself with a shrug. Maier walked away with the Nolde and for several minutes the two men conferred, with frequent glances in Cugel's direction. Then the Nolde departed and the innkeeper returned to Cugel's table. "A somewhat brusque man, the Nolde of Gundar," he told Cugel, "but very competent withal."

"It would be presumptuous of me to comment," said Cugel. "What, precisely, is his function?"

"At Gundar we place great store upon precision and methodicity," explained Maier. "We feel that the absence of order encourages disorder; and the official responsible for the inhibition of caprice and abnormality is the Nolde. . . What was our previous conversation? Ah yes, you mentioned our notorious baldness. I can offer no definite explanation. According to our savants, the condition signifies the final perfection of the human race. Other folk give credence to an ancient legend. A pair of magicians, Astherlin and Mauldred, vied for the favor of the Gunds. Astherlin promised the boon of extreme hairiness, so that the folk of Gundar need never wear garments. Mauldred, to the contrary, offered the Gunds baldness, with all the consequent advantages, and easily won the contest; in fact Mauldred became the first Nolde of Gundar, the post now filled, as you know, by Huruska." Maier the innkeeper pursed his lips and looked off across the garden. "Huruska, a distrustful sort, has reminded me of my fixed rule to ask all transient guests to settle their accounts on a daily basis. I naturally assured him of your complete reliability, but simply in order to appease Huruska, I will tender the reckoning in the morning."

"This is tantamount to an insult," declared Cugel haughtily. "Must we truckle to the whims of Huruska? Not I, you may be assured! I will settle my account in the usual manner."

The innkeeper blinked. "May I ask how long you intend to stay at Gundar?"

"My journey takes me south, by the most expeditious transport available, which I assume to be riverboat."

"The town Lumarth lies ten days by caravan across the Lirrh Aing. The Isk river also flows past Lumarth, but is judged inconvenient by virtue of three intervening localities. The Lallo Marsh is infested with stinging insects; the tree-dwarfs of the Santalba Forest pelt passing boats with refuse; and the Desperate Rapids shatter both bones and boats."

"In this case I will travel by caravan," said Cugel. "Meanwhile I will remain here, unless the persecutions of Huruska become intolerable."

Maier licked his lips and looked over his shoulder. "I assured Huruska that I would adhere to the strict letter of my rule. He will surely make a great issue of the matter unless —"

Cugel made a gracious gesture. "Bring me seals. I will close up my purse which contains a fortune in opals and alumes. We will deposit the purse in the strong-box and you may hold it for surety. Even Huruska cannot now protest!"

Maier held up his hands in awe. "I could not undertake so large a responsibility!"

"Dismiss all fear," said Cugel. "I have protected the purse with a spell; the instant a criminal breaks the seal the jewels are transformed into pebbles."

Maier dubiously accepted Cugel's purse on these terms. They jointly saw the scales applied and the purse deposited into Maier's strong-box.

Cugel now repaired to his chamber, where he bathed, commanded the services of a barber and dressed in fresh garments. Setting his cap at an appropriate angle, he strolled out upon the square.

His steps led him to the Solar Emosynary station. As before, two young men worked diligently, one stoking the blaze and adjusting the five lamps, while the other held the regulatory beam fixed upon the low sun.

Cugel inspected the contrivance from all angles, and presently the person who fed the blaze called out: "Are you not that notable traveler who today expressed doubts as to the efficacy of the Emosynary System?"

Cugel spoke carefully: "I told Maier and Huruska this: that Brazel is sunk below the Melantine Gulf and almost gone from memory; that the walled city Munt was long ago laid waste; that I am acquainted with neither Blue Azor, nor Vir Vassilis. These were my only positive statements."

The young fire-stoker petulantly threw an arm-load of logs into the fire-pit. "Still we are told that you consider our efforts impractical."

"I would not go so far," said Cugel politely. "Even if the other Emosynary agencies are abandoned, it is possible that the Gundar regulator suffices; who knows?"

"I will tell you this," declared the stoker. "We work without recompense, and in our spare time we must cut and transport fuel. The process is tedious."

The operator of the aiming device amplified his friend's complaint. "Huruska and the elders do none of the work; they merely ordain that we toil, which of course is the easiest part of the project. Janred and I are of a sophisticated new generation; on principle we reject all dogmatic doctrines. I for one consider the Solar Emosynary system a waste of time and effort."

"If the other agencies are abandoned," argued Janred the stoker, "who or what regulates the sun when it has passed beyond the horizon? The system is pure balderdash."

The operator of the lenses declared: "I will now demonstrate as much, and free us all from this thankless toil!" He worked a lever. "Notice I direct the regulatory beam away from the sun. Look! It shines as before, without the slightest attention on our part!"

Cugel inspected the sun, and for a fact it seemed to glow as before, flickering from time to time, and shivering like an old man with the ague. The two young men watched with similar interest, and as minutes passed, they began to murmur in satisfaction. "We are vindicated! The sun has not gone out!"

Even as they watched, the sun, perhaps fortuitously, underwent a cachectic spasm, and lurched alarmingly toward the horizon. Behind them sounded a bellow of outrage and the Nolde Huruska ran forward. "What is the meaning of this irresponsibility? Direct the regulator aright and instantly! Would you have us groping for the rest of our lives in the dark?"

The stoker resentfully jerked his thumb toward Cugel. "He convinced us that the system was unnecessary, and that our work was futile."

"What!" Huruska swung his formidable body about and confronted Cugel. "Only hours ago you set foot in Gundar, and already you are disrupting the fabric of our existence! I warn you, our patience is not illimitable! Be off with you and do not approach the Emosynary agency a second time!"

Choking with fury, Cugel swung on his heel and marched off across the square.

At the caravan terminal he inquired as to transport southward, but the caravan which had arrived at noon would on the morrow depart eastward the way it had come.

Cugel returned to the inn and stepped into the tavern. He noticed three men playing a card game and posted himself as an observer. The game proved to be a simple version of Zampolio, and presently Cugel asked if he might join the play. "But only if the stakes are not too high," he protested. "I am not particularly skillful and I dislike losing more than a terce or two."

"Bah," exclaimed one of the players. "What is money? Who will spend it when we are dead?"

"If we take all your gold, then you need not carry it further," another remarked jocularly.

"All of us must learn," the third player assured Cugel. "You are fortunate to have the three premier experts of Gundar as instructors."

Cugel drew back in alarm. "I refuse to lose more than a single terce!"

"Come now! Don't be a prig!"

"Very well," said Cugel. "I will risk it. But these cards are tattered and dirty. By chance I have a fresh set in my pouch."

"Excellent! The game proceeds!"

Two hours later the three Gunds threw down their cards, gave Cugel long hard looks, then as if with a single mind rose to their feet and departed the tavern. Inspecting his gains, Cugel counted thirty-two terces and a few odd coppers. In a cheerful frame of mind he retired to his chamber for the night.

In the morning, as he consumed his breakfast, he noticed the arrival of the Nolde Huruska, who immediately engaged Maier the innkeeper in conversation. A few minutes later Huruska approached Cugel's table and stared down at Cugel with a somewhat menacing grin, while Maier stood anxiously a few paces to the rear.

Cugel spoke in a voice of strained politeness: "Well, what is it this time? The sun has risen; my innocence in the matter of the regulatory beam has been established."

"I am now concerned with another matter. Are you acquainted with the penalties for fraud?"

Cugel shrugged. "The matter is of no interest to me."

"They are severe and I will revert to them in a moment. First, let me inquire: did you entrust to Maier a purse purportedly containing valuable jewels?"

"I did indeed. The propery is protected by a spell, I may add; if the seal is broken the gems become ordinary pebbles."

Huruska exhibited the purse. "Notice, the seal is intact. I cut a slit in the leather and looked within. The contents were then and are now —" with a flourish Huruska turned the purse out upon the table "— pebbles identical to those in the road yonder."

Cugel exclaimed in outrage: "The jewels are now worthless rubble! I hold you responsible and you must make recompense!"

Huruska uttered an offensive laugh. "If you can change gems to pebbles, you can change pebbles to gems. Maier will now tender the bill. If you refuse to pay, I intend to have you nailed into the enclosure under the gallows until such time as you change your mind."

"Your insinuations are both disgusting and absurd," declared Cugel. "Innkeeper, present your account! Let us finish with this farrago once and for all."

Maier came forward with a slip of paper. "I make the total to be eleven terces, plus whatever gratuities might seem in order."

"There will be no gratuities," said Cugel. "Do you harass all your guests in this fashion?" He flung eleven terces down upon the table. "Take your money and leave me in peace."

Maier sheepishly gathered up the coins; Huruska made an inarticulate sound and turned away. Cugel, upon finishing his breakfast, went out once more to stroll across the square. Here he met an individual whom he recognized to be the pot-boy in the tavern, and Cugel signaled him to a halt. "You seem an alert and knowledgeable fellow," said Cugel. "May I inquire your name?"

"I am generally known as 'Zeller'."

"I would guess you to be well-acquainted with the folk of Gundar."

"I consider myself well-informed. Why do you ask?"

"First," said Cugel, "let me ask if you care to turn your knowledge to profit?"

"Certainly, so long as I evade the attention of the Nolde."

"Very good. I notice a disused booth yonder which should serve our purpose. In one hour we shall put our enterprise into operation."

Cugel returned to the inn where at his request Maier brought a board, brush and paint. Cugel composed a sign:

THE EMINENT SEER CUGEL

COUNSELS, INTERPRETS, PROGNOSTICATES.

ASK! YOU WILL BE ANSWERED!

CONSULTATIONS: THREE TERCES.

Cugel hung the sign above the booth, arranged curtains and waited for customers. The pot-boy, meanwhile, had inconspicuously secreted himself at the back.

Almost immediately folk crossing the square halted to read the sign. A woman of early middle-age presently came forward.

"Three terces is a large sum. What results can you guarantee?"

"None whatever, by the very nature of things. I am a skilled voyant, I have acquaintance with the arts of magic, but knowledge comes to me from unknown and uncontrollable sources."

The woman paid over her money. "Three terces is cheap if you can resolve my worries. My daughter all her life has enjoyed the best of health but now she ails, and suffers a morose condition. All my remedies are to no avail. What must I do?"

"A moment, madam, while I meditate." Cugel drew the curtain and leaned back to where he could hear the pot-boy's whispered remarks, then once again drew aside the curtains.

"I have made myself one with the cosmos! Knowledge has entered my mind! Your daughter Dilian is pregnant. For an additional three terces I will supply the father's name."

"This is a fee I pay with pleasure," declared the woman grimly. She paid, received the information and marched purposefully away.

Another woman approached, paid three terces, and Cugel addressed himself to her problem: "My husband assured me that he had put by a canister of gold coins against the future, but upon his death I could find not so much as a copper. Where has he hidden the gold?"

Cugel closed the curtains, took counsel with the pot-boy, and again appeared to the woman. "I have discouraging news for you. Your husband Finister spent much of his hoarded gold at the tavern. With the rest he purchased an amethyst brooch for a woman named Varletta."

The news of Cugel's remarkable abilities spread rapidly and trade was brisk. Shortly before noon, a large woman, muffled and veiled, approached the booth, paid three terces, and asked in a high-pitched, if husky, voice: "Read me my fortune!"

Cugel drew the curtains and consulted the pot-boy, who was at a loss. "It is no one I know. I can tell you nothing."

"No matter," said Cugel. "My suspicions are verified." He drew aside the curtain. "The portents are unclear and I refuse to take your money." Cugel returned the fee. "I can tell you this much: you are an individual of domineering character and no great intelligence. Ahead lies what? Honors? A long voyage by water? Revenge on your enemies? Wealth? The image is distorted; I may be reading my own future."

The woman tore away her veils and stood revealed as the Nolde Huruska. "Master Cugel, you are lucky indeed that you returned my money, otherwise I would have taken you up for deceptive practices. In any event, I deem your activities mischievous, and contrary to the public interest. Gundar is in an uproar because of your revelations; there will be no more of them. Take down your sign, and be happily thankful that you have escaped so easily."

"I will be glad to terminate my enterprise," said Cugel with dignity. "The work is taxing."

Huruska stalked away in a huff. Cugel divided his earnings with the pot-boy, and in a spirit of mutual satisfaction they departed the booth.

Cugel dined on the best that the inn afforded, but later when he went into the tavern he discovered a noticeable lack of amiability among the patrons and presently went off to his chamber.

The next morning as he took breakfast a caravan of ten wagons arrived in town. The principal cargo appeared to be a bevy of seventeen beautiful maidens, who rode upon two of the wagons. Three other wagons served as dormitories, while the remaining five were loaded with stores, trunks, bales and cases. The caravan master, a portly mild-seeming man with flowing brown hair and a silky beard, assisted his delightful charges to the ground and led them all to the inn, where Maier served up an ample breakfast of spiced porridge, preserved quince, and tea.

Cugel watched the group as they made their meal and reflected that a journey to almost any destination in such company would be a pleasant journey indeed.

The Nolde Huruska appeared, and went to pay his respects to the caravan-leader. The two conversed amiably at some length, while Cugel waited impatiently.

Huruska at last departed. The maidens, having finished their meal, went off to stroll about the square. Cugel crossed to the table where the caravan-leader sat. "Sir, my name is Cugel, and I would appreciate a few words with you."

"By all means! Please be seated. Will you take a glass of this excellent tea?"

"Thank you. First, may I inquire the destination of your caravan?"

The caravan-leader showed surprise at Cugel's ignorance. "We are bound for Lumarth; these are the 'Seventeen Virgins of Symnathis' who traditionally grace the Grand Pageant."

"I am a stranger to this region," Cugel explained. "Hence I know nothing of the local customs. In any event, I myself am bound for Lumarth and would be pleased to travel with your caravan."

The caravan-leader gave an affable assent. "I would be delighted to have you with us."

"Excellent!" said Cugel. "Then all is arranged."

The caravan-leader stroked his silky brown beard. "I must warn you that my fees are somewhat higher than usual, owing to the expensive amenities I am obliged to provide these seventeen fastidious maidens."

"Indeed," said Cugel. "How much do you require?"

"The journey occupies the better part of ten days, and my minimum charge is twenty terces per diem, for a total of two hundred terces, plus a twenty terce supplement for wine."

"This is far more than I can afford," said Cugel in a bleak voice. "At the moment I command only a third of this sum. Is there some means by which I might earn my passage?"

"Unfortunately not," said the caravan-leader. "Only this

morning the position of armed guard was open, which even paid a small stipend, but Huruska the Nolde, who wishes to visit Lumarth, has agreed to serve in this capacity and the post is now filled."

Cugel made a sound of disappointment and raised his eyes to the sky. When at last he could bring himself to speak he asked: "When do you plan to depart?"

"Tomorrow at dawn, with absolute punctuality. I am sorry that we will not have the pleasure of your company."

"I share the sorrow," said Cugel. He returned to his own table and sat brooding. Presently he went into the tavern, where various card games were in progress. Cugel attempted to join the play, but in every case his request was denied. In a surly mood he went to the counter where Maier the innkeeper unpacked a crate of earthenware goblets. Cugel tried to initiate a conversation but for once Maier could take no time from his labors. "The Nolde Huruska goes off on a journey and tonight his friends mark the occasion with a farewell party, for which I must make careful preparations."

Cugel took a mug of beer to a side table and gave himself to reflection. After a few moments he went out the back exit and surveyed the prospect, which here overlooked the Isk River. Cugel sauntered down to the water's edge and discovered a dock at which the fishermen moored their punts and dried their nets. Cugel looked up and down the river, then returned up the path to the inn, to spend the rest of the day watching the seventeen maidens as they strolled about the square, or sipped sweet lime tea in the garden of the inn.

The sun set; twilight the color of old wine darkened into night. Cugel set about his preparations, which were quickly achieved, inasmuch as the essence of his plan lay in its simplicity.

The caravan-leader, whose name, so Cugel learned, was Shimilko, assembled his exquisite company for their evening meal, then herded them carefully to the dormitory wagons, despite the pouts and protests of those who wished to remain at the inn and enjoy the festivities of the evening.

In the tavern the farewell party in honor of Huruska had already commenced. Cugel seated himself in a dark corner and presently attracted the attention of the perspiring Maier. Cugel produced ten terces. "I admit that I harbored ungrateful thoughts toward Huruska," he said. "Now I wish to express my good wishes — in absolute anonymity, however! Whenever Huruska starts upon a mug of ale, I want you to place a full mug before him, so that his evening will be incessantly merry. If he asks who has bought the drink you are only to reply: 'One of your friends wishes to pay you a compliment.' Is this clear?"

"Absolutely, and I will do as you command. It is a large-hearted gesture, which Huruska will appreciate."

The evening progressed. Huruska's friends sang jovial songs and proposed a dozen toasts, in all of which Huruska joined. As Cugel had required, whenever Huruska so much as started to drink from a mug, another was placed at his elbow, and Cugel marveled at the scope of Huruska's internal reservoirs.

At last Huruska was prompted to excuse himself from the company. He staggered out the back exit and made his way to that stone wall with a trough below, which had been placed for the convenience of the tavern's patrons.

As Huruska faced the wall Cugel stepped behind him and flung a fisherman's net over Huruska's head, then expertly dropped a noose around Huruska's burly shoulders, followed by other turns and ties. Huruska's bellows were drowned by the song at this moment being sung in his honor.

Cugel dragged the cursing hulk down the path to the dock, and rolled him over and into a punt. Untying the mooring line, Cugel pushed the punt out into the current of the river. "At the very least," Cugel told himself, "two parts of my prophecy are accurate; Huruska has been honored in the tavern and now is about to enjoy a voyage by water."

He returned to the tavern where Huruska's absence had at last been noticed. Maier expressed the opinion that, with an early departure in the offing, Huruska had prudently retired to bed, and all conceded that this was no doubt the case.

The next morning Cugel arose an hour before dawn. He took a quick breakfast, paid Maier his score, then went to where Shimilko ordered his caravan.

"I bring news from Huruska," said Cugel. "Owing to an unfortunate set of personal circumstances, he finds himself unable to make the journey, and has commended me to that post for which you had engaged him."

Shimilko shook his head in wonder. "A pity! Yesterday he seemed so enthusiastic! Well, we all must be flexible, and since Huruska cannot join us, I am pleased to accept you in his stead. As soon as we start, I will instruct you in your duties, which are straightforward. You must stand guard by night and take your rest by day, although in the case of danger I naturally expect you to join in the defense of the caravan."

"These duties are well within my competence," said Cugel. "I am ready to depart at your convenience."

"Yonder rises the sun," declared Shimilko. "Let us be off and away for Lumarth."

Ten days later Shimilko's caravan passed through the Methune Gap, and the great Vale of Coram opened before them. The brimming Isk wound back and forth, reflecting a sultry sheen; in the distance loomed the long dark mass of the Draven Forest. Closer at hand five domes of shimmering nacreous gloss marked the site of Lumarth.

Shimilko addressed himself to the company. "Below lies what remains of the old city Lumarth. Do not be deceived by the domes; they indicate temples at one time sacred to the five demons Yaunt, Jastenave, Phampoun, Adelmar and Suul, and hence were preserved during the Sampathissic Wars.

"The folk of Lumarth are unlike any of your experience. Many are small sorcerers, though Chaladet the Grand Thearch has proscribed magic within the city precincts. You may conceive these people to be languid and wan, and dazed by excess sensation, and you will be correct. All are obsessively rigid in regard to ritual, and all subscribe to a Doctrine of Absolute Altruism, which compels them to virtue and benevolence. For this reason they are known as the 'Kind Folk'. A final word in regard to our journey, which luckily has gone without untoward incident. The wagoneers have driven with skill; Cugel has vigilantly guarded us by night, and I am well pleased. So then: onward to Lumarth, and let meticulous discretion be the slogan!"

The caravan traversed a narrow track down into the valley,

then proceeded along an avenue of rutted stone under an arch of enormous black mimosa trees.

At a mouldering portal opening upon the plaza the caravan was met by five tall men in gowns of embroidered silks, the splendid double-crowned headgear of the Coramese Thurists lending them an impressive dignity. The five men were much alike, with pale transparent skins, thin high-bridged noses, slender limbs and pensive gray eyes. One who wore a gorgeous gown of mustard-yellow, crimson and black raised two fingers in a calm salute. "My friend Shimilko, you have arrived securely with all your blessed cargo. We are well-served and very pleased."

"The Lirrh-Aing was so placid as almost to be dull," said Shimilko. "To be sure, I was fortunate in securing the services of Cugel, who guarded us so well by night that never were our slumbers interrupted."

"Well done, Cugel!" said the head Thurist. "We will at this time take custody of the precious maidens. Tomorrow you may render your account to the bursar. The Wayfarer's Inn lies yonder, and I counsel you to its comforts."

"Just so! We will all be the better for a few days rest!"

However, Cugel chose not to so indulge himself. At the door to the inn he told Shimilko: "Here we part company, for I must continue along the way. Affairs press on me and Almery lies far to the west."

"But your stipend, Cugel! You must wait at least until tomorrow, when I can collect certain monies from the bursar. Until then, I am without funds."

Cugel hesitated, but at last was prevailed upon to stay.

An hour later a messenger strode into the inn. "Master Shimilko, you and your company are required to appear instantly before the Grand Thearch on a matter of utmost importance."

Shimilko looked up in alarm. "Whatever is the matter?"

"I am obliged to tell you nothing more."

With a long face Shimilko led his company across the plaza to the loggia before the old palace, where Chaladet sat on a massive chair. To either side stood the College of Thurists and all regarded Shimilko with somber expressions.

"What is the meaning of this summons?" inquired Shimilko. "Why do you regard me with such gravity?"

The Grand Thearch spoke in a deep voice: "Shimilko, the seventeen maidens conveyed by you from Symnathis to Lumarth have been examined, and I regret to say that of the seventeen, only two can be classified as virgins. The remaining fifteen have been sexually deflorated."

Shimilko could hardly speak for consternation. "Impossible!" he sputtered. "At Symnathis I undertook the most elaborate precautions. I can display three separate documents certifying the purity of each. There can be no doubt! You are in error!"

"We are not in error, Master Shimilko. Conditions are as we describe, and may easily be verified."

"'Impossible' and 'incredible' are the only two words which come to mind," cried Shimilko. "Have you questioned the girls themselves?"

"Of course. They merely raise their eyes to the ceiling and whistle between their teeth. Shimilko, how do you explain this heinous outrage?"

"I am perplexed to the point of confusion! The girls embarked upon the journey as pure as the day they were born. This is fact! During each waking instant they never left my area of perception. This is also fact."

"And when you slept?"

"The implausibility is no less extreme. The teamsters invariably retired together in a group. I shared my wagon with the chief teamster and each of us will vouch for the other. Cugel meanwhile kept watch over the entire camp."

"Alone?"

"A single guard suffices, even though the nocturnal hours are slow and dismal. Cugel, however, never complained."

"Cugel is evidently the culprit!"

Shimilko smilingly shook his head. "Cugel's duties left him no time for illicit activity."

"What if Cugel scamped his duties?"

Shimilko responded patiently: "Remember, each girl rested secure in her private cubicle with a door between herself and Cugel."

"Well then — what if Cugel opened this door and quietly entered the cubicle?"

Shimilko considered a dubious moment, and pulled at his silky beard. "In such a case, I suppose the matter might be possible."

The Grand Thearch turned his gaze upon Cugel. "I insist that you make an exact statement upon this sorry affair."

Cugel cried out indignantly: "The investigation is a travesty! My honor has been assailed!"

Chaladet fixed Cugel with a benign, if somewhat chilly, stare. "You will be allowed redemption. Thurists, I place this person in your custody. See to it that he has every opportunity to regain his dignity and self-esteem!"

Cugel roared out a protest which the Grand Thearch ignored. From his great dais he looked thoughtfully off across the square. "Is it the third or fourth month?"

"The chronolog has only just left the month of Yaunt, to enter the time of Phampoun."

"So be it. By diligence, this licentious rogue may yet earn our love and respect."

A pair of Thurists grasped Cugel's arms and led him across the square. Cugel jerked this way and that to no avail. "Where are you taking me? What is this nonsense?"

One of the Thurists replied in a kindly voice: "We are taking you to the temple of Phampoun, and it is far from nonsense."

"I do not care for any of this," said Cugel. "Take your hands off of me; I intend to leave Lumarth at once."

"You shall be so assisted."

The group marched up worn marble steps, through an enormous arched portal, into an echoing hall, distinguished only by the high dome and an adytum or altar at the far end. Cugel was led into a side-chamber, illuminated by high circular windows and paneled with dark blue wood. An old man in a white gown entered the room and asked: "What have we here? A person suffering affliction?"

"Yes; Cugel has committed a series of abominable crimes, of which he wishes to purge himself."

"A total mis-statement!" cried Cugel. "No proof has been

adduced and in any event I was inveigled against my better judgment."

The Thurists, paying no heed, departed, and Cugel was left with the old man, who hobbled to a bench and seated himself. Cugel started to speak but the old man held up his hand. "Calm yourself! You must remember that we are a benevolent people, lacking all spite or malice. We exist only to help other sentient beings! If a person commits a crime, we are racked with sorrow for the criminal, whom we believe to be the true victim, and we work without compromise that he may renew himself."

"An enlightened viewpoint!" declared Cugel. "Already I feel regeneration!"

"Excellent! Your remarks validate our philosophy; certainly you have negotiated what I will refer to as Phase One of the program."

Cugel frowned. "There are other phases? Are they really necessary?"

"Absolutely; these are Phases Two and Three. I should explain that Lumarth has not always adhered to such a policy. During the high years of the Great Magics the city fell under the sway of Yasbane the Obviator, who breached openings into five demon-realms and constructed the five temples of Lumarth. You stand now in the Temple of Phampoun."

"Odd," said Cugel, "that a folk so benevolent are such fervent demonists."

"Nothing could be farther from the truth. The Kind Folk of Lumarth expelled Yasbane, to establish the Era of Love, which must now persist until the final waning of the sun. Our love extends to all, even Yasbane's five demons, whom we hope to rescue from their malevolent evil. You will be the latest in a long line of noble individuals who have worked to this end, and such is Phase Two of the program."

Cugel stood limp in consternation. "Such work far exceeds my competence!"

"Everyone feels the same sensation," said the old man. "Nevertheless Phampoun must be instructed in kindness, consideration and decency; by making this effort, you will know a surge of happy redemption."

"And Phase Three?" croaked Cugel. "What of that?"

"When you achieve your mission, then you shall be gloriously accepted into our brotherhood!" The old man ignored Cugel's groan of dismay. "Let me see now: the month of Yaunt is just ending, and we enter the month of Phampoun, who is perhaps the most irascible of the five by reason of his sensitive eyes. He becomes enraged by so much as a single glimmer, and you must attempt your persuasions in absolute darkness. Do you have any further questions?"

"Yes indeed! Suppose Phampoun refuses to mend his ways?"

"This is 'negativistic thinking' which we Kind Folk refuse to recognize. Ignore everything you may have heard in regard to Phampoun's macabre habits! Go forth in confidence!"

Cugel cried out in anguish: "How will I return to enjoy my honors and rewards?"

"No doubt Phampoun, when contrite, will send you aloft by a means at his disposal," said the old man. "Now I bid you farewell."

"One moment! Where is my food and drink? How will I survive?"

"Again we will leave these matters to the discretion of Phampoun." The old man touched a button; the floor opened under Cugel's feet; he slid down a spiral chute at dizzying velocity. The air gradually became syrupy; Cugel struck a film of invisible constriction which burst with a sound like a cork leaving a bottle, and Cugel emerged into a chamber of medium size, illuminated by the glow of a single lamp.

Cugel stood stiff and rigid, hardly daring to breathe. On a dais across the chamber Phampoun sat sleeping in a massive chair, two black hemispheres shuttering his enormous eyes against the light. The grey torso wallowed almost the length of the dais; the massive splayed legs were planted flat to the floor. Arms, as large around as Cugel himself, terminated in fingers three feet long, each bedecked with a hundred jeweled rings. Phampoun's head was as large as a wheelbarrow, with a huge snout and an enormous loose-wattled mouth. The two eyes, each the size of a dishpan, could not be seen for the protective hemispheres.

Cugel, holding his breath in fear and also against the stench which hung in the air, looked cautiously about the room. A cord ran from the lamp, across the ceiling, to dangle beside Phampoun's fingers; almost as a reflex Cugel detached the cord from the lamp. He saw a single egress from the chamber: a low iron door directly behind Phampoun's chair. The chute by which he had entered was now invisible.

The flaps beside Phampoun's mouth twitched and lifted; a homunculus growing from the end of Phampoun's tongue peered forth. It stared at Cugel with beady black eyes. "Ha, has time gone by so swiftly?" The creature, leaning forward, consulted a mark on the wall. "It has indeed; I have overslept and Phampoun will be cross. What is your name and what are your crimes? These details are of interest to Phampoun — which is to say myself, though from whimsy I usually call myself Pulsifer, as if I were a separate entity."

Cugel spoke in a voice of brave conviction: I am Cugel, inspector for the new regime which now holds sway in Lumarth. I decended to verify Phampoun's comfort, and since all is well, I will now return aloft. Where is the exit?"

Pulsifer asked plaintively: "You have no crimes to relate? This is harsh news. Both Phampoun and I enjoy great evils. Not long ago a certain sea-trader, whose name evades me, held us enthralled for over an hour."

"And then what occurred?"

"Best not to ask." Pulsifer busied himself polishing one of Phampoun's tusks with a small brush. He thrust his head forth and inspected the mottled visage above him. "Phampoun still sleeps soundly; he ingested a prodigous meal before retiring. Excuse me while I check the progress of Phampoun's digestion." Pulsifer ducked back behind Phampoun's wattles and revealed himself only by a vibration in the corded grey neck. Presently he returned to view. "He is quite famished, or so it would appear. I had best wake him; he will wish to converse with you before. . . ."

"Before what?"

"No matter."

"A moment," said Cugel. "I am interested in conversing with you rather than Phampoun."

"Indeed?" asked Pulsifer, and polished Phampoun's fang

with great vigor. "This is pleasant to hear; I receive few compliments."

"Strange! I see much in you to commend. Necessarily your career goes hand in hand with that of Phampoun, but perhaps you have goals and ambitions of your own?"

Pulsifer propped up Phampoun's lip with his cleaning brush and relaxed upon the ledge so created. "Sometimes I feel that I would enjoy seeing something of the outer world. We have ascended several times to the surface, but always by night when heavy clouds obscure the stars, and even then Phampoun complains of the excessive glare, and he quickly returns below."

"A pity," said Cugel. "By day there is much to see. The scenery surrounding Lumarth is pleasant. The Kind Folk are about to present their Grand Pageant of Ultimate Contrasts, which is said to be most picturesque."

Pulsifer gave his head a wistful shake. "I doubt if ever I will see such events. Have you witnessed many horrid crimes?"

"Indeed I have. For instance I recall a dwarf of the Batvar Forest who rode a pelgrane —"

Pulsifer interrupted him with a gesture. "A moment. Phampoun will want to hear this." He leaned precariously from the cavernous mouth to peer up toward the shuttered eyeballs. "Is he, or more accurately, am I awake? I thought I noticed a twitch. In any event, though I have enjoyed our conversation, we must get on with our duties. Hm, the light cord is disarranged. Perhaps you will be good enough to extinguish the light."

"There is no hurry," said Cugel. Phampoun sleeps peacefully; let him enjoy his rest. I have something to show you, a game of chance. Are you acquainted with 'Zambolio'?"

Pulsifer signified in the negative, and Cugel produced his cards. "Notice carefully! I deal you four cards and I take four cards, which we conceal from each other." Cugel explained the rules of the game. "Necessarily we play for coins of gold or some such commodity, to make the game interesting. I therefore wager five terces, which you must match."

"Yonder in two sacks is Phampoun's gold, or with equal propriety, my gold, since I am an integral adjunct to this vast hulk. Take forth gold sufficient to equal your terces."

The game proceeded. Pulsifer won the first sally, to his delight, then lost the next, which prompted him to fill the air with dismal complaints; then he won again and again until Cugel declared himself lacking further funds. "You are a clever and skillful player; it is a joy to match wits with you! Still, I feel I could beat you if I had the terces I left above in the temple."

Pulsifer, somewhat puffed and vainglorious, scoffed at Cugel's boast. "I fear that I am too clever for you! Here, take back your terces and we will play the game once again."

"No; this is not the way sportsmen behave; I am too proud to accept your money. Let me suggest a solution to the problem. In the temple above is my sack of terces and a sack of sweetmeats which you might wish to consume as we continue the game. Let us go fetch these articles, then I defy you to win as before!"

Pulsifer leaned far out to inspect Phampoun's visage. "He appears quite comfortable, though his organs are roiling with hunger."

"He sleeps as soundly as ever," declared Cugel. "Let us hurry. If he wakes our game will be spoiled."

Pulsifer hesitated. "What of Phampoun's gold? We dare not leave it unguarded!"

"We will take it with us, and it will never be outside the range of our vigilance."

"Very well; place it here on the dais."

"So, and now I am ready. How do we go aloft?"

"Merely press the leaden bulb beside the arm of the chair, but please make no untoward disturbance. Phampoun might well be exasperated should he awake in unfamiliar surroundings."

"He has never rested easier! We go aloft!" He pressed the button; the dais shivered and creaked and floated up a dark shaft which opened above them. Presently they burst through the valve of the constrictive essence which Cugel had penetrated on his way down the chute. At once a glimmer of scarlet light seeped into the shaft and a moment later the dais glided to a halt level with the altar in the Temple of Phampoun.

"Now then, my sack of terces," said Cugel. "Exactly where did I leave it? Just over yonder, I believe. Notice! Through the great arches you may overlook the main plaza of Lumarth, and those are the Kind Folk going about their ordinary affairs. What is your opinion of all this?"

"Most interesting, although I am unfamiliar with such extensive vistas. In fact, I feel almost a sense of vertigo. What is the source of the savage red glare?"

"That is the light of our ancient sun, now westering toward sunset."

"It does not appeal to me. Please be quick about your business; I have suddenly become most uneasy."

"I will make haste," said Cugel.

The sun, sinking low, sent a shaft of light through the portal, to play full upon the altar. Cugel, stepping behind the massive chair, twitched away the two shutters which guarded Phampoun's eyes, and the milky orbs glistened in the sunlight.

For an instant Phampoun lay quiet. His muscles knotted, his legs jerked, his mouth gaped wide, and he emitted an explosion of sound: a grinding scream which propelled Pulsifer forth to vibrate like a flag in the wind. Phampoun lunged from the altar to fall sprawling and rolling across the floor of the temple, all the while maintaining his cataclysmic outcries. He pulled himself erect, and pounding the tiled floor with his great feet, he sprang here and there and at last burst through the stone walls as if they were paper, while the Kind Folk in the square stood petrified.

Cugel, taking the two sacks of gold, departed the temple by a side entrance. For a moment he watched Phampoun careering around the square, screaming and flailing at the sun. Pulsifer, desperately gripping a pair of tusks, attempted to steer the maddened demon, who, ignoring all restraint, plunged eastward through the city, trampling down trees, bursting through houses as if they failed to exist.

Cugel walked briskly down to the Isk and made his way out upon a dock. He selected a skiff of good proportions, equipped with mast, sail and oars, and prepared to clamber aboard. A punt approached the dock from upriver, poled vigorously by a large man in tattered garments. Cugel turned away, pretending no more than a casual interest in the view, until he might board the skiff without attracting attention.

The punt touched the dock; the boatman climbed up a ladder.

Cugel continued to gaze across the water, affecting indifference to all except the river vistas.

The man, panting and grunting, came to a sudden halt. Cugel felt his intent inspection, and finally turning, looked into the congested face of Huruska, the Nolde of Gundar, though his face was barely recognizable for the bites Huruska had suffered from the insects of the Lallo Marsh.

Huruska stared long and hard at Cugel. "This is a most gratifying occasion!" he said huskily. "I feared that we would never meet again. And what do you carry in those leather bags?" He wrested a bag from Cugel. "Gold from the weight. Your prophecy has been totally vindicated! First honors and a voyage by water, now wealth and revenge! Prepare to die!"

"One moment!" cried Cugel. "You have neglected properly to moor the punt! This is disorderly conduct!"

Huruska turned to look, and Cugel thrust him off the dock into the water.

Cursing and raving, Huruska struggled for the shore while Cugel fumbled with the knots in the mooring-line of the skiff. The line at last came loose; Cugel pulled the skiff close as Huruska came charging down the dock like a bull. Cugel had no choice but to abandon his gold, jump into the skiff, push off and ply the oars while Huruska stood waving his arms in rage.

Cugel pensively hoisted the sail; the wind carried him down the river and around a bend. Cugel's last view of Lumarth, in the dying light of afternoon, included the low lustrous domes of the demon temples and the dark outline of Huruska standing on the dock. From afar the screams of Phampoun were still to be heard and occasionally the thud of toppling masonry.

2

THE BAGFUL
OF DREAMS

THE RIVER ISK, departing Lumarth, wandered in wide curves across the Plain of Red Flowers, bearing generally south. For six halcyon days Cugel sailed his skiff down the brimming river, stopping by night at one or another of the river-bank inns.

On the seventh day the river swung to the west, and passed by erratic sweeps and reaches through that land of rock spires and forested hillocks known as the Chaim Purpure. The wind blew, if at all, in unpredictable gusts, and Cugel, dropping the sail, was content to drift with the current, guiding the craft with an occasional stroke of the oars.

The villages of the plain were left behind; the region was uninhabited. In view of the crumbled tombs along the shore, the groves of cypress and yew, the quiet conversations to be overheard by night, Cugel was pleased to be afloat rather than afoot, and drifted out of the Chaim Purpure with great relief.

At the village Troon, the river emptied into the Tsombol Marsh, and Cugel sold the skiff for ten terces. To repair his fortunes he took employment with the town butcher, performing the more distasteful tasks attendant upon the trade. However, the pay was adequate and Cugel steeled himself to his undignified duties. He worked to such good effect that he was called upon to prepare the feast served at an important religious festival.

Through oversight, or stress of circumstance, Cugel used two sacred beasts in the preparation of his special ragout. Halfway through the banquet the mistake was discovered and once again Cugel left town under a cloud.

After hiding all night behind the abattoir to evade the hysterical mobs, Cugel set off at best speed across the Tsombol Marsh.

275

The road went by an indirect route, swinging around bogs and stagnant ponds, veering to follow the bed of an ancient highway, in effect doubling the length of the journey. A wind from the north blew the sky clear of all obscurity, so that the landscape showed in remarkable clarity. Cugel took no pleasure in the view, especially when, looking ahead, he spied a far pelgrane cruising down the wind.

As the afternoon advanced the wind abated, leaving an unnatural stillness across the marsh. From behind tussocks water-wefkins called out to Cugel, using the sweet voices of unhappy maidens: "Cugel, oh Cugel! Why do you travel in haste? Come to my bower and comb my beautiful hair!"

And: "Cugel, oh Cugel! Where do you go? Take me with you, to share your joyous adventures!"

And: "Cugel, beloved Cugel! The day is dying; the year is at an end! Come visit me behind the tussock, and we will console each other without constraint!"

Cugel only walked the faster, anxious to discover shelter for the night.

As the sun trembled at the edge of Tsombol Marsh Cugel came upon a small inn, secluded under five dire oaks. He gratefully took lodging for the night, and the innkeeper served a fair supper of stewed herbs, spitted reed-birds, seed-cake and thick burdock beer.

As Cugel ate, the innkeeper stood by with hands on hips. "I see by your conduct that you are a gentleman of high place; still you hop across Tsombol Marsh on foot like a bumpkin. I am puzzled by the incongruity."

"It is easily explained," said Cugel. "I consider myself the single honest man in a world of rogues and blackguards, present company excepted. In these conditions it is hard to accumulate wealth."

The innkeeper pulled at his chin, and turned away. When he came to serve Cugel a dessert of currant cake, he paused long enough to say: "Your difficulties have aroused my sympathy. Tonight I will reflect on the matter."

The innkeeper was as good as his word. In the morning, after Cugel had finished his breakfast, the innkeeper took him into the stable-yard and displayed a large dun-colored beast with powerful hind legs and a tufted tail, already bridled and saddled for riding.

"This is the least I can do for you," said the innkeeper. "I will sell this beast at a nominal figure. Agreed, it lacks elegance, and in fact is a hybrid of dounge and felukhary. Still, it moves with an easy stride; it feeds upon inexpensive wastes, and is notorious for its stubborn loyalty."

Cugel moved politely away. "I appreciate your altruism, but for such a creature any price whatever is excessive. Notice the sores at the base of its tail, the eczema along its back, and, unless I am mistaken, it lacks an eye. Also, its odor is not all it might be."

"Trifles!" declared the innkeeper. "Do you want a dependable steed to carry you across the Plain of Standing Stones, or an adjunct to your vanity? The beast becomes your property for a mere thirty terces."

Cugel jumped back in shock. "When a fine Cambalese wheriot sells for twenty? My dear fellow, your generosity outreaches my ability to pay!"

The innkeeper's face expressed only patience. "Here, in the middle of Tsombol Marsh, you will buy not even the smell of a dead wheriot."

"Let us discard euphemism," said Cugel. "Your price is an outrage."

For an instant the innkeeper's face lost its genial cast and he spoke in a grumbling voice: "Every person to whom I sell this steed takes the same advantage of my kindliness."

Cugel was puzzled by the remark. Nevertheless, sensing irresolution, he pressed his advantage. "In spite of a dozen misgivings, I offer a generous twelve terces!"

"Done!" cried the innkeeper almost before Cugel had finished speaking. "I repeat, you will discover this beast to be totally loyal, even beyond your expectations."

Cugel paid over twelve terces and gingerly mounted the creature. The landlord gave him a benign farewell. "May you enjoy a safe and comfortable journey!"

Cugel replied in like fashion. "May your enterprises prosper!"

In order to make a brave departure, Cugel tried to rein the

beast up and around in a caracole, but it merely squatted low to the ground, then padded out upon the road.

Cugel rode a mile in comfort, and another, and taking all with all, was favorably impressed with his acquisition. "No question but what the beast walks on soft feet; now let us discover if it will canter at speed."

He shook out the reins; the beast set off down the road, its gait a unique prancing strut, with tail arched and head held high.

Cugel kicked his heels into the creature's heaving flanks. "Faster then! Let us test your mettle!"

The beast sprang forward with great energy, and the breeze blew Cugel's cloak flapping behind his shoulders.

A massive dire oak stood beside a bend in the road: an object which the beast seemed to identify as a landmark. It increased its pace, only to stop short and elevate its hind-quarters, thus projecting Cugel into the ditch. When he managed to stagger back up on the road, he discovered the beast cavorting across the marsh, in the general direction of the inn.

"A loyal creature indeed!" grumbled Cugel. "It is unswervingly faithful to the comfort of its barn." He found his green velvet cap, clapped it back upon his head and once more trudged south along the road.

During the late afternoon Cugel came to a village of a dozen mud huts populated by a squat long-armed folk, distinguished by great shocks of whitewashed hair.

Cugel gauged the height of the sun, then examined the terrain ahead, which extended in a dreary succession of tussock and pond to the edge of vision. Putting aside all qualms he approached the largest and most pretentious of the huts.

The master of the house sat on a bench to the side, whitewashing the hair of one of his children into radiating tufts like the petals of a white chrysanthemum, while other urchins played nearby in the mud.

"Good afternoon," said Cugel. "Are you able to provide me food and lodging for the night? I naturally intend adequate payment."

"I will feel privileged to do so," replied the householder. "This is the most commodious hut of Samsetiska, and I am known for my fund of anecdotes. Do you care to inspect the premises?"

"I would be pleased to rest an hour in my chamber before indulging myself in a hot bath."

His host blew out his cheeks, and wiping the whitewash from his hands beckoned Cugel into the hut. He pointed to a heap of reeds at the side of the room. "There is your bed; recline for as long as you like. As for a bath, the ponds of the swamp are infested with threlkoids and wire-worms, and cannot be recommended."

"In that case I must do without," said Cugel. "However, I have not eaten since breakfast, and I am willing to take my evening meal as soon as possible."

"My spouse has gone trapping in the swamp," said his host. "It is premature to discuss supper until we learn what she has gleaned from her toil."

In due course the woman returned carrying a sack and a wicker basket. She built up a fire and prepared the evening meal, while Erwig the householder brought forth a two-string guitar and entertained Cugel with ballads of the region.

At last the woman called Cugel and Erwig into the hut, where she served bowls of gruel, dishes of fried moss and ganions, with slices of coarse black bread.

After the meal Erwig thrust his spouse and children out into the night, explaining: "What we have to say is unsuitable for unsophisticated ears. Cugel is an important traveler and does not wish to measure his every word."

Bringing out an earthenware jug, Erwig poured two tots of arrak, one of which he placed before Cugel, then disposed himself for conversation. "Whence came you and where are you bound?"

Cugel tasted the arrak, which scorched the entire interior of his glottal cavity. "I am native to Almery, to which I now return."

Erwig scratched his head in perplexity. "I cannot divine why you go so far afield, only to retrace your steps."

"Certain enemies worked mischief upon me," said Cugel. "Upon my return, I intend an appropriate revenge."

"Such acts soothe the spirit like no others," agreed Erwig.

"An immediate obstacle is the Plain of Standing Stones, by reason of asms which haunt the area. I might add that pelgrane are also common."

Cugel gave his sword a nervous twitch. "What is the distance to the Plain of Standing Stones?"

"Four miles south the ground rises and the Plain begins. The track proceeds from sarsen to sarsen for a distance of fifteen miles. A stout-hearted traveler will cross the plain in four to five hours, assuming that he is not delayed or devoured. The town Cuirnif lies another two hours beyond."

"An inch of foreknowledge is worth ten miles of afterthought —"

"Well spoken!" cried Erwig, swallowing a gulp of arrak. "My own opinion, to an exactitude! Cugel, you are astute!"

"— and in this regard, may I inquire your opinion of Cuirnif?"

"The folk are peculiar in many ways," said Erwig. "They preen themselves upon the gentility of their habits, yet they refuse to whitewash their hair, and they are slack in their religious observances. For instance, they make obeisance to Divine Wiulio with the right hand, not on the buttock, but on the abdomen, which we here consider a slipshod practice. What are your own views?"

"The rite should be conducted as you describe," said Cugel. "No other method carries weight."

Erwig refilled Cugel's glass. "I consider this an important endorsement of our views!"

The door opened and Erwig's spouse looked into the hut. "The night is dark. A bitter wind blows from the north, and a black beast prowls at the edge of the marsh."

"Stand among the shadows; divine Wiulio protects his own. It is unthinkable that you and your brats should annoy our guest."

The woman grudgingly closed the door and returned into the night. Erwig pulled himself forward on his stool and swallowed a quantity of arrak. "The folk of Cuirnif, as I say, are strange enough, but their ruler, Duke Orbal, surpasses them in every category. He devotes himself to the study of marvels and prodigies, and every jack-leg magician with two spells in his head is feted and celebrated and treated to the best of the city."

"Most odd!" declared Cugel.

Again the door opened and the woman looked into the hut. Erwig put down his glass and frowned over his shoulder. "What is it this time?"

"The beast is now moving among the huts. For all we know it may also worship Wiulio."

Erwig attempted argument, but the woman's face became obdurate. "Your guest might as well forego his niceties now as later, since we all, in any event, must sleep on the same heap of reeds." She opened wide the door and commanded her urchins into the hut. Erwig, assured that no further conversation was possible, threw himself down upon the reeds, and Cugel followed soon after.

In the morning Cugel breakfasted on ash-cake and herb tea, and prepared to take his departure. Erwig accompanied him to the road. "You have made a favorable impression upon me, and I will assist you across the Plain of Standing Stones. At the first opportunity take up a pebble the size of your fist and make the trigrammatic sign upon it. If you are attacked, hold high the pebble and cry out: 'Stand aside! I carry a sacred object!' At the first sarsen, deposit the stone and select another from the pile, again make the sign and carry it to the second sarsen, and so across the plain."

"So much is clear," said Cugel. "But perhaps you should show me the most powerful version of the sign, and thus refresh my memory."

Erwig scratched a mark in the dirt. "Simple, precise, correct! The folk of Cuirnif omit this loop and scrawl in every which direction."

"Slackness, once again!" said Cugel.

"So then, Cugel: farewell! The next time you pass be certain to halt at my hut! My crock of arrak has a loose stopper!"

"I would not forego the pleasure for a thousand terces. And now, as to my indebtedness —"

Erwig held up his hand. "I accept no terces from my guests!" He jerked and his eyes bulged as his spouse came up and prodded him in the ribs. "Ah well," said Erwig. "Give the woman a terce or two; it will cheer her as she performs her tasks."

Cugel paid over five terces, to the woman's enormous satisfaction, and so departed the village.

After four miles the road angled up to a gray plain studded at intervals with twelve-foot pillars of gray stone. Cugel found a large pebble, and placing his right hand on his buttock made a profound salute to the object. He scratched upon it a sign somewhat similar to that drawn for him by Erwig and intoned: "I commend this pebble to the attention of Wiulio! I request that it protect me across this dismal plain!"

He scrutinized the landscape, but aside from the sarsens and the long black shadows laid by the red morning sun, he discovered nothing worthy of attention, and thankfully set off along the track.

He had traveled no more than a hundred yards when he felt a presence and whirling about discovered an asm of eight fangs almost on his heels. Cugel held high the pebble and cried out: "Away with you! I carry a sacred object and I do not care to be molested!"

The asm spoke in a soft blurred voice: "Wrong! You carry an ordinary pebble. I watched and you scamped the rite. Flee if you wish! I need the exercise."

The asm advanced. Cugel threw the stone with all his force. It struck the black forehead between the bristling antennae, and the asm fell flat; before it could rise Cugel had severed its head.

He started to proceed, then turned back and took up the stone. "Who knows who guided the throw so accurately? Wiulio deserves the benefit of the doubt."

At the first Sarsen he exchanged stones as Erwig had recommended, and this time he made the trigrammatic sign with care and precision.

Without interference he crossed to the next sarsen and so continued across the plain.

The sun made its way to the zenith, rested a period, then descended into the west. Cugel marched unmolested from sarsen to sarsen. On several occasions he noted pelgrane sliding across the sky, and each time flung himself flat to avoid attention.

The Plain of Standing Stones ended at the brink of a scarp overlooking a wide valley. With safety close at hand Cugel relaxed his vigilance, only to be startled by a scream of triumph from the sky. He darted a horrified glance over his shoulder, then plunged over the edge of the scarp into a ravine, where he dodged among rocks and pressed himself into the shadows. Down swooped the pelgrane, past and beyond Cugel's hiding place. Warbling in joy, it alighted at the base of the scarp, to evoke instant outcries and curses from a human throat.

Keeping to concealment Cugel descended the slope, to discover that the pelgrane now pursued a portly black-haired man in a suit of black and white diaper. This person at last took nimble refuge behind a thick-boled olophar tree, and the pelgrane chased him first one way, then another, clashing its fangs and snatching with its clawed hands.

For all his rotundity, the man showed remarkable deftness of foot and the pelgrane began to scream in frustration. It halted to glare through the crotch of the tree and snap out with its long maw.

On a whimsical impulse Cugel stole out upon a shelf of rock; then, selecting an appropriate moment, he jumped to land with both feet on the creature's head, forcing the neck down into the crotch of the olophar tree. He called out to the startled man: "Quick! Fetch a stout cord! We will bind this winged horror in place!"

The man in the black and white diaper cried out: "Why show mercy? It must be killed and instantly! Move your foot, so that I may hack away its head."

"Not so fast," said Cugel. "For all its faults, it is a valuable specimen by which I hope to profit."

"Profit?" The idea had not occurred to the portly gentleman. "I must assert my prior claim! I was just about to stun the beast when you interfered."

Cugel said: "In that case I will take my weight off the creature's neck and go my way."

The man in the black-and-white suit made an irritable gesture. "Certain persons will go to any extreme merely to score a rhetorical point. Hold fast then! I have a suitable cord over yonder."

The two men dropped a branch over the pelgrane's head and bound it securely in place. The portly gentleman, who had introduced himself as Iolo the Dream-taker, asked: "Exactly what value do you place upon this horrid creature, and why?"

Cugel said: "It has come to my attention that Orbal, Duke of Ombalique, is an amateur of oddities. Surely he would pay well for such a monster, perhaps as much as a hundred terces."

"Your theories are sound," Iolo admitted. "Are you sure that the bonds are secure?"

As Cugel tested the ropes he noticed an ornament consisting of a blue glass egg on a golden chain attached to the creature's crest. As he removed the object, Iolo's hand darted out, but Cugel shouldered him aside. He disengaged the amulet, but Iolo caught hold of the chain and the two glared eye to eye.

"Release your grip upon my property," said Cugel in an icy voice.

Iolo protested vigorously. "The object is mine since I saw it first."

"Nonsense! I took it from the crest and you tried to snatch it from my hand."

Iolo stamped his foot. "I will not be domineered!" He sought to wrest the blue egg from Cugel's grasp. Cugel lost his grip and the object was thrown against the hillside where it broke in a bright blue explosion to create a hole into the hillside. Instantly a golden-gray tentacle thrust forth and seized Cugel's leg.

Iolo sprang back and from a safe distance watched Cugel's efforts to avoid being drawn into the hole. Cugel saved himself at the last moment by clinging to a stump. He called out: "Iolo, make haste! Fetch a cord and tie the tentacle to this stump; otherwise it will drag me into the hill!"

Iolo folded his arms and spoke in a measured voice: "Avarice has brought this plight upon you. It may be a divine judgment and I am reluctant to interfere."

"What? When you fought tooth and nail to wrench the object from my hand?"

Iolo frowned and pursed his lips. "In any case I own a single rope: that which ties my pelgrane."

"Kill the pelgrane!" panted Cugel. "Put the cord to its most urgent use!"

"You yourself valued this pelgrane at a hundred terces. The worth of the rope is ten terces."

"Very well," said Cugel through gritted teeth. "Ten terces for the rope, but I cannot pay a hundred terces for a dead pelgrane, since I carry only forty-five."

"So be it. Pay over the forty-five terces. What surety can you offer for the remainder?"

Cugel managed to toss over his purse of terces. He displayed the opal ear-bangle which Iolo promptly demanded, but which Cugel refused to relinquish until the tentacle had been tied to the stump.

With poor grace Iolo hacked the head off the pelgrane, then brought over the rope and secured the tentacle to the stump, thus easing the strain upon Cugel's leg.

"The ear-bangle, if you please!" said Iolo, and he poised his knife significantly near the rope.

Cugel tossed over the jewel. "There you have it: all my wealth. Now, please free me from this tentacle."

"I am a cautious man," said Iolo. "I must consider the matter from several perspectives." He set about making camp for the night.

Cugel called out a plaintive appeal: "Do you remember how I rescued you from the pelgrane?"

"Indeed I do! An important philosophical question has thereby been raised. You disturbed a stasis and now a tentacle grips your leg, which is, in a sense, the new stasis. I will reflect carefully upon the matter."

Cugel argued to no avail. Iolo built up a campfire over which he cooked a stew of herbs and grasses, which he ate with half a cold fowl and draughts of wine from a leather bottle.

Leaning back against a tree he gave his attention to Cugel. "No doubt you are on your way to Duke Orbal's Grand Exposition of Marvels?"

"I am a traveler, no more," said Cugel. "What is this 'Grand Exposition'?"

Iolo gave Cugel a pitying glance for his stupidity. "Each year Duke Orbal presides over a competition of wonder-workers. This year the prize is one thousand terces, which I intend to win with my 'Bagful of Dreams'."

"Your 'Bagful of Dreams' I assume to be a jocularity, or something on the order of a romantic metaphor?"

"Nothing of the sort!" declared Iolo in scorn.

"A kaleidoscopic projection? A program of impersonations? A hallucinatory gas?"

"None of these. I carry with me a number of pure unadulterated dreams, coalesced and crystallized."

From his satchel Iolo brought a sack of soft brown leather, from which he took an object resembling a pale blue snowflake an inch in diameter. He held it up into the firelight where Cugel could admire its fleeting lusters. "I will ply Duke Orbal with my dreams, and how can I fail to win over all other contestants?"

"Your chances would seem to be good. How do you gather these dreams?"

"The process is secret; still I can describe the general procedure. I live beside Lake Lelt in the Land of Dai-Passant. On calm nights the surface of the water thickens to a film which reflects the stars as small globules of shine. By using a suitable cantrap, I am able to lift up impalpable threads composed of pure starlight and water-skein. I weave this thread into nets and then I go forth in search of dreams. I hide under valances and in the leaves of outdoor bowers; I crouch on roofs; I wander through sleeping houses. Always I am ready to net the dreams as they drift past. Each morning I carry these wonderful wisps to my laboratory and there I sort them out and work my processes. In due course I achieve a crystal of a hundred dreams, and with these confections I hope to enthrall Duke Orbal."

"I would offer congratulations were it not for this tentacle gripping my leg," said Cugel.

"That is a generous emotion," said Iolo. He fed several logs into the fire, chanted a spell of protection against creatures of the night, and composed himself for sleep.

An hour passed. Cugel tried by various means to ease the

grip of the tentacle, without success, nor could he draw his sword or bring 'Spatterlight' from his pouch.

At last he sat back and considered new approaches to the solution of his problem.

By dint of stretching and straining he obtained a twig, with which he dragged close a long dead branch, which allowed him to reach another of equal length. Tying the two together with a string from his pouch, he contrived a pole exactly long enough to reach Iolo's recumbent form.

Working with care Cugel drew Iolo's satchel across the ground, finally to within reach of his fingers. First he brought out Iolo's wallet, to find two hundred terces, which he transfered to his own purse; next the opal ear-bangle, which he dropped into the pocket of his shirt; then the bagful of dreams.

The satchel contained nothing more of value, save that portion of cold fowl which Iolo had reserved for his breakfast and the leather bottle of wine, both of which Cugel put aside for his own use. He returned the satchel to where he had found it, then separated the branches and tossed them aside. Lacking a better hiding place for the bagful of dreams, Cugel tied the string to the bag and lowered it into the mysterious hole. He ate the fowl and drank the wine, then made himself as comfortable as possible.

The night wore on. Cugel heard the plaintive call of a night-jar and also the moan of a six-legged shamb, at some distance.

In due course the sky glowed purple and the sun appeared. Iolo roused himself, yawned, ran his fingers through his tousled hair, blew up the fire and gave Cugel a civil greeting. "And how passed the night?"

"As well as could be expected. It is useless, after all, to complain against inexorable reality."

"Exactly so. I have given considerable thought to your case, and I have arrived at a decision which will please you. This is my plan. I shall proceed into Cuirnif and there drive a hard bargain for the ear-bangle. After satisfying your account, I will return and pay over to you whatever sums may be in excess."

Cugel suggested an alternative scheme. "Let us go into

Cuirnif together; then you will be spared the inconvenience of a return trip."

Iolo shook his head. "My plan must prevail." He went to the satchel for his breakfast and so discovered the loss of his property. He uttered a plangent cry and stared at Cugel. "My terces, my dreams! They are gone, all gone! How do you account for this?"

"Very simply. At approximately four minutes after midnight a robber came from the forest and made off with the contents of your satchel."

Iolo tore at his beard with the fingers of both hands. "My precious dreams! Why did you not cry out an alarm?"

Cugel scratched his head. "In all candor I did not dare disturb the stasis."

Iolo jumped to his feet and looked through the forest in all directions. He turned back to Cugel. "What sort of man was this robber?"

"In certain respects he seemed a kindly man; after taking possession of your belongings, he presented me with half a cold fowl and a bottle of wine, which I consumed with gratitude."

"You consumed my breakfast!"

Cugel shrugged. "I could not be sure of this, and in fact I did not inquire. We held a brief conversation and I learned that like ourselves he is bound for Cuirnif and the Exposition of Marvels."

"Ah, ah ha! Would you recognize this person were you to see him again?"

"Without a doubt."

Iolo became instantly energetic. "Let us see as to this tentacle. Perhaps we can pry it loose." He seized the tip of the golden-gray member and bracing himself worked to lift it from Cugel's leg. For several minutes he toiled, kicking and prying, paying no heed to Cugel's cries of pain. Finally the tentacle relaxed and Cugel crawled to safety.

With great caution Iolo approached the hole and peered down into the depths. "I see only a glimmer of far lights. The hole is mysterious! . . . . What is this bit of string which leads into the hole?"

"I tied a rock to the string and tried to plumb the bottom of the hole," Cugel explained. "It amounts to nothing."

Iolo tugged at the string, which first yielded, then resisted, then broke, and Iolo was left looking at the frayed end. "Odd! The string is corroded, as if through contact with some acrid substance."

"Most peculiar!" said Cugel.

Iolo threw the string back into the hole. "Come, we can waste no more time! Let us hasten into Cuirnif and seek out the scoundrel who stole my valuables."

The road left the forest and passed through a district of fields and orchards. Peasants looked up in wonder as the two passed by: the portly Iolo dressed in black and white diaper and the lank Cugel with a black cloak hanging from his spare shoulders and a fine dark green cap gracing his saturnine visage.

Along the way Iolo put ever more searching questions in regard to the robber. Cugel had lost interest in the subject and gave back ambiguous, even contradictory, answers, and Iolo's questions became ever more searching.

Upon entering Cuirnif, Cugel noticed an inn which seemed to offer comfortable accommodation. He told Iolo: "Here our paths diverge, since I plan to stop at the inn yonder."

"The Five Owls? It is the dearest inn of Cuirnif! How will you pay your account?"

Cugel made a confident gesture. "Is not a thousand terces the grand prize at the Exposition?"

"Certainly, but what marvel do you plan to display? I warn you, the Duke has no patience with charlatans."

"I am not a man who tells all he knows," said Cugel. "I will disclose none of my plans at this moment."

"But what of the robber?" cried Iolo. "Were we not to search Cuirnif high and low?"

"The Five Owls is as good a vantage as any, since the robber will surely visit the common room to boast of his exploits and squander your terces on drink. Meanwhile, I wish you easy roofs and convenient dreams." Cugel bowed politely and took his leave of Iolo.

At the Five Owls Cugel selected a suitable chamber, where he refreshed himself and ordered his attire. Then, repairing to the common room, he made a leisurely meal upon the best the house could provide.

The innkeeper stopped by to make sure that all was in order and Cugel complimented him upon his table. "In fact, all taken with all, Cuirnif must be considered a place favored by the elements. The prospect is pleasant, the air is bracing, and Duke Orbal would seem to be an indulgent ruler."

The innkeeper gave a somewhat noncommittal assent. "As you indicate, Duke Orbal is never exasperated, truculent, suspicious, nor harsh unless in his wisdom he feels so inclined, whereupon all mildness is put aside in the interests of justice. Glance up to the crest of the hill; what do you see?"

"Four tubes, or stand-pipes, approximately thirty yards tall and one yard in diameter."

"Your eye is accurate. Into these tubes are dropped insubordinate members of society, without regard for who stands below or who may be coming after. Hence, while you may converse with Duke Orbal or even venture a modest pleasantry, never ignore his commands. Criminals, of course, are given short shrift."

Cugel, from habit, looked uneasily over his shoulder. "Such strictures will hardly apply to me, a stranger in town."

The innkeeper gave a skeptical grunt. "I assume that you came to witness the Exposition of Marvels?"

"Quite so! I may even try for the grand prize. In this regard, can you recommend a dependable hostler?"

"Certainly." The innkeeper provided explicit directions.

"I also wish to hire a gang of strong and willing workers," said Cugel. "Where may these be recruited?"

The innkeeper pointed across the square to a dingy tavern. "In the yard of the 'Howling Dog' all the riffraff in town take counsel together. Here you will find workers sufficient to your purposes."

"While I visit the hostler, be good enough to send a boy across to hire twelve of these sturdy fellows."

"As you wish."

At the hostler's Cugel rented a large six-wheeled wagon and a team of strong farlocks. When he returned with the wagon to the Five Owls, he found waiting a work-force of twelve individuals of miscellaneous sort, including a man not only senile but also lacking a leg. Another, in the throes of intoxication, fought away imaginary insects. Cugel discharged these two on the spot. The group also included Iolo the Dream-taker, who scrutinized Cugel with the liveliest suspicion.

Cugel asked: "My dear fellow, what do you do in such sordid company?"

"I take employment so that I may eat," said Iolo. "May I ask how you came by the funds to pay for so much skilled labor? Also, I notice that from your ear hangs that gem which only last night was my property!"

"It is the second of a pair," said Cugel. "As you know, the robber took the first along with your other valuables."

Iolo curled his lips. "I am more than ever anxious to meet this quixotic robber who takes my gem but leaves you in possession of yours."

"He was indeed a remarkable person. I believe that I glimpsed him not an hour ago, riding hard out of town."

Iolo again curled his lip. "What do you propose to do with this wagon?"

"If you care to earn a wage, you will soon find out for yourself."

Cugel drove the wagon and the gang of workers out of Cuirnif along the road to the mysterious hole, where he found all as before. He ordered trenches dug into the hillside; crating was installed, after which that block of soil surrounding and including the hole, the stump and the tentacle, was dragged up on the bed of the wagon.

During the middle stages of the project Iolo's manner changed. He began calling orders to the workmen and addressed Cugel with cordiality. "A noble idea, Cugel! We shall profit greatly!"

Cugel raised his eyebrows. "I hope indeed to win the grand prize. Your wage, however, will be relatively modest, even scant, unless you work more briskly."

"What!" stormed Iolo. "Surely you agree that this hole is half my property!"

"I agree to nothing of the sort. Say no more of the matter, or you will be discharged on the spot."

Grumbling and fuming Iolo returned to work. In due course Cugel conveyed the block of soil, with the hole, stump and tentacle, back to Cuirnif. Along the way he purchased an old tarpaulin with which he concealed the hole, the better to magnify the eventual effect of his display.

At the site of the Grand Exposition Cugel slid his exhibit off the wagon and into the shelter of a pavilion, after which he paid off his men, to the dissatisfaction of those who had cultivated extravagant hopes.

Cugel refused to listen to complaints. "The pay is sufficient! If it were ten times as much, every last terce would still end up in the till at the 'Howling Dog'."

"One moment!" cried Iolo. You and I must arrive at an understanding!"

Cugel merely jumped up on the wagon and drove it back to the hostelry. Some of the men pursued him a few steps; others threw stones, without effect.

On the following day trumpets and gongs announced the formal opening of the exposition. Duke Orbal arrived at the plaza wearing a splendid robe of magenta plush trimmed with white feathers, and a hat of pale blue velvet three feet in diameter, with silver tassels around the brim and a cockade of silver puff.

Mounting a rostrum, Duke Orbal addressed the crowd. "As all know, I am considered an eccentric, what with my enthusiasm for marvels and prodigies, but, after all, when the preoccupation is analyzed, is it all so absurd? Think back across the aeons to the times of the Vapurials, the Green and Purple College, the mighty magicians among whose number we include Amberlin, the second Chidule of Porphyrhyncos, Morreion, Calanctus the Calm, and of course the Great Phandaal. These were the days of power, and they are not likely to return except in nostalgic recollection. Hence this, my Grand Exposition of Marvels, and withal, a pale recollection of the way things were.

"Still, all taken with all, I see by my schedule that we have a stimulating program, and no doubt I will find difficulty in awarding the grand prize."

Duke Orbal glanced at a paper. "We will inspect Zaraflam's

'Nimble Squadrons', Bazzard's 'Unlikely Musicians', Xallops and his 'Compendium of Universal Knowledge'. Iolo will offer his 'Bagful of Dreams', and, finally, Cugel will present for our amazement that to which he gives the tantalizing title: 'Nowhere'. A most provocative program! And now without further ado we will proceed to evaluate Zaraflam's 'Nimble Squadrons'."

The crowd surged around the first pavilion and Zaraflam brought forth his 'Nimble Squadrons': a parade of cockroaches smartly turned out in red, white, and black uniforms. The sergeants brandished cutlasses; the foot soldiers carried muskets; the squadrons marched and countermarched in intricate evolutions.

"Halt!" bawled Zaraflam.

The cockroaches stopped short.

"Present arms!"

The cockroaches obeyed.

"Fire a salute in honor of Duke Orbal!"

The sergeants raised their cutlasses; the footmen elevated their muskets. Down came the cutlasses; the muskets exploded, emitting little puffs of white smoke.

"Excellent!" declared Duke Orbal. "Zaraflam, I commend your painstaking accuracy!"

"A thousand thanks, your Grace! Have I won the grand prize?"

"It is still too early to predict. Now, to Bazzard and his 'Unlikely Musicians'!"

The spectators moved on to the second pavilion where Bazzard presently appeared, his face woebegone. "Your Grace and noble citizens of Cuirnif! My 'Unlikely Musicians' were fish from the Cantic Sea and I felt sure of the grand prize when I brought them to Cuirnif. However, during the night a leak drained the tank dry. The fish are dead and their music is lost forever! I still wish to remain in contention for the prize; hence I will simulate the songs of my former troupe. Please adjudicate the music on this basis."

Duke Orbal made an austere sign. "Impossible. Bazzard's exhibit is hereby declared invalid. We now move on to Xallops and his remarkable 'Compendium'."

Xallops stepped forward from his pavilion. "Your Grace, ladies and gentlemen of Cuirnif! My entry at this exposition is truly remarkable; however, unlike Zaraflam and Bazzard, I can take no personal credit for its existence. By trade I am a ransacker of ancient tombs, where the risks are great and rewards few. By great good luck I chanced upon that crypt where several aeons ago the sorcerer Zinqzin was laid to rest. From this dungeon I rescued the volume which I now display to your astounded eyes."

Xallops whisked away cloth to reveal a great book bound in black leather. "On command this volume must reveal information of any and every sort; it knows each trivial detail, from the time the stars first caught fire to the present date. Ask; you shall be answered!"

"Remarkable!" declared Duke Orbal. "Present before us the Lost Ode of Psyrme!"

"Certainly," said the book in a rasping voice. It threw back its covers to reveal a page covered with crabbed and interlocked characters.

Duke Orbal put a perplexed question: "This is beyond my comprehension; you may furnish a translation."

"The request is denied," said the book. "Such poetry is too sweet for ordinary ears."

Duke Orbal glanced at Xallops, who spoke quickly to the book: "Show us scenes from aeons past."

"As you like. Reverting to the Nineteenth Aeon of the Fifty-second Cycle, I display a view across Linxfade Valley, toward Kolghut's Tower of Frozen Blood."

"The detail is both notable and exact!" declared Duke Orbal. "I am curious to gaze upon the semblance of Kolghut himself."

"Nothing could be easier. Here is the terrace of the Temple at Tanutra. Kolghut stands beside the flowering wail-bush. In the chair sits the Empress Noxon, now in her hundred and fortieth year. She has tasted no water in her entire lifetime, and eats only bitter blossom, with occasionally a morsel of boiled eel."

"Bah!" said Duke Orbal. "A most hideous old creature! Who are those gentlemen ranked behind her?"

"They constitute her retinue of lovers. Every month one

of their number is executed and a new stalwart is recruited to take his place. Competition is keen to win the affectionate regard of the Empress."

"Bah!" muttered Duke Orbal. "Show us rather a beautiful court lady of the Yellow Age."

The book spoke a petulant syllable in an unknown language. The page turned to reveal a travertine promenade beside a slow river.

"This view reveals to good advantage the topiary of the time. Notice here, and here!" With a luminous arrow the book indicated a row of massive trees clipped into globular shapes. "Those are irix, the sap of which may be used as an effective vermifuge. The species is now extinct. Along the concourse you will observe a multitude of persons. Those with black stockings and long white beards are Alulian slaves, whose ancestors arrived from far Canopus. They are also extinct. In the middle distance stands a beautiful woman named Jiao Jaro. She is indicated by a red dot over her head, although her face is turned toward the river."

"This is hardly satisfactory," grumbled Duke Orbal. "Xallops, can you not control the perversity of your exhibit?"

"I fear not, your Grace."

Duke Orbal gave a sniff of displeasure. "A final question! Who among the folk now residing in Cuirnif presents the greatest threat to the welfare of my realm?"

"I am a repository of information, not an oracle," stated the book. "However, I will remark that among those present stands a fox-faced vagabond with a crafty expression, whose habits would bring a blush to the cheeks of the Empress Noxon herself. His name —"

Cugel leapt forward and pointed across the plaza. "The robber! There he goes now! Summon the constables! Sound the gong!"

While everyone turned to look, Cugel slammed shut the book and dug his knuckles into the cover. The book grunted in annoyance.

Duke Orbal turned back with a frown of perplexity. "I saw no robber."

"In that case, I was surely mistaken. But yonder waits Iolo

with his famous 'Bagful of Dreams'!"

The Duke moved on to Iolo's pavilion, followed by the enthralled onlookers. Duke Orbal said: "Iolo the Dream-taker, your fame has preceded you all the distance from Dai-Passant! I hereby tender you an official welcome!"

Iolo answered in an anguished voice: "Your Grace, I have sorry news to relate. For the whole of one year I prepared for this day, hoping to win the grand prize. The blast of midnight winds, the outrage of householders, the terrifying attentions of ghosts, shrees, roof-runners and fermins: all of these have caused me discomfort! I have roamed the dark hours in pursuit of my dreams! I have lurked beside dormers, crawled through attics, hovered over couches; I have suffered scratches and contusions; but never have I counted the cost if through my enterprise I were able to capture some particularly choice specimen."

"Each dream trapped in my net I carefully examined; for every dream cherished and saved I released a dozen, and finally from my store of superlatives I fashioned my wonderful crystals, and these I brought down the long road from Dai-Passant. Then, only last night, under the most mysterious circumstances, my precious goods were stolen by a robber only Cugel claims to have seen."

"I now point out that the dreams, whether near or far, represent marvels of truly superlative quality, and I feel that a careful description of the items —"

Duke Orbal held up his hand. "I must reiterate the judgment rendered upon Bazzard. A stringent rule stipulates that neither imaginary nor purported marvels qualify for the competition. Perhaps we will have the opportunity to adjudicate your dreams on another occasion. Now we must pass on to Cugel's pavilion and investigate his provocative 'Nowhere'."

Cugel stepped up on the dais before his exhibit. "Your Grace, I present for your inspection a legitimate marvel: not a straggle of insects, not a pedantic almanac, but an authentic miracle." Cugel whisked away the cloth. "Behold!"

The Duke made a puzzled sound. "A pile of dirt? A stump? What is that odd-looking member emerging from the hole?"

"Your Grace, I have here an opening into an unknown space, with the arm of one of its denizens. Inspect this tentacle! It pulses with the life of another cosmos! Notice the golden luster of the dorsal surface, the green and lavender of these encrustations. On the underside you will discover three colors of a sort never before seen!"

With a nonplussed expression Duke Orbal pulled at his chin. "This is all very well, but where is the rest of the creature? You present not a marvel, but the fraction of a marvel! I can make no judgment on the basis of a tail, or a hindquarters, or a proboscis, whatever the member may be. Additionally, you claim that the hole enters a far cosmos; still I see only a hole, resembling nothing so much as the den of a wysen-imp."

Iolo thrust himself forward. "May I venture an opinion? As I reflect upon events, I have become convinced that Cugel himself stole my Dreams!" "Your remarks interest no one," said Cugel. "Kindly hold your tongue while I continue my demonstration."

Iolo was not to be subdued so easily. He turned to Duke Orbal and cried in a poignant voice: "Hear me out, if you will! I am convinced that the 'robber' is no more than a figment of Cugel's imagination! He took my dreams and hid them, and where else but in the hole itself? For evidence I cite that length of string which leads into the hole."

Duke Orbal inspected Cugel with a frown. "Are these charges true? Answer exactly, since all can be verified."

Cugel chose his words with care. "I can only affirm what I myself know. Conceivably the robber hid Iolo's dreams in the hole while I was otherwise occupied. For what purpose? Who can say?"

Duke Orbal asked in a gentle voice: "Has anyone thought to search the hole for this elusive 'bag of dreams'?"

Cugel gave an indifferent shrug. "Iolo may enter now and search to his heart's content."

"You claim this hole!" retorted Iolo. "It therefore becomes your duty to protect the public!"

For several minutes an animated argument took place, until Duke Orbal intervened. "Both parties have raised persuasive points; I feel, however, that I must rule against Cugel. I therefore decree that he search his premises for the missing dreams and recover them if possible."

Cugel disputed the decision with such vigor that Duke Orbal turned to glance along the skyline, whereupon Cugel moderated his position. "The judgment of your Grace of course must prevail, and if I must, I will cast about for Iolo's lost dreams, although his theories are clearly absurd."

"Please do so, at once."

Cugel obtained a long pole, to which he attached a grapple. Gingerly thrusting his contrivance into the hole, he raked back and forth, but succeeded only in stimulating the tentacle, which thrashed from side to side.

Iolo suddenly cried out in excitement. "I notice a remarkable fact! The block of earth is at most six feet in breadth, yet Cugel plunged into the hole a pole twelve feet in length! What trickery does he practice now?"

Cugel replied in even tones: "I promised Duke Orbal a marvel and a wonderment, and I believe that I have done so."

Duke Orbal nodded gravely. "Well said, Cugel! Your exhibit is provocative! Still, you offer us only a tantalizing glimpse: a bottomless hole, a length of tentacle, a strange color, a far-off light — to the effect that your exhibit seems somewhat makeshift and impromptu. Contrast, if you will, the precision of Zaraflam's cockroaches!" He held up his hand as Cugel started to protest. "You display a hole: admitted, and a fine hole it is. But how does this hole differ from any other? Can I in justice award the prize on such a basis?"

"The matter may be resolved in a manner to satisfy us all," said Cugel. "Let Iolo enter the hole, to assure himself that his dreams are indeed elsewhere. Then, on his return, he will bear witness to the truly marvelous nature of my exhibit."

Iolo made an instant protest. "Cugel claims the exhibit; let him make the exploration!"

Duke Orbal raised his hand for silence. "I pronounce a decree to the effect that Cugel must immediately enter his exhibit in search of Iolo's properties, and likewise make a careful study of the environment, for the benefit of us all."

"Your Grace!" protested Cugel. "This is no simple matter! The tentacle almost fills the hole!"

"I see sufficient room for an agile man to slide past."

"Your Grace, to be candid, I do not care to enter the hole, by reason of extreme fear."

Duke Orbal again glanced up at the tubes which stood in a row along the skyline. He spoke over his shoulder to a burly man in a maroon and black uniform. "Which of the tubes is most suitable for use at this time?"

"The second tube from the right, your Grace, is only one-quarter occupied."

Cugel declared in a trembling voice: "I fear, but I have conquered my fear! I will seek Iolo's lost dreams!"

"Excellent," said Duke Orbal with a tight-lipped grin. "Please do not delay; my patience wears thin."

Cugel tentatively thrust a leg into the hole, but the motion of the tentacle caused him to snatch it out again. Duke Orbal muttered a few words to his constable, who brought up a winch. The tentacle was hauled forth from the hole a good five yards.

Duke Orbal instructed Cugel: "Straddle the tentacle, seize it with hands and legs and it will draw you back through the hole."

In desperation Cugel clambered upon the tentacle. The tension of the winch was relaxed and Cugel was pulled into the hole.

The light of Earth curled away from the opening and made no entrance; Cugel was plunged into a condition of near-total darkness, where, however, by some paradoxical condition he was able to sense the scope of his new environment in detail.

He stood on a surface at once flat, yet rough, with rises and dips and hummocks like the face of a windy sea. The black spongy stuff underfoot showed small cavities and tunnels in which Cugel sensed the motion of innumerable near-invisible points of light. Where the sponge rose high, the crest curled over like breaking surf, or stood ragged and crusty; in either case, the fringes glowed red, pale blue and several colors Cugel had never before observed. No horizon could be detected and the local concepts of distance, proportion, and size were not germane to Cugel's understanding.

Overhead hung dead Nothingness. The single feature of

note, a large disk the color of rain, floated at the zenith, an object so dim as to be almost invisible. At an indeterminate distance — a mile? ten miles? a hundred yards? — a hummock of some bulk overlooked the entire panorama. On closer inspection Cugel saw this hummock to be a prodigious mound of gelatinous flesh, inside which floated a globular organ apparently analogous to an eye. From the base of this creature a hundred tentacles extended far and wide across the black sponge. One of these tentacles passed near Cugel's feet, through the intracosmic gap, and out upon the soil of Earth.

Cugel discovered Iolo's sack of dreams, not three feet distant. The black sponge, bruised by the impact, had welled a liquid which had dissolved a hole in the leather, allowing the star-shaped dreams to spill out upon the sponge. In groping with the pole, Cugel had damaged a growth of brown palps. The resulting exudation had dripped upon the dreams and when Cugel picked up one of the fragile flakes, he saw that its edges glowed with eery fringes of color. The combination of oozes which had permeated the object caused his fingers to itch and tingle.

A score of small luminous nodes swarmed around his head, and a soft voice addressed him by name. "Cugel, what a pleasure that you have come to visit us! What is your opinion of our pleasant land?"

Cugel looked about in wonder; how could a denizen of this place know his name? At a distance of ten yards he noticed a small hummock of plasm not unlike the monstrous bulk with the floating eye.

Luminous nodes circled his head and the voice sounded in his ears: "You are perplexed, but remember, here we do things differently. We transfer our thoughts in small modules; if you look closely you will see them speeding through the fluxion: dainty little animalcules eager to unload their weight of enlightenment. There! Notice! Directly before your eyes hovers an excellent example. It is a thought of your own regarding which you are dubious; hence it hesitates, and awaits your decision."

"What if I speak?" asked Cugel. "Will this not facilitate matters?"

"To the contrary! Sound is considered offensive and everyone deplores the slightest murmur."

"This is all very well," grumbled Cugel, "but —"

"Silence, please! Send forth animalcules only!"

Cugel dispatched a whole host of luminous purports: "I will do my best. Perhaps you can inform me how far this land extends?"

"Not with certainty. At times I send forth animalcules to explore the far places; they report an infinite landscape similar to that which you see."

"Duke Orbal of Ombalique has commanded me to gather information and he will be interested in your remarks. Are valuable substances to be found here?"

"To a certain extent. There is proscedel and diphany and an occasional coruscation of zamanders."

"My first concern, of course, is to collect information for Duke Orbal, and I must also rescue Iolo's dreams; still I would be pleased to acquire a valuable trinket or two, if only to remind myself of our pleasant association."

"Understandable! I sympathize with your objectives."

"In that case, how may I obtain a quantity of such substances?"

"Easily. Simply send off animalcules to gather up your requirements." The creature emitted a whole host of pale plasms which darted away in all directions and presently returned with several dozen small spheres sparkling with a frosty blue light. "Here are zamanders of the first water," said the creature. "Accept them with my compliments."

Cugel placed the gems in his pouch. "This is a most convenient system for gaining wealth. I also wish to obtain a certain amount of diphany."

"Send forth animalcules! Why exert yourself needlessly?"

"We think along similar lines." Cugel dispatched several hundred animalcules which presently returned with twenty small ingots of the precious metal.

Cugel examined his pouch. "I still have room for a quantity of proscedel. With your permission I will send out the requisite animalcules."

"I would not dream of interfering," asserted the creature.

The animalcules sped forth, and before long returned with sufficient proscedel to fill Cugel's pouch. The creature said thoughtfully: "This is at least half of Uthaw's treasure; however, he appears not to have noticed its absence."

"'Uthaw'?" inquired Cugel. "Do you refer to yonder monstrous hulk?"

"Yes, that is Uthaw, who sometimes is both coarse and irascible."

Uthaw's eyes rolled toward Cugel and bulged through the outer membrane. A tide of animalcules arrived pulsing with significance. "I notice that Cugel has stolen my treasure, which I denounce as a breach of hospitality! In retribution, he must dig twenty-two zamanders from below the Shivering Trillows. He must then sift eight pounds of prime proscedel from the Dust of Time. Finally he must scrape eight acres of diphany bloom from the face of the High Disk."

Cugel sent forth animalcules. "Lord Uthaw, the penalty is harsh but just. A moment while I go to fetch the necessary tools!" He gathered up the dreams and sprang to the aperture. Seizing the tentacle he cried through the hole: "Pull the tentacle, work the winch! I have rescued the dreams!"

The tentacle convulsed and thrashed, effectively blocking the opening. Cugel turned and putting his fingers to his mouth emitted a piercing whistle. Uthaw's eye rolled upward and the tentacle fell limp.

The winch heaved at the tentacle and Cugel was drawn back through the hole. Uthaw, recovering his senses, jerked his tentacle so violently that the rope snapped; the winch was sent flying; and several persons were swept from their feet. Uthaw jerked back his tentacle and the hole immediately closed.

Cugel cast the sack of dream-flakes contemptuously at the feet of Iolo. "There you are, ingrate! Take your vapid hallucinations and go your way! Let us hear no more of you!"

Cugel turned to Duke Orbal. "I am now able to render a report upon the other cosmos. The ground is composed of a black spongelike substance and flickers with a trillion infinitesimal glimmers. My research discovered no limits to the extent of the land. A pale disk, barely visible, covers a quarter of the sky. The denizens are, first and foremost, an ill-natured hulk

named Uthaw, and others more or less similar. No sound is allowed and meaning is conveyed by animalcules, which also
procure the necessities of life. In essence, these are my dis-
coveries, and now, with utmost respect, I claim the grand prize
of one thousand terces."

From behind his back Cugel heard Iolo's mocking laughter.
Duke Orbal shook his head. "My dear Cugel, what you
suggest is impossible. To what exhibit do you refer? The boxful
of dirt yonder? It lacks all pretensions to singularity."

"But you saw the hole! With your winch you pulled the tentacle! In accordance with your orders, I entered the hole and
explored the region!"

"True enough, but hole and tentacle are both vanished. I do
not for a moment suggest mendacity, but your report is not easily verified. I can hardly award honors to an entity so fugitive
as the memory of a non-existent hole! I fear that on this occasion I must pass you by. The prize will be awarded to Zaraflam
and his remarkable cockroaches."

"A moment, your Grace!" Iolo called out. "Remember, I am
entered in the competition! At last I am able to display my products! Here is a particularly choice item, distilled from a
hundred dreams captured early in the morning from a bevy of
beautiful maidens asleep in a bower of fragrant vines."

"Very well," said Duke Orbal. "I will delay the award until I
test the quality of your visions. What is the procedure? Must I
compose myself for slumber?"

"Not at all! The ingestion of the dream during waking hours
produces not a hallucination, but a mood: a sensibility fresh,
new and sweet: an allurement of the faculties, an indescribable
exhilaration. Still, why should you not be comfortable as you
test my dreams? You there! Fetch a couch! And you, a cushion
for his Grace's noble head. You! Be good enough to take his
Grace's hat."

Cugel saw no profit in remaining. He moved to the outskirts
of the throng.

Iolo brought forth his dream and for a moment seemed puzzled by the ooze still adhering to the object, then decided to
ignore the matter, and paid no further heed, except to rub his
fingers as if after contact with some viscid substance.

Making a series of grand gestures, Iolo approached the great chair where Duke Orbal sat at his ease. "I will arrange the dream for its most convenient ingestion," said Iolo. "I place a quantity into each ear; I insert a trifle up each nostril; I arrange the balance under your Grace's illustrious tongue. Now, if your Grace will relax, in half a minute the quintessence of a hundred exquisite dreams will be made known."

Duke Orbal became rigid. His fingers clenched the arms of the chair. His back arched and his eyes bulged from their sockets. He turned over backward, then rolled, jerked, jumped and bounded about the plaza before the amazed eyes of his subjects.

Iolo called out in a brassy voice: "Where is Cugel? Fetch that scoundrel Cugel!"

But Cugel had already departed Cuirnif and was nowhere to be found.

CHAPTER VI

FROM CUIRNIF TO PERGOLO

1
THE
FOUR WIZARDS

CUGEL'S visit to Cuirnif was marred by several disagreeable incidents, and he left town with more haste than dignity. At last he pushed through an alder thicket, jumped a ditch and scrambled up on the Old Ferghaz High-road. Pausing to look and listen, and discovering that pursuit apparently had been abandoned, he set off at best speed to the west.

The road lay across a wide blue moor patched here and there with small forests. The region was eerily silent; scanning the moor, Cugel found only distance, a wide sky and solitude, with no sign of hut or house.

From the direction of Cuirnif came a trap drawn by a one-horned wheriot. The driver was Bazzard, who, like Cugel, had exhibited at the Exposition of Marvels. Bazzard's entry, like Cugel's 'Nowhere', had ben disqualified for technical reasons.

Bazzard halted the trap. "So, Cugel, I see that you decided to leave your exhibit at Cuirnif."

"I had no real choice," said Cugel. "With the hole gone, 'Nowhere' became a massive boxful of dirt, which I was happy to leave in the custody of Duke Orbal."

"I did the same with my dead fish," said Bazzard. He looked around the moor. "This is a sinister district, with robber asms watching from every forest. Where are you bound?"

"Ultimately, to Azenomei in Almery. As of now, I would be happy to find shelter for the nignt."

"In that case, why not ride with me? I will be grateful for your company. Tonight we will stop at the Iron Man Inn, and tomorrow should bring us to Llaio where I live with my four fathers."

307

"Your offer is welcome," said Cugel. He climbed to the seat; Bazzard touched up the wheriot and the trap moved along the road at good speed.

After a period Bazzard said: "If I am not mistaken, Iucounu the Laughing Magician, as he is known, makes his resort at Pergolo, which is near Azenomei. Perhaps you and he are acquainted?"

"We are indeed," said Cugel. "He has enjoyed several choice jokes at my expense."

"Aha then! I gather that he is not one of your most trusted comrades."

Cugel looked over his shoulder and spoke in a distinct voice. "Should any casual ears be listening, let it be known that my regard for Iucounu is of a high order."

Bazzard made a sign of comprehension. "Whatever the case, why are you returning to Azenomei?"

Again Cugel looked in all directions. "Still in reference to Iucounu: his many friends often report overheard messages, but sometimes in garbled form; hence I am careful to avoid loose talk."

"That is correct conduct!" said Bazzard. "At Llaio, my four fathers are equally prudent." After a moment Cugel asked: "Many times I have known a father with four sons, but never before a son with four fathers. What is the explanation?"

Bazzard scratched his head in puzzlement. "I have never thought to ask," he said. "I will do so at the earliest opportunity."

The journey proceeded without incident and late in the afternoon of the second day, the two arrived at Llaio, a large manse of sixteen gables.

A groom took the trap into charge; Bazzard conducted Cugel through a tall iron-bound door, across a reception hall and into a parlour. High windows, each of twelve violet panes, dimmed the afternoon sunlight; fusty magenta beams, slanting down across the room, warmed the dark oak wainscoting. A long table rested on dark green carpeting. Close together, with their backs to the fire, sat four men of unusual aspect, in that they shared between them a single eye, a single ear, a single arm and a single leg. In other respects the four were much alike: small and slight, with round serious faces and black hair cut short.

Bazzard performed the introductions. As he spoke the four men deftly passed arm, eye and ear back and forth, so that each was able to appraise the quality of their visitor.

"This gentleman is Cugel," said Bazzard. "He is a minor grandee of the Twish River Valley, who has suffered the jokes of someone who shall remain nameless. Cugel, allow me to present my four fathers! They are Disserl, Vasker, Pelasias and Archimbaust: at one time wizards of repute until they too ran afoul of a certain prankster magician."

Pelasias, who at this moment wore both the eye and ear, spoke: "Be assured of our welcome! Guests at Llaio are all too rare. How did you chance to meet our son Bazzard?"

"We occupied close pavilions at the Exposition," said Cugel. "With due respect for Duke Orbal, I feel that his rulings were arbitrary, and neither Bazzard nor I won the prize."

"Cugel's remarks are not exaggerated," said Bazzard. "I was not even allowed to simulate the songs of my unfortunate fish."

"A pity!" said Pelasias. "Still, the Exposition no doubt provided memorable experiences for you both, so the time was not wasted. Am I right in this, Bazzard?"

"Quite right, sir, and while the subject is fresh in my mind, I would like you to resolve a perplexity. A single father often boasts four sons, but how does a single son boast four fathers?"

Disserl, Vasker and Archimbaust rapidly tapped the table; the eye, ear and arm were interchanged. At last Vasker made a curt gesture. "The question is nuncupatory."

Archimbaust, providing himself with eye and ear, examined Cugel with care. He seemed especially interested in Cugel's cap, to which Cugel had again attached 'Spatterlight'. "That is a remarkable ornament," said Archimbaust.

Cugel bowed politely. "I consider it very fine."

"As to the origin of this object: do you care to provide us any information?"

Cugel smilingly shook his head. "Let us change the subject to more interesting topics. Bazzard tells me that we have a number of friends in common, including the noble and popular Iucounu."

Archimbaust blinked his eye in puzzlement. "Are we speaking of that yellow, immoral and repulsive Iucounu, sometimes known as the 'Laughing Magician'?"

Cugel winced and shuddered. "I would never make such insulting references to dear Iucounu, especially if I thought that he or one of his loyal spies might overhear."

"Aha!" said Archimbaust. "Now I understand your diffidence! You need not worry! We are protected by a warning device. You may speak freely."

"In that case I will admit that my friendship with Iucounu is not deep and abiding. Recently, at his command, a leather-winged demon carried me across the Ocean of Sighs and dropped me sprawling upon a dreary beach known as Shanglestone Strand."

"If that is a joke, it is in poor taste!" declared Bazzard.

"That is my opinion," said Cugel. "In regard to this ornament, it is actually a scale known as the 'Pectoral Sky-break Spatterlight', from the prow of the demiurge Sadlark. It exhibits power which, frankly, I do not understand, and is dangerous to the touch unless your hands are wet."

"All very well," said Bazzard, "but why did you not wish to discuss it before?"

"By reason of a most interesting fact: Iucounu owns all the rest of Sadlark's scales! He will therefore covet 'Spatterlight' with all of that intense and excitable yearning which we associate with Iucounu."

"Most interesting!" said Archimbaust. He and his brothers tapped a flurry of messages back and forth, interchanging their single eye, ear and arm with swift precision. Cugel, watching, at last was able to hazard a guess as to how four fathers might sire a single son.

Vasker presently asked: "What are your plans in connection with Iucounu and this extraordinary scale?"

"I am both uncertain and uneasy," said Cugel. "Iucounu covets 'Spatterlight': true! He will approach me and say: 'Ah, dear Cugel, how nice that you bring me 'Spatterlight'! Hand it over, or prepare for a joke!' So then: where is my recourse? My advantage is lost. When one deals with Iucounu, he must be prepared to jump nimbly from side to side. I have quick wits and agile feet, but are these enough?"

"Evidently not," said Vasker. "Still —"

A hissing noise made itself heard. Vasker at once imposed upon his voice the tremolo of fond recollection: "Yes, dear Iucounu! How strange, Cugel, that you should also number him among your friends!"

Noting Bazzard's secret sign, Cugel spoke in tones equally melodious. "He is known far and wide as an excellent fellow!"

"Just so! We have had our little differences, but is this not sometimes the way? Now, all is forgotten, on both sides, I am sure."

Bazzard spoke: "If you should chance to see him in Almery, please convey our very warmest regards!"

"I will not be seeing Iucounu," said Cugel. "I plan to retire to a snug little cabin beside the River Sune and perhaps learn a useful trade.'

"On the whole, this seems a sensible plan," said Archimbaust. "But come now, Bazzard, tell us more of the Exposition!"

"It was grandly conceived," said Bazzard. "No doubt as to that! Cugel displayed a remarkable hole, but Duke Orbal disallowed it on grounds of fugacity. Xallops showed a 'Compendium of Universal Knowledge' which impressed everyone. The cover depicted the Gnostic Emblem, in this fashion. . . ."

Taking up stylus and paper, Bazzard scribbled: *Do not look now, but Iucounu's spy hangs above, in a wisp of smoke.* "There, Cugel! Am I not correct?"

"Yes, in the main, although you have omitted several significant flourishes."

"My memory is not the best," said Bazzard. He crumpled the paper and threw it into the fire.

Vasker spoke. "Friend Cugel, perhaps you would enjoy a sip of dyssac, or might you prefer wine?"

"I will be happy with either," said Cugel.

"In that case, I will suggest the dyssac. We distill it ourselves from local herbs. Bazzard, if you will."

While Bazzard served the liquor, Cugel glanced as if casually around the chamber. High in the shadows he noticed a wisp of smoke from which peered a pair of small red eyes.

In a droning voice Vasker spoke of the Llaio fowl-run and the high price of feed. The spy at last bcame bored; the smoke slipped down the wall, into the chimney and was gone.

Pelasias looked through the eye to Bazzard. "The alarm again is set?"

"Quite so."

"Then once again we can speak freely. Cugel, I will be explicit. At one time we were wizards of reputation, but Iucounu played us a joke which still rankles. Our magic for the most part is forgotten; nothing remains but a few tendrils of hope and, of course, our abiding detestation of Iucounu."

"Clarity itself! What do you propose to do?"

"More to the point: what are your plans? Iucounu will take your scale without remorse, laughing and joking all the while. How will you prevent him?"

Cugel pulled uneasily at his chin. "I have given some attention to the matter."

"To what effect?"

"I had thought perhaps to hide the scale, and confuse Iucounu with hints and lures. Already I am troubled by doubts. Iucounu might simply ignore my conundrums in favor of Panguire's Triumphant Displasms. No doubt I would be quick to say: 'Iucounu, your jokes are superb and you shall have your scale.' My best hope may be to present the scale to Iucounu face to face, as a purported act of generosity."

"In this case, how are your goals advanced?" asked Pelasias.

Cugel looked around the room. "We are secure?"

"Definitely so."

"Then I will reveal an important fact. The scale consumes whomever it touches, save in the presence of water, which dulls its voracity."

Pelasias regarded Cugel with new respect. "I must say that you wear this lethal trinket with aplomb."

"I am always aware of its presence. It has already absorbed a pelgrane and a female hybrid of bazil and grue.

"Aha!" said Pelasias. "Let us put this scale to the test. At the fowl run we trapped a weasel who now awaits execution: why not by the power of your ornament?"

Cugel assented. "As you like."

Bazzard fetched the captive predator, which snarled and hissed in defiance. Wetting his hands, Cugel tied the scale to a stick and thrust it down upon the weasel, which was instantly absorbed. The node showed new coruscations of red, vibrating to such vivid fervor that Cugel was reluctant to pin it again to his cap. he wrapped it in several layers of heavy cloth and tucked it into his pouch.

Disserl now wore eye and ear. "Your scale has shown its power. Nonetheless, it lacks projective scope. You need our help, sickly though it may be. Then, if you are successful, perhaps you will restore our orphan members."

"They may no longer be in useful condition," said Cugel dubiously.

"We need not worry on this score," replied Disserl. "The organs, fully sound and competent, reside in Iucounu's vault."

"That is good news," said Cugel. "I agree to your terms, and I am anxious to hear how you can help me."

"First and most urgently, we must ensure that Iucounu cannot take the scale either through force or intimidation, or by means of Arnhoult's Sequestrous Digitalia, or by a time stoppage, such as the Interminable Interim. If he is so thwarted, then he must play the game by your rules, and victory is at your command."

Vasker took the organs. "Already I am cheered! In Cugel we have a man who can confront Iucounu nose to nose and never flinch!"

Cugel jumped to his feet and paced nervously back and forth. "A truculent posture may not be the best approach. Iucounu, after all, knows a thousand tricks. How will we prevent him from using his magic? Here is the nub of the matter."

"I will take counsel with my brothers," said Vasker. "Bazzard, you and Cugel may dine in the Hall of Trophies. Be mindful of spies."

After a dinner of fair quality, Bazzard and Cugel returned to the parlour, where the four wizards sipped in turn from a great mug of tea. Pelasias, now wearing eye, arm and ear, spoke: "We have consulted Boberg's *Pandaemonium* and also the Vapurial Index. We now are convinced that you carry something more than just a handsome scale. Rather, it is Sadlark's cerebral nexus itself. It has ingested several creatures of strong personality, including our own good weasel, and now displays signs of vitality, as if recovering from an estivation. No more strength may be allowed Sadlark at this time."

Archimbaust took the organs. "We think in terms of pure logic. Proposition One: in order to achieve our goals, Cugel must confront Iucounu. Proposition Two: Iucounu must be deterred from seizing the scale out of hand."

Cugel frowned. "Your propositions are orderly, but I envision a program somewhat more subtle. The scale will bait a trap; Iucounu will run eagerly forward and be rendered helpless."

"Inept, on three counts! First: you will be watched by spies, or by Iucounu himself. Second: Iucounu recognizes bait from afar and will send either a casual passer-by or you yourself into the trap. Third: in preference to negotiation, Iucounu uses Tinkler's Old-fashioned Froust, and you would find yourself running from Pergolo on thirty-foot strides to retrieve the scale for Iucounu."

Cugel held up his hand. "Let us return to the propositions of pure logic. As I recall, Iucounu must not be allowed to seize the scale out of hand. What follows?"

"We have several dependent corollaries. To slow the quick grasp of his avarice, you must feign the submission of a cowed dog, a pose which Iucounu in his vanity will readily accept. Next we will need an article of confusion, to give us a range of options from which to choose. Tomorrow, therefore, Bazzard will duplicate the scale in fine gold, with a good red hypolite for the node. He will then cement the false scale to your cap in a bed of explosive diambroid."

"And I am to wear the cap?" asked Cugel.

"Of course! You will then have three strings to your bow. All will be destroyed if Iucounu tries even the least of his tricks. Or you can give Iucounu the cap itself, then go somewhat apart and wait for the blast. Or, if Iucounu discovers the diambroid, other avenues appear. For instance, you can temporize, then make play with the authentic scale."

Cugel rubbed his chin. "Propositions and corollaries to the side, I am not anxious to wear a charge of high explosive attached to my cap."

Archimbaust argued the program, but Cugel remained dubious. Somewhat sulkily Archimbaust relinquished the organs to Vasker who said: "I propose a somewhat similar plan. As before, Cugel, you will enter Almery in an unobtrusive manner. You will stroll quietly by the side of the road with the cloak pulled across your face, using any name but your own. Iucounu will be intrigued, and come out in search of you. At this point your policy will be restrained courtesy. You will politely decline all offers and go your own way. This conduct will surely prompt Iucounu to unwise excess! Then you will act!"

"Just so," said Cugel. "What if he simply seizes cap and scale, false or real, and preempts it to his own use?"

"That is the virtue of Archimbaust's scheme," Vasker pointed out.

Cugel gnawed at his lower lip. "Each plan seems to lack a certain full elegance."

Archimbaust, taking the organs, spoke with emphasis: "My plan is best! Do you prefer Forlorn Encystment at a depth of forty-five miles to an ounce or two of diambroid?"

Bazzard, who had spoken little, put forward an idea: "We need only use a small quantity of diambroid, and thus allay the worst of Cugel's fears. Three minims is enough to destroy Iucounu's hand, arm and shoulder, in the case of improper conduct."

Vasker said: "This is an excellent compromise! Bazzard, you have a good head on your shoulders! The diambroid, after all, need not come into use. I am sure that Cugel will deal with Iucounu as a cat plays with a mouse."

Disserl spoke to the same effect: "Show only diffidence! His vanity will then become your ally!"

Pelasias said: "Above all, accept no favors! Or you will find yourself in his obligation, which is like a bottomless pit. At one time —"

A sudden hiss, as the alarm web detected a spy.

" — packet of dried fruits and raisins for your pouch," droned Pelasias. "The way is long and tiring, especially if you use the Old Ferghaz Way which traces every swing and meander of the River Sune. Why not make for Taun Tassel on the Waters-gleam?

"A good plan! The way is long and Forest Da is dark, but I hope to evade even the whisper of notoriety, and all my old friends as well."

"And your ultimate plans?"

Cugel gave a wistful laugh. "I will build a little hut beside the river and there live out my days. Perhaps I will do a small trade in nuts and wild honey."

"There is always a market for home-baked loaves," Bazzard pointed out.

"A good thought! Again, I might search out scraps of old calligraphy, or just give myself to meditation and watch the flow of the river. Such, at least, is my modest hope."

"It is a pleasant ambition! If only we could help you along your way! But our magic is small; we know a single useful spell: Brassman's Twelve-fold Bounty, by which a single terce becomes a dozen. We have taught it to Bazzard, that he may never want; perhaps he will share the sleight with you."

"With pleasure," said Bazzard. "You will find it a great comfort!"

"That is most kind," said Cugel. "What with the packet of fruit and nuts, I am well-provided for my journey."

"Just so! Perhaps you will leave us your cap ornament as a keepsake, so that when we see it we will think of you."

Cugel shook his head in distress. "Anything else is yours! But I could never part with my lucky talisman!"

"No matter! We will remember you in any case. Bazzard, foster the fire! Tonight is unseasonably cold."

So went the conversation until the spy departed, whereupon, at Cugel's request, Bazzard instructed him in that cantrap controlling the Twelve-fold Bounty. Then, upon sudden thought, Bazzard addressed Vasker, now wearing eye, ear and arm. "Another of our small magics which might help Cugel on his way: the Spell of the Tireless Legs."

Vasker chuckled. "What a thought! Cugel will not care to be visited with a spell customarily reserved for our wheriots! Such a spell does not accord with his dignity."

"I give dignity second place to expedience," said Cugel. "What is this spell?"

Bazzard said half-apologetically: "It guards the legs from the fatigue of a long day's march, and as Vasker indicates, we use it mainly to encourage our wheriots."

"I will consider the matter," said Cugel, and there the subject rested.

In the morning Bazzard took Cugel to his work-shop, where, after donning wet gloves, he duplicated the scale in fine gold, with a central node of flaming red hypolite. "Now then," said Bazzard. "Three minims of diambroid, or perhaps four, and Iucounu's fate is as good as sealed."

Cugel watched glumly as Bazzard cemented diambroid to the ornament and attached it to his cap by a secret clasp. "You will find this a great comfort," said Bazzard.

Cugel gingerly donned the cap. "I see no obvious advantage to this false, if explosive, scale, save for the fact that duplicity is valuable for its own sake." He folded 'Spatterlight' into the flap of a special glove provided by the four wizards.

"I will provide you with a packet of nuts and fruit, and then you will be ready for the road," said Bazzard. "If you move at a good pace, you should arrive at Taun Tassel on Water's-gleam before nightfall."

Cugel said thoughtfully: "As I consider the way ahead, I become ever more favorably inclined to the Spell of the Untiring Legs."

"It is the work of a few minutes only," said Bazzard. "Let us consult my fathers."

The two repaired to the parlour, where Archimbaust consulted an index of spells. Encompassing the syllables with effort, he released the salutary force toward Cugel.

To the amazement of all, the spell struck Cugel's legs, rebounded, struck again without effect, then clattered away, reverberated from wall to wall, and finally lapsed in a series of small grinding sounds.

The four wizards consulted together at length. Finally Disserl turned to Cugel: "This is a most extraordinary happening! It can only be explained by the fact that you carry 'Spatterlight', whose alien force acts as a crust against earthly magic!"

Bazzard cried out in excitement: "Try the Spell of Internal Effervescence upon Cugel; if it proves fruitless, then we shall know the truth!"

"And if the spell is efficacious?" asked Disserl coldly. "Is this your concept of hospitality?"

"My apologies!" said Bazzard in confusion. "I failed to think the matter through."

"It seems that I must forego the 'Untiring Legs'," said Cugel. "But no matter: I am accustomed to the road, and now I will take my leave."

"Our hopes go with you!" said Vasker. "Boldness and caution: let them work hand in hand!"

"I am grateful for your wise counsel," said Cugel. "Everything now depends upon Iucounu. If avarice dominates his prudence, you shall soon know the enjoyment of your missing organs. Bazzard, our chance acquaintance has yielded profit, so I hope, for all concerned." Cugel departed Llaio.

2
SPATTERLIGHT

WHERE a bridge of black glass crossed the River Sune, Cugel found a marker announcing that he had once again come into the Land of Almery.

The road forked. Old Ferghaz Way followed the Sune, while the Kang Kingdom Marchway, swinging south, crossed the Hanging Hills and so descended into the valley of the River Twish.

Cugel held to the right and so fared west through a countryside of small farmsteads, demarcated one from the other by lines of tall mulgoon trees.

A stream flowed down from the Forest Da to join the Sune; the road crossed over by a bridge of three arches. At the far side, leaning against a damson tree and chewing a straw stood Iucounu.

Cugel halted to stare, and at last decided that he saw, not an apparition nor a yellow-faced hallucination with pendulous jowls, but Iucounu himself. A tawny coat contained the pear-shaped torso; the thin legs were encased in tight pink- and black-striped trousers.

Cugel had not expected to see Iucounu so soon. He leaned forward and peered, as if in doubt. "Am I correct in recognizing Iucounu?"

"Quite correct," said Iucounu, rolling his yellow eyes in every direction except toward Cugel.

"This is a true surprise!"

Iucounu put his hand to his mouth to conceal a smile. "A pleasant surprise, I hope?"

"Needless to say! I never expected to find you loitering along the wayside, and you quite startled me! Have you been

319

fishing from the bridge? But I see that you carry neither tackle nor bait."

Iucounu slowly turned his head and surveyed Cugel from under drooping eyelids. "I too am surprised to see you back from your travels. Why do you walk so far afield? Your former depredations took place along the Twish."

"I am purposely avoiding my old haunts, and my old habits as well," said Cugel. "Neither have brought me profit."

"In every life comes a time for change," said Iucounu. "I too consider metamorphosis, to an extent which might surprise you." He discarded the straw from his mouth and spoke with energy. "Cugel, you are looking well! Your garments become you, as does that cap! Where did you find so handsome an ornament?"

Cugel reached up and touched the duplicated scale. "This little piece? It is my lucky talisman. I found it in a mire near Shanglestone Strand."

"I hope that you brought me another of the same sort, as a memento?"

Cugel shook his head as if in regret. "I found but a single specimen of this quality."

"Tsk. I am disappointed. What are your plans?"

"I intend a simple life: a cabin on the banks of the Sune, with a porch overhanging the water, and there I will devote myself to calligraphy and meditation. Perhps I will read Stafdyke's *Comprehensive Survey of All the Aeons*, a treatise to which everyone alludes, but which no one has read, with the probable exception of yourself."

"Yes, I know it well. Your travels, then, have brought you the means to gratify your desires."

Cugel smilingly shook his head. "My wealth is scant. I plan a life of simplicity."

"The ornament in your cap is very showy. Is it not valuable? The nexus, or node, gleams as brightly as a good hypolite."

Cugel once more shook his head. "It is only glass refracting the red rays of sunlight."

Iucounu gave a noncommittal grunt. "Footpads are common along this road. Their first objective would be this famous ornament of yours."

Cugel chuckled. "So much the worse for them."

Iucounu became attentive. "How so?"

Cugel fondled the gem. "Whoever tried to take the jewel by force would be blown to bits, along with the jewel."

"Rash but effective," said Iucounu. "I must be off about my business."

Iucounu, or his apparition, vanished. Cugel, assured that spies watched his every move, gave a shrug and went his own way.

An hour before sundown Cugel arrived at the village Flath Foiry, where he took lodging at the Inn of Five Flags. Dining in the common room, he became acquainted with Lorgan, a dealer in fancy embroideries. Lorgan enjoyed both large talk and generous quantities of drink. Cugel was in no mood for either and pleading fatigue retired early to his chamber. Lorgan remained in bibulous conversation with several merchants of the town.

Upon entering his chamber, Cugel locked the door, then made a thorough inspection by lamp-light. The couch was clean; the windows overlooked a kitchen garden; songs and shouts from the common room were muted. With a sigh of satisfaction, Cugel dimmed the lamp and went to his couch.

As Cugel composed himself for slumber, he thought to hear an odd sound. He raised his head to listen, but the sound was not repeated. Cugel once again relaxed. The odd sound came again, somewhat louder, and a dozen large whispering bat-like creatures flew out of the shadows. They darted into Cugel's face and climbed on his neck with their claws, hoping to distract his attention while a black eel with long trembling hands worked to steal Cugel's cap.

Cugel tore aside the bat-things, touched the eel with 'Spatterlight', causing its instant dissolution, and the bat-things flew crying and whispering from the room.

Cugel brought light to the lamp. All seemed in order. He reflected a moment, then, stepping out into the hall, he investigated the chamber next to his own. It proved to be vacant, and he took immediate possession.

An hour later his rest was again disturbed, this time by Lorgan, now thoroughly in his cups. Upon seeing Cugel he blinked in surprise. "Cugel, why are you sleeping in my chamber?"

"You have made a mistake," said Cugel. "Your chamber is next door over."

"Ah! All is explained! My profuse apologies!"

"It is nothing," said Cugel. "Sleep well."

"Thank you." Lorgan staggered off to bed. Cugel, locking the door, once more threw himself down on the couch and passed a restful night, ignoring the sounds and outcries from the room next door.

In the morning, as Cugel took his breakfast, Lorgan limped downstairs and described to Cugel the events of the night: "As I lay in a pleasantly drowsy state, two large madlocks with heavy arms, staring green eyes and no necks entered by the window. They dealt me any number of heavy blows despite my appeals for mercy. Then they stole my hat and made for the window as if to leave, only to turn back and strike further blows. 'That is for causing so much trouble,' they said, and finally they were gone. Have you ever heard the like?"

"Never!" said Cugel. "It is an outrage."

"Strange things happen in life," mused Lorgan. "Still, I will not stop at this inn again."

"A sensible decision," said Cugel. "Now, if you will excuse me, I must be on my way."

Cugel paid his score and set off along the high-road, and the morning passed uneventfully.

At noon Cugel came upon a pavilion of pink silk, erected upon a grassy place beside the road. At a table laden with fine food and drink sat Iucounu, who, at the sight of Cugel, jumped up in surprise. "Cugel! What a happy occasion! You must join me at my meal!"

Cugel measured the distance between Iucounu and the spot where he would be obliged to sit; the distance would not allow him to reach across the space holding 'Spatterlight' in his gloved hand.

Cugel shook his head. "I have already taken a nutritious lunch of nuts and raisins. You have chosen a lovely spot for your picnic. I wish you a happy appetite, and good day."

"Wait, Cugel! One moment, if you please! Taste a goblet of

this fine Fazola! It will put spring in your steps!"

"It will, more likely, put me to sleep in the ditch. And now —"

Iucounu's ropy mouth twitched in a grimace. But at once he renewed his affability. "Cugel, I hereby invite you to visit me at Pergolo; surely you have not forgotten the amenities? Every night we will host a grand banquet, and I have discovered a new phase of magic, by which I recall remarkable persons from across the aeons. The entertainments are splendid at Pergolo!"

Cugel made a rueful gesture. "You sing siren songs of inducement! One taste of such glamour might shatter my resolve! I am not the rakehelly Cugel of old!"

Iucounu strove to keep his voice even. "This is becoming all too clear." Throwing himself back in his chair, he glowered morosely at Cugel's cap. Making a sudden impatient gesture, he muttered a spell of eleven syllables, so that the air between himself and Cugel twisted and thickened. The forces veered out toward Cugel and past, to rattle away in all directions, cutting russet and black streaks through the grass.

Iucounu stared with yellow eyes bulging, but Cugel paid no heed to the incident. He bade Iucounu a civil farewell and continued along the way.

For an hour Cugel walked, using that loping bent-kneed gait which had propelled him so many long leagues. Down from the fells on the right hand came the Forest Da, softer and sweeter than the Great Erm to the far north. River and road plunged into the shade, and all sound was hushed. Long-stemmed flowers grew in the mold: delice, blue-bell, rosace, cany-flake. Coral fungus clung to dead stumps like cloths of fairy lace. Maroon sunlight slanted across the forest spaces, creating a gloom saturated with a dozen dark colors. Nothing moved and no sound could be heard but the trill of a far bird.

Despite the apparent solitude, Cugel loosened the sword in its scabbard and walked with soft feet; the forests often revealed awful secrets to the innocent.

After some miles the forest thinned and retreated to the north. Cugel came upon a cross-roads; here waited a fine double-sprung carriage drawn by four white wheriots. High on the coachman's bench sat a pair of maidens with long orange hair, complexions of dusky tan and eyes of emerald green. They wore a livery of umber and oyster-white and, after quick side-glances toward Cugel, stared haughtily ahead.

Iucounu threw open the door. "Hola, Cugel! By chance I came this route and behold! I perceive my friend Cugel striding along at a great rate! I had not expected to find you so far along the way!"

"I enjoy the open road," said Cugel. "I march at quick-step because I intend to arrive at Taun Tassel before dark. Forgive me if, once again, I cut our conversation short."

"Unnecessary! Taun Tassel is on my way. Step into the carriage; we will talk as we ride."

Cugel hesitated, looking first one way, then another, and Iucounu became impatient. "Well then?" he barked. "What now?"

Cugel attempted an apologetic smile. "I never take without giving in return. This policy averts misunderstandings."

Iucounu's eyelids drooped at the corners in moist reproach. "Must we quibble over minor points? Into the carriage with you, Cugel; you may enlarge upon your qualms as we ride."

"Very well," said Cugel. "I will ride with you to Taun Tassel, but you must accept these three terces in full, exact, final, comprehensive and complete compensation for the ride and every other aspect, adjunct, by-product and consequence, either direct or indirect, of the said ride, renouncing every other claim, now, and forever, including all times of the past and future, without exception, and absolving me, in part and in whole, from any and all further obligations."

Iucounu held up small balled fists and gritted his teeth toward the sky. "I repudiate your entire paltry philosophy! I find zest in giving! I now offer you in title full and clear this excellent carriage, inclusive of wheels, springs and upholstery, the four wheriots with twenty-six ells of gold chain and a pair of matched maidens. The totality is yours! Ride where you will!"

"I am dumbfounded by your generosity!" said Cugel. "What, may I ask, do you want in return?"

"Bah! Some trifle, perhaps, to symbolize the exchange. The kickshaw that you wear in your hat will suffice."

Cugel made a sign of regret. "You ask the one thing I hold dear. That is the talisman I found near Shanglestone Strand. I have carried it through thick and thin, and now I could never give it up. It may even exert a magical influence."

"Nonsense!" snorted Iucounu. "I have a sensitive nose for magic. The ornament is as dull as stale beer."

"Its spark has cheered me through dreary hours; I could never give it up."

Iucounu's mouth drooped almost past his chin. "You have become over-sentimental!" Glancing past Cugel's shoulder, Iucounu uttered a shrill cry of alarm. "Take care! A plague of tasps is upon us!"

Turning, Cugel discovered a leaping horde of green scorpion-things the size of weasels close upon the carriage.

"Quick!" cried Iucounu. "Into the carriage! Drivers, away!"

Hesitating only an instant Cugel scrambled into the carriage. Iucounu uttered a great sigh of relief. "A very near thing! Cugel, I believe that I saved your life!"

Cugel looked throgh the back window. "The tasps have disappeared into thin air! How is that possible?"

"No matter; we are safely away, and that is the main point. Give thanks that I was on hand with my carriage! Are you not appreciative? Perhaps now you will concede me my whim, which is the ornament on your hat."

Cugel considered the situation. From where he sat he could not easily apply the authentic scale to Iucounu's face. He thought to temporize. "Why would you want such a trifle?"

"Truth to tell, I collect such objects. Yours will make a famous centerpiece for my display. Be so good as to hand it over, if only for my inspection."

"That is not easily done. If you look closely you will see that it is fixed to my cap on a matrix of diambroid."

Iucounu clicked his tongue in vexation. "Why would you go to such lengths?"

"To deter the hands of thieves; why else?"

"Surely you can detach the article in safety?"

"While we bump and sway in a speeding carriage? I would not dare make the attempt."

Iucounu turned Cugel a lemon-yellow side-glance. "Cugel, are you trying to 'twiddle my whiskers', as the saying goes?"

"Naturally not."

"Just so." The two sat in silence while the landscape flashed past. All in all, thought Cugel, a precarious situation, even though his plans called for just such a progression of events. Above all, he must not allow Iucounu the close scrutiny of the scale; Iucounu's lumpy nose indeed could smell out magic, or its lack.

Cugel became aware that the carriage traversed, not forest, but open countryside. He turned toward Iucounu. "This is not the way to Taun Tassel! Where are we going?"

"To Pergolo," said Iucounu. "I insist upon extending you my best hospitality."

"Your invitation is hard to resist," said Cugel.

The carriage plunged over a line of hills and descended into a valley well-remembered by Cugel. Ahead he glimpsed the flow of the Twish River, with a momentary flash of red sunlight on the water, then Iucounu's manse Pergolo appeared on the brow of a hill, and a moment later the carriage drew up under the portico.

"We have arrived," said Iucounu. "Cugel, I welcome you once again to Pergolo! Will you alight?"

"With pleasure," said Cugel.

Iucounu ushered Cugel into the reception hall. "First, Cugel, let us take a glass of wine to freshen our throats after the dust of the journey. Then we will tie up the loose strands of our business, which extend somewhat further into the past than you may care to remember." Here Iucounu referred to a period during which Cugel had held him at a disadvantage.

"Those days are lost in the mists of time," said Cugel. "All is now forgotten."

Iucounu smiled behind pursed lips. "Later in your visit we will reminisce, to our mutual amusement! As for now, why not remove your cap, cloak and gloves?"

"I am quite comfortable," said Cugel, gauging the distance between himself and Iucounu. One long step, a swing of the arm, and the deed would be done.

Iucounu seemed to divine the quality of Cugel's thoughts

and moved back a pace. "First, our wine! Let us step into the small refectory."

Iucounu led the way into a hall panelled in fine dark mahogany, where he was greeted effusively by a small round animal with long fur, short legs and black button eyes. The creature bounded up and down and voiced a series of shrill barks. Iucounu patted the beast. "Well then, Ettis, how goes your world? Have they been feeding you enough suet? Good! I am glad to hear such happy tidings, since, other than Cugel, you are my only friend. Now then! To order! I must confer with Cugel."

Iucounu signaled Cugel to a chair at the table, and seated himself opposite. The animal ran back and forth barking, pausing only long enough to gnaw at Cugel's ankles.

A pair of young sylphs floated into the room with trays of silver which they set before Cugel and Iucounu, then drifted once more back the way they had come.

Iucounu rubbed his hands together. "As you know, Cugel, I serve only the best. The wine is Angelius from Quantique, and the biscuits are formed from the pollen of red clover blossom."

"Your judgment has always been exquisite," said Cugel.

"I am content only with the subtle and the refined," said Iucounu. He tasted the wine. "Matchless!" He drank again. "Heady, tart, with a hint of arrogance." He looked across the table at Cugel. "What is your opinion?"

Cugel shook his head in sad abnegation. "One taste of this elixir and I never again could tolerate ordinary drink." He dipped a biscuit into the wine and tendered it to Ettis, who again had paused to gnaw at his leg. "Ettis of course has a wider discrimination than I."

Iucounu jumped to his feet with a protest, but Ettis had already gulped down the morsel, thereupon to perform a curious contortion and fall down on its back, with feet raised stiffly into the air.

Cugel looked questioningly at Iucounu. "You have trained Ettis well in the 'dead dog' trick. He is a clever beast."

Iucounu slowly subsided into his chair. Two sylphs entered the chamber and carried Ettis away on a silver tray.

Iucounu spoke through tight lips. "Let us get down to business. While strolling Shanglestone Strand, did you meet a certain Twango?"

"I did indeed," said Cugel. "An extraordinary individual! He became perturbed when I would not sell him my little trinket."

Iucounu fixed Cugel with the keenest of scrutinies. "Did he explain why?"

"He spoke of the demiurge Sadlark, but in such an incoherent fashion that I lost interest."

Iucounu rose to his feet. "I will show you Sadlark. Come! To the work-room, which of course is dear to your memory."

"'Work-room'? These episodes are lost in the past."

"I remember them distinctly," said Iucounu in an easy voice. "All of them."

As they walked toward the work-room, Cugel tried to sidle close to Iucounu, but without success; Iucounu seemed always a yard or so beyond the reach of Cugel's gloved hand, in which he held 'Spatterlight' at the ready.

They entered the work-room. "Now you shall see my collection," said Iucounu. "You will wonder no longer as to my interest in your talisman." He jerked up his hand; a dark red cloth was whisked away, to reveal the scales of Sadlark, arranged upon an armature of fine silver wire. From the evidence of the restoration, Sadlark would have been a creature of moderate size, standing on two squat motilators, with two pairs of jointed arms ending each in ten clasping fingers. The head, if the term were at all appropriate, was no more than a turret surmounting the keen and taut torso. The belly scales were white-green, with a dark green keel tinged with vermilion swinging up to end at the frontal turret in a blank and eye-catching vacancy.

Iucounu made a grand gesture. "There you see Sadlark, the noble over-world being, whose every contour suggests power and velocity. His semblance fires the imagination. Cugel, do you agree?"

"Not altogether," said Cugel. "Still, by and large, you have recreated a remarkably fine specimen, and I congratulate you." He walked around the structure as if in admiration, all the while hoping to come within arm's-length of Iucounu, but as Cugel moved, so did the Laughing Magician, and Cugel was thwarted in his intent.

"Sadlark is more than a mere specimen," said Iucounu in a voice almost devout. "Now notice the scales, each fixed in its proper place, except at the thrust of the keel where a staring vacancy assaults the eye. A single scale is missing, the most important of all: the protonastic centrum, or, as it is called, the 'Pectoral Sky-break Spatterlight'. For long years I thought it lost, to my unutterable anguish. Cugel, can you imagine my surge of gladsomeness, the singing of songs in my heart, the crepitations of pure joy along the appropriate passages, when I looked at you, and discovered there in your cap the missing scale? I rejoiced as if the sun had been conceded another hundred years of life! I could have leapt in the air from sheer exhilaration. Cugel, can you understand my emotion?"

"To the extent that you have described it — yes. As to the source of this emotion, I am puzzled." And Cugel approached the armature, hoping that Iucounu in his enthusiasm would step within reach of his arm.

Iucounu, moving in the other direction, touched the armature to set the scales jingling. "Cugel, in some respects you are dense and dull; your brain is like luke-warm porridge, and I say this without heat. You understand only what you see, and this is the smallest part." Iucounu emitted a whinny of laughter, so that Cugel sent him a questioning look. "Observe Sadlark!" said Iucounu. "What do you see?"

"An armature of wires and a number of scales, in the purported shape of Sadlark."

"And what if the wires were removed?"

"The scales would fall into a heap."

"Quite so. You are right. The protonastic centrum is the node which binds the other scales with lines of force. This node is the soul and force of Sadlark. With the node in place, Sadlark lives once again; indeed Sadlark was never dead, but merely disassociated."

"What of, let us say, his inner organs?"

"In the overworld, such parts are considered unnecessary and even somewhat vulgar. In short, there are no inner parts.

Have you any other questions or observations?"

"I might politely venture to point out that the day is waning and that I wish to arrive at Taun Tassel before dark."

Iucounu said heartily: "And so you shall! First, be good enough to place upon the work-table the 'Pectoral Sky-break Spatterlight', with all traces of diambroid detached. No other option is open to you."

"Only one," said Cugel. "I prefer to keep the scale. It brings me luck and wards off acrid magic, as you have already learned."

Yellow lights flickered behind Iucounu's eyes. "Cugel, your obstinacy is embarrassing. The scale indeed holds a proud crust between you and enemy magic of the casual sort. It is indifferent to overworld magic, some of which I command. Meanwhile, please desist from this constant skulking forward in the attempt to bring me within range of your sword. I am tired of jumping backward every time you sidle in my direction."

Cugel spoke haughtily: "Such an ungracious act never so much as crossed my mind." He drew his sword and laid it on the work-bench. "There! See for yourself how you have misjudged me!"

Iucounu blinked at the sword. "Still, keep your distance! I am not a man who welcomes intimacies."

"You may expect my full cooperation," said Cugel with dignity.

"I will be frank! Your deeds have long cried out for retribution, and as a man of conscience I am forced to act. Still, you need not aggravate my task."

"This is harsh language!" said Cugel. "You offered me a ride to Taun Tassel. I did not expect treachery."

Iucounu paid no heed. "I will now make my final request: give me the scale at once!"

"I can not oblige you," said Cugel. "Since that was your final request, we can now leave for Taun Tassel."

"The scale, if you please!"

"Take it from my cap, if you must. I will not assist you."

"And the diambroid?"

"Sadlark will protect me. You must take your chances."

Iucounu uttered a cry of laughter. "Sadlark also protects me, as you will see!" He threw aside his garments and with a quick movement inserted himself into the center of the matrix, so that his legs fitted into Sadlark's motilators and his face showed behind the gap in the turret. The wires and scales contracted around his pudgy body; the scales fit him as if they were his own skin.

Iucounu's voice rang lke a choir of brass horns: "Well then, Cugel: what do you think now?"

Cugel stood gaping in wonder. At last he said: "Sadlark's scales fit you remarkably well."

"It is no accident, of this I am certain!"

"And why not?"

"I am Sadlark's avatar; I partake of his personal essence! This is my destiny, but before I can enjoy my full force, I must be whole! Without further quibbling you may fit 'Spatterlight' into place. Remember, Sadlark will no longer protect you against my magic, since it is his magic, as well."

A crawling sensation in Cugel's glove indicated that Sadlark's protonastic centrum 'Spatterlight' endorsed the remark. "So it must be," said Cugel. He carefully detached the ornament from his cap and removed the diambroid. He held it in his hand a moment, then placed it against his forehead.

Iucounu cried out: "What are you doing?"

"For the last time I am renewing my vitality. Often this scale has helped me through my trials."

"Stop at once! I will be needing every iota of force for my own purposes. Hand it over!"

Cugel let the true scale slip into his gloved palm and concealed the false ornament. He spoke in a melancholy voice: "With pain I give up my treasure. May I for a final few moments hold it to my brow?"

"By no means!" declared Iucounu. "I plan to put it to my own brow. Lay the scale on the work-bench, then stand back!"

"As you wish," sighed Cugel. He placed 'Spatterlight' on the work-bench, then, taking his sword, walked mournfully from the room.

With a grunt of satisfaction, Iucounu applied the scale to his brow.

Cugel went to stand by the fountain in the foyer, with one

foot raised to the lip of the basin. In this position he listened gravely to the awful noises rising from Iucounu's throat.

Silence returned to the work-room.

Several moments passed.

A thudding clashing sound reached Cugel's ears.

Sadlark propelled himself by clumsy hops and jumps into the foyer, using his motilators in the manner of feet, with only fair success, so that he fell heavily from time to time, to wallow and roll with a great rattling of scales.

Late afternoon light streamed through the door; Cugel made no move, hoping that Sadlark would blunder out into the open and return to the overworld.

Sadlark came to a halt and spoke in a gasping voice. "Cugel! Where is Cugel? Each of the forces I have consumed, including eel and weasel, requests that they be joined by Cugel! Where are you? Cugel, announce yourself! I cannot see by this peculiar Earth-light, which explains why I plunged into the mire."

Cugel remained silent, scarcely daring to breathe. Sadlark slowly turned the red node of his sky-breaker around the foyer. "Ah, Cugel, there you are! Stand without motion!"

Sadlark lurched forward. Disobeying the order, Cugel ran to the far side of the fountain. Angry at Cugel's insubordination, Sadlark gave a great bound through the air. Cugel seized a basin, scooped up water and flung it upon Sadlark, who thereby misjudged his distance and fell flat into the fountain.

The water hissed and bubbled as Sadlark's force was spent. The scales fell apart and swirled idly about the bottom of the fountain.

Cugel stirred among the scales until he found 'Spatterlight'. He wrapped the scale in several thicknesses of damp cloth and taking it into the work-room placed it into a jar of water, which he sealed and stored away.

Pergolo was silent, but Cugel could not rest easy; Iucounu's presence hung in the air. Could the Laughing Magician be watching from some secret place, stifling his merriment with great effort while he planned a set of humorous pranks?

Cugel searched Pergolo with care but discovered no significant clues except Iucounu's black opal thumb-ring, which he found in the fountain among the scales, and at last Cugel felt assured that Iucounu was no more.

At one end of the table sat Cugel; at the other, Bazzard. Disserl, Pelasias, Archimbaust and Vasker ranged at either side. The missing parts had been recovered from the vaults, sorted and restored to their owners, to the general satisfaction.

Six sylphs served the banquet, which, while lacking the bizarre condiments and impobable juxtapositions of Iucounu's 'novel cuisine', was nevertheless enjoyed by the company.

Various toasts were proposed: to Bazzard's ingenuity, to the fortitude of the four wizards, to Cugel's brave deceits and duplicities. Cugel was asked, not once but several times, as to where his ambitions might now take him; on each occasion he responded with a glum shake of the head. "With Iucounu gone, there is no whip to drive me. I look in no direction and I have no plans."

After draining his goblet, Vasker voiced a generalization: "Without urgent goals, life is insipid!"

Disserl also tilted his goblet high, then responded to his brother: "I believe that this thought has been enunciated before. A surly critic might even use the word 'banality'."

Vasker replied in even tones: "These are the ideas which true originality rediscovers and renews, for the benefit of mankind. I stand by my remark! Cugel, do you concur?"

Cugel signalled the sylphs to the better use of their decanters. "The intellectual interplay leaves me bewildered; I am quite at a loss. Both viewpoints carry conviction."

Vasker said: "Perhaps you will return with us to Llaio and we will explain our philosophies in full detail."

"I will keep your invitation in mind. For the next few months I will be busy at Pergolo, sorting through Iucounu's affairs. Already, a number of his spies have submitted claims and invoices which almost certainly are falsified. I have dismissed them out of hand."

"And when all is in order?" asked Bazzard. "What then? Is it to be the rustic hut by the river?"

"Such a cabin, with nothing to do but watch sunlight moving on the water, exerts an attraction. But I fear that I might become restless."

Bazzard ventured a suggestion. "There are far parts of the world to be seen. The floating city Jehaz is said to be splendid. There is also the Land of the Pale Ladies, which you might care to explore. Or will you pass your days in Almery?"

"The future is blurred as if in a fog."

"The same is true for all of us," declared Pelasias. "Why make plans? The sun might well go out tomorrow."

Cugel peformed an extravagant gesture. "That thought must be banished from our minds! Tonight we sit here drinking purple wine! Let tonight last forever!"

"This is my own sentiment!" said Archimbaust. "Now is now! There is never more to experience than this single 'now', which recurs at an interval exactly one second in length."

Bazzard knit his brows. "What of the first 'now', and the last 'now'? Are these to be regarded as the same entity?"

Archimbaust spoke somewhat severely: "Bazzard, your questions are too profound for the occasion. The songs of your musical fish would be more appropriate."

"Their progress is slow," said Bazzard. "I have appointed a cantor and a contralto choir, but the harmony is not yet steady."

"No matter," said Cugel. "Tonight we will do without. Iucounu, wherever you are, in underworld, overworld or no world whatever: we drink to your memory in your own wine! This is the final joke, and, feeble though it may be, it is at your expense, and hence, enjoyed by the company! Sylphs, make play with the decanters! Once again to the goblets! Bazzard, have you tried this excellent cheese? Vasker: another anchovy? Let the feast proceed!"